DARK ONE'S BRIDE

Dark One's Trilogy - Book Two

Aldrea Alien

Thardrandian Publications

ISBN: 0992264561
ISBN-13: 978-0992264567

www.aldreaalien.com

To my #1 fan.
She knows who she is.

CHAPTER ONE

*T*he carriage clattered and wobbled down the road, forcing Clara to set aside her embroidery or be pricked. Once again, she was reminded of a certain talk she needed to have with the Citadel's blacksmith about his laxity on carriage maintenance. Still, as she sat there, quietly suffering the jarring in her spine, she noticed the bumps were too even and numerous to be potholes.

Cobblestones. And that had to mean they'd entered another city. Were they finally in Endlight?

She peered out the window. Buildings filled her view in a shock of off-white and red, a relief from the mottled browns and greens of the autumn countryside. In style, the brick and plaster-covered buildings looked no different to the countless others she'd seen in her journey. Nothing to suggest they'd reached anything but another cluster of shops and homes.

Clara pressed her cheek against the glass, straining to see everything her narrow vantage point afforded her. It was a manner very much unsuited to the future Great Lady, but she cared not a whit.

She'd done a lot of reading up on the kingdom's larger cities. Endlight sat on the doorstep of seven gargantuan pillars. If she could just see the skyline, then maybe...

People lined the road, busy with their lives of work or begging or just plain keeping back from the Great Lord's black carriage. Nothing different about them to give away where they were. It was oddly disappointing. For years, anything beyond her home village of Everdark had seemed so exotic, but the journey here had swiftly shown her how wrong she'd been.

With every mile they travelled, she had hoped Endlight would prove different.

Sighing, Clara flopped back into the seat. She wanted to hammer on the roof and demand the driver reveal their present destination. Only the stranglehold she kept on her impatience stopped her. That and Lucias' men took it upon themselves to ignore her completely unless it conflicted with the Great Lord's wishes. She would be having words with him about *that*. She'd honestly thought the soulless men would treat her differently than they'd done before she had saved Lucias' life.

She frowned at the empty seats gracing the other side of the carriage. They had slowed, caught up in traffic by the sounds of it, and the jolting turned to an uneven rocking that always threatened to pitch her forward. Bracing herself with a hand on either side of the carriage was the only way to stop the dreadful jostling.

Perhaps it would take their wedding for her status to be recognised amongst the Great Lord's men. Or maybe her authority over them would be little more than words until she was pregnant with the next Great Lord.

Her stomach fluttered at the thought of carrying a child to term. She wasn't even halfway through her seventeenth year, was she truly ready for motherhood? What if she was just like her own mother? Clara bit her lip, her cheek tingling with the memory of the last time she'd spoken to the woman who had given birth to her.

"No," she muttered into the silence. She'd never subject a child to that. She would be far more compassionate to her children than her mother had ever been to her. More like her father. Stern but loving.

Of course, that all depended on her husband remaining

in her presence long enough for more than chaste kisses. She may not have a full understanding of the act, but she knew how children were made even if her face heated at the mere thought of him... and her... *Please, Goddess, give me strength*. She would need all the willpower she could muster in order to get through the coming week with her nerves intact.

Shadows fell across the carriage, drawing her back to the window. A large building dominated the world beyond the smoky glass. The view of huge grey slabs of stone remained unchanged for some time. Too long to be a gateway. Some sort of internal fortification?

Her heart leapt. That meant a city big enough to warrant a castle.

They *had* arrived at Endlight.

Lucias would be waiting for her, of that she was certain. *My darling*. To be able to see his face again, to hear his voice...

Unable to contain her excitement, Clara hugged herself and beat the heels of her boots against the bench's base, uncaring in how childlike such abandon seemed. After three months of his absence, her dear husband-to-be was so close now.

She'd spent weeks wishing for his return, even if it was only for a few days. Had wished harder that he had hadn't left her behind to begin with. The Citadel had been colder without his presence. It'd been agony seeing him go, being forced to wait out the time apart wondering how he fared nearer the border.

Of course, he never turned up no matter how hard she wished. There was no practicality behind him making the trip down from Endlight only to come back weeks later for their wedding, but it still would've been nice to receive a letter. How hard could it be to send a pigeon? Or maybe he hadn't the time. Part of the reason he'd left so far in advance of her was to deal with the court.

The heavy, iron-bound planks of a gate briefly altered

the scenery visible through the window before the view opened out into the bustling centre of a castle courtyard. Clara flattened her cheek against the glass and searched the crowd for any sign of Lucias, her heart pounding.

Nothing.

She returned to her seat, softly chiding herself under her breath. Lucias had more important things to do than wait for the exact moment of her arrival. He could be out patrolling with the troops. And whilst Endlight was considered a border city, the true edge of the kingdom was close to half a day's ride from the city. If he was up there, then he wouldn't learn of her arrival until much later.

And we are to be married soon. Just a week left to her now and she would be able to call him her husband. She could weather a few more hours before seeing him again.

The dreadful swaying slowed. Then, at last, they came to a halt. The carriage rocked further as the driver stepped down and several thuds on the carriage wall at her back spoke of her luggage being removed from the storage rack above.

Clara hastened to smooth her skirts, gave up and focused on her sleeves. She was dressed from head to toe in rich black silk. The hems and sleeves were heavy with grey embroidery, dark echoes of the Great Lord's fiery symbol.

Content that everything was presentable, she sat on the edge of her seat and waited for someone to open the carriage door, all the while desperately fighting the urge to do it herself.

The latch clicked and the door swung out into the bustle beyond.

"Clara?" Tommy called. Her page stood by the door, his sweet face pulled into a puzzled frown as she failed to all but leap from the carriage as she'd done during the last few stops.

No matter how much she longed to see everything, there was a certain code of conduct she would have to adhere to. At least, according to the books she'd unearthed in the Citadel's dusty library.

Without thought, her hand slid to the small sheathed dagger nestled in the laces of her bodice. Her fingers had barely secured themselves around the crosspiece by the time she became aware of the action. *Silly girl*, she chided, carefully relinquishing her hold. There was no danger to be had here.

Still, her stomach fluttered as she sidled closer to the exit. This wasn't like the inns of the tiny villages and hamlets they'd stopped at on their way here. Lucias was adamant that all of the kingdom's nobility would be here for their wedding, for who wouldn't want to witness the first time a Great Lord had married in centuries?

A nomadic wedding. She'd memorised the words she must speak, but it was like the times her family used to visit the temple. Speaking and understanding seemed very far off. Perhaps Lucias would be able to explain the significance behind some of the more puzzling phrases. He, of all people, wouldn't want her looking like a fool in front of everyone.

Here we go. Steeling herself, Clara stepped out into the courtyard.

The surrounding men paid more attention to the chests they manhandled off the carriage than her presence. No one beyond Tommy seemed to notice her at all. Even then, he paused only long enough to give her a bow before trotting off to the head of the horses. No other man was allowed to unhitch them whilst in his presence. His voice was lost in the collective noise, but she could see his mouth moving as he explained the horses' needs in great detail.

She turned to eye her transport. Alone, the bleak plainness of the Great Lord's carriage would garner little attention. That'd been the point of travelling in it, after all. She supposed those escorting her could likewise come from any post harbouring the Great Lord's men.

Was she so easy to overlook?

A strand of her hair waved in the breeze and tickled her

nose. She went to tuck it behind her ear, jerking her hand away as her gloved fingers rustled against cloth. Of course, she'd been covering up her rather unmistakable rich red hair since leaving the Citadel. It'd been the last word of caution she'd heard from Lucias.

To think she once would've thought such prudence as paranoia, but even in the heart of the kingdom, there was no telling who could turn out to be an enemy.

Surely it was safe to show her true self here. Lucias would not have chosen to have them wed in a place which wasn't secure.

She unwound the scarf, shaking her head and discreetly rubbing at her sweat-soaked scalp. Even this did not draw the attention she was hoping. Clara glanced over her shoulder, the unmarked carriage stood empty. The men who'd unloaded her things had dispersed.

A fine reception for the future Great Lady. Well, if no one was going to greet her, she might as well make her own way inside and to whatever room they'd reserved for her arrival.

She strode off towards a set of stairs leading up to what was certainly the castle's main entrance.

A group of women appeared through the wide, arched doorway as she reached the bottom step. They halted at the top, staring down at her with such intensity that she froze at the bottom of the stairs as if she were back to being a child of seven years caught fiddling with her mother's sewing machine.

Clara resisted the urge to shuffle her feet as the group descended. Closer and she could make out the distinct bulge of pregnancy distorting several of the women's gowns.

One such woman, with a faint tinge of grey in her otherwise brown hair, appeared close to giving birth. Was she a servant? The simple dress of green and muted gold certainly suggested such. Or perhaps she was a maid to one of the noblewomen she walked alongside?

Clara peered at the other women, before returning her gaze to the green and gold garbed woman. The way she carried herself was at odds with the modest cut of her clothes.

The heavily-pregnant woman halted before her. Dark brown eyes—a shade that was echoed in the roots of her hair—surveyed Clara with a sharpness that banished all thought of this woman being anyone's servant. Could this be Thad's wife? She looked to be in her early forties. If that were so, then she'd grossly misjudged the Endlight lord's age.

The woman smiled and clasped Clara's forearm. "You must be Clarabelle," she said as the rest of the group surrounded them. "Your hair is exactly as he described it."

Clara eyed the pregnant woman. Her skin was the soft brown she'd heard was common of those born along the eastern border of the kingdom, where the land slipped beneath the sea. The woman's nose was proud and held high even though she appeared at ease. She must enquire as to whether this was indeed Thalia.

"Amazing," another woman murmured, fingering a deep red curl of Clara's hair without even a by your leave. "So bright and rich."

"Is it?" Clara muttered as she cast a wary eye over the women encircling her. She timidly laid a hand upon her bosom, her fingers inching towards the dagger. The men down in the village of Darkwood had learnt the hard way that Clara no longer suffered being hemmed in. Where was Brenna? She thought a woman with her ambitions would prefer to linger with the other noblewomen, but she couldn't spy the young woman's pale face amongst the group.

"We've heard so much about you," the pregnant woman breathed. Her arm linked with Clara's, wordlessly steering her up the stairs. She clung like a stray dog to her last morsel. Was the woman expecting Clara to sprint off upon her release? "Our dear Great Lord speaks of little else."

He does? Clara smiled to herself.

"Of course," the woman continued, seemingly paying no heed to Clara. "Our Great Lord is out on patrol at the moment. That boy never seems to want to stay still for long.

May the Goddess protect him, his wedding day is so near and he insists on joining the common guards for a trip around the city limits. It must be nerves, my son was the same." She patted Clara's arm. "But he'll be in for the evening meal."

The thought of Lucias putting himself in such a dangerous position knotted Clara's stomach. All the easy passages through the mountains were guarded, with the widest gorge emptying out at the foot of the legendary Pillars of Endlight, but accidents happened and the loss of Lucias' life endangered the whole kingdom.

The shadow of the castle fell over them as they passed beneath the arch of the entrance. Much like the Citadel, the doorway opened out into a huge entrance that branched off into smaller hallways and winding stairs.

"You must want to freshen up after such a journey," the woman continued. "I'll see that the servants prepare your room. I trust you didn't have much trouble on the roads here."

"None at all." But then, the roads wouldn't have posed a problem even if she chose to go without an armed escort. It was the villages along the way that tended to offer up trouble. She opened her mouth to speak further before the woman could—

The clatter of hooves echoed through the courtyard, drowning out every noise bar one. "Clara!"

Lucias. She spun at the voice, pulling herself free of the woman's arm. He was here! So soon? He must have seen the carriage arrive.

She tried to make her way back to the courtyard. The other women barred her way, their bustling only adding to their impediment. She bit back a snarl. If they would merely stay still for a moment, then she'd already be through.

The racket grew louder. Standing on her toes to peer over the women, she spied a massive black horse barrelling through the gates, foam flying off its flanks. The beast slid to a stop before a footman, its hindquarters mere inches from the flagstones.

Lucias leapt from the saddle before the panting animal could finish righting itself. He raced towards the group.

She squeezed her way between the remaining women, almost tumbling down the stairs, to meet him halfway across the courtyard. Clara flung her arms around him and sagged against his chest. After three months without his presence, it felt unbelievably good to hold him again.

"I've missed you," he whispered, his breath warming more than her ear. He brushed his thumb across her jaw, coaxing her head up. His lips sought out hers, hungrily claiming them.

Her legs shook. Everything else faded from her thoughts. Her hands slid up his back, curling over his shoulders.

Someone clicked their tongue, attempting to make little tsk-tsk noises between chuckles.

The pregnant woman in green and gold shuffled between them, her belly forging the path. "Now, now, my lord." She batted Lucias away as if he was a child forbidden to touch the Feast Day sweets and, much to Clara's surprise, he stepped back. Although he still kept a firm grip on Clara's hand. This woman definitely had to be Thalia. "She's just arrived. Give your lady a chance to freshen up before you ravish her."

Lucias grinned, his eyes seeming to glitter as they alighted on Clara's face. "But of course, my lady, and I must return to my duties." After so many months apart, taking in his features afresh had Clara easily spotting the subtle lines that could only mean a consistent lack of sleep. "I simply had to see my beloved before tonight. I trust your journey was uneventful."

Clara nodded. "Moderately so."

The wrinkles around his eyes deepened as fresh delight sparkled in his dark gaze. "I am glad to hear that," he murmured. The breath of his words heated the back of her hand a moment before his lips brushed it, the whispering touch tingling through her. "Until later, my dear."

She tightened her hold on his fingers, wishing she could command him to stay. "Until tonight," she agreed, her face heating at the woman's scrutiny. She wasn't sure what he had on his mind, but if it meant she'd spend some time at his side, she wouldn't object to waiting a little while longer.

Giving a bow to the pregnant woman, Lucias waved aside the man who held his black brute of a horse. He vaulted over the beast's rump and into the saddle. Clara swore her heart skipped a few beats as, with a dip of Lucias' head in her direction, his destrier bowed low.

Then he was off, cantering back out into the street.

Beside her, the pregnant woman snorted. "Show off." Her hands fastened around Clara's wrist in a grip that threatened to cut off her circulation. "Let us retire to the solarium whilst my girls make the final preparations to your chambers."

Forced to keep up with the woman or let the both of them fall, Clara stumbled her way up the stairs in silence.

"Lucias insisted you have your own space until the wedding," the woman went on, seemingly oblivious to everything else. "It has sparked such fuss with the court. So many wish to know why."

Another woman took her place on Clara's other side, claiming her free arm in a similar possessive grip. "He's got to have somewhere to steal her from." Her accent had the words being pulled out in such a soft, careful fashion; akin to the melodious way Thad spoke. "You're going to love the room."

"I will?" she managed to squeak. The pair had already guided her through the castle entrance and they were now ascending a smaller set of stairs. Was this really the way to her chambers? Should they not have been using the main stair opposite the carved archway?

"Oh yes." The woman inclined her head. Strands of brown hair fell over her face. "Your chosen chambers are high enough to give one a perfect view of the moors." Her lips, thickly painted an unnatural red, curved into what

Clara guessed was meant to be a smile. "Not that you'll be doing much looking out the window."

It wasn't until the rest of the women behind them fell to a bout of giggling that Clara realised just what the woman was alluding to. She ducked her head, trying to hide her burning cheeks. She supposed Lucias wouldn't have cared to announce to the people that he wouldn't be fully adopting the nomadic marriage customs. Or that she was a virgin and planned to remain that way until their wedding night.

And who would believe either claim? The words Lucias' had cautioned her with some months back tumbled through her head. He was right. After spending months alone in his company, they would've expected him to have already slept with her.

"Hush your tongues this instant!" the first woman—Thalia, no doubt of that anymore—snapped over her shoulder. "You know the traditions beyond Endlight are different." She patted Clara's face. "Look at that, you've made the poor girl blush. Be off with you all! If you cannot be civil, then be gone!" She flapped a hand at the surrounding women as if they were naught but pesky birds and batted at the painted woman still clutching onto Clara's arm. "Go!"

The women scurried off, subtly casting dark glances at Thalia before vanishing around various corners. Such looks had undoubtedly been noticed, but the woman paid no heed to them now. Her distended belly seemed to be her sole focus.

"I do apologise for them, my lady. They can be right jackals at times." She frowned and rubbed her belly one last time. "This way, if you please." The woman waddled off down the hall, leaving Clara with the choice of following or becoming utterly lost.

Chapter Two

Clara turned on the spot in the middle of the solarium. She stood between the two long tables that filled the middle of the room. Natural light streamed through the tall windows adorning the left wall, illuminating every inch of the space. Dying embers glowed in the cavernous fireplace embedded in the wall opposite the entrance.

The room was easily twice as big as the one back in the Citadel. Homier, too. The Citadel's solarium had likely never seen a family anywhere near the size of Farris' horde. Three sons had apparently been the limit when it came to Lucias' ancestors and children. And none of those siblings had survived their older brother's coronation to produce their own offspring.

Clara ran her hand along the top of a table. The surface was polished in a warm, patchy fashion that could only be achieved through years of loving use. Very few things in the Citadel had such a patina. Everything there was old, but dusty. Abandoned. Back there, she could've stood in a room bustling with activity and still feel utterly alone. Here, even though it was just the two of them, there was a welcoming hum to the air.

Although, now she thought about it, the lack of warmth in her home was likely due to the Citadel's residents. All of the men and women working in the Citadel were, technically, part of the Great Lord's army and just as soulless.

Beyond Tommy, she'd only the Citadel's Steward, Gettie, for company. And even the elderly woman had no soul.

"Come, come." Thalia ushered her into one of the hearth-side chairs in a series of gentle nudges as if shooing a wayward child. "Please, sit whilst I get you something to drink. The water should still be warm."

Clara leapt to her feet before the chair could fully accept her weight. "That won't be necessary, my lady." She eyed the woman's belly. The Lady of Endlight had to be close to gifting her lord with another baby. Standing so near, Thalia looked ready to burst, the folds of her gown straining over the bulge. "I wouldn't want you exerting yourself on my account."

"Nonsense. A poor host I would be to not offer you a thing. Now sit. Sit! I'll make you a cup of tea."

Clara slowly lowered herself back into the chair. The leather arms were worn in places and bore patches in others, but the cushions still had some padding. A fact she was most grateful for after the journey in the carriage's less-than-comfortable seating.

She'd vague memories of sneaking a sip of tea from her mother's cup. It was a flavour she had come to enjoy over the years, but such luxuries had been expensive even then and her exploratory sips had been few and far between. That'd been back when her family had the coin for her mother to entertain the occasional wealthy customers whilst her father did the final adjustments to their gowns.

Seemingly satisfied that Clara wouldn't get back up, Thalia set about making tea. She took up a short, blackened hook and hoisted a small kettle from where it'd been hanging over the ashes and embers in the fireplace. The woman then waddled over to a table sitting just behind where Clara sat, puffing with every step.

Clara dug her fingers into the leather. In the back of her mind, the reedy little voice of her mother's past berating echoed on. *How dare you let someone wait on you,* it screeched. *A pregnant noblewoman, no less! Did I not teach you better manners?*

Biting the inside of her cheek, Clara sank deeper into the chair. Things were different now. The venom of her mother's tongue was little more than a memory, just like the blows Clara had often suffered at the woman's hands. But soon, she would be the Great Lady and nothing would be able to touch her.

She listened to the soft trickle of water and the musical clink of porcelain coming from over her shoulder. The smell of brewing leaves tweaked her nose. She fidgeted in the chair. A part of her still ached to help, but she'd managed to keep the urge confined. This wasn't home. Here on the western fringes of the kingdom, offering to assist again when the offer had already been declined was considered an insult.

Thalia tottered back into her line of sight, a cup and saucer gracefully balanced in each hand. "Here we are. I do hope the tea is to your liking."

Clara seized the proffered saucer, the cup shaking treacherously in her grasp. She clutched the handle and took a sip of the warm liquid. Overpowering sweetness hit her tongue. Honey. Her eye twitched as she fought down the urge to shudder and, somehow, managed a smile.

To Clara's utmost relief, the woman didn't seem to notice. She'd no clue whether it was the same all over the kingdom, but showing any dislike of offered food was considered impolite. At least, that's what her mother had taught her. "It is lovely, my lady," she mumbled, keeping her head down in the off chance that initiating eye contact might reveal her true thoughts. "Very refreshing. Thank you."

Thalia waddled over to the chair opposite Clara's, giving a small sigh as she settled. "Please, please, you will soon be our Great Lady, let us not stick to the formalities of titles in private. Call me Thalia. I insist." She sipped at her own tea and smiled, deepening the wrinkles around her eyes. "So," she murmured, elegantly resting both cup and saucer on her belly. "You and Lucias?"

Clara mimicked the woman's action by placing her saucer on her lap. Keeping it steady wasn't as easy as it looked. "Yes?"

The woman glanced about them. They were still the room's only occupants. "I was a little surprised to learn that you two, despite choosing Endlight as the stage for your wedding ceremony, will not be indulging in her more... risqué customs." A soft, almost questioning, note tinged her words.

Clara took a deep breath. *So it starts.* After five months, she had expected Lucias to search for some way around the promise he'd made at the beginning of their engagement. The one where he'd sworn she'd remain a virgin until their wedding night. She just hadn't anticipated that way to come via another.

Why did he tell her? And how much of what she'd thought of as deeply personal details did he confide in this woman? Or had Lucias confided in another not knowing it would also be passed to the man's wife? Thalia was married to Thad, after all, and the man was like a brother to Lucias.

Still, the idea that anyone else knew made her stomach turn. At least it was the Lady of Endlight enquiring rather than the Lord. "I know how it must sound," Clara said, straightening her back in what she hoped was a pose that radiated authority. "But we—"

Thalia gasped and laid a hand on Clara's knee, almost upsetting both their cups. "I hope I'm not overstepping my boundaries, my lady, but allow me to explain myself first." She eyed Clara expectantly.

It took a moment for Clara to realise the woman was waiting for approval. She inclined her head in a way she hoped didn't appear too eager.

"May I start by saying I'm not a native to this city." She patted Clara's arm. "I grew up on the eastern border and—"

"Port Dank?" Clara blurted, momentarily forgetting herself at the thought of other places. The little she'd seen of

Endlight might not have been what she expected, but surely something as enormous and magnificent as the ocean couldn't be lessened by reality.

Thalia lifted a brow at her, the soft quirk to her smile taking the edge off the otherwise harsh expression. "My family's estate had seaside views, but no, I did not live in Port Dank. Rather, Port Dyre."

Clara blushed. She took another sip of the sickly-sweet tea in an attempt to conceal her face behind the cup. "Sorry," she mumbled.

The woman laughed. "You remind me so much of me when I was your age. My home was a peaceful place. The Dyre Estate is perched almost in the ocean and I always had a clear line of sight to the water, but I'd never wandered further than the city markets." She waved her hand, taking in the room with one wide sweep over her arm. "All this was so much more than I'd ever dreamed, but then Thad came and..." Thalia clutched at the pendant resting on her breast. A soft smile, brimming with the fondness of memories, curved the woman's lips.

Clara easily recalled the day when she had first met Thad. Even with her mind preoccupied with trying to flee the Citadel, she'd been momentarily stunned by the Endlight Lord's looks and manners. She could easily imagine that, when he'd been a far younger man in search of a bride, he must've seemed like something from a fable.

"I know how terribly daunting the prospect of their customs can be if you're not brought up in their ways. I certainly found it so."

A hereto unknown tension slipped free of Clara's spine. *That* was the reason Thalia had chosen to speak of this. But were the woman's intentions merely to calm Clara about the upcoming proceedings or did Thalia seek to sway her into thinking otherwise about the choice not to adhere to the custom of betrothed couples being with one another on the eve of their wedding?

Clara cleared her throat. "No one seems willing to tell

me, and I wonder if you would be so kind... Why do the people of Endlight practice the...?" Clara's tongue faltered as she searched for the words that would not set her face aflame.

"Hmm?" Thalia mumbled around her teacup. "Oh. They believe a virgin at the altar is unlucky."

"Unlucky?" Clara echoed. When countless women across the kingdom married without bedding their betrothed prior to their marriage? She supposed some of those couples might've had a poor run with their luck, but she'd be willing to bet that the larger percentage lived their married lives quite contently. She certainly wasn't going to change her mind based on superstition.

Thalia giggled. It was a sound that seemed more at home coming from a girl of seven rather than one who must've been twice Clara's age, but it also brought to life a faint blush to the woman's lightly-powdered cheeks as Thalia clearly fought to restrain herself. "Sounds preposterous, doesn't it? I didn't believe it myself at first, but the people here still believe in this old folktale that dates back to when the moors belonged to themselves."

"A folktale?" She could see some people putting such stock in stories, but all?

Thalia nodded, setting aside her cup and saucer. An act Clara swiftly mimicked in the hopes of fobbing off any more offers of sweet tea. "I can't recall it precisely and—" Thalia sat back, a faraway smile gracing her lips. "Well, Thad tells it far better than I, you understand?"

He probably does, Clara mused. The man likely used his people's lore to coax his betrothed into following along with Endlight's customs.

"It goes something along the lines that there was this couple, a nomadic version of nobility that the Endlight lordship is said to have originated from. The pair decided to shun their people's custom. The woman did not receive a visit from her soon-to-be husband on the eve of her wedding. Instead, she was kidnapped."

Clara frowned before she caught herself. It took a large degree of control, but she managed to smooth her forehead and keep her mouth from pursing. "I'd hardly consider that as unlucky. An ill-timed twist of fate, perhaps. Who's to say she wouldn't have been taken even if they had been together?"

"If the husband had been in the tent with her, I'm sure he would've fought off her kidnapper."

She nodded. "But he also could've died in the act of defending her. It could've happened even after the couple were wed. Or later still. Would the people still have linked it to that day?"

Thalia shrugged. "You would do better asking Thad that question. Or even Lucias. I hear he's very knowledgeable in nomadic traditions."

Clara hoped that, what with him being the Great Lord, Lucias was well versed in all of his kingdom's traditions and not just those of one border city. She had certainly attempted to educate herself on any differences across the land.

The woman picked up her empty teacup. "More?"

She shook her head. Her tongue was still trying to recover from the previous cup. "No, thank you. But what about the story? Was that the end? Did he ever find her?"

Laughter shook Thalia's whole body. She laid a hand upon her belly, rubbing it in a seemingly absent manner. "Oh yes. The husband supposedly spent five years searching for his bride, only to discover she'd chosen to marry her kidnapper and had given the man several sons."

Clara could see how that might happen. It all depended on what sort of person the kidnapper was in comparison to the man the woman was supposed to marry. *Like Lucias.* Clara had almost believed him to be a beast until the Endlight lords came. He'd been gruff at first, clearly still trying to process the death of his father and his new position as ruler. Adding her unexpected presence alongside knowing his own mother lusted for his death couldn't have made things any better.

The presence of Count Farris and Lord Thad had brought out an almost different man in Lucias. A warmer, kinder person had peeked out from beneath the cold shell and she had fallen. Enough so to save his life when his mother finally came to take it.

The gentle rattle of a teacup balancing on its saucer drew Clara out of her musing. Thalia had left her seat and, by the trickling sound of liquid at her back, was pouring herself another cup.

"Of course," the woman said as she returned to her chair. "There was no doubt more to it than that, but if it was ever true, then it probably would've helped in justifying their reasoning for continuing."

If it was ever true. Clara eyed the woman. "Lucias said no one would believe we don't already... know each other in that way." The noblewomen Thalia had chased away were either unaware or refused to think it possible that the Great Lord could spend several months in his mistress' presence and not lay with her.

No one seemed to care if he chose to keep her as his mistress, for most of the Great Lords hadn't married those who bore them their heirs. But to supposedly deflower her *then* wed her somehow became an invitation for scandalous accusations about her purity. *Except for here.*

Clara bit her lip. Was that the real reason Lucias had chosen to marry her at Endlight? To avoid having her name be unduly tarnished?

"You should've heard Thad when he found out. He's very insistent on Lucias having a child as quickly as possible. But then, he was also curiously taken aback when Lucias declared his intention to marry you. He seemed to be of the opinion that you weren't interested in such an arrangement."

Clara's face heated faster than the dampened fire and hot tea could provide. She let her gaze drift towards the dimming embers poking out of the ashes. "That was probably my fault." After everything she'd said and done in Thad's presence—from her mistaken accusation of Lucias' intention to rape her, to fleeing for home at the first chance she got—the man had probably been dumbfounded to discover just who his lord planned to marry.

"Nonsense." Thalia flapped her hand in the air as if batting the thought away. "He was probably shocked that, after so many generations, a Great Lord would choose to marry his mistress." She lifted her cup to her lips and hummed. "I don't know what went on between you and our Great Lord—unlike some of my ladies, I'm aware such talk is none of my business." She leant forward and laid her hand atop Clara's. "But truth be told, when he greeted you just now, I've never seen him happier."

"He missed me." That knowledge alone made her trip here bearable.

The woman sat back with a grunt. "Of course he has, the man's been insufferable since he arrived. Hardly ever rests. Barely talks about anything beyond you and tactics. Thankfully, the border attacks have been brief and relatively bloodless. For our side, at least."

Clara felt the blood rushing from her face. She glanced at the floor, fully expecting to find a puddle of it pooling around her boots. "He's been patrolling the border?" When the woman mentioned patrols, the very idea of him being anywhere near the border hadn't crossed her mind.

Now that it had, her stomach knotted at the thought of him barrelling headlong into battle, knowing full well what his death would do to the kingdom. Of how many soulless men and women would suddenly be in full command of themselves. She'd already saved this kingdom from a fate of being torn apart by its own criminals bent on vengeance towards those who'd sent them to their worse-than-death sentences. She had no desire to repeat such an act.

Was his very-much-direct involvement in defence the reason he'd kept communications between Endlight and the Citadel to a minimum? So she wouldn't find out? They were going to have some very long talks about that. "Since when?" The question came out far sharper than she intended, but she had to know. "And how often?"

"Daily since he arrived. And there are his biweekly visits to the Pillars..." Thalia shook her head. "And my darling husband tags along every time. I'm certain he's convinced that it's *his* duty alone to keep his lord safe."

"And *have* there been any attacks whilst he's there?" If Thad had enough sense to know Lucias should not be putting himself in such danger, then he also should've been using whatever brother-like influence he claimed to have on his Great Lord to direct Lucias *away* from the enemy.

Thalia grimaced. "I haven't asked. But I would suspect they get into the usual conflict the patrols all face nearer the mountains."

Minor skirmishes, then. It was still too dangerous. All it'd take to kill Lucias would be one well-aimed arrow, or one lucky sword swing, and the kingdom would tear itself apart. She rubbed at her temple. *Lucias dear, you are a fool.* Had she not come to that conclusion months ago? *Yes.* But he was *her* fool. Or, at least, he would be by the end of this week.

"Oh!" Thalia hastily set her cup aside to clasp Clara's knee. "But I am upsetting you."

"Not at all." The grip on her knee was quite strong, stronger than she expected from a woman of noble birth. She twisted her leg to and fro, unable to find a means of relaxing the fingers holding her fast. "Really." She should've expected Lucias to fling himself into battle alongside his men instead of sitting idly by.

"I'm certain our Great Lord is taking every precaution towards keeping himself safe. He's not an easy man to anger."

Clara thought back to her first few weeks in the Citadel. Even when riled, he'd been beyond patient with her, certainly more so than she would've been if the situation was reversed. "And *you* must know a lot about him to be confident in that assessment."

The fine lines around Thalia's eyes deepened. "I may not have known him for as long as my husband, but I know him well enough."

The door at the far end of the room creaked open, the diversion enough to let Clara win her knee free of Thalia's grip.

A woman, likely the same age as herself, appeared around the door and scurried to their side. "My ladies." She curtsied deeply before them. "I was instructed to bring word to the Great Lord's Mistress that her room is ready and to escort her there at her convenience."

Clara sighed. *Great Lord's Mistress.* How she hated the sound of her title. As if she'd suddenly stopped having an identity of her own the very second word had leaked out of the newly-made Great Lord having already chosen the woman who was to produce his much-needed heir. It would only get worse once they were married.

At least Great Lord's Wife was a title she could live with.

She stood, smiling her thanks to Thalia. "I should go freshen up." She faced the servant as Thalia babbled her understanding and farewells. "Lead the way."

"Yes, my lady," the woman said, bobbing another curtsy.

Clara followed the servant through the winding halls. Unlike the dim, enclosed halls of the Citadel, they breezed through wide, airy sections lit by way of large windows or a line of bright candles.

There were people everywhere. Most of them were garbed in the muted greens of the castle staff and they went silently about their duties without a glance in their direction, but a handful of the men and women she saw had the look of nobility about them. It was these people who watched their passage with great interest.

My passage. They had to know all about her by now. She coiled a finger around a lock of hair, morosely tugging it before realising even that action was being noted. *I have to be careful.* This was to become her life from now on. Her every movement, every single word she uttered... just fodder for these people.

Small wonder Lucias held little fondness for social events. He probably used the patrols as an excuse to keep away from these people for as long as was possible without arousing suspicion. *I wonder if I can join him.* She'd grown quite accustomed to wielding a sword over the past few months.

"Not much further, mistress," the woman said as they ascended a short set of stairs and began their way down another lavishly decorated corridor.

There weren't many doors down this stretch, what with one side being mostly windows. A large portion of the doorways were shut. However, through the open doors, she spied rooms that appeared empty of residents. Was she to have this section of the castle to herself?

"Here we are." The woman stopped before a dark door. Unlike the others, the wood was engraved with the stylised fire of the Great Lord.

Clara eyed the door directly opposite. It was one of the empty rooms. "Will my page be nearby?" She wasn't likely to require Tommy's services during her stay here, but she'd certainly feel better having someone she knew and trusted within earshot. Just in case. They were near the border, after all, it couldn't be considered as being paranoid to prepare oneself for the possibility of danger.

"Your page will be stationed across the hall, my lady." The woman opened the door and bowed. "I've been instructed to tell you the key to your chambers is on the bedside table."

She stepped past the woman and into the room, softly grumbling to herself upon taking in the decor. Throughout the castle, she'd seen greens and golds adorning the walls and flooring. But here, it was like someone had taken a small chunk of the Citadel, using the dark colours to decorate this one room.

Large windows took over most of the outer wall. The autumn sunlight glowed softly against the warm wood of the furniture only to be captured in the darkness of the bedding and the curtains. At the foot of her bed sat the two chests she had journeyed with, both of them blending into the shadows. *And here I thought I'd escaped the black and reds for just one week.*

"I do hope it is acceptable for her ladyship." The servant cleared her throat. "A bath has been drawn to your preferred specifications." She indicated a second door.

"A bath?" She whirled on the woman. "It'll be ready right now?" After a week travelling across the kingdom, such a luxury would be bliss.

The servant flinched and then curtsied. "Of course, my lady. The count prides his staff on our efficiency." She dipped her head. "Someone will be up in the evening to escort you to dinner. Unless her ladyship requires anything else…?"

Escorted to a meal. She had not required such formalities for many months. But then, with only the pair of them sharing the Citadel's great hall alongside the soulless servants, neither Lucias nor herself saw much point in any sort of ceremony. And when he left her side for Endlight, she ate every meal in the kitchen whilst the servants continued their tasks around her.

"No, thank you, that'll be all."

Clara waited until the woman was gone before further exploring her accommodations. True to the servant's word, a key sat on the bedside table. Seeing it didn't bring as much comfort as she hoped. There were undoubtedly other copies.

The bed itself was quite large. Bigger than the one she slept in back at the Citadel, yet not as wide as the bed filling the Great Lord's windowless bedchamber. *Big enough for two.* But she wouldn't be sharing this bed with Lucias, would she? He'd surely carry her off to his own chambers—wherever *that* was—and ravish his newly-made wife there.

Clara snatched up the key and, with her face heating something fierce at the thought of their wedding night, hastily locked herself in before making for the adjoining door. Would it be too much to ask for the bathwater to be cold?

The red and black motif carried on in the second room. Even the bath, standing in the middle of the room with steam issuing from the sudsy water, did not escape the stark treatment; its outer shell having been coated in black enamel.

Lured by the perfume and gentle warmth caressing her cheeks, Clara quickly stripped and sank into the bath's welcoming embrace. She stared up at the ceiling, her mind unable to keep still. No one would be requiring anything of her until this evening, where she'd encounter the majority of the court for the first time.

This is it. Her stomach twisted. No more hiding away in the Citadel for her. Tonight, she would stand before them and be known as nothing else except the Great Lord's Mistress.

Clara slipped further into the water. *Goddess*, she pleaded. *Don't let me embarrass myself.*

Chapter Three

"Aren't you hungry?"

Clara looked up from her bowl and to her right, instantly meeting Lucias' eyes. Such a warm, dark shade of brown and brimming with concern. "I *was*," she confessed. The journey had made her so nervous that she'd barely eaten much of anything.

And yet, as ravenous as she had been...

She lifted her spoon to timidly stir the pale gloop which she sincerely hoped was meant to be some sort of fish soup. Her stomach twisted, threatening a revolt if she put even a spoonful into her mouth. "I guess I'm not one for seafood." Clara winced as the words left her lips. Her mother would've whipped her backside and sent her off to bed hungry for refusing good food.

She took a deep breath. This wasn't the little house she'd once called home and there was more than just her mother and herself here. Whatever wasn't consumed by the court wouldn't go to waste.

Her gaze lifted from the bowl to the tables filling the castle's great hall. No matter how hard she tried to ignore the flurry of motion coming from the tables arrayed before them, she couldn't. Each mighty row of wood had its fair share of men and women. *I didn't think there'd be so many.* There had to be over a hundred people seated before her. *The whole court.* It had to be.

Those who sat closer to the head table were bedecked in finer clothing than she was. Several of them glittered in the candlelight as they moved. Most of them appeared engaged in their own little conversations. Even so, she couldn't shake the feeling that they were also secretly watching her.

It didn't help that she'd been seated at the head table, sharing it with not only Lucias but Count Farris and his family. Or at least a handful of his older children. Despite knowing the count had been married several times, she hadn't expected his family to be quite so large. Sixteen children if she'd heard right, the youngest being only three years of age.

At least she didn't have to share the table with all of them. Not that it would've mattered if Farris' entire family had surrounded her. Like Thad's blond mop of hair, she still would've stood out like a lit torch amongst so many dark-haired people. *I should've worn the scarf.* It would've been hot and uncomfortable, but she wouldn't be so easily spotted. The perfect target for an assassination if the neighbouring kingdoms were so inclined. *Bit late for such regrets.*

Another person's hand grasped the rim of her bowl.

Clara jerked upright, instinctively clutching her chest in search of her dagger. Her fingers had closed around the hilt when she realised it was merely Lucias.

"If you're only going to play with your food," he said, "then here..." In one swift move, he switched his empty bowl for her full one and proceeded to devour the contents, lifting the bowl ever nearer his mouth to speed the process.

She snickered into her gloved hand as he slurped down the last of her soup, forgoing the spoon altogether. In their time apart, she'd forgotten the amount of food he could consume in one sitting.

Clara poked his side. "You'll get fat if you keep eating so much." It was thrice the amount she'd seen any one man eat for a single meal, even during the Feast Days back in Everdark.

Lucias snorted and plonked the bowl back onto the table.

"I've been eating like this for half my life." He patted his stomach. "Haven't gained anything yet. *You*, on the other hand." His gaze swept over her, clearly pleased with what he saw. "I see Gettie has been making sure you eat well enough."

Growing warmth took hold of her cheeks. After months of being under the old woman's care and eating far more than she used to back in the village, Clara's body had definitely done much towards filling out a few of the hollows in her figure. Her daily routine of sparring with the guards—both in unarmed combat and with a short sword—was steadily aiding in shaping the rest.

Servants bustled around the table, collecting the empty bowls. More people pushed carts laden with domed platters into the room. Clara's nose twitched at the smell of roasted flesh wafting from them. It wasn't a familiar scent. Whilst Lucias and herself had eaten modestly enough in the Citadel, she rather doubted the court would follow suit.

Even so, her stomach gave what she hoped was a hungry grumble.

A pair of servants pushing one of the many carts advanced on the head table. A few more followed, each with an additional platter in hand. One from the latter group bowed to Lucias and presented him with one of the platters. At Lucias' nod, the servant lifted the lid. The steaming dish underneath was piled high and festooned with bright decorations.

Clara froze as a similar dish was set before her. The servants back in the Citadel never did this and, after months, they'd become so accustomed to her preferences that she never needed to ask them to prepare her anything more lavish than a stew.

The men bowed and moved down the table.

No longer so focused on the pair, Clara gradually became aware of how other servants were engaged in similar tasks around the room. They went along the tables in pairs, unveiling a domed platter for each guest. Quite different to how the food at the Citadel was served during the last feast. There, it had all been laid out on the table for anyone to grab in whatever portion they wished.

The blade of a knife clanked terribly against the rim of her plate—which she now saw was etched with swirls of gilding. Clara jumped, a startled squeak escaping her throat. She followed the knife to the hand holding it, then up the arm. Eventually glaring at Lucias.

Infuriatingly, he merely stared back, a tight smile gracing his lips. With that insufferable look on his face, he picked up his goblet and shook it at a passing servant.

It wasn't until the woman had refilled the goblet with wine and moved on that he spoke.

"Clara." His voice was pitched so quietly that her name escaped as little more than a sigh. "I rather doubt you've eaten a single thing today. You must be starving. If you don't start eating fairly soon, I shall summon a doctor."

She blinked, following his gaze to take in the half-consumed bulk of his meal and the untouched heap on her plate. Did he truly think her ill enough to warrant a doctor? *Most likely*. And such an action would garner all sorts of talk that she could do without.

Giving him a brief smile, she tried her best to ignore the servants still flitting about and turned her attention to the food. It was a bird of some sort, a *whole* roasted bird about half the size of the chickens she'd seen hanging in the butchery window down the street from her mother's home. The bird sat upon a slice of crisp bread, which seemed to be getting less crisp by the second, and was encircled by an assortment of steaming vegetables.

Clara poked the bird with her fork before plucking a slice of carrot from the base. At least that was recognisable. She frowned at the first bite. It didn't taste like any carrot she'd ever had. Not bad, a little sweeter than she liked, but not inedible. Emboldened, she moved on to the meat. That, too, surprised her by being not so different from the rabbits her father used to bring home.

On the edge of her vision, she could see Lucias watching her eat with visible relief.

Guilt twisted her stomach. She'd only refused the soup because she'd been unsure of the contents. She hadn't realised such refusals still upset him. Had she not made herself clear enough that she'd no intention of leaving his side, much less stage the same act of refusing food to get her way?

It was probably for the best to get his thoughts far from any idea of her being unwell. Clara clasped her goblet and washed down her mouthful with a sip of tart wine. Her stomach bubbled. She took a larger gulp of the wine, grimacing at the aftertaste. Whilst she only indulged in alcohol on the odd occasion, none of the wine back at the Citadel had been so foul.

Her gaze slid down the table. Farris was chatting with two of his three eldest children, at least those who were in the city, which meant there was the familiar presence of Thad amongst the strange faces. Thalia sat next to her husband, their oldest boy, Leonard, on her other side and next to him... Brenna.

"So," Clara said, her mind settling on the only detail it could. "Explain this to me again." She leant closer to Lucias, pressing her cheek against his shoulder so as to speak without being heard by anyone except him. "Brenna wasn't meant to marry Farris?"

She'd heard not long before Lucias' departure for Endlight of the change in the woman's engagement. Brenna was no longer destined to become another of the old count's wives, but rather a Lady of Endlight in the distant future. And considering the obvious swell of her belly—no doubt approaching five months now—had already gone to some length to ensure her future title remained that way.

Lucias grinned and dipped his head until his breath tickled her nose. "No, she was."

Clara tilted to discretely eye the woman from beneath Lucias' jaw. Brenna seemed quite at ease, obliviously chatting away to an older woman Clara hadn't been introduced to, smiling and laughing as the stranger spoke. On the surface, Brenna looked no different from when Clara had last seen her. But there was something about her face, the softness of her smile, that had her almost glowing. Was that due to her pregnancy or her recent marriage to Thad's oldest son?

Lucias took a sip from his goblet, blocking her view. He twisted to face her a little, resting an elbow on the table for balance and whispered against his shoulder. "It is my understanding that, after how they found them, Farris more or less conceded the girl to his grandson."

How they found them. Clara didn't need any more detail to imagine precisely how they had been discovered. "And I assume that is how she got into her current state?"

"Mhmm." His gaze dropped, it was only for a second, but it had definitely rested on her own unfertilized belly.

The food in her stomach turned leaden, rolling in the most disturbing fashion. She hastened to hide any show of unease on her face by forcing down another mouthful of sweetened carrots. Foolish to think that he wouldn't wish she was already carrying his child, especially after the attack on his life. Everyone, save for a select few, probably expected her to be pregnant by now, if not as far along as Brenna. "Do you regret not picking her?"

Lucias straightened in his seat, grinning. "Why would I possibly regret my choice?"

"You would've secured an heir by now." If he had chosen Brenna instead of Clara—or any of the other women except for Penny, really—then he could already be on his way to fatherhood. *And probably without marrying them.* Or would the lack of her presence mean he would've died during the barbarian's attack that almost *did* take his life?

His head twitched from side to side, his dark eyes rolling slightly back into his head as if he considered the same possibilities. "I suppose that could be true." He returned his full focus to her and his grin softened. "Except then I wouldn't be betrothed to such a woman as you. I cannot imagine any-one else having the courage to confront my mother un-armed, let alone that giant she brought with her."

Clara's face grew steadily hotter as he spoke. She flat-tened a hand on her chest in a vain attempt to steady the sudden wild beat of her heart.

Lucias brushed her cheek with the back of his fingers, so cool against the inferno of her skin. Tiny spots of silvery-blue light danced in his eyes. He bent close as if to kiss her.

For one brief moment, the world seemed to blur.

The cessation of movement caught her eye and Clara turned her head from him. That subtle action set her head spinning. "Not here," she whispered. "Not in front of all these people."

Those with seats closest to the head table had paused in their idle chatter. Men and women alike turned their heads in a casual fashion that spoke of staring without trying to appear as if they did so.

Lucias' gaze mimicked her own in inspecting the court before returning to her, his brow scrunched. "No kissing in public?" he murmured. His frown deepened. "You didn't seem so concerned when you first arrived."

Uncertain, and a little embarrassed as to what else she could possibly say, she picked at her food. Yes, she'd done poorly when it came to restraining herself in the courtyard. It'd been a tiring journey and seeing his face again after all those months had been enough to make her forget anyone else in the courtyard even existed. But here? Now? "They're *staring* at us."

He shrugged, which was about what she should've ex-pected from him. "Let them." Lucias drew her closer and tilted her head to one side. His breath tickled her ear, send-ing a pleasant shiver down her back. "Would it help if I told you what they're thinking?"

Clara twisted out of his grasp. "You can read minds, now?" Or was that just another facet of his magic that he'd neglected to inform her of?

Lucias chuckled. "Thank the Goddess I've no such power. Granted, it would be advantageous in certain situations, but I do believe *that* alone would be enough to drive a man mad." He leant back, steepling his fingers on the table. "But I can tell you they are curious about you."

"You don't say?" she muttered under her breath. She was the first woman in seven successions to become a wife instead of remaining as a mistress. Of course they were curious.

A faint smirk tweaked his lips. "Is there any doubt?" His eyes left her face for a split second to take in the room. "They sit there, their heads full of stories about this woman who saved their Great Lord from our murderous neighbours and *still* they wonder what's so special about her." He clasped her hand beneath the table. "Don't concern yourself with them. Better yet, show them that fire I fell in love with."

A part of her wanted to forget about those watching them and comply, for the rumours certainly had her doing far more than kissing. They'd the better part of a week until the wedding, then she would be required to kiss Lucias before the altar to seal their vows, in front of these very same men and women.

"I…" Clara wet her suddenly dry lips. Married before all these people; taking vows she'd rehearsed until her throat was sore. *What if I get them wrong?* Her already churning stomach clenched at the thought. How she wished Gettie was here instead of back at the Citadel. The old woman always seemed to know exactly what to say to calm Clara's nerves.

Lucias gave her hand a reassuring pat before returning to his meal, the absence of his fingers leaving her skin chill. He stared straight out at the crowd, his jaw twitching. One brow jerked upwards in her direction. Concern flickered across his face. The silvery-blue specks in his eyes had grown, twirling in the centres. Not quite one spinning glow, but close. "Clara? Are you all right?"

She'd barely opened her mouth when someone rapped their knuckles on the table.

"I request a quieting of the tables," Farris demanded of the room.

Clara glanced past her betrothed to find the old count on his feet with his goblet lifted high in the air. What was this? Her gaze flicked to Lucias, who seemed a little apprehensive of the man's movements, but vastly more interested in hers.

Lucias' hand alighted on her wrist. With one finger, he discretely pulled her glove down enough to expose her skin. He stared at her, his eyes almost white with light.

Her heart hammered faster. Was something wrong?

The collective chatter along the tables quietened and then died. Every face turned towards the head table. She took a deep breath, struggling against the urge to fan her uncomfortably warm cheeks. Nothing left to do but to remain aloof, show them that nothing could faze her. That was how the nobility handled these situations, wasn't it?

With the room silent, Farris continued, "It is our custom for a groom's father to address the clan before his son's wedding, to speak of his deeds and declare him as a suitable warrior for any woman. But, my lords and ladies, this right of our forefathers is not possible for our Great Lord." Farris tipped his goblet in Lucias' direction. "He has gifted me with the privilege of taking his father's place." He held the chalice to his chest and bowed his head.

Most of the men and women in the other tables mimicked him.

Clara watched on, puzzled and all too aware of Lucias' unwavering scrutiny in her. By the look in his face, he expected her to faint at any moment.

That wasn't an entirely foolish thought. She certainly felt hot enough. It had to be all the people crammed into one room. *One enormous room.* Her gaze rolled to the candles and the fireplaces flanking the tables.

Discretely unfastening the top button of her gown, Clara turned her attention to Farris. She'd expected the count to adhere to his people's customs, but not for a speech to come so soon. Was she also meant to be doing as they all did?

She went to follow and was stopped from lifting her arm by a faint pressure on her wrist. Beneath the table, Lucias clasped her hand. He shook his head, a small bemused smile tweaking his lips. At least he'd stopped his unnerving studying of her and his eyes had returned to their normal dark colour.

Clara squeezed his fingers, smiling when he replied in kind.

Farris cleared his throat. "I know some of you are here only to become a part of history, to watch our Great Lord take the forever vows with his mistress, but *I* am here for a higher reason." He held up his hand as troubled murmurs rose through the crowd. "I have watched this boy grow into a man. It is no secret that he spent many years here, training on the front lines."

"He trained on our borderline too, my old friend," a man called out from somewhere in the crowd.

"That he did," Farris conceded. "Fought long and hard. Unflinching like a true warrior of the moors." He jabbed a finger at the now enthralled audience. It somewhat reminded Clara of the old man back on the streets of Everdark who'd tried to warn the village of what the previous Great Lord's death would mean to them. "I stand here before you all to declare I have seen our Great Lord's worth and judge this man as being no less a warrior than one of my own sons." He clapped a hand on Thad's shoulder, whose whole face was flushed red. "Who among you would dare to say the same?"

"I would dare!" a different man yelled from somewhere towards the far end of the room. "He single-handedly kept the savages at bay when our outer defences fell last winter."

"As would I." A woman, bedecked in a wealth of pale blue silk and sitting at the front of the tables, jumped to her feet. "Instead of diverting his men from their rounds, he tracked down the bandits responsible for the attack on my carriage." Her chin lifted. "By himself."

More cries followed the pair. Some just shouted their declaration, whilst others revealed what Lucias had done to protect their part of the kingdom.

Clara dared another glance at her betrothed, surprised to find Lucias seemed rather embarrassed by the display. He'd never mentioned any of this before. Oh, he would regale her with tales of the places he'd been to and of the sights he longed to show her. But what he *did* there?

Well, according to him, he trained and patrolled like any guard. Not once had he talked about stopping an invasion or hunting down bandits single-handedly.

Lucias caught her staring and grimaced. "I see Farris has had too much wine already." He got to his feet and raised his hands along with his voice. "People, please."

The cries of the crowd died.

"These words are not necessary. It is my duty to keep our kingdom safe, whether the enemy comes from beyond our borders or within our very lands." He smiled down at her and she knew her cheeks matched his in redness. "Think of these coming days as history if you wish. To me, it is simply an affirmation of how I feel for my dear Clarabelle, who I'm sure you've just overwhelmed."

Clara stared incredulously up at him. After everything she'd been through, he dared to claim a few dozen proclamations of his past actions would overwhelm her?

She stood, her palms slapping against the table. Her legs shook as they took her weight, causing the room to spin. Wrapping her arm about his waist helped steady her, but it did nothing to still the room.

Lucias twisted in her hold and she grabbed his cravat, pulling his mouth within reach whilst he was ensnared by shock. Their lips touched and he instantly pulled her tighter into his embrace. There wasn't the same tingly magic of the kiss they'd shared in the courtyard, but with the thrill of knowing everyone watched on—a few cheering as Lucias tipped her back and deepened the kiss—it came surprisingly close.

Hauling her upright, he parted them enough to breathe and allowed her to regain her footing. "I thought we weren't up to public kisses?" He gently brushed the hair from her face. "Was it something I said?" His grin widened. "If so, please do tell me what it was and I'll keep on saying it."

Clara leant against him and laughed breathlessly, stopping as the room gave a little twirl. *Oh no.* Was this the wine's doing? But she'd been so careful, indulging only in a single goblet-full and half of that still sat on the table. It had to be the lack of food. She probably shouldn't have drunk so much on a near-empty stomach.

Still feeling lightheaded, she pressed their foreheads together. "I don't feel so good," she whispered. She'd thought the breathless feeling had come from their kiss, but her heart still beat like her mother's sewing machine working at full pace and her chest heaved with each shuddering breath. "Get me out of here."

The drag of his brows against her skin spoke of a frown. He pulled back. "You do seem to be getting paler. Do you want me to call for a doctor?"

Clara shook her head, instantly regretting it. Not here. She couldn't possibly linger here, underneath the keen stares of the court, for more than a couple of minutes. She rocked back on her heels. How odd that her head had seemed perfectly fine when she was seated. "To be honest, I'm just a little lightheaded."

His face creased with concern and his gaze flicked down to the table. What thoughts crossed his mind? This was merely a case of mild drunkenness. "Maybe you just need some fresh air." Lucias grasped her elbow, steadying her. "Come, we'll take a stroll around the gardens. You'll love them."

The servants, as if responding to some command Clara hadn't seen him give, scurried up to move the heavy chairs out of the way.

"My lord?" Farris called out as they went to leave the table. "Do you retire so soon? There is still more to be had."

In one smooth motion, Lucias guided her off the dais and gave the count a bow. "My apologies, Farris. It is late and my lady *did* only arrive today."

"But of course." Farris waved his hand in the air, brushing aside the apology as if it hadn't needed to be said. "I forget how weary travel can make a person not used to it and she'll need all the rest she can get, eh?" His polite smile twisted suggestively and he gave a meaningful chuckle as Lucias led her away.

Clara silently cursed her heating cheeks for burning so readily at the count's notion of what was to happen this coming week. A dead man could tell he spoke of the night before her wedding, when Lucias was meant to come to her room and steal her away or, at least, lie with her. Few knew that would not be so and it seemed Farris was not one of them.

Whispers flew in their wake, just as they'd done earlier whenever she set foot outside her chambers. The words they spoke need not be heard, for the faces they came from could've filled volumes no matter how hard those very people tried to conceal their thoughts behind a facade of politely worried smiles.

No doubt they believed their Great Lord planned to retire to his bed for the night, dragging her along with him. The very idea of them coming to such a conclusion was an unsettling one. But why wouldn't they? She was leaving in the presence of her betrothed after having initiated a public kiss. Rumour alone had made her far more scandalous than she'd ever dare to be.

Lucias' expression remained unchanged as he slowly aimed her towards the closest door. That had to mean they were headed for the kitchens.

She shrunk from the thought of entering a place blazing with more heat. Already, what had originally been a cosy warmth was too much. She opened her mouth, the suggestion of an alternative route already on her tongue, when the churning of her stomach returned. It grew stronger the longer they walked. More rebellious.

Clara lengthened her steps. The last thing she was prepared to let happen was vomit in front of the whole court. Not for anything.

Chapter Four

They wove through the crowd of servants, both those in the room and others waiting on the far side of the doors. The rattle and jumbled chatter of a busy kitchen hit her. Clara winced at the noise, shrinking into Lucias' arms. He rubbed her shoulder, gently guiding her onwards. She stifled a groan. Forward meant heading towards the growing heat of the ovens.

"It's just a little further," Lucias murmured in her ear.

Sweat sprung across her forehead. Her stomach clenched. Bile slid up her throat, gagging her as she fought to keep it down. Tears increased their flow, turning the world into shimmering light. It didn't matter how far away the gardens were, she wasn't going to make it.

She pushed Lucias aside, stumbling blindly in search of a bucket... a bowl... anything.

Her fingers latched onto the rim of something round.

Liquid and chewed chunks of food poured out her mouth the very second she bent her head. Her whole body shuddered in its efforts to expel everything she'd eaten for the night. And possibly the previous night's meal as well.

Then it was over, leaving her wrung out.

Her legs shook. Faced with the prospect of being dumped onto the floor, she bent over the table. It required pushing aside the bowl before her. That was what she'd grasped, a big metal bowl similar to the one the Citadel cooks used for mixing bread dough. Mercifully empty before she'd gotten hold of it.

There was a faint tug on her head as she moved. Belatedly, she realised someone had grabbed her hair and pulled it back from the bowl. Turning her head a fraction brought Lucias' carefully neutral face into view.

Someone on her left touched her shoulder. "Miss? Here." The woman pressed a cool glass into Clara's hand. "Just the thing to soothe the stomach, Miss," the woman added as she grabbed the bowl and swiftly replaced it with an empty one.

Clara sipped at the cloudy liquid half-filling the glass. The sharp tang of ginger hit her tongue, mingling with the acrid taste already in the back of her throat. She shuddered, but took another sip. Did she still look so poorly that the woman thought Clara would repeat the act? She certainly didn't feel much better.

"Don't drink too much at once," Lucias cautioned, handing her a length of cloth that dripped water. "You don't want it coming back up."

With her hands still shaking, Clara cleaned herself up between taking carefully measured sips. She took a final swallow of the ginger-tinged water and set it aside. Her legs wobbled anew as they took her weight.

"Come, my dear." Lucias took up her hand, gently cupping her elbow. "Walk with me a while. Perhaps some fresh air will help ease your stomach." He guided her to another doorway before she had the wherewithal to nod her agreement, patiently letting her dictate the pace.

The door took them out into a narrow, vacant corridor. Cool air caressed her face and took the edge off the wretched sogginess that had grasped her limbs. Clara breathed deeply as they walked, willing her stomach to stop fluttering and disgusted it wouldn't obey such a command. It was empty bar a half-cup of liquid. What was left for it to protest?

Lucias ran his hand up and down her back in light, reassuring strokes. The action was somewhat at odds with the concern plastered across his face and the anger evident in the flicker of silvery-blue light in his eyes. Small though they were, the sparks still flashed in the gloom. "How are you feeling now?"

"Still terrible," she mumbled. Even away from the warmth of the kitchens, the unbearable heat continued to plague her.

He nodded as if expecting that very reply. There was a hitch in his stride as he fumbled with something in a small pouch on his belt. "Here," he whispered, pressing a slim glass vial into her hand. "Drink this. It should fix that."

Clara uncorked the vial and downed the brown sludge without a second thought. Her very hair seemed to shudder at the bitterness coating her tongue. She gagged. Her stomach rolled, still deciding on whether to reject this strange concoction. "What was that?" The words barely escaped her without her biting her tongue.

"It's the antidote for a large variety of poisons." He took the vial back from her and returned it to the pouch. "I always keep a few on me."

Heat drained from her face. She wasn't certain if it was due to the vial's effects or the implication that... "Someone tried to poison me?" She hadn't even been here a day. How could there already be people in place to make an attempt on her life? And why hadn't they gone straight for Lucias?

"Well, it was either that or the food was far too rich for you. But I'd prefer to err on the side of caution when it comes to your wellbeing. I'll bring a few vials for you in the morning. Right after I send a few of my people to interrogate the kitchen staff."

Clara silently ran her tongue over her teeth. *His people.* He had to mean the soulless men who made up the Great Lord's army. Several such troops would currently be patrolling the castle grounds alongside Endlight's usual guard.

He rubbed at his chin. "Discretely, I would think. In the meantime, it would probably be best if we keep your food on the blander side until we can determine the culprit. It'll be far harder for them to mask poison without the help of spices. It might take a few days, though. I hope you don't mind."

Clara shook her head, her thoughts still caught up in the reality of someone wanting *her* dead more than the Great Lord. It had to be one of the neighbouring kingdoms, most likely an order from the Ebony Court at Ne'ermore. "I thought this was supposed to be a safe place," she murmured.

His lips twisted sourly. "The only place in the kingdom for me, for *us*, that comes close to being safe is the Citadel."

She frowned, recalling how the Citadel had been breached, and Lucias almost slain, by that giant of a man Lenora brought with her. "So suspect everyone is what you're saying?" And hope they didn't have a horde of barbarians to call upon.

Lucias gave a soft chuckle. "Not *everyone*, you can trust Farris and his family, but on the whole? If you're the slightest bit uncertain, then yes. Come." He indicated a high, carved archway leading out into the night. "This way."

The gardens opened out before her as she stepped through. Torches illuminated an ambling trail through the gloom, throwing strange shadows amongst the stark flower-beds. The space beyond the flickering light seemed to stretch forever in the dark, yet she sensed the even darker masses of the castle walls looming over them. Guards no doubt prowled such heights, their attention fixated on the sleeping city beyond the stone barrier.

She strolled along the path in silence with Lucias at her side, their every footfall crunching amongst the gravel. Few new plants sought to grow in the cold soil, although a number of shrubs were making a valiant effort in sprouting a handful of tiny leaves in expectation of the coming spring.

Lucias watched her, frowning. "I noticed your mother isn't amongst the people accompanying you." His breath misted in the air as he spoke.

Idly rubbing at her bare arms, Clara grimaced. "She

didn't respond." Not directly, at least. They may not have parted in the most amenable of ways, but the woman was still her mother. They were the only family each other still had and she'd been foolish enough to believe her mother would want to witness Clara's wedding.

She'd sent her page down to the village to deliver the news to her mother some months back. *Poor Tommy.* In hindsight, she should've expected her mother to take out her anger on the lad, should've sent a guard to protect him. She would've gone herself had Lucias not already have left for Endlight. She would *not* make such a mistake again.

"She still hasn't forgiven you for getting chosen by my people?"

Clara shook her head. Anyone listening to her mother rant on about Clara's disrespect of her would've thought Clara had a choice in entering the Great Lord's carriage all those months ago.

I can't believe she's still bitter over it. Given what her mother had planned, she was fortunate in swapping a marriage she didn't want for one she'd chosen. Lucias was a far better choice than some cobbler who was old enough to be her grandfather. Even without the trappings of being the Great Lord.

"Perhaps it's better this way."

She shrugged and rubbed a little harder at her arms. *Perhaps.* She would've preferred having family here, but if her mother wasn't prepared to lay aside her poisonous tongue for one day and be happy for her daughter, then maybe Lucias was right.

The longer they lingered in the cold night air, the more it burrowed into her skin. How she regretted not choosing one of the other gowns she'd brought with her. They may not have been as extravagant as the one she currently wore, having far less lace and embroidery than a formal occasion would demand of the soon-to-be Great Lady, but several of the gowns had full-length sleeves. Next time, she would do the prudent thing and bring a stole.

Lucias removed his coat, the shadows turning the dark red of his vest almost black. "Feeling the cold is a good sign," he said, draping the heavy coat around her shoulders. "I take it that we're starting to feel better?"

She nodded and drew the coat tighter around her shoulders, the fabric still warm with his body heat. Despite the soft churning in her gut, she was indeed feeling far better than she had whilst under scrutiny in the Great Hall, or even in the kitchen.

They'd almost completed a full circuit of the garden when Lucias cleared his throat. "I am sorry... about Farris, that is. He's never been one to hold his tongue."

Clara grunted and lengthened her stride, aiming for the small amount of warmth the hallways offered. She'd already surmised such an opinion of the man, but there were far greater things to occupy her mind than what the count had said. Five months was certainly long enough for word of Lucias' survival, and his impending wedding, to reach Ne'ermore. But to have someone sent into the castle? Someone who would prepare the Great Lord's meals? "I take it you've not divulged the little titbit about us not fully observing Endlight's customs."

Lucias scuffed his boot along the path, sending up a spray of pebbles. "No," he said, sighing. "He's a bit... set in his ways. I didn't want to bother him with that bit when he's been so accommodating about having the wedding here."

Of course he would be willing to assist, you're their Great Lord. Sometimes, she wondered if Lucias had actually forgotten he ruled these people. Or was it more a case of him preferring to forget that he did? "Won't everyone realise when you don't spirit me from my chambers on the eve of our wedding?"

Lucias smiled and wrapped an arm companionably around her shoulders.

Clara peered at him. There was something about the way his mouth twitched that gave her pause. "Except you *are* intending on doing just that, aren't you?" She shook her head, softly chiding herself. How had she not anticipated such an answer sooner?

"Do I plan to spirit you off to my quarters? No. But, I *did* promise to teach you a few things before we were married. Besides, if it *looks* like we're adhering to Endlight's custom, then everyone will believe—"

"—that we had sex?" She pulled free of his grip, tugging the coat tighter about her as a different sort of chill settled in her stomach. He sought to stoke the fires of rumour rather than let the embers die?

All those eyes. The way they watched her, waiting for her to do something to feed their gossip. Well, she'd certainly given them *that. And then some.* And once word got out of her display in the kitchen. They'd probably believed her to be deathly ill or…

Pregnant.

Clara slowed. Five months had passed since Lenora failed to kill her son. That was plenty of time for something to happen. No one would believe they hadn't been intimate months before the eve of their wedding. Lucias had warned her often enough of what people would think, more times than she wished to count. He likely found all the whispers flying about amusing.

Well, she'd come to accept that changing their thoughts on such a matter was simply not within her power.

"You wish to deceive everyone rather than let them know the truth?" Whether or not she deliberately allowed the truth to be warped in such a way was the only thing she'd some measure of control over. "I'm not sure I could—"

"We've been over this," Lucias said. "I'm not asking for you to change your wish, nor do I seek to break my promise that you will go before the altar a virgin. Simply that none of them will believe me if I told them we'd never been intimate. *Thad* barely believed it and he has no reason to doubt my words. I see little harm in us sharing a room for the night; it's not as if we won't become husband and wife the next day. If anything, it would ease my concerns regarding your safety."

Clara crossed her arms, trying to hide it in tugging the coat tighter around her. She'd not begun to think about what manner of harm could come whilst she was abed. Until now.

He frowned, the wavering torchlight throwing odd shadows across his face. "But my being there's not what's worrying you, is it?" Lucias shook his head. "I don't understand. Why does it matter to you what they think?"

She stared out at the garden hiding in the darkness beyond the light, her eyes adjusting to the gloom until she made out the trees huddled against the walls. Her mother may not have put much faith in gossip, but if Clara ever had a chance to control even a fraction of the rumours, she'd rather be known as the woman who bullied their Great Lord into marriage before sex instead of the one who begged to become his wife *after* the act. "It doesn't matter what they think," she whispered.

"Not to me but, clearly, *you* care."

She whirled on him. "You *don't?*" Her gaze dropped as she grabbed great fistfuls of her skirt. "Or are you telling me you are fine with what they think of me?" Hearing the current rumours of what they supposedly did behind closed doors was bad enough, but who knew what else they thought of them that the people *didn't* voice.

Lucias grasped her hands, his calloused fingers gently prying her skirts free of her grip. "The worst they will think of you is that we've made love before our wedding. Most of them will have done the *exact* same thing, sometimes with those they're not even destined to marry. And a handful of *those* people will currently be cheating on their husband or wife. So, no, I don't see the point in distressing myself with what they'll think of us." His grip loosened. One hand caressed her cheek. "I am more concerned with your thoughts."

She cocked her head, prolonging the touch. "*My* thoughts?"

"Yes, yours." He released her other hand to pace before her, his boots pounding across the gravel in deep, murderous strides. "Is this your way of saying you've changed your mind? I know I shouldn't have left you alone at the Citadel, but if I'd stayed…" He raked his fingers through his hair, pulling several strands free of where it was tied at the neck. "Well… if my mother had returned, I would've felt better knowing she couldn't get hold of you so easily. Leaving was the only way I could possibly keep my promise to protect you."

She rolled her eyes. He'd made the same claim before leaving her with only a handful of the soulless servants and her page for company.

Lucias grabbed her shoulders, nearly lifting her off the ground in his urgency. "If—" His throat constricted with a faint gulp. Silvery-blue light danced in the centre of his eyes, then vanished. "If you are having reservations about marrying me—about anything at all—then please, don't wait until we're before the altar to let me know. Tell me now."

She caressed his cheek, felt the tightness of his jaw. He was fully prepared for her answer to be an unfavourable one. And why not? He'd been raised to believe that the love of another was something he'd never know. That securing an heir was meant to precede everything else, even if it also meant giving up on what he craved the most.

What you want, you simply cannot hope to possess. Her face heated at the memory. It seemed like a lifetime since she'd last spoken those words, lashing out like a child seeking to hurt out of spite and fear. What did it matter that for most of his life it had been all too true?

On the other hand, everyone was in agreement that the Great Lords went mad in the end. Lucias had been the one to tell her that the last Great Lord to marry had killed his own wife, and that man's son had gone on to be the first one labelled as a Dark Lord by the other kingdoms. It seemed to her that the descendants had only embraced the title.

Yet, staring up into Lucias' eyes, dark without the silvery-blue specks of light... No madness lurked in their depths. Fear, yes. The terror of losing what he'd only begun to accept he could gain. But also love and unending patience.

Clara flung herself against him, readjusting herself as his sword hilt dug into her side. "You're a fool," she mumbled into his shoulder, her arms encircling his chest. *My fool*. How remarkable it was to watch a man who possessed the power to destroy a city become so timid in her arms.

He tentatively wrapped his arms around her. "Does that mean you haven't changed your mind? Because I can have a carriage prepared for you within the hour. You could go wherever you desire."

"Tempting," she teased. "But I'd much rather wait until after the wedding to travel the kingdom."

"*Our* kingdom," he murmured. His arms tightened, all but crushing her. Only the stiff panels of her corset saved her from the full force of his embrace. "You swear?"

Clara wriggled in the small space left to her, gaining enough room to thread her fingers into his hair. With very little coaxing, he dropped the inch she needed to be level with him. She looked him straight in the eye. "I swear," she whispered.

His eyes closed and a small relieved sigh gusted out his mouth. He pressed his lips against her temple and, as they stood there in the cool torch-lit gloom of the garden, she swore his mouth twitched into a smile.

CHAPTER FIVE

$\mathcal{T}$he chime of the temple bells filled the air. Their tuneless song hammered in Clara's head. Wincing, she turned from the wardrobe, temporarily abandoning her search for a respectable daytime gown. She parted the heavy window curtains just enough to let in the first fingers of sunlight.

The sun was barely high enough to illuminate the city rooftops. Even with the journey here and the sickness of last night taxing her, she couldn't sleep much beyond dawn.

From up here, Endlight didn't look any different to her village. The same roofs, tile or thatch depending on the wealth of the owners. The styles barely differed from home, the roofs might've been a little steeper and the chimney tops were bulkier, but it was the same wood, stone and plaster walls. Nothing to really denote a change in places.

She leant on the window frame and glowered at the sight. *I can't believe I slept in.* Her mother would've switched her for the very audacity of her idleness. Down there, people would be beginning their day. Some would've already started it before the sun was even up, much like she'd done when still living with her mother.

The temple bells chimed again and she rubbed her forehead until the dreadful clanging stopped. Her throbbing head was bearable as long as quiet reigned. She took a small amount of comfort in knowing that she at least didn't share the malady of those who had heavily indulged during dinner and were unfortunate enough to greet this morning with a head sore from wine.

Not that being possibly poisoned was any better.

She sauntered back to the wardrobe, her boot heels clacking against the bare floor, and continued her endeavour of dressing. A little thrill shivered down her back as her fingers brushed the soft linen of her travel dress. She'd spent much of her time in the dark, nondescript gown. It had little in the way of adornments, no lace, barely any form... Just the thing for travelling across the land without drawing too much notice.

Sighing, she pushed the outfit aside for another. With its fair share of embroidery along the apron skirts and the bodice sleeves, the red and black fabric might not leave her as easily hidden in the crowd, but it was no less comfortable. More importantly, it was an outfit befitting the Great Lady.

Sadly, dressing in it took a little more time than usual. Unlike in the Citadel, no one had come to check on her. It was possible the servants had been given orders not to disturb the Great Lord's mistress or, more likely, no one thought she'd be awake this early. Whatever the reason, it'd left her with the option of tightening the laces of her corset on her own or remaining here until someone showed up.

The opportunity to dress in solitude had become an increasingly rare one since Lucias' departure from the Citadel. The women there treated her like a wealthy child's doll, all but dressing her each morning despite her numerous protests. Never had she considered that she might actually want their help but, whilst caught in the midst of a brief battle with the laces of her corset, she *did* wish there was someone to aid with the back.

It took quite a bit of grumbling and fussing as she peeked over her shoulder at the full-length mirror. She'd only recently started to come to terms with the idea of such fashion and, usually, she would forgo the corset if she could for the comfortable familiarity of a bodiced petticoat. That garment had the added bonus of lacing at the sides, too. But this wasn't the Citadel and her wedding gown required such an item to be presentable. She might as well start getting accustomed to the blasted thing.

Her skirts and bodice were far easier to manage, even with the fiddly buttons. Although, she did forgo the silly bustle cage that the Citadel women insisted she pack. What did she care that it was coming into fashion? The ruffles of her petticoat and apron skirt already had her backside looking big enough. She didn't need any more help there.

She fastened the last of her jacket's little buttons and took in her reflection, twisting every which way to ensure she wasn't flashing her petticoat. The skirt tail dragged slightly with each swish, but everything seemed to be in place. *Finally*. It must've taken a good half-hour. She was definitely losing touch with her technique if she couldn't do something as simple as dressing herself.

Still, the next time she travelled, it wouldn't hurt to have one—just *one*—of the servants nearby to help her. *Maybe...* Clara frowned. What was the woman's name? The brunette from the Citadel kitchen. Gettie called her...

Clara huffed. She knew the woman's face, could picture it clearly as if the woman stood before her, but the name continued to elude her thoughts.

Grumbling under her breath, she plonked herself before the vanity and set about taming the mess that a night of restless sleep had made of her hair. The woman's name was going to bug her. But surely she couldn't be expected to know the name of *every* servant that came through the Citadel, could she?

She tugged viciously at her hair, forcing the knots out and gritting against the pain. *I should know*. She was not going to become one of those snobbish nobles everyone in the village despised. She would learn as many names as she could. It didn't matter that those serving in the Citadel no longer had their souls, they were still people.

Dressed and groomed, she belted on her dagger and secured it beneath the voluminous, satin folds of her apron. The castle had already proven itself less safe than the Citadel, she was not about to wander the halls without some form of defence.

She opened the door leading out into the corridor.

Lucias stood in the hallway, his hand poised to knock. Rare were the chances she got to see anything other than carefully controlled emotion adorn his face, but the mildly surprised expression could hardly be contrived.

His shock wasn't there for long before his lips swiftly curved into that delightfully cocky smile she'd begun to miss. "Good morning, love." In one smooth motion, he stepped away from the door and swept her into the hallway. "You're up earlier than I was anticipating. I trust you are well?"

She nodded. Although her head still faintly throbbed, little else ailed her. "I couldn't sleep another second," she confessed, deliberately omitting that her restlessness state was due to the after-effects of last night. If she had been poisoned, then the little vial of antidote seemed to have done its job.

Instead, she grasped his arm, taking almost possessive hold of the limb, and allowed him to steer her along the corridors. "It's the first city I've ever visited."

Lucias' shoulders trembled with silent laughter. He smiled fondly. "I've been here so many times, seen everything this place has to offer, that I forget how different it feels to newcomers."

Clara felt her cheeks warm. She probably sounded like some oik off a farm.

"However," he continued, "Thalia has expressed a desire to have you join her and the rest of the noblewomen in the solarium. She seems to think a day of gossip and needlework and whatever else they do there would be prudent after your unfortunate reaction to the food last night."

Is that what we're calling it? She hummed thoughtfully. It probably was for the best if talks of poison didn't leak to castle staff before Lucias could enquire further. But would it not be easier for someone to poison her amongst all those women when they'd already proven capable of doing so in the middle of a banquet? "Is that why you're here? To escort me there?"

He grinned and the years seem to vanish from his face. "Actually, I thought you'd much rather prefer to see Endlight than being holed up in some room where..." His eyes suddenly widened and he fumbled with a small pouch. "I almost forgot. Here." Lucias pressed the pouch into her hands. "Some more of the vials."

Clara silently accepted the pouch and discreetly fastened it beneath her skirts, gifting her easy access to them via a pocket. "See... Endlight?" she mumbled once the ties were fastened, hoping that was what he'd been about to speak of. The carriage's tinted windows hadn't afforded her the best view of the streets.

Lucias' head bobbed like a rambunctious boy recently cut loose from his mother's side. "We could take a trip around the city. I'd love to show you some of it up close."

"On foot?" Her feet tingled at the thought. Although they were artfully booted to suit a noble's personal guard more than the demure noblewoman she was expected to become, she doubted it would take much walking before all her excitement was sapped.

He grunted. "Of course not." Placing his hand in the small of her back and cupping her elbow, he guided her down a flight of steps. "I wouldn't risk the ear-lashing Thalia would give me if I had you walk the distance I have in mind."

Clara shook her head. "As much as I would love to see the city, I don't think I could stand looking at another carriage just now, much less ride in one." Not even if it was open-topped. "Maybe another time." They'd a few days of being in this city before the wedding and likely several more afterwards. Surely there would be plenty of opportunities for her to see some of Endlight's sights.

Lucias' lips twitched into a secretive little smile. They turned a corner and began their descent of another set of stairs. "Actually, I wasn't thinking of taking a carriage either."

"Then how?" There were only a handful of options in regards to transport.

The corners of his eyes crinkled further. "*That*, my dear, is a surprise."

He continued to lead her through the winding hallways, remaining in smug silence. They saw few people along the way and those she *did* spy wore the attire of the castle servants. It was possible that a great deal of the nobility were still nursing sore heads.

With nothing else to distract her, she considered the options of transportation left to them. Only one made sense. "You plan for me to travel via horseback, don't you?" She'd gone into Everdark perched upon his destrier's wide rump a handful of times, but the trip didn't take long. He surely wouldn't expect her to do so whilst sightseeing.

Lucias huffed dramatically. "You know, it takes all the fun out of surprising someone if they guess it beforehand."

"So it *will* be on horseback, then?" she pressed. Her stomach flopped at the thought of being the one in sole control of such a beast. "You know I can't ride." And her dress was hardly suited for the act.

He chuckled. "You'll be perfectly safe with me. And I would've tried to sway your mind about the carriage, but horseback really is the best way to see the Pillars."

She clamped her free hand upon his sleeve. The famed Pillars of Endlight. It was the one view she longed to see out her window. Sadly, her chambers faced the moors rather than the mountain range. All this he must've known. "You..." Clara glared at Lucias only to have him smirk back and waggle his eyebrows. "Fine, we'll take your black brute of an animal." She could suffer clinging to him if her reward was seeing the Pillars up close.

"*That* wasn't quite what I had in mind." The pressure of

his hand on her back increased, giving Clara no other option but to trot along with him as they slipped beneath the massive archway of the main entrance and descended the stairs.

I know. But she could hope that wasn't so. The alternative didn't bear thinking about.

Out in the courtyard, men milled around in a parody of the efficient stablemen she'd left back at the Citadel. They scurried about their business, seeming to get into each other's way more often than not.

Three men stood near the base of the stairs. Two of them wore the muted green and gold livery of Endlight. The pair fought to keep Lucias' stallion from moving as the beast pawed at the ground in obvious objection to their handling.

Tommy was the third man and he held the reins of another, rather more docile, horse. It nuzzled her dear page, seemingly searching for whatever he kept in his pockets. He smiled up at them as they neared, absently stroking the animal's neck.

Lucias left her side to assist the two men with his destrier. He laid a hand on his mount. The animal instantly stilled at his master's touch and Lucias waved the men away. "What do you think?" he asked her, indicating the other horse.

Clara eyed the second animal as she joined them at the foot of the stairs. It was smaller, yet more solid-looking, than Lucias' black destrier. Not as dark either, its rump speckled with a pattern of light grey rosettes. "It's a horse." What else could he possibly expect her to say? She knew very little about these creatures.

"It's a pony," Tommy clarified.

Lucias took up her hand and drew her closer to the grey beast. "He was to be one of your wedding gifts, but..." He shrugged. "As I said, Endlight *is* best seen on horseback."

She stared at the pony. It looked back at her with a vacant, almost bored, gleam in his eyes. Compared to the brute standing beside it, the animal was certainly less intimidating, but she still didn't trust such a look. Not when she'd seen so-called placid carthorses cave in a dog's skull with a single kick. *What am I supposed to do with a horse?*

"I can't ride," she repeated in the vain hope that the surrounding company would have Lucias reconsider. Granted, it hadn't been too bad sitting behind Lucias on his destrier, but what was she supposed to do if this creature suddenly took it upon itself to take command? What if it ran off with her on its back?

He shrugged. "You will learn."

"But—"

"Clara." Her name reached her ears in such a lifeless tone that she scarcely believed it had passed his lips. He tugged her arm, tipping her against him. "There may come a time where you will need to run," he whispered. "And when it does, I don't wish for your only choice to be on foot."

She stared up at him, swearing her blood had just run cold through her veins. *When?* Not if. He truly believed her life could be put in such danger.

The steady pressure of his hands upon her shoulders scooted her towards the animal. "I picked him just for you." The words boomed through the courtyard, far too cheerful given his previous words. "He's gentle, solid but fast and, should you ever so happen to fall, it's not that far to the ground." He clicked his fingers.

One of the castle servants trotted over with a wooden block and set it beside the pony.

Smiling, Tommy held the reins out to her. "He won't bite."

That's not the bit I'm worried about. Clara placed a boot on the block, her stomach cramping in a distinct threat towards emptying itself. Was she really prepared to ride this unruly creature? She gave the thick neck a half-hearted pat, surprised when the pony continued standing there. *Very well, not unruly...* Yet. But how would it behave once she was atop its back?

At least it bore a decent saddle, with the style reminiscent to the gear Lucias' destrier wore, and not the scant pad of leather they expected most ladies to use. "Maybe we could visit the Pillars some other day?" she suggested, hoping the promise of a future ride would be enough.

Lucias' dark brows lowered in disappointment. "I am *not* negotiable on this." The firm coil of his magic embraced her waist, lifting her off the ground and leaving her straddling the pony's back with the leather sticking and grating against her legs.

She wriggled in the seat, silently cursing herself for not choosing to wear her long bloomers. And her dress, not suited to riding in the slightest, bunched about her something fierce. *I should've suggested changing.* Her travelling attire wasn't nearly as bulky as this.

Except voicing such a thing would've been seen as another excuse to not ride at all. At least her corset didn't adhere to the longer fashion that could lead to hindering her movements and her skirts still covered a great deal of her legs. She tilted to one side to check. What the fabric didn't conceal was encased in the supple leather of her boots.

The pony shuffled on the spot as she attempted to adjust her attire, his hooves clicking against the cobblestone. Giving a yelp, Clara clawed at the reins and hauled on them until the thin strips of leather bit into her fingers.

Beside her, Lucias shook his head and tut-tutted. "Don't hold the reins so tightly, my dear." He carefully arrayed her skirts so they draped over the pony's rump and still allowed her to remain decent. "He won't bolt on you."

"And if he does?" she countered. It couldn't take much. She risked a glance his way and saw him grinning back at her.

"Then I will stop him." Giving the pony's neck a pat, he turned to his horse and vaulted onto the massive animal's back. "Let the poor pony have his head."

Taking a deep breath, she carefully lowered her arms until the pony's neck wasn't quite as bunched up. The pony shook his head, sending his black mane flying and causing Clara to squeak, before he settled back to his original still state with a sigh.

Lucias nudged the destrier closer. "*Now* will you permit me the honour of showing you about the city?"

Swallowing the sudden prickly terror bobbing in her stomach, Clara nodded. How did they get these creatures to move? Kicking? *Of course.* She tapped her heels against the pony's barrel-like ribs and the animal took a shuffling step forward. Another, stronger, boot turned the shuffle into a swaying plod.

Lucias urged his eager mount beside her as they exited the courtyard. "See?" His horse was not being anywhere near as accommodating in keeping to the slow pace, preferring to all but jog on the spot in order to comply with his rider's order. "Sable's about as quiet as they come without being near death."

"Sable?" Clara echoed. She knew some people named their animals. Not having had the luxury of a pet, or even a working beast, the idea had always sounded a little strange.

The pony's ears swivelled back at the sound of his name.

Feeling a little bolder, she leant forward and patted the soft neck. "Good Sable," she murmured and, again, the ears twitched. Perhaps not *all* of these beasts weren't to be trusted.

Straightening in the saddle, she turned her gaze to the streets beyond the castle walls.

This early in the morning, the sun hadn't crept high enough to remove the faint, glittering layer of frost the winter-crisp air had left on the buildings. It didn't deter those already up and about. People resigned to travelling the day on foot wandered the road edges, leaving the main section open for carts and those who were, like Lucias and herself, on horseback.

Both drivers and riders ignored them as they ambled along the well-worn cobbles. The same couldn't be said for the city's pedestrians. Clara blushed as people turned their heads to watch them pass by. Even after the multiple trips to the council hall in Everdark, before Lucias had departed for Endlight, she hadn't gotten used to the attention her presence garnered. It was the red and black gown that drew their eye. *And my hair.* She'd proven that on her way here.

Even with the gaping citizens, the ride was quite pleasant. Sable retained a steady, rocking gait, obeying the gentlest tug of the reins. And to think she'd hauled on the poor boy's mouth. *I'll make sure you've extra...* What?

Frowning, she patted the pony's neck. Whatever did they feed horses besides hay? The carthorses in Everdark used to be given apples by the bolder children. Perhaps she could have Tommy sneak a few down to the stables for Sable. "How far are the Pillars from here?"

With his face scrunched in confusion, Lucias bent close and cupped a hand around his ear, prompting her to repeat her question louder.

"It'll take us half the day to get there," he shouted back over the chatter of the streets. "But first, what would you say to a spot of breakfast?"

She nodded, her stomach grumbling in affirmation. At least out here, no would-be poisoner could possibly predict where they would stop.

Chapter Six

She followed Lucias as he wove through streets both wide and narrow. The crowd thinned as they left the castle's looming presence. With Lucias leading the way and the pony content to follow the destrier, she was free to relax a little into the saddle and take in the city.

Bright stalls with their fancy awnings came and went. Meagre signs and a few modest crates to hold their wares swiftly took their place. The sight was almost soothing and familiar enough to home for her to forget she rode an animal with a mind of its own.

Even so, she craned her neck around every new corner, hoping to see something that she wouldn't come across on the streets of Everdark. Every time, she was disappointed to see more of the same. Truly, beyond the Pillars peeking over the rooftops every so often, Endlight felt so very... ordinary.

They rode through several market squares. Like the rest of the city, the stalls and people filling the areas seemed no different to those she'd once walked by back home. If a little more opulent than the last few they'd bypassed, the stalls here being somewhat less rickety. A number being extensions of shop fronts with big, intricately painted signs.

The people were no different. The further they got from the castle, the less the crowd seemed to care about their presence. Most walked with their heads down, their minds clearly occupied with their daily tasks. A few were so inwardly intent that they almost collided with Lucias' destrier before noticing the snorting beast. Lucias seemed to take all this in stride.

Still, every now and then, they would round a corner that put them in view of the city watch. And every time, he would abruptly lead her away until the oblivious watchmen were once again out of sight.

Upon the seventh time of him avoiding them, Clara couldn't stop herself from laughing. It seemed ridiculous, but it almost looked as if he was playing a massive game of 'keep away' without the other players knowing and with her as the item in question. "You're deliberately keeping me from everyone, aren't you?" That was why he'd been at her door so early, why he'd insisted on the pony and had dismissed several worthy places to grab breakfast.

Lucias chuckled, confirming her suspicions. "I haven't seen you in months," he said, his words nearly lost to the creak and clatter of a passing cart. "Thalia would see you tied up in social niceties, whilst the rest of the court would have me bogged down with documents and disputes." Shaking his head, he slowed his mount to a shuffling pace. "My father left quite the mess behind."

"Then maybe we should return if it's that bad." Her stomach grumbled. The sun was steadily creeping higher, enough to chase away much of the shadows in the square, and she'd still not had anything to eat. A quick sweep of the crowd revealed no watch, for the moment at least, and the castle towers were some distance away. Perhaps she could convince Lucias to make a stop for food. She eyed the shops as their mounts sauntered by, spying several that looked promising.

"No." Lucias kneed his destrier on and Sable matched the bigger horse's pace. They quickly left the shops behind. "Some have waited months to resolve their difference of opinions, they can wait another day." He flashed her a lopsided grin. "They will just have to forgive me for preferring to be the sole focus of my dear lady's attention for more than a few minutes rather than weathering their demands."

We'll be by ourselves soon enough. The thought darted across her mind like a sparrow along the eaves. She tipped her head to the sky, her cheeks heating something fierce. *Neutral thoughts.* She would either have to keep her mind off the idea of their wedding night or manage to get her blushing under control. "You honestly think Thalia would seek to keep us apart?"

Lucias nodded. "She is quite the traditionalist. If she had her way, we wouldn't be allowed near each other. Or at least not without an escort. They still practice that along the eastern border, you know."

She hadn't the faintest notion that Thalia put such stock in tradition, although that did answer why the woman had been swayed by her betrothed, Thad, to follow the Endlight wedding customs. Still... "You're her lord. You could ask her to not interfere."

Lucias threw back his head and laughed. "You don't think I haven't? I've known her so long that I'm certain she sees me as a little brother. There's only so much I could do without resorting to an actual command, which would re-quire my men to enforce and—disregarding my unwilling-ness to dissuade anyone from thinking of my, or your, well-being—doing so will bring more of those rumours you dislike hearing. Besides..." He flashed her a rather boyish grin. "It's more fun this way."

Clara twisted in the saddle, trying to spy any sign of the city watch. No one seemed at all concerned with their pas-sage. They were far from the castle, perhaps far enough for people not to realise they'd come from within its walls. "So who knows we're out here?"

His upper lip quivered into a sneer. "Everyone by now, I would think. *And* I'll likely get an earful from Thad later because I chose to come out here without an armed escort." He issued a dramatic sigh. "Such is the life of a Great Lord."

She smiled up at him. "You *poor* thing. It must be *so* try-ing."

He chuckled. "You may jest, my dear, but you're also right. If I lean too far one way or the other, then I'm either incompetent or a tyrant. Worst case? I'm both. It's not easy maintaining such balance. My grandfather learnt that the hard way."

They entered another square. This one bustling with people and their clashing cries as sellers hawked their wares. A large, bronze statue of the Goddess stood in the centre of the square. Clara peered around it, looking for a place to suggest for breakfast, but there was something about the statue that had her gaze continually drawn to it.

She frowned at the figure as they circled the square. The Goddess' delicate features were framed by long curls of hair that flowed about much of her naked body. Not the first such depiction she'd seen in her short journey here, although more common the closer she got to the border. And this one was—

Oh! Blushing, she turned her face. The sculptor had been very precise in what the hair did *not* cover. And extremely detailed. *That's new.* As were the children milling about the statue's base. A number of the smaller ones had clambered up the sculpted features to sit atop the Goddess' shoulders or stand amidst the great folds of her hair. She wouldn't have dared such an act in Everdark. Yet, no one here seemed to mind.

Lucias aimed for the statue where the street traffic was thinner, their passing catching the eye of several children. They pointed and talked amongst themselves, likely drawn to the gleaming image of the black destrier.

They halted at the foot of the statue where Lucias dismounted. "I'll grab us something to eat." He patted his horse's thick neck. "Wait here for me." With that, he took off in the direction of a man wandering through the crowd with a small pushcart.

"I will," Clara replied, although she wasn't quite certain if his departing words were for her or the horse. She took the opportunity to shuffle in the saddle and work feeling into her backside. It had grown tender during their ride, then a little numb. She'd vastly prefer to dismount and stretch her legs. It had to be safe enough. Why else would Lucias have chosen to stop here?

A quick look at her immediate surroundings revealed no place to rest, just the bronze depiction of the Goddess sitting atop its plinth. Apart from the children, few people lingered near the statue beyond an elderly couple intent on each other and a lone woman who looked to be praying.

Clara slithered off Sable's back, gasping as her legs returned to their usual position beneath her. Why hadn't anyone warned her that her thighs would ache this much?

She managed a few tottering steps to lean against the low wall surrounding the plinth. A small, long-forgotten, garden had been laid out between wall and plinth. What remained of those distant intentions was naught but compacted dirt almost as hard as stone.

Struggling with the bulk of her skirts and keeping a firm hand on the reins, Clara managed to perch herself on the wall to wait. It put her no higher than the crowd. She peered into the throng nevertheless, idly kicking her legs and scratching Sable's ears as the pony lipped at her skirts.

What if Lucias got himself into trouble? She carefully unsheathed her dagger. Would she be able to make her way back to the castle without his guidance? They'd taken a lot of corners that looked so similar. *Hurry back.*

Her stomach grumbled in anticipation, clearly not bearing the same concerns.

Lucias' destrier stood on her other side, patiently waiting for his master to return. The black beast effectively kept the majority of the people around them from venturing any closer. No doubt her toying with the dagger kept the rest from lingering. Surely the horse knew the way back to his stables.

Clara had returned the blade to its sheath and was in the middle of weighing the merits of clambering to her feet atop the wall, and possibly climbing the statue itself, when

Lucias appeared through the crowd.

He shuffled between people, his arms held high as if brandishing a prized kill instead of two small parcels.

"Here we are!" Grinning, he deposited one of the small cloth-encased bundles into her hands. Warmth soaked through the cloth and the smell of baked goods wafted up from the parcel.

Peeling back the cloth unleashed the full aroma of pastry-encased meat. "Pasties?" Clara squeaked before taking a large bite. Soft chunks of meat and thick jellified vegetables danced along her tongue. Moaning, she chewed the mouthful and chomped down another. "Do you know how long it's been since I had one of these?"

He chuckled, hopping onto the wall to sit beside her. "Judging by the way you're devouring it, I would say some time." He leant back, propping himself on the plinth and tipping his head back on the outward curve of a bronze curl of hair from the statue. "If you enjoy them so much, you could've arranged for Gettie to make them standard fare for you."

She grimaced around the pasty. The thought of asking for anything beyond the simple meals the kitchen already prepared for her had never crossed her mind. It wouldn't really be much different to the pies and roasts they already made.

Lucias mumbled unintelligibly around a mouthful of pasty before swallowing to continue. "What do you think of fair Endlight so far?"

"It's so..." Her gaze slid across the market as she sought for the right word. This place was as much of a home to Lucias as the Citadel had been, if not more so.

"Imposing?" he pressed. "Magnificent?"

"Ordinary," she confessed. "The streets look no different to the ones I walked back home. But it's all so big." She spread her arms wide. "You could fit Everdark inside these walls and lose it."

Lucias smiled. "Wait until you see Port Dank. You won't

be able to mistake her streets for that of another village."

Clara paused in the act of taking another bite. "We'd be going to Port Dank?"

"Eventually. I plan on..." Lucias fell silent as the crowd pressed around the horses. A little shuffling of the destrier's rump kept away all but the boldest. "I need to travel through the kingdom anyway, repair any defences or ties that might've degraded during my father's reign. I was hoping you'd want to come with me rather than being left behind. We could perhaps..." He waved a hand about. "I don't know. Spend a little more time in touring the kingdom than is really necessary?"

Tour the kingdom? Throughout her childhood, she would hear of the old Great Lord's passing as he went to and from the great Citadel, sometimes leaving the fortress for months. Rumour always put him on the front line of a battle with this or that enemy. "But isn't the Citadel where the Great Lord lives?"

"Most of the time," he agreed with a nod. "Not always. And if you came along, I could show you, if not the world beyond our kingdom's border, then the one within."

Our kingdom. How she loved the ease in which he spoke such words. No hesitation whatsoever in sharing what was his. "And visit all the places you spoke of?"

"Yes!" His hand swept over the square. "Places even better than this. You could see the merchant fleets at Port Dank with your own eyes."

"I don't know..." He'd done his best to explain places like Port Dank, but the idea of ships the size of houses seemed mere fantasy.

Lucias dug into the pouch at his hip and withdrew a small bottle—a canister fit for a guard, judging by the battered look of it. "Talk to Thalia and you'd think it was never a good idea for a lady to travel on horseback, especially not an expectant one, but there are ways around that." He took a swig from the bottle before handing it to her. "I'd love nothing more than to show my Great Lady around her kingdom."

She drank from the bottle, slightly disappointed to find only lukewarm water. "And, of course, you would also be showing the kingdom their Great Lady Clarabelle?" She snickered as the name passed her lips. What a mouthful.

"Dark," Lucias said, picking something from his pasty and flicking it to the sparrows flitting about the statue. "Come our wedding, you will be the Great Lady Clarabelle Dark."

Clara snorted and went to take another bite of her pasty. The seriousness of his expression stopped her. "Really?" she blurted. "*That's* your family's name?"

He frowned at her. "What did you think it was?"

"I—" She faltered. The Great Lords had always just been the Great Lords as far as anyone at Everdark was ever concerned. Only now that the full extent of his name was said did she realise she'd no prior knowledge of it. "I've never given it much thought, really." The more she did think about it, the more she chastised herself for not thinking otherwise. Or even guessing. "Just not... *that.*"

Clara bit her tongue as the urge to giggle bubbled in her chest. Her mind was nowhere near as gracious. *Great Lord Lucias Dark, the Dark Lord*, her traitorous thoughts sang over and over. She shielded her lips with a hand and nibbled on the pasty in an effort to stifle her laughter. "It *is* rather... unfortunate," she mumbled.

"It's not funny, you know."

I beg to differ. Laughter snorted out her nose. She tried to muffle it with her hand and found herself unable to contain her mirth any longer. "I'm sorry," she wheezed. "It's just that it sounds so—"

His frown returned, but deeper. "I *am* aware of how it sounds. Would it help if I said it didn't start that way? That our enemies began referring to us as the Dark Lords well before my ancestors embraced the name?"

"What was your family known as before then?" she asked around a mouthful of pasty.

Lucias sighed. "We took our name from the village, like many of the surrounding nobility of the age. Great Lord Kerwin was originally the Count of Everdark before he got it into his head to—"

"—attack the neighbouring lands?" she finished for him. "Absorbing people's souls as he went?" The thought came so naturally to her now. Strange how a few months learning Lucias' family line had done to accepting certain magics as being second nature.

He pursed his lips. "Quite. The title of Dark Lord was a moniker the neighbouring kingdoms used around the fourth Great Lord and was adopted by his son soon after his succession."

Clara chewed thoughtfully, trying to recall what had happened during the fourth Great Lord's reign that would be so horrible in comparison to the previous Great Lords.

Kerwin the Vanquisher had fallen to his son's blade after trying to take the man's soul. His son went mad early on, all but drowning the land in its own blood before falling in battle around his fiftieth year.

The third Great Lord had fared better, holding off the madness plaguing those who commanded the souls of the army. Yet he had very nearly died heirless, his wife conceiving on their wedding night. *And the fourth...* The fourth Great Lord was also the last one to marry the mother of his heir. She knew he'd killed his wife, she assumed it had been in a fit of insanity like the first two suffered from. But one death rather paled alongside the slaughters done in the past.

"Couldn't you change your name back?" How difficult could it be? She'd be willing to bet most people were unaware of their Great Lord's full title. *Just as I'd been.* Likely only those in high standing would need informing. "You shouldn't be lumped with your ancestors." He wasn't like the men who'd forged the surrounding lands into a kingdom, attacking all who opposed them and stealing the souls of the innocent.

Lucias shook his head. "I *am* the Dark Lord. To deny that is to deny a part of history, a part of *me*. You heard the court go on last night. They'd lift me up to the Goddess' side if they thought I'd allow it. They've already done so in the past."

Clara all but choked on her food. She doubled over, coughing up bits of flaky pastry.

Lucias shuffled along the wall, gently patting her back until she'd regained her breath. He offered her the bottle.

She snatched it from his grasp and greedily sucked down the water. "They have?" she rasped, giving one brief cough to clear her throat. "Why haven't I heard of this before?"

He snorted. "Not with *me*." His nose wrinkled, clearly not amused at the prospect. "I'd be a poor god. Could you imagine?"

She could. Quite easily. With the abilities he'd inherited from both parents, he was already halfway there. "An absolute terror, your Holiness."

Shock took his face, there for the trilling squawk of an aggressive blackbird overhead, then gone. The gentle huff of his laughter brushed her cheeks. "What wicked profanity you speak, love. Whenever did I say I was anywhere near holy?"

Clara stuck out her tongue.

He shook his head, the sun-etched wrinkles around his eyes deepening. "At any rate. The fifth Great Lord waged war with the people who make up the eastern part of the kingdom. They weren't prepared for an invasion such as he gave. He trounced any opposition so thoroughly, took the souls of everyone who dared to stand against him, that the people became convinced they fought a god. They kept on believing so until he fell, and by then the lands were ours."

"I don't believe you ever told me that part."

His lips kept their curve, just enough that those from afar to mistake the action for a smile, but the good-natured humour that'd been behind it had vanished. "It's not a part of my family's history I like to linger on." His gaze drifted across the square, his focus distant. "There are extremely good reasons why he deserved the title he claimed. No doubt the people he conquered have a different outlook on him, but I consider that time as just another warning of what could happen if I'm not vigilant."

"What did he do?"

Lucias blinked, drawn back from whatever thoughts he'd wandered into. "This is hardly the place for such a discussion and I wouldn't dare mar the memory of this day with sinister tales of my ancestors." He wrapped an arm around her shoulders, drawing her closer. "Ask me another time, my dear. I will endeavour to answer all your questions then."

Clara laid her head on his shoulder, breathing deeply of the subtle musk of linen and warm skin. She had missed this simple intimacy, the sureness of his grasp. How it was tight enough to hold her firm but with a hint of hesitance, as if he still expected her to shy from him at any second. It wouldn't do to have this moment wrecked because of questions that could wait. The past wasn't about to change on her. "Agreed."

On this side of the statue, they were remarkably sheltered from the breeze. She closed her eyes and snuggled herself against Lucias. The sun's warmth leaked through the clouds at just the right temperature to lull the unsuspecting.

She'd begun to doze when a thundering cough jolted her awake.

Gasping, Clara jerked herself upright, her face aflame. "Sorry," she mumbled. Sweet Goddess, she hadn't fallen asleep in public since her age could be counted with single digits.

Lucias peered at her and her cheeks grew hotter. "How has riding Sable been for you so far? Not as terrifying as you thought it would be?"

Clara swung her feet. They'd been in the saddle for a few hours and, although they'd not sat here for long, her backside was nowhere near as tender as it had been. However would she cope with a longer journey atop the pony? "He's lovely. But—"

He arched a brow at her. "*But?*"

"I do wonder why you got him." Even if she wasn't going to be ushered off to the Citadel via carriage soon after their wedding ceremony, she couldn't picture herself spending a great deal of time travelling. Not like what was required of the Great Lord. And, whilst Everdark might not be that far from the Citadel gates, any visits she made wouldn't be frequent enough to warrant her own mount. "He would spend most of his time in the stables once we return home."

Lucias scoffed. "Nonsense. I don't plan to keep you cooped up. It could take us a year to travel the kingdom's borders if we so chose. I intend to remain in Port Dank for at least a month. That should give you plenty of opportunities to sample some of the more exotic wares as they're unloaded."

Clara gently stroked Sable's soft nose, flipping the tufts of her reins out of the pony's inquisitive mouth. "You must be more than familiar with the exotic wares the docks must hold, yes?"

He frowned, clearly puzzled, then his shoulders shook in a soundless laugh as he seemed to come to the understanding that she spoke of the certain houses he admitted to visiting in the past. "We would steer clear of *those* particular wares. They're not exactly situated where a noble should be seen anyway."

That didn't stop you. Her gaze slid to the front of sable's saddle and her thoughts turned to how large Brenna had gotten after only a few months into her pregnancy, as well as how she'd been greeted with Thalia's massive girth upon her arrival yesterday. "I wouldn't be able to ride for very long."

"Hmm?" Lucias tore his gaze from the nearby buildings. "Maybe not immediately, but once you've gotten used to riding... Well, you'll easily be able to keep up with the guard."

"I meant when I'm pregnant," she muttered between clenched teeth, grinding each word before they could leave her lips. "After all, isn't getting me with child your goal?"

His eyes widened and he clutched at his chest. "Miss Weaver, you wound me. Do you think I intend to lock you away from the world the very minute you conceive? If that'd been my sole aim, I wouldn't have let you leave the Citadel until I'd sired a son."

She winced. It had almost come to that only a few months ago.

Instead, he would celebrate his twenty-sixth year once winter was done with the world and well before his child was born. Neither being a milestone he'd believed he would reach. Nor would he have if she hadn't stayed to help him reach the Citadel's training grounds where he could heal.

Yet, she knew of men who already claimed several children before even reaching their twentieth year. *Maybe nobles wait longer*. She didn't think that was true, but still... "Why haven't you?"

Lucias eyed her, his brows raised. "Firstly, I thought I had more time. My father was not particularly old or ill. If he hadn't been so idiotic in thinking he could personally escort my mother to the border without endangering himself, then there's a good chance he would still be alive." He caressed her cheek, softly coaxing her head back. "But then, I never would've met you."

Clara rolled her eyes. "Your men wouldn't have kidnapped me, you mean."

He grimaced. "Yes, *that*."

"If that was the Goddess' plan," she mumbled. "Then I'm sure we—"

Lucias snorted and stared at the buildings on the opposite side of the square. Now they had her attention, one of them looked very much like a temple entrance, only lacking the usual statues of the Goddess flanking the entrance. "Don't tell me you believe that whole 'every soul has a mate' nonsense."

The chill air caught in her throat. How could he dare to call it nonsense? "Don't *you?*"

His examination of the stalls seemed to deepen. Then, he sighed. "I stopped believing in a lot of things at a very young age." He eyed her with an oddly fervent glint permeating his gaze. "That whole talk the priests do about how the Goddess ensures every soul has a twin? Do you honestly think *that's* true?"

She nodded. She'd believed for as far back as she could remember. Everyone she'd ever spoken to in Everdark believed and the village priests practically guaranteed it as truth. Why would they lie?

His face screwed up briefly. "Whilst thinking that you ending up at my side because we were meant to be together *is* an attractive thought, if I believed it then I—"

A young man fell between them. He collided into Lucias. "Sorry, sir," he mumbled.

Swallowing a scream, Clara scrabbled for her dagger and had barely unsheathed the blade when the young man rocked back atop the wall to bump into her arm. The dagger slipped from her fingers to clatter against the cobblestones.

"My apologies, my lady." With a touch to his forehead as if tipping a hat, the young man raced into the crowd.

Lucias righted himself and set about adjusting his clothes. "That was..." His free hand fell to his belt where two thin cords hung. A long line of hushed expletives passed his lips. "Stay here."

Before she could speak, he'd leapt aboard his destrier and was racing across the square after the young man. People screamed and dove out of the way. Those who didn't were swept aside by some invisible force long before the warhorse's hooves could reach them. A few were plucked into the air, followed by their swift descent.

Clara clutched at Sable's reins, keeping the pony from following. Sable tugged back. He whinnied but, mercifully didn't try too hard to follow. She peered around the pony's head to spy the destrier vanishing down some side street.

Even if she could find her way back into the saddle unassisted, the chances of getting lost following them grew with every second.

Best to wait. As soon as Lucias had a clear line of sight to the young man, the chase would be over.

She dropped to the cobblestones to scoop up her dagger. Holding the blade before her might not have been much of a threat to those passing by, but it steadied her nerves.

No one else sought to come near her. Not even the children sitting still and quiet atop the statue. They watched her and cast meaningful looks between themselves, yet remained out of reach and relatively unthreatening.

Clara tilted her head to stare around the statue. The castle towers peeked over the rooftops. She would be able to find her way back, even if she wasn't entirely sure of the streets she'd need to take, but travelling on her own would take some time and surely Lucias wouldn't take long to deal with what seemed to be a common pickpocket. If the remaining half of her pasty hadn't also fallen to the ground alongside her dagger, she might've attempted a few more bites.

As things stood, she would just have to resign herself to waiting for his return.

CHAPTER SEVEN

The crowd had only begun to resume their normal day-to-day business after Lucias' departure when one of the children sitting on the Goddess' statue dropped from their high perch. They crept towards Clara, clearly unaware they'd been spotted.

Clara fingered her dagger hilt. She wasn't certain what the child was up to, but she wasn't about to be caught unawares again. "Stop right there!" She whirled on them with her dagger raised to a chorus of frightened shrieks.

Five sets of eyes watched her. Wary and a little bit fearful, like scolded dogs. None of them looked to be any older than nine. Nor did they appear to have been acquainted with a bath for some time.

Clara lowered the dagger, keeping the blade hidden within her skirts rather than sheathing it. "Before any of you as much as think of trying anything, don't bother. I've nothing worth stealing." She glanced over her shoulder at Sable and frowned. How much did a horse go for in Endlight? Especially one as compliant as the dappled grey pony. *Enough.* Even if the buyer only paid a fraction of Sable's worth, it was still likely to be more than this lot had seen in their lifetimes. "And if you try to take my horse, I'll see that your parents have you thoroughly disciplined."

"We don't have any parents, Miss," said the smallest boy of the group, a grubby kid likely no more than five years of age. He'd been the one creeping up on her. The sun had left its harsh mark on his pasty face, turning it ruddy and flaky.

One of the older children, a pale-faced girl of perhaps nine years, snorted and rolled her eyes. "You don't call her *Miss*, Trubs," she said. "The proper term is 'my lady'." The girl swung one arm wide and attempted a bow whilst she dangled from the crook of the statue's elbow.

Trubs lowered his head. Redness flooded his face, further darkening his sunburnt cheeks. He hunched his shoulders, knobbly things that could only be mostly bone beneath his thin, tattered shirt. The boy almost seemed to be expecting some sort of physical reprimand.

Clara's stomach twisted. Even during her unruliest babysitting task, she'd never struck a child. "It's all right," she said, sheathing her dagger. "I'm not a noble." Not until she was married. "You just gave me quite the fright sneaking up like you did." She tucked a lock of greasy hair behind the boy's ear, grimacing as the act revealed more sun-ravaged skin.

No parents. Did that mean there was an orphanage nearby? She'd heard the priests back in Everdark would take in fit young men to bring them up. Surely, Endlight couldn't be that different. Or were they truly on their own? "What are you doing out here?"

Trubs shuffled his feet. At least he wore shoes. If the battered strips of leather wrapped around his feet could really be called such. "We were waiting for Derek," he mumbled. "That man's not going to hurt him, is he?"

"Him?" she echoed, her thoughts still mired in deciphering their predicament. "You mean the young man who took off? He's a friend of yours, this Derek?"

Trubs nodded.

"Well..." Clara bit her lip. She wasn't entirely certain what the lad had taken from Lucias, although she could make a confident guess at it being money. And whilst Lucias was within the law to do so, she didn't think he'd take the boy's soul for petty thievery. "Your friend might be punished, but then he shouldn't have taken something that wasn't his."

"It wasn't his fault," a small voice piped up. A sixth face appeared from within the folds of the statues flowing hair. The girl struggled to stay in place on the slope. "I was hungry."

Clara took a step back from the statue to take in all six of the children. They rather reminded her of Tommy, although her page had collected quite a few more years of experience in living on the streets than any of these children had been alive. Still, she recalled the younger years of him rummaging through garbage and stealing from stalls rather than people. "Your friend still made a foolish decision."

The girl scrunched herself back into the fold of the statue's hair.

"Here." Clara picked up the discarded remains of her pasty, dropped in the original scramble along with the bottle of water, and held it out to the girl. The pasty was a little dirty on the outside, but the filling seemed clean. "It's not much, but—"

Trubs swiped it from her hands and hustled back up the statue. The other children crowded around him, carefully picking pieces off and shovelling it into their mouths before giving the larger chunk to the girl.

The other boy in the group eyed the bottle of water. He licked his lips, which reminded Clara of sacking in both colour and texture. None of them appeared to be in any way protected from the elements.

Clara rummaged in her pockets, pulling out a small wooden pot of cream she'd grown rather attached to during her short journey to Endlight. "Come here." With a few brisk waves of her hand, she ushered the boy to hop off the low wall surrounding the statue base. "This will help with the cracking." She crouched before the boy and, after scooping up a generous dollop of cream from the pot, smeared the salve over the boy's mouth.

The boy rubbed his lips together once she was done. His

sandy brows rose and his dark eyes widened.

She took out her handkerchief and, using a small dab of water from the battered bottle, gently wiped a layer of grime from the boy's sunburnt cheeks. "I'm Clara," she said, using a clean section of the handkerchief's fine linen on his forehead before handing the boy the bottle. "What's your name?"

The boy swallowed the tepid water in long, breathless gulps. He watched her the whole time, peering around the bottle as he tipped it to get the last few drops. His gaze flicked past her, his eyes widening anew.

At her back, the murmur of the crowd grew. It could only mean Lucias had returned and, judging by the draining of colour to the boy's heavily tanned face, he'd caught their thief.

"Derek!" the oldest girl screamed from her place still atop the statue.

Clara slowly stood and, absently brushing the dirt from her skirts, turned to see what the rest of them had spotted.

Lucias rode through the crowd. The black, gleaming bulk of his destrier high-stepping across the cobblestones would've been enough to draw most eyes. That the lad the children called Derek floated before them like a cat held by the scruff didn't do much to lessen the pull of people's attention.

Now that the would-be thief was more person than blur, the young man looked very young indeed. Not even old enough to have facial hair. What the boy did have were pale patches on his face and, whilst his arms were mostly brown, his hands were whiter than the olive brown tone of her own skin.

Clara had only seen such a sight in one other person and that had been the old baker down the street from her mother's house back in Everdark. Some had thought him diseased, but most knew him as owning the cleanest, most honest, bakery in the village.

Lucias halted before the statue, never once relinquishing his hold on his captive. "I'm sorry," he said, giving no indication he recognised the children crowding the statue. "But it looks like we are going to have to postpone our little venture to the Pillars. I need to see that this pickpocket is suitably punished."

"You can't!" the oldest girl blurted. She dropped from her perch and had taken a step towards Lucias before common sense seemed to grab hold of her limbs. Instead, she wrapped an arm around the shoulders of the boy she'd called Trubs. "Sir, if you take him, who will look after us?"

Something dragged on the left side of Clara's skirt. She glanced down to find the sunburnt boy clinging to the fabric with his grubby little fingers. Her chest tightened as she took in their pleading faces. "Lucias," she managed through a throat that seemed intent on closing up on itself. "Put the boy down."

"I will not," he gruffly replied before directing his attention to the children. "Where are your parents?"

The pale girl's shoulders sagged. "Dead," she mumbled. "Dad got crushed by a wagon and a fever took mum."

Clara gently prised the sunburnt boy's hands from her skirts and stepped around the still-floating form of Derek to stand beside the destrier. The black beast snorted and pinned his ears back at her approach, but made no move to harm her. "Do you think we could..." She laid a hand on the horse's shoulder and stared up at Lucias. "I don't know, take them in? Maybe?"

Lucias raised an eyebrow at her. He dismounted and slowly lowered his captive onto the wall. "Stay put."

Derek scrunched himself into a ball, nodding vehemently. "Yes, sir."

Still keeping one eye on the boy, Lucias hooked his hand into the crook of Clara's elbow and drew her a little ways from the children. "You know nothing about them."

That was true. But, whilst she might not know something as intimate as their names, she did know one very important detail. "They're orphans. That poor boy only stole from us to feed them. Isn't that enough?"

Sighing, Lucias pinched the bridge of his nose. "I understand what you're trying to accomplish, dear, I do. And that is partially why I fell for you. However..." He lowered his hand and his eyebrows knotted together. "You cannot take in every homeless child you stumble across."

"If the Great Lord will not help them, then who else will?" she countered. True, she'd not given the idea thorough consideration, but nor could she see any reason to turn away and continue to let these children roam the streets rather than take them under her wing. "The Citadel's big enough to house hundreds of men. Seven children would hardly be underfoot." Especially once settled in enough to be given tasks, whether that be in the form of schooling or apprenticeships.

Lucias folded his arms. His brows grew tighter together, almost fully merging into one. "The Citadel's that size because it's designed as a fortified building to hold and protect the Great Lord, not as a nursery."

"Of course it is." She clasped his arm. "But what about when our baby comes? Children deserve to be around other children. Our son will be all alone in such a big place. With them around, to play with him, to protect him, our son can just be a child."

Slowly, those dark brows unknotted as she spoke. "Clara," Lucias breathed. His gaze flicked to the children and he shook his head. "Look, I didn't mind you having Tommy, the boy is a quick learner and he is more than fit enough to work as your page but—"

Clara tightened her grip on his arm. She was not leaving these children behind to fend for themselves. "You've been saying for months of how you want to train Tommy to be your new stable master. It wouldn't take long for—" Without a thought to her actions, she whirled to face the children, taking in their bewildered expressions before her gaze settled on the oldest girl. "What's your name, sweetie?"

"Yes," the girl replied. "That's what my brother called me."

"Your name is Sweetie?" Clara repeated, not sure whether she'd misunderstood or the girl had.

The girl nodded.

Her brother named her? She ran a critical eye over the other boys. None beyond Derek seemed older than the girl. Was that another family member she'd also lost? Just how long had these poor souls been without the basics of life?

No more. She stood behind Sweetie and clasped the girl's slender shoulders. A glance at Lucias' face spoke of crumbling defences. One more precise blow should get them to fall. "I could train Sweetie here to be my new page. It wouldn't take long and you'd have your stable master."

A small smile tweaked his lips. Lucias shook his head. "All right, I concede. Bring the girl along and—"

"No." Sweetie jerked out of Clara's grasp and planted herself before Derek with all the tenacity of a mother cat guarding her kittens. She crossed her arms, holding them tightly across her little chest. "I'm not leaving without my brother."

Clara opened her mouth, prepared to declare how implausible it was for them to be related, for the girl's skin was far too pale, but now she saw them side-by-side, there was a stark similarity in their features. The shape of their jaws, their mouths, the darkness of their eyes.

And the girl wasn't just pale in skin. What Clara had first taken as blonde hair actually bordered on white.

"And if you're taking my brother and me, then you take all of us," the girl continued. "We go together or not at all."

"Sweetie!" Derek said, wrapping his arms around her shoulders. Judging by the way he eyed Lucias and Clara, this wasn't the first time his sister had spoken her mind so brazenly. "You can't just— I'm so sorry, my lord, she—"

A burst of laughter erupted from Lucias and halted the boy's tongue.

Clara whipped her head around to find her betrothed leaning against his horse, his mouth split wide in a grin. Just what had he found so amusing?

"I see why you're so keen to adopt them," Lucias wheezed between bouts of chuckling. "It's like seeing a miniature of you." He bowed low in Sweetie's direction. "Do you have any other demands, little lady? Or is having all seven of you safe under the protection of the Great Lord a satisfactory alternative to sleeping on the streets?"

Clara clapped her hands together. "Really?" Only the wet tightness of her throat stopped the word from coming out as anything but a squeal. "All of them?"

"I can't very well break up a family, now can I?" He waggled a finger at her. "But be warned, Miss Weaver, I will not be so easily swayed a third time. You'll have your hands full enough with this lot."

She bowed her head, still not quite able to control her smile. Whilst she wasn't quite so sure about Lucias' stance on not adopting more orphaned children should she press, if her time as an unpaid babysitter had taught her anything, it was that seven children would definitely be tough to wrangle. "I promise."

"Of course, taking them to the castle ourselves will cut your tour of the city short," he grumbled half-heartedly.

Clara bit her lip, trying to keep the brief spike of disappointment from her face. Yes, taking these children in would mean missing out on seeing the Pillars up close. "There will be other days," she said, partly to herself. It wasn't as if Endlight or her Pillars were going to vanish anytime soon. "Or we could see the children safely to the castle and continue on?"

Lucias screwed up his nose as if he'd taken a whiff of something left for dead in an alley. She guessed that particular thought had already occurred to him before he'd opened his mouth. "Thad will have gotten word that we're missing from within the castle walls by now. If we go near the castle, we won't be leaving without a fully armoured escort."

Clara grunted. Having a bunch of armed men encircling her and Lucias would definitely dampen the carefree mood her tour of the city had carried with it thus far.

A small cough drew their attention back to the children.

Derek stood at the fore, his hand clasped behind him. "Are you actually serious, my lord? You want to adopt us? All of us?"

"That was our intention," Lucias replied whilst Clara nodded empathically. "Are you voicing your objection? As you can see, my lady is very keen to get all of you off the streets rather than have you punished for your attempted thievery." He straightened to his full height and silvery-blue sparks of light flickered across his eyes. "That's still an option, if you'd prefer."

The boy stepped back, dragging his sister with him.

"Lucias," Clara said, grabbing his sleeve to pull all his focus on her. "Don't frighten them."

"I'm not objecting," Derek mumbled.

Sweetie squirmed in her brother's grasp. "The last man who said he wanted to take us in tried to sell us."

Clara knelt before the girl. "I know it probably doesn't mean much, but I promise, this is nothing like that." She brushed the soft, springy hair from the girl's face. "You'll live with us. Be fed and clothed. Taught and trained in whatever you desire to learn. But you'll need to be my page for a little while first."

The girl wrinkled her button nose. Clara could see the resemblance there with the boy Sweetie claimed was her brother. "What's a page do?"

"Well, I don't know what other pages are made to do, but my current one runs little errands for me. He also learnt to fight." Clara took in the girl's slightly piqued expression and added, "With a sword. But, we tend to start off with one of these." She withdrew her dagger and closed the girl's pale fingers around the hilt.

Sweetie clutched the weapon like a rope thrown down a well. Her already huge eyes grew even bigger. She looked from Clara to Lucias and back.

Clara glanced over her shoulder to find Lucias thoughtfully rubbing his chin as he surveyed the children.

"Do any of you know how to read?" he asked them. "Or know the route to the castle gates?"

Their reply was mixed. Most of them nodded, although the youngest one shook her head, whilst the boy called Trubs looked a little perplexed and the very quiet girl—that Clara pegged as being no older than six—shook her head in wide swings.

"My brother taught us a few words," Sweetie said, wringing her hands. "Street names, so we could find our way back if we ever got separated."

"I can read the Goddess' Gospel, my lord," Derek said. "The priests let us stay in the temple on cold days. I know the way to the castle, too."

"I suppose that'll be enough to get them there for now." Lucias climbed back into his saddle. "Round up your children, love," he ordered Clara. "One of these shops is bound to have some parchment and wax. I'm sure they won't mind if I borrow them."

Clara frowned.

The action must've been noticed for Lucias continued, "My seal should get our little troop through the gates and to Thalia's door, she'll see to the rest whilst we continue on with our tour." He kneed his destrier around, riding off into the hastily-parting crowd.

Derek watched the horse's passage, his brow furrowing as he gently drew Sweetie closer. "You're dumping us in the castle?"

"Only until tonight," Clara insisted. "Don't worry. I'm sure they'll treat you well in our absence."

"And if they don't?" Derek countered. One of the young boys had ventured closer, he too was added to the older boy's grasp.

"You said that you've read the Goddess' Gospel?" Clara waited until Derek gave a puzzled nod. She'd dim memories of the priests and their lectures. Her mother had vastly preferred Clara to work in the shop rather than attend sermons and Lucias, whilst devout in his own way, saw a throng like that as merely another place for his enemies to stage an assassination. "Then you'll know of the Great Lord?"

Again, Derek nodded. The rest of the children had descended the statue. They circled him like chicks around a mother hen. "He said we'd be under the Great Lord's protection. Does he work for him?"

Clara shook his head. "Not exactly. That man—the one you tried to steal from and whose eyes just glowed a moment ago—*is* your Great Lord. And I am to become his wife in four days from now. Believe me when I say those in the castle will take the utmost care with you and your siblings."

Chapter Eight

*C*lara glanced over her shoulder as her pony happily ambled behind Lucias' destrier. The children were well and truly out of sight, having vanished into the crowd almost at the very second Derek was handed the letter stamped with the Great Lord's insignia. She'd almost thought they'd fled back to wherever they spent their days, but the boy had seemed intrigued enough to follow Lucias' orders.

Then again...

"We should've gone with them," she mumbled to herself. Despite Lucias insisting otherwise, there were a great many things that could go wrong in letting them enter the castle unescorted.

"They'll be fine," Lucias replied, snapping her attention back to him. He'd slowed his mount's pace to walk alongside her. The horse high-stepped, his neck arched and tail flicking in what she assumed was displeasure at their slow speed. "Thalia will see to them. And if they're not there when we return later in the afternoon, then I'll personally help you find them, all right?"

She absently chewed on the corner of her mouth and nodded.

"But right now, you're missing out on the sight before you." He pointed over the rooftops.

Clara straightened in the saddle. Although they were

still some distance from the Pillars of Endlight, they dominated the sky, their presence growing with every nearing step.

A pair of ordinary towers became visible as they rounded a corner. The sight set her stomach to bubbling and fluttering like a child faced with the approaching Feast Day celebrations. The structures might not have been as imposing as their destination, but they were a signal that a city gate neared. And that could only mean an unobstructed view of the ancient structures.

Sure enough, the next corner afforded her a view of an exit to the walled-in houses and bustling streets. Clara tightened her grip on the reins, willing herself to remain calm. Not as easy as she'd hoped.

People filled the cobbled way between her and the open road, but this didn't seem to pose an obstacle to Lucias. His horse surged forward, parting the crowd through sheer presence. She trailed after him, her face growing hotter with every perceived stare.

Armed men sporting the livery of the watch stood at either side of the entrance, their faces trained on the men and women passing through. They appeared far more diligent at their job than the men back at Everdark. But then, little of note happened in her village and those who joined the watch there seemed to consider it an easy job. Being part of the watch within a city at the border had to be a far more exciting life.

A man separated from the group to their left. As he grew closer, she spied the customary knotwork upon his cuffs and shoulders, although in a design she'd not seen before.

The man stamped to a halt before them. His gauntleted fist hit his breastplate with a heart-stopping bang that drew attention to those who had previously paid them little mind. "Hail, Great Sword of the South."

Lucias swung his mount around and bowed his head. "Lieutenant Dean, it's good to see you again. How is the road to the Pillars?"

"Peaceful, my lord," the man replied, his gaze sliding her way. One brow lifted quizzically as she was... evaluated. It was such a fleeting expression that she thought she'd been mistaken, but no, she had definitely just been assessed. The lieutenant swiftly returned his attention to Lucias. "Shall I have my men mount and escort you?"

Clara bit her tongue to keep herself from objecting. Yes, she would rather travel solely in Lucias' company, even if it was for a time, but if the man deemed such measures as a necessity, then disagreeing with him would hardly be wise.

"I applaud your concern, lieutenant, but your men aren't required."

Indecision flickered across the man's face and, for a moment, Clara thought he might maintain his stance on the escort. Then the lieutenant seemed to recall just who he would address this objection to and instead opted to salute, turn on his heel and stride back to his men. The little display was enough to part the remainder of the crowd, leaving a clear path to the road. And the Pillars.

Lucias led the way down this gap, his mount jerking its legs high with every step.

People bowing in his passage. Our *passage*. Hard to miss that the genuflections came in her wake just as much as their Great Lord's. So unlike the villagers of Everdark who would barely glance her way as she walked the streets.

The full blast of pre-spring air hit them as they passed beneath the arch connecting the gate towers. Harsh and icy from its trip down the mountains, it buffeted those who dared the slush-covered cobbles. Shivering, Clara tugged on the reins, her stomach clenching as the pony fought the command before edging closer to Lucias' black destrier.

No longer hemmed in by walls and buildings, the crowd spread out. Those on foot generally opted to leave the road altogether and walk along either side, whilst the carthorses were urged into a faster pace. The occasional rider joined the throng, their passage firing mud and water in all directions.

Ahead, the gleaming Pillars beckoned, the road they guarded winding across the plains and disappearing into the mountains. Strange that people seemed so eager to traverse the way when the enemy lurked on the other side. Q'oth was the closest according to the maps. *And home to the Raven Estate.* Had Lucias' mother settled there or did she return to Ne'ermore to come up with another plot to end her son's life?

Her gaze flicked to Lucias, marking how he fidgeted in the saddle, always looking around, his right hand constantly checking his sword. She hadn't seen him this suspicious since they'd first left the Citadel some months ago. Back then, it was the all-too-pressing matter of his mother's impending arrival that plagued his mind. And she was beyond the very border they now made their way towards.

Clara cleared her throat, drawing his attention. "Did I hear the lieutenant call you Great Sword of the South?"

A whisper of a laugh passed his lips, but even that held a tinge of nervousness to it. Hard to detect unless expected. "You did. The nomads gave me the name during my year roaming the moors with them." He twisted in his saddle and frowned at the city gates. "Although the 'Great' bit is new." Settling back down, he urged his horse into a slow trot. "Come, before they decide to follow regardless."

She gritted her teeth and clung tightly to the pony's mane as they proceeded to bounce along the road. If the lieutenant chose to send an escort after them, she wasn't certain how a little distance would stop the watch from catching up.

With each step jarring every inch of her, Clara lost track of their progress until the road began to climb over the foothills. She hauled on the reins, relieved when Sable fell back into a swaying plod.

Lucias veered off the road. His horse came to a halt at the top of a mound with barely a twitch of the reins, her pony stopping after a few shambling steps. "There they are: the Pillars of Endlight."

Clara craned her neck, taking the sight in one breath-taking sweep. Every passage she'd ever read about the Pillars didn't do them justice. "I wasn't expecting them to be so... big." Each glistening white tower stood strong before the gorge. Together, they formed a perfect arc, ready to defend the land from whatever suicidal enemy dared to brave this entrance.

"They predate the kingdom, no contesting that," Lucias said. "Scholars believe them to be older than the nomads' claiming of the moors."

And they've owned the land for over two thousand years. At least, that's what the books in the Citadel's library said. She eyed the towers, the stone so white in the cool winter sun, like something from a legend. She could well believe they claimed such an age. "What were they defending?"

Lucias shrugged and kneed his mount onward. "Come on, no point dawdling here. You wanted to get closer, didn't you?"

Her gaze dropped to the road winding towards the towers as their horses high-stepped across the grass. Despite the trail leading out of the kingdom and into that of their lord's enemy, people still populated the way in an endless ribbon of carts, riders and pedestrians. Both in and out. "Is it safe?"

Grinning, he nodded. "Perfectly. The Pillars are well manned, as are the scout towers atop the ridge. Our enemies know this. No one has dared to march through the gorge in decades, it'd be too perilous and no sane leader would lead his men to certain death."

That didn't say much for those who were considered less sane. She could well imagine a person like Lucias' mother driving men to their deaths in order to see her son slain. Clara tore her gaze from the gleaming stone of the Pillars to scan the mountain, half expecting to find danger rearing its head from every bush and tree.

The land either side of the passage stood bare, its stony surface dotted with lesser towers roosting on ledges like chickens. *No places to hide.* Still, she couldn't shake the skin-itching sensation that they tempted fate just sitting here. "I've changed my mind. Let's go back to the city." Whilst she saw no logical way for anyone to attack them where they were, being behind Endlight's walls would soothe her nerves.

Lucias frowned. His mouth opened as if he was about to object, before twisting into a rueful smile. "It seems I can't escape being the Great Lord out here with you. If it'll make you feel better, then we will return to the castle." He turned his mount and led the way back, joining the road to plod alongside a pair of caravans.

The hitched horses of one slowed, clearly an order from the driver than the animals for the beasts issued some objection to the command, before the other on her right sped up. A strange choice to make with the gate just cresting over the brow of the hill, for surely a traveller would want to reach their destination swiftly.

Still, Clara dismissed it. Her imagination must've been running off with her common sense again, seeing danger in every minor act.

Although the way the driver on her right looked at Lucias...

She doubted the man recognised his Great Lord. Whilst Lucias put off the air of a noble or wealthy merchant's son, there was no definitive sign that he was different to any other man. Nor were they the only people upon horseback.

The driver finally seemed to realise his less-than-pleasant stare had been noticed. He returned to glaring at the road ahead and went for his whip, tapping something fierce on the roof with the butt of the handle.

Clara couldn't tear her gaze from the driver's actions. There was something about him. The whip appeared to be unstuck, yet the man kept up the rhythmic banging, and he seemed to haul on the reins every so often rather than trying to encourage the horses onwards. She risked a glance towards Lucias, seeking answers.

He, too, eyed the driver. His customary grasp on his sword hilt had become tight enough for his knuckles to go white. Even his destrier seemed agitated, high-stepping its way up the road. "Clara," he whispered, indicating she closed the distance between them with a twitch of his head. When she managed to aim Sable in that direction, Lucias continued, "I want you to go on ahead. Alert the guards at the gate."

Dread settled in her stomach like a brick. Nodding, Clara and urged the pony to increase its ambling pace. Sable's ears swung back and the pony offered a few shambling steps before returning to the lazy strides. She urged him harder, feeling the hollow thump as her booted heels connected with his side. "I'm really sorry about this, boy." Another kick and Sable leapt into a bone-shaking trot.

Both carriage drivers seemed to ignore her as she bounced by. The one on her right gave a final bang on the footwell of his seat, echoed by the other on her left. There was the click of a door latch, faint enough over the crunch of hooves and wheels on gravel that she almost missed it.

"Die, devil!" a man roared. The cry was met with more bellows.

In one swift movement, Clara wheeled her pony around.

Men poured from the carriages, so many that they must've packed themselves like a well-stuffed pie. They surrounded Lucias' horse, harrying it with swords and daggers.

Lucias slashed at the men, whirling the great black destrier so that its hooves were always flying.

Howls of pain joined the grunts and cries whenever the horse let loose. The beast screamed alongside the men, sounding more like an enraged boar than a horse. His head thrashed from one side to the other, grabbing whatever he could.

Clara scrabbled for her dagger, her trembling fingers finding only an empty scabbard. *The gate guards.* Lucias might hold his own for now, but it would only take one blow, one lucky grab to haul him from the saddle. Turning back towards the gate, Clara urged Sable on.

The pony paid little mind to her attempts to move him. Giving a neigh that belied his small size, he skittered sideways towards the fight.

A scream slashed through the air. Man or beast, she couldn't be sure.

Beneath her, Sable snorted. His rump dropped and a dreadful fluttering started up in her stomach. "S-steady, boy," Clara murmured. She hauled on the pony's mouth, hoping to stall the terrible image of him galloping across the plains with her clinging to his back like a flea. At least he was now aimed in the right direction.

"Get to the gate!" Lucias roared, swiping the air with his free hand. The air between them rippled.

There was an almighty thwack against Sable's rump. The pony squealed and bolted.

Screaming, Clara grabbed great fistfuls of the thick mane and prayed she'd the strength to hold on. They dove through the crowd on the road, the surrounding people little more than blurs, their cries all but blocked by the racket of the pony's hooves upon the gravel and her heart pounding furiously in her ears.

She blinked, trying to see her way through the tears. The wind of their passage stung her face. The gate couldn't be far. As fast as they were travelling, they'd have to be close. Her gaze fastened on the sight of them bearing down upon a laden cart. She hauled on the reins.

Sable swung to one side, stumbling and sliding. Clara bounced in the saddle, a shriek slithering through her gritted teeth. Unbalanced, she slammed into the pony's neck and felt herself tipping. She adjusted her grip, abandoning the reins altogether to snatch new fistfuls of mane.

It didn't help.

Clara hit the cobblestones and rolled until her back slammed up against something as equally unforgiving. Her breath rushed through her lips, leaving her chest burning. Through the ringing in her ears, she caught the muddied chatter of a gossiping crowd.

"My lady!"

Lucias? No, he wasn't nearby and he'd only ever spoken her name with such concern.

She rolled her eyes, searching for the source of the sound. All she could see was the shimmering grey of the clouds and buildings. Moving anything else seemed impossible. Everything ached. Her mouth silently opened and closed, the fire in her chest desperate for air. Tears blurred her vision, their passage down her cheeks turning icy in the chill breeze.

Finally, in one massive gasp, she could breathe again. Clara raised an arm, stiff from the tumble, to dash her tears across her sleeve. More took their place. She sniffed in an effort to halt their flow to no avail. Sitting up proved a far harder task, her back stiff. Something wet hit her neck. She patted her hair, cringing as her fingers came into contact with something slimy.

People suddenly filled her vision. Concerned faces floating above the uniform of the Endlight guard. One helped her to her feet. "Are you badly injured, my lady?" he asked her before shouting over his shoulder. "Someone get a doctor!"

"No," she croaked. The stiffness in her right hip suggested it had taken the majority of the impact, but she could deal with that later. She clutched at the man who still supported her. "The Great Lord!" she blurted, pointing the way Sable had come. There was no sign of the battle, hidden by the press of the crowd and the land. "Over the hill. Bandits. You've got to help him!"

"Easy, my lady," the man said. "You hit the ground pretty hard. We can't all just... leave our post at your word. Why don't you rest and tell us what happened?"

Clara stared at the guard, her mouth dropping open. The bandits could have Lucias knocked to the ground by now, barely warding off blows and they wanted her to chat like she was describing some back-city thief? "A fine lot you are." She shoved the man, although it was herself who took a few staggering paces back.

"My lady," the man protested. "We can't help if you don't—"

"If you won't help, then I'll do it myself. Where's my pony!" She searched the immediate area for the animal, finding him in the possession of another guard. Snatching up the reins, she attempted to mount him. Her skirts tugged at her legs, hindering any chance of lifting them high enough without exposing herself to all and sundry.

Clara dropped back to the cobblestones. There was only one thing for it. She whirled on the nearest guard. "You!" Her ankle twinged with each step and had her silently lamenting how the Citadel, with the training ground's healing magic, was so far away. "Your dagger," she demanded.

The guard objected in a stream of incoherent babbles.

Snarling, Clara plucked the dagger from his belt. She sawed through the hem of her dress. After that, tearing a long enough slit through the skirts was a swift matter. Unhindered, she clambered aboard the pony and aimed it the way she'd come. Her body protested. She wiggled, searching in vain for the same comfortable position she'd used for half the day. It only seemed to increase the ache in her legs.

Higher up, she spied the man Lucias had spoken to during their departure. "You there!" The crowd parted around the man as she singled him out with a wave of her hand. "Lieutenant..." Had Lucias said the man's name? "You! You saw me leave through this gate with the Great Lord, correct?"

The lieutenant nodded as he halted at Sable's shoulder. "Yes, my lady." He looked around them, puzzled at first, then panic took over his face as he seemed to realise Lucias was not with her. He twisted to eye the road leading to the Pillars with sick dismay. "Is he still—?"

"Out there." She levelled her pilfered dagger at the road. "An ambush." How many men had swarmed out of those carriages? Eight? Ten? Even with the destrier's might at his control, she'd no idea how Lucias could fight off so many.

The man's ruddy, olive face grew pale. "To arms, men!" the lieutenant bellowed. He scrambled towards a horse tied up at the guard post and leapt into the saddle.

"But sir," one of the guards protested whilst, all around him, other guards were procuring horses from shop fronts and riders.

"No buts, man," the lieutenant snapped back, drawing his sword as he turned the horse. "Our Great Lord needs us!" He drew his mount alongside Sable. "Show us," he demanded of Clara.

Her pony leapt forward with barely a twitch of her heels. They thundered along the road, leaving the crowd at their back and seemingly going nowhere at once. Her heart pounded in time to the hoofbeats. The wind stung her eyes, but she didn't dare close them. *Don't be dead. Please, Goddess, don't let him be dead.*

They crested the hill to find Lucias dismounted and standing over the bodies of his attackers. A blue glow rose from one of the men, gone before Clara had a chance to dash the tears from her eyes. If this were the Citadel, she would've said Lucias was in the process of taking one of the men's souls, but she'd never seen him do so beyond the glyph-covered room of the Citadel dungeons.

Sable came to a shambling halt beside the black destrier. The animal seemed no worse off for having been in the midst of battle. Sweaty perhaps, but whole. That boded well for his rider.

Lucias turned as guards caught up and, one by one, dismounted. He regarded them suspiciously, silvery-blue flecks dancing across the surface of his eyes, before recognition lit his face. "Lieutenant," he said, greeting the man with a nod of his head. "It seems I was wrong about needing the escort."

Clara half-dismounted, half tumbled out of her saddle. Relief sapped what energy remained in her legs, dropping onto the road at Lucias' feet. "You're alive!" She clung to him, barely believing the truth. She'd been so certain that he couldn't possibly hold off so many men on his own.

"Of course I am, they weren't prepared to face—" He crouched at her side. "You look— What happened? Did you fall?" He twisted her this way and that before she could answer, searching for injuries. "Are you all right? Is anything broken?"

"Am *I* all right?" she echoed. *No.* Her legs sharply objected to any movement. Even stiff as she was, she didn't think anything was broken. But she was sore in more places than the impact could account for. How long had they been riding through the city? Clara blinked up at the sky. Through her unshed tears, the world was little more than a blur of colours and light. It'd been midday, hadn't it? "What about *you*?"

"They didn't get a chance to touch me. I should've realised it'd been too quiet." Sighing, he gently wrapped her arm around his neck. "Come on. I'm rather done tempting fate today. Let's get you back to the castle." The soft pressure of Lucias' magic helped her to regain her footing and then lifted her back into the saddle. He stared up at her once she was settled aboard Sable, his brow creased with worry. "You *are* all right, aren't you?"

She nodded, not convinced she could trust her voice beyond more than a few words.

The concern in his eyes deepened, taking over his whole face. "But... you're crying."

"I am *not*." Clara waved him away, waiting until he was about to remount before hurriedly wiping the dampness from her cheeks. She shuffled in the saddle, desperately trying to ignore the ache in her hip. What she needed was a little liniment like her father used to apply to his joints every morning and night.

"My lord," the lieutenant called. "A word, if I may."

"Certainly." Lucias dropped back onto the worn cobbles with liquid grace. "I didn't manage to garner much information from them, but I'm willing to bet they came at Ne'ermore's insistence." He circled one of the carriages with the lieutenant following close on his heels, even peeking into the open door. "I don't see anything unusual. No identifiers." He turned back to Clara, one brow raised querulously. "What do you think, dear?"

Clara nudged her pony closer, wincing at a particularly jarring step. "I think they were looking to sneak into the city." There was no chance the group knew Lucias would be outside the city walls at this time and with nothing in the way of an escort. "The way the driver thumped on the roof? That was a definite signal to those inside."

The lieutenant eyed the slain men, frowning and idly rubbing his chin in thought. "Could be a mercenary company," he mumbled. "She's getting reckless. They'll likely have orders waiting for them elsewhere. It will be harder to track." He grinned, the expression lacking the usual cheeriness. "A shame you didn't leave one alive, my lord."

With a hearty thump, Lucias laid a hand on the man's shoulder. "I'm certain you're up to the job regardless, Lieutenant. I'll leave this mess in your capable hands and see to my lady's injuries."

The lieutenant straightened. "Yes, my lord. I'll be sure to have every inch of the carriages and the men searched. If they've left anything of note, I'll see to it that Lord Thad gets word to you." Giving Lucias a sharp salute, he turned to his men. "I want this filth removed from the road and into the stables as quickly as possible."

Lucias left the man's side to climb aboard his destrier and join Clara. "We should return to the city."

"Without an escort?" The protest was out before she could think how to voice her concerns. All the lieutenant's men seemed occupied in their task, but surely if their Great Lord requested it of them, they'd see them safely through the gates.

"I doubt there are any more between here and the city walls. My concern for the moment is your wellbeing. If you're stiff may I suggest going one better and making use of the local bathhouse? If anything, it'll bring about less talk if we wash the dirt off you *before* returning to the castle."

"A bathhouse?" Everdark didn't possess any that she was aware of. She *had* heard of such places and they mostly sounded like a different class of brothel. Now, she wasn't so sure. She doubted he would suggest visiting such a place if they truly were as she believed. "Why would I ever want to set foot in one of those?"

"Because I'm betting that your legs were hurting even before your fall and a good soak in hot water would do them some good. I remember what it was like when I first started riding. The unfamiliar effort of keeping your thighs apart for long periods of time does eventually take its toll. You'll get used to it, I'm sure."

She leant over to swat at his side, her cheeks burning. She was certain his lips had taken on a suggestive twist at that last sentence. That her action was rewarded with a laugh did little to soothe her irritation. "Are you going to be like this all day?"

"All day? No." His grin widened. "I plan to be like this all week." He took up the pony's reins, slowly leading her up the road.

Now the waves of concern and panic were no longer driving her onwards, her body objected to every one of Sable's steps. "Couldn't you just... make the injuries go away?" she asked, wriggling her fingers in the air.

He shook his head. "It's not simple. Such magic would require me to ring an area in glyphs and they are not ones that can be so easily removed." His grip on the tightened as Sable stumbled, drawing her closer. "It would fast become a drain on my power."

An entirely different concern had her stomach bubbling away like an over-boiled broth. "Aren't bathhouses a little..." She scrunched deeper into the saddle. "...public?"

The heat of Lucias' chuckle dug into her gut. "Most of them are, but I know of one where I can procure a private room for you, so don't worry about that. We can't have you still complaining about aching legs at tonight's ball. People might get the wrong idea even when the rumours of your tumble reach them. And they *will* hear about it."

She eyed him, half expecting to find Lucias grinning like an alley cat that'd made off with a whole fish. He *was* indeed smirking.

But, curse him, he was also right. Even if the guards at the gate didn't natter amongst their peers. She'd fallen right in front of a huge crowd. Small chance of the court not discovering that. "As you pointed out, I could do with a wash." She took up Sable's reins. "Lead the way." Whatever was said about her actions, she vastly preferred getting rid of the filth clinging to her hair as quickly as possible.

CHAPTER NINE

Most of the fond memories Clara had of home were of the tales her father would tell as she drifted off to sleep, lulled by his voice. A handful of those stories involved nobles and balls. On those nights, she would dream of peeking through the window of a huge room glittering with candlelight to watch as people swarmed the floor, all moving in unison.

In all her life, she'd never dared to dream of attending such an affair.

Now she lingered in the doorway to a room dedicated to them, admiring the warm glow. Candlelight glittered upon everything, from the polished metal adorning the ceiling to the white stone underfoot. The room was a strange shape; the walls were too many for it to be a simple square and lacked the curves that would make the area circular. Music drifted through the air, the notes flowing lazily from wood and string. Already, couples danced to the tune.

"Keeping the court gossiping about your adventures today by being fashionably late, I see."

Clara turned at Lucias' voice to find him walking up the hallway, grinning.

He halted before her, the faint gleam of concern creasing the corner of his eyes. "You look no worse for wear, all things considered. Are you certain of being all right in doing this?"

Nodding, she patted her hair—all very much clean and still slightly damp—checking every curl was still in place. "I wouldn't miss it for the world." Sitting out her first ball hadn't even been a consideration. Although, spending most of the afternoon soaking in a private pool at the bathhouse, before returning to the castle in fresh clothes, had left her with precious little time to prepare for tonight's festivities.

Lucias, on the other hand, seemed rather less dishevelled than she would've expected. It always amazed her at how nicely he cleaned up. Like the previous night, the practical leather she'd grown used to seeing him in was nowhere to be found. Instead, he was almost a shadow in a black jacket and breeches. The only alleviation to this darkness was his deep red vest, which showed a flash of embroidery along the hems, and the silver glitter of the sword he still wore at his hip.

"Am I to take it by your staring, that my attire meets your approval?" He spread his arms wide and twirled for her. Whoever had tailored his jacket had certainly been fond of the current trend to emphasise a man's shoulders and backside. Fortunately, he'd the frame for such flattery.

Clara nodded. "My dad would've approved." If there was one thing she remembered correctly about her father, it was his appreciation for a well-made outfit. "And you certainly look less barbaric in that attire."

A question lurked in the twitch of Lucias' arched brow.

"You rather frightened me the first time we met," she clarified.

"Are we referring to our more formal meeting or the time before, when you caught me unawares in naught but a towel?"

Heat flooded her face upon the recollection of him dripping wet in the candlelight with only a flimsy length of cloth wrapped around his waist. "The former, when you were in your..." She fluttered a hand before him, trying to find the right words to describe the attire Lucias had donned the morning he'd chosen her as his mistress. "Leather ensemble," she finally settled.

Clasping her hand in his, Lucias bowed low and brushed his lips over her knuckles. "My utmost apologies, my lady. I will endeavour to not startle you in such a manner again." Straightening, he offered his left arm. "Shall we?"

Clara glanced over her shoulder to peer through the gap in the door. Everyone else waited for them to make an appearance. "I didn't have a chance to find out," she murmured as a new thought came to mind. "Did the children from the market square make it here all right?"

A small smile lifted the corners of Lucias' mouth as he escorted her to the ballroom entrance. "They are here, I made sure of that. Arrived in the afternoon, apparently. Last I heard of them, Thalia was in the middle of ensuring they'd been bathed and ushered off towards the kitchen. I think the worst we might hear of them tonight is that they managed to empty the castle larders."

She nodded. "Good." Not that she hoped they'd devoid the whole castle of food, but that they were at least getting a decent meal. Probably the first in a very long time for several of them, if not *the* first. "I'll want to see them later."

"Of course."

They stepped through the doorway. The man standing just on the other side of the opening stiffened. Already standing tall, Clara couldn't see how he managed to stand taller, but he seemed to find another inch or two.

She winced in anticipation of the bellow she knew was to come in their presence. It'd been enough of a shock to have her entry into the Great Hall met with such yelling. Last night, she'd arrived after most of the guests, but there would certainly have been more ceremony made of Lucias' entrance than hers.

"And now, presenting: his esteemed lordship, Great Lord Lucias Dark. Great Sword of the South, vanquisher of our western enemies, protector of the eastern seas and defender against the savages of the Ebony Court at Ne'ermore..."

Clara's attention drifted off, half-hearing the rest of the

man's talk. Would she be saddled with so many titles upon their marriage? Becoming the Great Lady was more than enough for her.

"And accompanying him: Mistress of the Great Lord, Clarabelle Weaver."

She flinched at the address. They'd said the same words the previous night. Even with them officially betrothed, being his mistress was still considered the higher title until the wedding. *Four more days.* She could weather it until then. It was only a word and soon others would take its place in the people's mind. *Great Lady Clarabelle Dark.* What a mouthful that was going to be.

The crowd filling the room had stilled, their attention swinging to Lucias. *To us.* Clara's cheeks heated and she tried to convince herself it was due to the warmth of the room.

She turned her gaze upwards, eyeing the large and heavy-looking chandeliers hanging over the dance floor, their gilt curves glittering like everything else. A flush of wonder suffused her bosom, cooling her cheeks and heating her core.

It truly was beyond anything she'd ever dreamt.

"Do remember to smile, my dear," Lucias whispered. "Some of these people have come a long way to see you."

She slowly pulled her gaze back to his face. For someone who'd admitted to not being all that fond of these sorts of gatherings, Lucias seemed very much at ease. More so than he'd been back at the Citadel. "I confess, I didn't expect you to be so relaxed around all these people." He hadn't even attempted to grasp his sword hilt once since entering.

A faint smile tweaked one corner of his mouth. "Your presence makes all this bearable." He gave her fingers a little squeeze, drawing her closer. "And I wouldn't want to pass up the chance to dance with you before our wedding."

They'd done a lot of dancing during their time in the Citadel. Most evenings would end with him teaching her the steps of several dances popular within the court. That's when he hadn't been teaching her how to use a blade, both equally necessary skills in his opinion. "You mean you want to show me off," Clara needled.

He chuckled. "What man could possibly resist such a temptation?" He toyed with a lock of her hair, gently curling it around his finger. "Like it or not, you will become the jewel of my court. I intend to ensure you glitter amongst the other gems."

Resisting temptation. That was his excuse in teaching her how to wield a sword; that they either duelled with their tongues or a blade. Ever since the attack on Lucias, they'd spent barely a waking moment apart in the months before he left for Endlight, be either within or without the Citadel's walls. True separation came only when it was time for them to sleep.

But this was the first time he'd referred to her as a jewel. "About the children—"

"Social duties first, my dear," he murmured, deliberately turning her towards the edge of the dance floor where clusters of noblemen and women lingered. "*Then* we may speak of other things."

Clara's stomach bubbled at the sudden prospect of mingling. She'd been aware of it, but it'd been a dim thought, a dream not quite remembered in full. Such duties hadn't been required of her since the impromptu banquet in the Citadel, and never with the entirety of the kingdom's nobility. The possible poisoning she'd suffered at last night's dinner had stalled any chance of that then.

Now?

Her gaze swept over the room. It was a lot of people. Far more than she'd ever imagined. That had to mean even the lowest of the noble ranks was in attendance. *To see me.* The little common woman who'd saved the Great Lord from death, and the kingdom from doom.

Clara took a deep breath and silently prayed that the Goddess would aid her in not making a fool of herself.

The first group they stopped at greeted them with bows

and mumbled pleasantries. Lucias accepted all this with the gentle nod of his head, a gesture Clara copied. They spoke, briefly and on frivolous things—admiration of her gown, a titter of wonder over Clara, and an invitation to their estate in the summer—before parting ways to another group to be greeted by similar words.

It seemed hours trickled away as they moved through the room, fluttering from one cluster of nobles to another. Names were spoken, titles too, she was certain of it. But the powdered faces and polite smiles blurred into such a muddle that she couldn't remember a single one.

Nevertheless, she clutched Lucias' arm, responding to every bow and curtsy with a soft smile. Sometimes, the people would attempt a little more than idle small talk, often in hushed, flustered tones that she barely took in. Not that it mattered, for Clara seldom replied with anything beyond a nod or shake of the head. It seemed enough for them.

Sadly, she could not get away doing so with the current pair of noblewomen. They continued to chitter away, their heads bobbing to and fro like sparrows along the eaves, following as Lucias pointedly guided Clara towards the dance floor.

"It's so very brave of you to join us, my lady," gushed one of the women, laying a gloved hand on Clara's elbow. "It must've been dreadfully frightening."

"A little," Clara replied, somewhat relieved someone had mentioned something beyond politics and fashion. At any other time, she would've been more than willing to gossip about dresses, and learning the state of the court would be useful towards helping Lucias mend whatever upheavals his father had caused, but not whilst surrounded by the glitter of candlelight on gilt and the melody of angels. "Still, Lucias is quite capable of—"

"That was such a wicked fall to have," the other woman blurted. She also laid a hand on Clara's arm. "Especially in your condition. You must've been awfully concerned about the baby."

"What con—?" Clara cut herself off as Lucias squeezed her hand.

"Consideration you give your future Great Lady," he hastily continued in her stead. "Of course, what mother wouldn't be alarmed? But if you two ladies would excuse us?" he enquired of the pair, gesturing to where a good dozen couples danced in the centre of the room.

The pair graciously accepted, although they continued to titter away to themselves as Lucias escorted her onto the dance floor.

Clara flashed him a relieved smile. The part of her that would vastly prefer seeking out her bed had grown substantially stronger. She didn't think she could stand any more of the saccharine chatter dribbling out their mouths. Not after everything else that had happened today.

The gentle beat of the music drew her feet and, after a quick check to see where the other woman stood in relation to their partners, Clara took up her position at his side.

Lucias bent close, his palm nestled upon the small of her back whilst his other hand clasped her left. "Now, what was it you wanted to speak about?" he asked as they begun their first circuit around the dance floor.

"Hmm?" Her gaze jerked back from where she'd been idly watching the musicians with their gleaming instruments. After all the talking, she'd almost forgotten what she'd said at any given time, never mind who to. Clara eyed the neighbouring dancers. Out on the floor, with everyone twirling to the music, anything she said would be lost. "What's this about my *condition?*" she whispered into his ear.

Lucias smiled as he guided them between the other dancers. "The current rumour is that you're carrying my child, especially after last night."

"I'm—" She faltered in her steps, and scrambled to regain her footing before it could be noticed. She covered her lips with a hand, trying to stifle any hint of mirth.

He drew her tighter, twirling her, and, as he tipped her

backwards, Clara became aware of his magic's gentle pressure cradling her torso. "Are you *laughing*, Miss Weaver?"

She fought to keep her face neutral, hoping it would be enough to convince him. "Of course not."

His lids lowered, but not before she caught a shimmer of light in the depths of his eyes. Not the silvery-blue power of the Great Lords, but an insidious gleam that sprang to life whenever she dared to speak anything beyond the truth. "You're a poor liar." He straightened and Clara bounced upright.

"My apologies." She'd found ways around his strange ability of catching lies—talking in a roundabout way, saying plenty without actually answering the question served the best. Doing so was also draining and scarcely worth the effort most times. She cleared her throat. "I meant to say that the rumours are quite preposterous and, from our knowledgeable standpoint, could be considered amusing if one has that sense of humour, which I may or may not possess."

He frowned. "You know I hate it when you do that."

The musicians changed to a different melody. Lucias moved her haphazardly across the floor whilst people adjusted to the new steps, giving Clara time to compose herself. She focused on the music, the delicate flurries and wandering lows that was the beat of the *Golden Path*. She'd barely grasped the intricate steps required for the dance before he left for Endlight and hadn't repeated them since.

They completed a circuit of the room in silence. The twirling motions weren't as difficult as she recalled. Learning the footwork involved in a swordfight had made her surer in her steps, more aware of where or how her feet landed and sprang off the floor.

What it didn't help with was the annoyance of dancing the *Golden Path* with a train, even one so short that it barely deserved such a name and wasn't designed to be lifted. Coupled with the quick backwards movements required of the dance, the heavy fabric swished with each twirl. Always at the wrong moment, threatening to tangle her legs.

Clara found herself having to focus harder on the steps, kicking her skirts whenever they tried to wrap around her. If there was one thing she couldn't risk tonight, it was tripping and making a fool of herself.

And my apparent unborn child. She hesitated midway through one of the twirls, giving her skirts another kick only to find her balance upset by the swish of fabric and having her almost trip over her own feet. A squeak of surprise left her lips before the subtle caress of magic tightened around her waist.

A gentle chuckle shook them. She glanced up from untangling her feet to the sight of Lucias' grin. "Careful," he murmured, one hand brushing the hair back from her face.

The tune of the *Golden Path* finished and, after a brief pause, the musicians started a dreamier melody. Her feet followed suit. Clara laid her head on Lucias' shoulder and let him gently sway her to the music. She'd missed this, the suppleness of his touch, of the sure way he led her around the room and the reassuring brush of his magic whenever her feet happened to fumble. Light enough to let her right herself, but there should she fail.

The melody finished all too soon. Her legs wobbled, the ache of the day's ride and subsequent fall digging deep into her flesh. Still, she clutched at his jacket as another slow-paced piece of music started up, hoping he would heed her silent wish to remain on the floor. It didn't matter her feet grew tired of carrying her, nor did she care about the many times she stumbled at even the simplest of steps until she was relying entirely on her dance partner's ability to keep her upright.

Lucias wrapped his arms around her. The cool touch of his magic cinched her waist, lifting her ever so slightly until her feet barely touched the ground. "Don't you think you should rest for a while, my dear?" he whispered, his breath skittering down her neck.

She grunted her disapproval of the very idea. The last

thing she wanted was anyone drawing his attention, even for a moment. *What an utterly selfish and childish thought.* She was still allowed those, wasn't she? Out here, the other dancers were as distant as stars. Resting meant letting the waiting world take hold. She wasn't ready to give him up to that just yet.

He directed her in gentle, sweeping steps to where others mingled near the edge of the dance floor. "We can retire for the night, if you want."

Clara desperately wanted to take up the offer, for they must've been here for several hours already. At least, if the tenderness of her feet were to judge. "Nonsense." Except she'd left early last night and doing the same thing again would only invite gossip she was in no mood to deal with. "I just need to rest for a spell." Clara huffed as she ambled at his side, searching for a spare seat. "Providing I can find a place not swarming with people."

Lucias led her through the crowd. The people parted like sheep faced with a horse; unthinking and with the softest hint of fear. Unlike the ordinary folk, the nobility seemed to have a far better idea of their Great Lord's abilities should he be so inclined as to use them. At least, that was what they believed. She wasn't even certain as to the extent of his power.

The room had a balcony with a good view of the floor and, as they ascended the stairs, she saw the seats full of elderly men and women. They chatted amongst themselves and watched the dancers whilst indulging in an evening drink.

"Ah, my lady!" Count Farris emerged from the centre of the elderly throng. He bowed low, prompting those around him to stand and do the same. "I see our dear Great Lord has deigned to release you from the dance floor." The count grinned at Lucias and gave his lord a wink. "Come." He gestured to his recently vacated chair. "Rest yourself awhile."

She graciously took up the offer, letting out a tiny sigh as she sat. Free of her weight, her feet took up a fresh call of abuse. She wiggled them as best as she could inside her slippers, sorely wishing she could remove her footwear altogether. Would it still be rude to excuse herself now?

"You must be thirsty, my dear." Farris waved over a serving boy bearing a tray of jugs and goblets. "Not wine, of course," he went on as the servant filled one of the goblets with an opaque amber liquid. "I hear it's bad for an expecting mother." He took up the goblet and presented it to her. "But I hope the juice of the orange fruit will be to your taste, our Thalia loves the stuff when she's with child."

Clara inclined her head at the gesture, taking great pains to ensure nothing but polite acceptance touched her face. After the over-sweetened tea Thalia had served upon Clara's arrival yesterday, she was wary of drinking anything the heavily pregnant woman enjoyed.

Still, well aware her every move was under the scrutiny of their company, she took a sip. The juice was surprisingly tart and refreshing. Orange fruit, was it? Where did they grow?

Her gaze drifted over the dancers and idle nobles on the floor below. Unlike back at the Citadel, where her Great Lord could get lost alongside his servants, plucking Lucias' image from the crowd was relatively simple. The red and black of his outfit stood out rather violently against the softer hues of those around him. *An easy target.*

Bile slid up her throat at the thought. Clara concentrated on keeping her face neutral, taking the occasional sip of juice in what she hoped was a nonchalant fashion. *He wouldn't put himself in danger.*

Her treacherous thoughts slipped back to when the barbarian stormed the Citadel some months prior. Lucias had faced the man, fully believing he would die. *Maybe then*, she silently conceded. He would offer up his life to give her the opportunity to flee—she fully believed he would gift her the very world if she asked for it—but not with any other reason.

And this wasn't the Citadel. If anywhere in this land

was safe for him, it was here. There were guards aplenty, from all over the kingdom. The castle was walled, as was the city beyond. Men patrolled both day and night. *He is safe.* He would stay that way. She'd make sure of it in whatever way she could.

It was her duty.

CHAPTER TEN

*C*lara leant against the balcony railing. She was alone for the moment. At least, as alone as a person could be in a room full of others. Small groups milled around on the edge of her vision, visibly straining to hear the slightest word from her lips, no matter how droll. Was this what Lucias had meant when he'd compared such gatherings as being akin to some trick show. *Hardly an honest face out there.*

Although the urge to chase off the people surrounding her grumbled in the back of her thoughts, Clara contented herself with quietly sipping at her second goblet of the tart orange-coloured juice and admiring the dancers below.

This high, the elaborate steps were lost to the myriad flashes of colour. Couples swapped partners, turning the distinct pairings into one spiralling line. Each one of the women's skirts became another link in a great of chain expensive cloth, twirling along.

It seemed word of the current fashion for corsets and bustles hadn't quite reached all the noblewomen, for quite a number of them still sported the poofy shoulders and bell-shaped skirt designs she remembered her mother sewing for some of the wealthy merchant women.

Lucias danced amongst the other nobles, leading this woman and that across the floor, but never for long. He would halt every so often, his face turning her way. No doubt checking she hadn't left. Every time he did so, she would raise her goblet in acknowledgement and he would incline his head before returning his attention to those surrounding him.

The presence of another person creeping up on her pulled Clara's attention from the dancers. She twisted slowly, lest her awareness tipped off an opportunistic assassin. Her hand casually strayed to where her dagger nestled in the folds of her skirt.

Relief drew her lips into a wide smile upon seeing it was merely Thad intruding on her small pocket of solitude.

"I had been wondering where Endlight's heir had disappeared to." He'd been at the feast earlier, and she knew the man's wife had retired after eating, joking about how the baby must be a boy for it to already exercise such demands over its mother. She had expected to see Thad amongst the first to greet her and Lucias in the ballroom, but his presence had been conspicuously absent.

"I apologise for my tardiness, my lady. Other duties took me from the festivities." Thad grasped the railing, his shoulders bunching as he stared at the dancers. "How have you found dear Endlight so far? I hear Lucias has already given you a personal tour around some of our fair city."

Clara winced as her mind drifted to the day's events. How likely was it that Thad knew the full story? *Extremely.* "He did," she confessed, her thoughts barely contained. She wanted to ask, to blurt out all the questions coming to mind.

Had Thad learnt something new about Lucias' would-be murderers? That would certainly explain why the man glared at the dance floor as if willing it to ignite. Was it really Lenora trying to enact her revenge once more? Or did she now have the backing of the entire Ebony Court at Ne'ermore?

Holding her tongue there took a great deal more control than Clara anticipated. She fingered her dagger hilt, finding peace in tracing the cool lines etched into the metal. The court appeared to know about the attack, but that didn't mean they were aware of the full details. "The city was every bit as enthralling as I'd imagined," she managed. "Especially the Pillars. They're as impressive up close as the tales tell."

Concern darted across Thad's face. "He took you as far as the Pillars?" He slid closer, his voice dropping to a whisper. "I believe I misheard you, my lady, because it sounded like you said he *went beyond the city border*? Unaccompanied? Did the attack not happen within Endlight's walls?"

"No?" She'd been so caught up in seeing the Pillars that she'd only thought of the risk once they were closer. "We didn't go very far outside the border," she continued, hoping to ease some of the lord's distress. "Just the last hill before the valley." The revelation seemed to have no effect on his expression. "Is something wrong?"

Thad muttered under his breath, the occasional impolite word reaching her ears. "He's not meant to leave the city without a full, and very much *armed*, escort. He *knows* this."

She hunched her shoulders, sharply recalling the lieutenant's hesitance at letting them through the gates unescorted. "If it's any consolation, the gate guard *did* try."

Sighing, he hung his head. "It was one thing for Lucias to be this reckless with his life when his father was alive, but now?" His blond hair shimmered in the candlelight as he shook his head. "I had hoped your presence would've curbed this... self-destructive behaviour." He glanced at her, those green eyes dark and angry. "You should've stopped him. That's your duty. To ensure he comes to no harm."

"And did he?" She'd been thorough in determining that for herself long before Thad knew of the attack, enduring Lucias' whimsical quips as she ensured he hadn't the slightest scratch on him. It seemed the big, black brute of a warhorse had done well in protecting his owner in her stead.

"He could have!" Thad snarled, still in a low enough voice that the words clawed their way out from between his teeth. "All it would've taken was one lucky blow, or one man getting hold of him and dragging him to the ground. You're fortunate none of those men bore crossbows."

Clara stiffened. Yes, he was correct in that Lucias had been lucky, but she couldn't let the tone slide, not in public. Keeping her back straight and head high, she swivelled on her heel to face the man. "I don't know who you think you are addressing, my lord, but—"

"A *child*, it would seem," he snapped, pressing closer until he towered over her.

Her heart thundered in her ears. This close, she was sharply reminded of Thad's bulk. "Are you trying to scare me?" she managed, struggling to shake the terror squeezing her chest. Thad might not be as imposingly large as the barbarian she'd faced some months back, but he was certainly strong enough to bodily lift her with ease. "Because I've seen scary and you're nowhere near as alarming."

Blinking, Thad seemed to become aware of their position near the balcony rail, of how several people below had halted in their dancing to stare up at them and lean towards each other to chatter amongst themselves.

Lucias is going to love that. As much as he teased her for being concerned about how the court viewed her, he still took certain steps to ensure they only gossiped about what he wished them to. Having his closest friend seemingly bully his betrothed would not be an act easily glossed over.

The same thoughts appeared to cross Thad's mind as the man took a few careful steps back. "I would not dare to intimidate you, my lady." Nevertheless, his gaze lowered to the dance floor where Lucias still mingled amongst the other nobles, outwardly oblivious. Whilst people had stopped paying them any obvious mind, Clara knew better than to assume her future husband hadn't caught her little exchange.

"That's good to hear," Clara muttered distractingly as she walked a few steps down the balcony's length, her hand gliding along the smooth railing. "Because I'm certain Lucias would be less than amused to discover his trusted right hand couldn't be."

Thad glared at her, those blond brows drawing tighter and further wrinkling the bridge of his nose. He gripped the railing next to her hand, the breadth of his fingers twice that of her own. "Is that a threat, my lady?"

"Why would I threaten you? We are friends here, aren't we?" Smiling, she patted the back of his hand. "Although, I must say you were much nicer when we first met in the Citadel."

"Well, I didn't have to deal with the threat of the Great Lord's death on my doorstep, nor was there some wayward waif of a girl leading my lord astray." He leant closer, keeping his posture in a carefully neutral display of deference whilst the tone of his voice gained a sliver of menace. "And whilst I am on the subject, what's this I hear about him allowing children off the street into the castle? The Great Lord is supposed to sire a child, not adopt them."

Clara's gaze drifted over the dancers, idly picking Lucias out of the crowd. "Since when were those things mutually exclusive?" No one else had mentioned the arrival of the children she'd bundled off the street. If Thad had merely heard, then there was the possibility that others had, too.

She'd rather hoped that the appearance of seven children, scruffy as they were, would've been overlooked. Although, that they were noted did say something about the vigilance of the castle's security, which did ease a certain tension. Here was safe, even if outside the city walls wasn't.

Thad's chest swelled as he inhaled mightily through his nose. Those green eyes flashed disapproval. "You've a duty to—"

"I am well aware of my duties." Whilst the prospect of a Great Lady was a novelty to the court, her presence meant more than dances and pretty words. Lucias had made it absolutely clear in regards to the practical reason of why she was needed long before he proposed marriage. "Lucias will have his heir at a time of *our* choosing." She whirled on him, fixing him with a cool stare that she was certain would've made her mother proud. "Although, I'm sure he would *love* to discuss the timing of such a matter with you."

Thad gnawed on the corner of his lip, those piercing green eyes burrowing into her as his brow scrunched in thought. "So, this is what the court will have to face after the wedding?" he murmured, almost to himself. "You've certainly changed from the meek woman I remember when we first met."

Her cheeks warmed a little at the remembrance of their first conversation, which had effectively been her begging Thad to aid in her escape the Citadel she now called home. "*Should* I remain the same?" She shook her head in answer before he could utter a word. "If I am to rule at Lucias' side, I refuse to have anyone believe I am an easy target for their will. These are my people, too. I'm prepared to do what I must to keep them safe. That is all I am concerned with."

"I think you might have underestimated how much influence you have over him." The harsh edge in his voice had softened, the same couldn't be said for the starkness of his face. "The court is hoping that his marriage to you means the kingdom has regained a stable ruler. Lucias might have been reckless with his life these past few months, but the same could never be said about the way he treats those under his command." Thad bowed his head. "And *I* am looking to see that he won't become..." He stalled, clearly looking for the right words.

"His father?" Clara supplied. Had the Endlight lord wondered, feared perhaps, that his friend—the man he likened to a brother—would become instantly mad? It must've crossed his mind at least once since the previous Great Lord's demise.

"Quite."

Clara laid a hand on his forearm, the corners of her lips curving in what she hoped was an empathic smile. "We've the same goal there." One day they may have to face a madman with unrivalled power at his command, but that time would, hopefully, be a long way off.

Thad cleared his throat with a brief, muffled cough. His

gaze dropped pointedly to her hand until she removed it. "Well, I'm sure the other nobles find it a refreshing change."

"And just what *was* his father like, if I may?" Lucias spoke so little of the man and always with a sense of disdain, as if the mere thought of his father nauseated him. The servants and guards in the castle were even less willing to broach the subject beyond a casual mention of the past. She knew only of the unsavoury deeds he'd committed in procuring an heir from Lucias' unwilling mother.

"I couldn't tell you much. My father dealt with him more than I. But I do know he'd a rather short temper."

She chewed on her lip. Several questions darted through her mind. She settled on the strongest blaring from the depths. "Always? Or only after he took up his inheritance?"

Those green eyes, which had bored so deeply into her only moments ago, now narrowed in fresh suspicion. "I couldn't rightly say one way or the other. The impression I got from my father was that the change wasn't a new thing." Thad smiled coolly. "But the night is getting late. You've had quite the day, it would seem, and I must retire." He retreated, bowing respectfully. "I wish you fair dreaming, my lady."

Clara watched him depart before returning her attention to the crowd below. Thad was right in it being quite late. It didn't seem to deter the dancers or their enthusiasm in twirling and stomping about. As much as she would've liked to stay and watch them, a nagging feeling in the back of her mind had her thoughts turning to the orphaned children.

I should check on them. Whilst she was confident in Lucias' appraisal of Thalia's care, she'd feel better after ensuring they had indeed been adequately looked after. Perhaps she could convince Lucias to come with her so they could introduce themselves properly.

Leaning over the balcony rail, she searched for Lucias amongst those on the dance floor and found him on the edge of the crowd. Clara tipped forward further, a heralding cry on her lips.

The words died before she voiced them.

A woman stood next to Lucias, not gleefully dancing with him as she'd seen each one do for most of the night. That brown hair and pasty skin seemed familiar. Lucias certainly knew her, for he appeared to be guiding her out a doorway into darkness with his hand firmly clamped upon her upper arm.

Clara hastened to follow, trotting down the stairs to the astonished gasp of onlookers. She slipped through the door. Only the dimly lit hallway greeted her. *Blast.* A scant handful of pathways and exits peeled off this route, leaving her with a few possibilities.

Whispers and softly-spoken grumbles echoed from ahead, barely audible with the raucous of the music and revelry at her back. She crept down the corridor to where it rounded a corner, her soft-soled slippers aiding in her silent steps upon the rug running the length of the stone floor.

The voices were a little more distinct. Not enough for her to make out what was being said, but it was definitely her wayward Great Lord.

Clara peeked around the corner, sticking only enough of her face out to see with one eye. The tip her nose scraped against the stone wall, jolting her back. Odd how rough the surface was when it looked so smooth. *Like a cat's tongue.* Rubbing her wounded nose on the back of a finger, she focused on the pair standing in the middle of the corridor.

The dark-haired woman clung to Lucias like a scorned puppy. "You need a woman's touch." Not much room for assumptions there; the woman was completely sure of her words.

Bitterness crept up Clara's throat. Gentle ire sealed away her voice and quavered through to her very bones.

Lucias turned his head and muttered something. When the woman didn't move, he shoved her back and turned on his heel to march Clara's way.

She flattened back against the wall. *Hide.* That was what she needed. Just a little place. A door or even a niche to tuck herself into.

Only walls greeted her questing gaze.

His footsteps grew ever nearer. A muffled, unhappy thud of heels hitting the rug.

No hiding spots. Nothing for it, then, but to own up to her eavesdropping. She squared her shoulders and stepped away from the wall.

Lucias rounded the corner and halted, visibly startled. "Clara? You—" He glanced over his shoulder before hastening to her side. "You shouldn't be here."

She stiffened her back, preparing herself for what was to come, silently reminding herself that if anyone was in the wrong here, it was him. *A woman's touch, indeed.* If he didn't explain himself swiftly, he was going to get one touch he didn't want. "I could say the same of you." The words left her lips so sweetly that she could almost taste honey on her tongue. "Who was that you were speaking to?"

"No one of import."

"Is that what you told her of me?" she muttered, side-stepping him. If he wasn't going to give her the truth, then she'd get it from the woman.

He grasped her wrist, holding her fast. "Stop."

Clara obeyed. It was either that or opt to forsake the limb entirely.

"I'm certain the conclusion you've reached seems perfectly logical to you at this moment and I wouldn't blame you for it, but if you think, you'll understand how it can't be right."

"So I saw wrongly, did I?" She retrieved the full use of her arm with a jerk. "You did *not* have a woman draping herself all over you, then?" Was this the true reason why he'd left the Citadel so soon? *Does he love another woman?* That sickening thought prowled her mind, picking off any other notions like a wolf amongst sheep. The question released a torrent of others. They darted about, stuck in a current of fear. If he forsook her, she'd nowhere else to go.

"Slow down and think, Clara. Please."

Huffing, she folded her arms. *Then why would he come after me?* She clung to that thought like a boulder in a flood. *Why look for a mistress if he already has one?* He wouldn't... would he? "Then why not tell me who she is?"

Sighing, Lucias rubbed at the back of his neck. "Because she's a..." His nose scrunched, exaggerating the beak-like curve. "An unwelcome element of my past. One I am fast regretting having. I could certainly have done without her poisonous presence tonight." He shook his head. "On the other hand, I'm not even certain the Goddess would know the outcome if we changed but one part of the life we've experienced."

She bit her tongue. So, the woman had been a past lover.

"Clara." He caressed her cheek. "Don't look at me like that. Please? I am yours through and through, I swear. I have been since I first laid eyes on you. I would not risk losing a woman of such indomitable spirit."

"Then tell me who she is."

He shook his head. "I already told you, she's no one. You can't possibly be jealous of no one."

"I'm not *jealous*." The words were out before she could stop them. She folded her arms. She was angry. Angry and upset. And... *Jealous.* "Stop smirking, it's not amusing."

His grin widened. "You're a terrible liar."

No, I'm not. He was just good at seeing the truth. *Like his mother.* He must be aware of inheriting the very power he claimed the Raven Household used to maintain their rule over the Ebony Court at Ne'ermore. "If I'm jealous, then *you—*" She pressed an accusing finger against the tip of his nose. "—are just as prone to the emotion."

"Am *not*," he scoffed.

"Oh? So was that an entirely different man who didn't trust the lords of Endlight when Farris came to the Citadel on his way to collect Brenna?" She recalled his expression well, the darkness lurking behind his eyes when he'd caught her innocently alone with Endlight's undeniably handsome, and very much married, heir. Not that Thad was her type.

"I was never jealous of Thad."

Clara made a show of rolling her eyes. "I don't need some fancy inherent magic to know who the liar is now."

Laughing, he wrapped his arms around her and held her close. "Oh no, my dear, I knew were you already mine."

She snorted. "A liar *and* delusional." Clara pressed her palm to his cool forehead. "I think you might be feverish."

"You just don't want to admit I'm right," he whispered into her hair.

"Definitely feverish," she mumbled. Over his shoulder, her gaze drifted to the corridor corner. She half-expected to see the woman standing there. A bitter part of her wished she had been.

But she'd seen that face before, she was certain of it. All she had to figure out was where. She'd feel better just having a name.

"Come." Lucias stepped back and offered his arm, waiting for her to place a hand into the crook of his elbow before continuing. "We must give the court our leave, then I shall escort you to your chambers."

Clara glanced over her shoulder as he led her towards the ballroom. She hadn't gotten an adequate enough answer of who that was. "But—"

"I know where your mind has led you, and there'd be quite a number who would think of it as great sport to send you further astray, but the night is growing late and the day has been long. Not to mention exceedingly more trying than I'd anticipated. Ask me in the morning, if you still find yourself troubled by it, and I will answer any question you ask. For now, I believe we've a gaggle of children that..." He arched a brow in question. "...I'm guessing you would like to see before retiring for the night?"

She nodded and opened the door to the ballroom. "Court first, then take me to my children. Wherever they've ended up," she muttered to herself. No one had mentioned them when she was readying for tonight, she'd given little thought to as where they were.

Lucias chuckled. "I believe you'll approve of the ar-
rangements I made in your stead."

Chapter Eleven

*C*lara's legs wobbled slightly as Lucias escorted her through the castle. Away from the bright candlelit room and heart-thumping music, the day's trials and excitement swiftly caught up with her. She could barely keep her eyes open. Each step came leadenly.

Nevertheless, she was aware of being led down the corridor to her quarters. Sure enough, they halted before the dark wood door marked with the Great Lord's flame-like emblem. "I thought we were seeing the children first." She wasn't entirely certain if making it to the children before falling asleep was even a possibility, but not even trying? Would they think the worst?

"We are," Lucias replied, giving her back a brief, vigorous rub. An act she barely felt through the corset. "And they should be resting not far from their new mother's chambers." He waved a hand, indicating the doors opposite Clara's. "I ordered the girls to be moved into the left room and the boys are now sharing with Tommy."

So close. She'd hoped for them to be ensconced somewhere befitting their new status as children of the Great Lord, but she hadn't considered they could be placed anywhere near her. "That's perfect, thank you." Giving him a little warning squeeze to remain where he stood, she strode up to the left door.

Silence greeted her as the door swung open.

Clara poked her head into the room. Darkness stole any chance of seeing more than a few feet clearly, but she could make out three beds. It was quite late. Perhaps the girls were sleeping soundly.

She crept further into the room, aiming for the closest bed. Even if the smallest of the three girls had chosen to sleep here, the mattress seemed far too flat for anything to be beneath the covers. Gently questing along the sheets with her fingers confirmed this. She moved on to the others and found them in a similar state.

The place was all laid out as it should be, just woefully empty.

Clara backed out of the room, the beat of her heart thumping wildly in her ears. *I promised.* Safety. Assurance. *I should've checked on them first.* The court could've waited another hour for her presence.

She had time to fix this, hadn't she? *Calm. Breathe. Think logical thoughts.* Not the easiest when her heart continued to beat faster than a drummer's stick. She whirled on Lucias, who watched her with a puzzled frown. "Did you say the girls should be in here?"

Shock widened his dark eyes. Lucias peeked into the room to confirm what Clara already knew. He glanced at the other room; where the boys would be if everything was all right. "Let's check on them first." He clasped her hand and led her to the other door.

Clara all but fell over her own feet in her eagerness to confirm the boys were precisely where they should be. The silence coming from the other side suddenly didn't seem quite so soothing.

Candlelight greeted them as they opened the door. That held no sense of relief either. Not when she knew Tommy could still be up. Whilst he usually slept the same hours as the rest of the people back in Everdark—awake at dawn and in bed at sunset—he suffered from patches of restlessness where sleep was impossible. He was currently attempting knitting as a means to calm his mind enough to rest.

Clara peered around the door, trusting that her page would still be there and perhaps know where the children were.

Several pairs of eyes looked her way with equal levels of alarm.

Relief jellified her legs. She clung to the door. "They're here," she called over her shoulder. "All of them." They appeared to have been playing some sort of game with various bottles and jars, and what looked suspiciously like a balled-up stocking.

Tommy twisted in his cross-legged position on the floor. "Clara!" he announced, hopping to his feet. He froze, shooting the children a worried look, then shifted that gaze to Clara. "A servant told me they were staying here?"

She nodded. "That's right. They don't have a home, so they're going to be living in the Citadel with us."

All at once, the worry melted from Tommy's face to be replaced with the warmest smile. "Gettie will like that." He returned to facing the children, sinking back to his place on the floor.

Derek gently lifted the youngest girl's sleeping head off his lap and stood, eyeing the older boy with the same slowly sweeping stare the majority of people did after spending some time with Tommy. Most seemed to believe Tommy was putting on some sort of act, but Clara had never known a time that the boy wasn't earnest. And if Tommy ever noticed the glances, he gave no indication.

"It's all true, then?" Derek asked.

Grumbling came from behind him. The heavily freckled girl sat up, yawning and scrubbing at her face. "What—?" Her brown eyes widened as they fell on Clara. "You came back." In one almighty burst of activity, she scrambled across the bed, tumbled onto the floor and scuttled over to throw her arms around one of Clara's legs.

Without thinking, she caressed the girl's hair. Now that the limp, dark mass was freshly washed, her hair had more of a light brown tint and stood out from her like a fuzzy halo. "Didn't I say I would?"

Movement on the edge of her vision caught her attention. Clara lifted her head to find the rest of the children standing in a row before her. They'd all been scrubbed clean during their time here and decked out in the red and black attire of Lucias' house.

Derek, who she now knew was only thirteen years old—thanks to Lucias' little chat with Thalia—stood the straightest. The rest mimicked him to the best of their abilities.

She surveyed them, taking in the timid looks and slightly poised stance that reminded her of the half-wild stray cats the roamed Everdark's streets. "It rather occurs to me that I know very little about any of you." She clasped her hands together and—after a touch of wrangling to have the freckled-faced girl release her grip on Clara's leg—lowered herself onto the end of the nearest bed.

One by one, the children turned their attention to the boy who'd been their sole carer for a great deal longer than any child should need to be. Derek's fingers worked furiously at his other wrist.

Clara held out a hand to him. "You're scratching. May I see why?"

"It's nothing, Miss." Still, the boy sidled up to kneel before her.

She delicately cradled Derek's hand, being careful not to touch the paler parts of his skin—white even against the olive brown backdrop of her palm—for it looked quite inflamed. Redness adorned his knuckles. It could've been mistaken for him having a violent nature at a glance.

Gently pushing up the cuffs of his shirt, Clara moved on to examine his wrist where the patch of white stopped haphazardly. He appeared to have scratched quite deeply along the joint, breaking the skin in some places. "How badly does it hurt?"

The boy's expression soured. Betrayal glittered in his eyes as, huffing, he rolled them. "It doesn't," he muttered, jerking his hand free. "And I'm not contagious either."

"I know that," she replied, trying to maintain an even tone, for this certainly couldn't be the first time someone had remarked on his skin. And few doing so positively judging by his reaction. "I meant the sunburn. It's clearly irritated."

Derek gave an uneasy grimace, his gaze dropping. "A little," he mumbled before pride had him lifting his chin. "I can handle it."

"You've gone and burnt yourself again?" Sweetie railed from her place alongside the others, her mouth puckering. "I've told you, if we've got to watch the sun, so do you."

"Not Ruby," crowed a slightly younger boy. "She just freckles, see?" One pale finger pointed to the third girl in the room, or more at the brown flecks that were barely visible upon the girl's cheeks.

In response, Ruby puffed out her chest and thumped it dramatically. Now that she was clean, the girl's lank hair displayed its muted tones of dark red.

Clara hummed to herself. "I've a balm that might help. Tommy?" She glanced over Derek's shoulder at her page. "Could you fetch it for me, please? It should be on my dressing table, just behind the screen. The blue jar."

Nodding, Tommy bounced to his feet and scurried through the open door.

She sought out the boy with the chapped lips before her gaze slid to the one with the peeling and terribly sun-reddened face. "It might help the both of you as well." She rocked back, tapping a little tune on her thighs. "Shall we start with names and ages whilst we wait? I already know you, Derek, and your sister." She peered around the boy to smile at his sibling, who offered the same in response. Her gaze returned to the small boy with the sunburnt face. "You too, although I don't believe your name really is *Trubs*."

"It's Trouble," the boy replied, a touch of defiance tightening his jaw. He squared his shoulders. "And I'm five and a half years old." He punctuated himself with a stiff nod.

"Sweetie found him out the back of the cattle yards," Derek said. "He's only been with us for a year or so. His dad left when his mum fell ill. She died." His voice fell at those last words, almost a whisper.

Clara felt the tips of her fingers gracing her lips before she realised she'd moved. She stood, taking a few staggering steps to fall to her knees before the young boy and wrap her arms tightly around his slender shoulders. "My dad fell to a wasting illness some years back," she confessed in a teary whisper.

The memory of watching the strong man her father had once been withering to a figure half his original size whilst under the illness' thrall was one she'd never be free of. She hadn't even been able to hug him in his final moments for fear of contracting the same sickness. Not many in Everdark had fallen to the illness that had beset her father, but not a single infected soul had survived. "It must've been terrible." To lose, not one, but both parents whilst so young.

Tiny hands gripped her gown, clinging tight. Trouble buried his face into her shoulder and the smallest of sniffles drifted up to her ear.

She gave him a little reassuring squeeze and tilted her head to catch Derek's eye. With the gentle tip of her chin, she indicated that he kept talking as though the boy in her arms wasn't quietly soaking her clothes with his tears.

Clearing his throat, Derek jerked a thumb at the boy with chapped lips. "That's Rascal. Reckon he's six years old. Found him wandering around the moor-side wall about two years back. He came to Endlight with his old man, but we've no idea where he went off to."

The boy with chapped lips smiled uncertainly, those dark eyes peeking out from beneath his sandy hair.

His father's probably back home. And likely heartbroken, for the man would surely be thinking his son had fallen afoul of someone and was either dead or out of reach. Maybe, with some help from the nomads, they could reunite them. She made a mental note to see if it was at all possible before announcing the idea to the boy.

The older boy moved up the line of children, laying a hand on one of the girl's shoulder. "Ruby's also six," Derek continued without missing a beat. "Her family was in the same sector as Trub's. The illness took a lot of people. Don't ask her to speak, she can't. Never been able to. Doesn't know why."

Clara held out her hand in supplication to Ruby. The scrawny girl eagerly accepted the silent invitation of a consoling hug.

Derek's hand had barely slipped from her shoulder before he clapped his other hand onto the last unnamed boy—the one who'd been proud of Ruby's skin freckling rather than burning. "Whereas Woden..." Derek grimaced. "His parents went out one day, left him playing with all us kids, and just didn't come back. He was four then and that was three years ago."

Woden was the palest of the bunch alongside Sweetie. He'd fine, almost white hair, and blue eyes that examined her likely as much as she did him. Whilst she didn't doubt the age Derek claimed, Woden's mannerisms gave him the air of being far older than the other boys. More reserved, too.

Finally, Derek stopped to tousle the youngest girl's brown hair. "And this is Poppet. She's four now, but she's been with us since Sweetie found her in an alley. She was just a baby."

"However did you manage to feed someone so young?" She could comprehend these children being able to care for a toddler, for they'd merely need to soften whatever food they scrounged. But an *infant*? Experience told her they required milk, be it their mother's or from another milk-giving animal.

"It was late spring," Sweetie replied. "Derek creeps into the cattle yards at night when the nomads bring their herds in. He milks enough from the cows for us."

Clara frowned. Whilst a bold move, she was well aware

of the power behind those beasts should they choose to lash out. "You're lucky to not have been injured by one of them. I hope not to see any foolish risks such as that taken whilst under my care."

Derek gave her a sheepish smile, his shoulders hunching. "No, Miss."

"Since we're on the subject of nourishment, I hear you've all been fed?"

Sweetie nodded. "They took us into the kitchen before sundown."

"It was *full* of food," Poppet added. "Like, this much!" She spread her little arms as wide as they could go.

Trouble jumped behind the girl and mimicked her. "More like *this*."

"That's a lot of food. I hope none of you stuffed yourselves." The last thing she needed was for the children to make themselves sick through eating more than their bodies could handle. She'd already been down that road when Lucias first insisted she wasn't eating nearly enough.

"The nice lady with the big belly told us to eat until we were full," Rascal said, tugging at the collar of his shirt. "The neck is tight, Miss."

"That's because it fits you better than your old clothes." Most of their old attire had been beyond slightly baggy. Poppet's garb, if it truly could be called that, had barely been more than a sack in comparison to the lovely chemise she currently wore. "Still..." Clara knelt before Rascal and gently loosened the top two buttons of his shirt. "No one'll mind."

"Did you see the tiny size of the roast birds?" Trouble asked of Ruby, the two still clearly back on the subject of food. "I could've fit a whole one in my mouth. The pigeons in the square were fatter."

Ruby wrinkled her nose. She clasped her thumbs and flapped her fingers like a bird whilst shaking her head. Indicating herself with a forefinger, she mimed stuffing her mouth before using the same finger to turn the end of her nose up and make a rough grunting noise.

"No way you could've eaten that whole roast pig," Rascal retorted, twisting whilst his shirt was still in Clara's grip. A third button popped open.

The girl defiantly tilted her chin.

"Well, *I* could eat a whole cow if I wanted to."

Sweetie snorted. "But that would mean you'd need to go *near* a cow again and we all know that'll never happen."

"I'll eat cooked cow."

"It's called beef, genius," Woden said, cocking his head and swinging those blue eyes inward until he peered at his own nose.

"I knew that," Rascal snapped, his little nose wrinkling with indignation.

Clara scrubbed at her face, using it as an excuse to cover her mouth and hide her laughter. She'd enjoyed minding the younger children in her street, not just for the few pennies or extra food each job would pay. She'd missed the simple banter and competition most of all.

Trouble sighed wistfully. His eyes had glazed over at the mention of beef and he continued to stare into whatever memory the conversation had taken him to. "I ate beef once," he murmured, his voice all but lost against the ruckus of the rest. "It was a festival, just before Papa and me came here."

Clearing her throat, Clara waited until each child had turned their attention to her. "I expect to see all of you in the dining hall come morning. *And* I want each and every one of you on your best behaviour."

"We get to eat two days in a row?" Poppet squealed, her brown eyes huge with wonder.

"Of course," she murmured reassuringly, her stomach dropping at the girl's words. Naturally, it would be difficult for them to find enough to feed all seven every single day, but it wasn't a thought she had lingered on for too long. "You'll get three meals a day, every day. The same as every-one else here."

"Three?" The high-pitched sound coming out of the little girl's mouth was almost beyond the range of hearing.

"Got it!" Tommy declared from out in the hall. He barrelled through the doorway, pausing only to squeeze by Lucias.

Thanking him, Clara took the jar from Tommy and unscrewed the lid. All the while, her gaze lingered on Lucias. As still and silent as he'd been, she'd forgotten his presence entirely. Even now, he seemed to prefer his stance of leaning casually in the doorway and observing. Was the distance because of the children? If so, then for the benefit of who?

Motioning the two younger boys closer, she applied a thick layer of the balm to Rascal's lips before moving on to smother Trouble's face. "I want each of you to apply this twice a day, that's both when you wake up and just before you go to bed." Handing the jar over the Derek, she fixed the younger children with a stern stare. "Which you all should've been doing rather than playing whatever game you've got here."

"What's going to happen to us?" Sweetie asked. The girl had returned to her perch on the end of a bed and seemed indifferent to the fact each forward rock had her dangling over the edge quite precariously. "The pregnant lady said you'll be leaving in a few days."

"Well, this isn't our home. But you're all going to travel to the Citadel with me. And Lucias, of course." She glanced over her shoulder, trying to gauge his reaction. It was possible that he'd continue on with his plan to visit the other border towns without her.

"They look after you there," Tommy said. "There's always plenty of food, clothes that'll fit and you can sleep in your own beds."

Clara nodded. Whilst she hadn't checked every inch of the Citadel like her page—not even during her attempts to flee the place—she knew there were more than enough spare bedrooms for the children to have one each if they desired. "You'll also be taught to read and write, along with whatever skills you'd like to learn."

"Like an academy?" Sweetie pressed. "The priests told us about them once, they didn't seem very exciting."

"I don't—" Words failed her. The only academies she had ever heard about were through the hushed mutterings of disgruntled folk back in Everdark. Usually, those mutters were directed at some young man with what her father used to term as fanciful ideas on how the world worked. They never stayed very long.

"It won't be like that at all," Lucias said, straightening to stand squarely within the doorframe. "For starters, we'll be family."

"Does that make you our big sister?" Poppet asked of Clara.

"I can be, if you'd like. I've never had siblings before." She waggled a finger in mock sternness. "But don't think that means I'll go easy on your studies."

"You don't sound like a sister," Sweetie said. "You sound more like a mum."

Poppet gasped. Her already wide eyes somehow seemed to grow even more so. "I've never had one of those," she whispered.

Clara knelt at the little girl's side and wrapped her arms around the bony frame. "If you'd prefer, I'd be honoured to be your mum."

Thin arms tightened around her shoulders. Too long to be Poppet's.

Clara lifted her head to find her face enveloped by the pale cloud that was Sweetie's hair.

More arms embraced her. The boys. A tightness welled in her chest. Tears threatened to pour forth. It would be hard for them all, but she was willing to find a way through that. For family.

Chapter Twelve

*H*er bathing chamber was freezing. She'd never considered before how a whole bath of steaming water could also heat the room to a bearably warm temperature. Her little bucket of tepid water really had no hope of matching such lofty ideals.

It also somewhat encouraged her to be swift with her bathing. Fortunately, she'd very little in the way of actual dirt to cleanse herself of after her late afternoon scrub down yesterday.

Clara eyed the black-enamelled bath whilst drying herself. It sat in the middle of the room like a hulking beast. Yes, she could've requested the servants fill it for her, but then what? Stand around in her nightgown whilst they trotted in with buckets of hot water? Asking for the simple one she currently used had been bad enough. At least they knew to leave a bucket outside her chambers back in the Citadel.

She rubbed vigorously at her damp skin, the softness of the cloth doing little beyond moving the water around. It was with much effort that she was finally able to call herself dry.

Setting the towel aside, she carefully hoisted the bucket of water over the bath rim. The water gurgled down the plug hole. Hopefully, it actually went somewhere and wasn't currently discharging all over the floor below.

Interior plumbing was a relatively new innovation. None

of the people she used to speak with in Everdark had such marvels in their houses, nor did even the most luxurious part of the Citadel harbour anything more than a basin.

Just how had whoever oversaw the Endlight Castle's upkeep also managed to integrate these modern touches?

It didn't stop at the drain. Taps protruded over the foot end of the tub. She hadn't been bold enough to turn them and find out if they worked or were merely for show. The castle had to be several centuries old, being built back at the time of the kingdom's formation, if not beforehand. She couldn't imagine they'd have the foresight to install pipes.

She watched the water drain away, her thoughts turning to what Lucias had said once they'd both ensured the children were safely tucked into their beds. She hadn't paid much mind to his words then, being too concerned with the girls preferring to sleep scrunched beneath one blanket rather than in individual beds—an act she rather hoped would change over time.

"It would seem that you pick up people the way others would stray dogs." Lucias chuckled, those dark eyes glittering with genuine joy. "First Tommy, now this lot."

"You don't mind, do you?" The thought of having to tell those poor children they couldn't actually stay was enough to make her stomach roll.

He shook his head. "If I had, they wouldn't have gotten this far into the castle. Naturally, Thad suggests caution in allowing you to adopt every urchin you come across, but all I see is a woman who will be an exceptionally good mother. I'm quite enamoured with the idea of filling the Citadel with children's laughter. I think it's been a long time since those walls heard such a sound. But I see no reason that they all need to be of my blood, and why should I deny those children a secure place to grow into who they're meant to be purely on that basis?"

She'd not been able to compose herself to answer within the

short time it took Lucias to escort her to the black door leading to her bedchamber. Everything beyond that, the mundane task of readying herself for sleep—and finally unlacing that dreadfully snug corset—had been a fuzzy mess of memory.

Was he suggesting adding more orphaned children to their brood? *Perhaps in time*. Settling seven new people into the Citadel's orderly schedule would take some shuffling. Lessons would have to be planned.

She absently curled her finger into her hair and ran the resulting tuft across her cheek. Perhaps it would be best to send for a governess to teach them. Not straight away, Clara could handle the basics, but she lacked certain skills and having those areas fleshed out could only gift the children with a wider choice.

The plug hole gave a gulping suck as the last of the water drained away, jerking Clara from her musing.

Throwing her dressing gown over her chemise and securely fastening the tie, she made her way into the comparatively brighter bedchamber. She'd flung back the dark curtains at first light and had cracked open a window to allow movement of the stale air. The wind had picked up during her time bathing, stirring the curtains and throwing odd shadows across the black walls.

Settling on the stool before her dressing table, she tackled the knots sleep had woven into her hair. She swept the brush mindlessly through the blood-red strands, her thoughts slowly returning to the children.

Just what should she focus on first? Reading seemed the logical choice. Maybe the castle library had something easy for them to start with.

Another sound reached her ears over the whisper of bristles. She paused, the brush poised delicately above her head. Nothing. Holding her breath, she gave the brush another sweep through, softly so as to not drown out any noise and—

There it was again. The faintest tap of a foot landing on the stone floor. Easily lost in the bustle of a morning routine.

Was she not alone?

Clara peered into her mirror, fussing absently with the wisps where her hair parted whilst her gaze ventured elsewhere. There was no movement in the reflection beyond her own, no hint of a person at her back.

How could they have gotten in? She'd ushered everyone out and locked the door with the very key that still sat in the lock. Maybe it was just her imagination, a piece of Lucias' paranoia settling on her shoulders.

The window. She had thought it safe to leave open, given that they were several stories up and it'd require quite the enterprising assassin to even dare think of climbing such a height, never mind how they'd manage it.

Nevertheless, the hairs at the nape of her neck stood to attention.

Her questing gaze fell on the dagger openly sitting on the bedside table, precisely where she'd put it upon exiting the blankets. So much for always keeping a weapon on her person. Could she reach it before they realised her intentions? If it was truly an assassin, they were certainly taking their time.

Grumbling and muttering under her breath as if she'd forgotten something vital, she set down the brush and swivelled on the stool. Even the new vantage point gave her nothing to go on. Where could a person hide?

Clara lurched to her feet to pad across the room in a display of frustrated searching. She eyed the dressing screen, innocently sectioning off a corner of the room. Like the ones back in the Citadel, it stood as high as the doorway with solid panels all the way up. The feet gave enough clearance to reassure her that nobody stood behind them, but that didn't leave off the fact they could be crouched on the chair.

She reached the plush rug running along the side of the bed. As the soft slap of her bare feet vanished, that same barely-perceptible tap of another's footfall continued at her back.

A ripple of coldness skittered down her spine. *Danger*, it seemed to whisper. *Behind you*. She fussed with the blankets, continuing to play the part of an oblivious victim searching for an object of minor import. All the while, allowing her search to slowly close the distance between her and the bedside table.

It took every ounce of willpower not to flee towards the dagger, but that would likely end in disaster. Whoever was in her room clearly planned to wait for the right moment. She didn't linger on why, just focused on using it to her advantage whilst keeping an ear on those ghostly footsteps.

At last, the weapon was within reach.

In one smooth movement, Clara swiped the dagger from the table and swung about. With the weapon gripped by the hilt, the sheath flew off the blade.

The dark figure shadowing her ducked.

Clara took the opportunity of the distraction to scuttle towards the door.

The figure—a man decked in black from the neck down—rolled across the floor and popped back onto his feet with far more speed than Clara had anticipated. He overtook her, drawing his weapon; a dagger that was considerably larger than her own.

The soles of her feet skated on the floor, all balance lost for a moment. She dared to lift her gaze from the man to glance at the door. The key still stuck out of the lock. *Good.* If she could just reach it. If she could somehow cause the man to not be in her way.

But how?

A candlestick also sat on her bedside table, thick and made entirely of iron. She took a step back towards it with her dagger held firmly in her fist, ready to stab at the first hint of the figure being within reach. Hopefully, all her training in the Citadel hadn't been in vain.

Her would-be assassin followed her step for step. She needed a distraction. She needed—

Tommy. If she yelled, he'd come bearing the sword

Lucias had gifted to him. He'd proven that through several of her more troublesome sleeps during the journey here. He wouldn't be able to enter, but perhaps his presence at the door would be enough to gift her with the brief chance to unlock it.

But if she called for her page, what guarantee did she have that the other children wouldn't follow in his wake? What if their combined efforts at entry broke down the door?

Clara took a deep breath, not willing to take her eyes off the man for another second. It was a risk she'd have to take. "Tommy!" The name blasted from her lips, loud enough to wake the dead.

Her would-be assassin paused. He turned his head partially as if to look over his shoulder, but his gaze remained trained on her like a cat on a rat.

She matched his glare with one of her own, hoping it didn't betray the quaking she felt deep in her gut. Clara slid her foot back in the slowest of glides. Her mouth went dry.

The air between them seemed to grow colder the longer they remained in place, rooted to the spot.

"Clara?" Tommy called from the hall. The door handle rattled and the puzzled cry was fast muffled by the panicked thump of a body against the door. He called her name again, growing more frantic as the wooden barrier remained unyielding.

The man turned, eyeing the entrance, and sneered.

"Get Lucias!" she roared, diving for the candlestick. *Hold him off.* That's all she needed to do. Once Lucias had arrived, then it would be over. That door would be no barrier to him and the man had nowhere to run beyond straight out the window to his death.

Her would-be assassin smirked as she raised the candlestick. He crept closer, his dagger held low. The man didn't seem all that big. Lean, perhaps, and possibly faster than herself. She supposed the fully-black attire would've been imposing to some, but she'd faced worse.

"Neither that nor the Dark Lord will save you, little

girl," the man said. Although his voice was gruff and thick with anger, the accent was unmistakably that of their northern enemy's. Not that Clara needed such proof; few would choose to send an assassin, fewer still would target her over the Great Lord. "Put down the candlestick and that ridiculous needle, I'll promise to make it quick."

"Touch me and I promise it'll be painful beyond measure for you once Lucias gets here." The man would either die like the man who'd attempted to rape her or he'd become another soldier in the Great Lord's soulless army.

And judging by the look on his face, the man knew just as well as she. That would make him desperate; a boon and a curse at the same time.

She laid a hand on the bed, prepared to vault over it if necessary. Keeping something sturdy between them seemed like the best plan. *Like the bath.* Her gaze flicked to the other door in the room. There was no lock and the door swung inwards, no chance of shutting him in there. But if she could get inside without him following, maybe she could hold the door for however long it took Lucias to arrive.

She took a step away from the bed. It couldn't be more than half the room's width between her and the door, but the distance seemed to stretch to the length of a ballroom. If she left the dubious safety of where she stood, then there'd be no chance to go back.

Hefting the candlestick, she took another step. Maybe if she lobbed the thing at him. Her throwing wasn't the most accurate, but it could certainly give the man pause long enough to see her across the room.

Another few half-steps got her even closer.

On the other hand, he might hurl the candlestick back. Getting hit in the back of the head was not a risk she wanted to take. Keeping hold of the candlestick and using it as a bludgeon seemed like a better stance.

The man's gaze slid to the bathroom door. Realisation flickered in his eyes and his brows lowered. He strode closer, no longer creeping but with the dagger still held low. Another few more strides and he'd be near enough to strike.

Clara feinted, lurching back the way she'd come with the candlestick held before her like a shield and her dagger at the ready. The man stepped back, then to the side in preparation to meet her mad dash to the exit.

She whirled and ran for the bathroom door.

"No, you don't." He grasped her sleeve, jerking her around.

She turned on a single heel. Her arm went slack, the candlestick's weight following the momentum of an upward arc. The bottom edge struck the man's face, breaking skin. At first, she thought she'd managed to hit his eye. But as he brought the back of a hand up to his face, she saw it wasn't so.

Slicing at the air with her dagger to keep him off her, Clara swung again.

His hand clamped around the candlestick. Baleful, dark eyes glared at her, one held near closed to ward off the blood dripping from his brow. "You little brat." Gone was the gruffness, replace by a deathly iciness.

It took all her defiance to spit in his face. She lashed out with a leg, her heel connecting with a knee.

Snarling, he flung her away from him, sweeping her legs out from under her as she stumbled.

Her back hit the floor, knocking the breath from her lungs. Her right hip objected to the landing, having not fully recovered from yesterday's fall. Both candlestick and dagger tumbled out of her grasp.

Gasping, she rolled for the dagger.

His rough fingers closed around her throat. Paralysing pressure stole the breath she'd only just regained. Her arm flailed wildly, spinning the dagger out of reach. She grabbed for the hand choking her, desperately trying to pry back so much as a finger.

Clara thrashed, seeking to throw off the assassin. Her flails had her empty fist connecting with the side of the man's head. His grip slipped enough for her to swallow another gasp.

"Stay down," he growled, kneeling over her. The man latched onto her neck tighter than before, pushing her against the floor, his dark eyes bulging with the effort.

She raked at them, streaking his face with long red scratches.

The pressure on her neck increased. Her vision blurred. Flickering specks of white and black seemed to dance before her eyes. Her heart hammered furiously, a stark contrast to the absence of pounding in her temples.

Blackness slunk its way across the edges of her sight, tunnelling her vision. *Hold on.* Her whole body convulsed, ridding her limbs of their strength. Even that didn't shake the man's grip free. The steady thump of her heels on the floor seemed to reverberate dully through the room.

A creaking groan, similar to that of protesting wood, filled her ears.

Splinters showered the room. The man sat up, his arms raised to protect his face.

Air flooded her lungs. She gasped, fresh tears pricking at the corners of her eyes.

The man was flung up against the ceiling before she could think beyond finding the strength to breathe, then slammed into the wall to fall to the floor like a rag doll.

"Clara!" Lucias dropped to his knees beside her. "No," he whispered. "Please, no." Terror paled his face. "Don't say I'm too late. I couldn't... I can't... don't be dead."

Pain continued to blossom in her chest. She breathed deep, happily welcoming the sensation, and clasped his hand.

"Thank the Goddess," he whispered, lifting her fingers to his lips. "Can you breathe all right? Talk? Any extreme pain?" Lucias helped her sit up as he rattled off the questions, then whirled on Tommy before she could answer a single one. "Fetch Lord Farris for me. And keep the children out of here."

The boy all but fell over himself to scamper back through

the doorway.

Clara gingerly felt along her throat.

"Permit me to see what damage he has caused," Lucias said, gently assisting her to the end of the bed.

With her elevated, her head spun something fierce. She laid a hand on Lucias' shoulder as he knelt before her to examine her neck.

He rocked back onto his heels. "Lots of swelling," he murmured, grimacing. "You can probably feel that. Definitely going to be some bruising. I wouldn't advise talking for a bit, either." He glanced at the remains on the door. "I suppose we should see you dressed in something a little less improper before anyone else arrives. I don't think you want to be sitting there in your undergarments."

Clara looked down at her attire. Until he had mentioned it, she hadn't realised her dressing gown hung off her shoulders. The tie must've loosened during her struggle or when the man had grabbed her. She tugged everything back into place, holding the edges snugly at her breast. Yes, she'd been clothed in less than this in Lucias' presence twice before. Except...

Her gaze drifted to her attacker. Whilst he certainly wasn't in the position to harm her any further, the idea of removing any layer of clothing—even if it were to don a more appropriate one—with him in the room was not a thought she'd considered entertaining.

Lucias looked over his shoulder and the man's limp form slid across the floor, facing away from them. "I wouldn't worry about him. Here." He stood, offering his hand. "How about you show me which attire is the easiest for you to get on in a hurry and I'll assist you in donning it. No corsets," he added.

Nodding, she let him lead her behind the dressing screen and had her settle on the stool. Via a series of grunts and much pointing, she was finally able to slip into a dress that was essentially an overlong tunic. It was one she typically wore whilst wandering the Citadel on lazy days rather than be seen in public, but it was better than standing around in her undergarments. And it was quite loose in the neck, leaving her bruised skin untouched by fabric.

Lucias aided her to the end of the bed where she sat whilst he turned to examine her would-be assassin. "He's still alive." He slapped the man's face, lifting an eyelid when the man didn't move. "If I can wake him, we might be able to get a few answers."

Clara frowned. Coming out of an attack like that alive was one thing. Being capable of understanding anything after Lucias had tossed the man about the room like hay in a storm was a whole other matter.

"I know," Lucias said, pulling a face. "I should've been more careful. I panicked. Can you blame me? Would you have been cautious in my place?"

She shook her head. If by some peculiar chance she'd seen Lucias in the same distress, she would've run the assassin through.

"Although I would say it's safe to assume this one doesn't require a trial before sentencing." That was a new measure he had begun to enforce, starting with Everdark. Most of the people sent to him for punishment were unmistakably guilty of their crimes, but rather than rely on them being on the iron wagon as proof of their guilt like the Great Lords before him, he required documents.

The man groaned, his head rocking to one side, but otherwise remained unresponsive.

Lucias opted to drag the man into the middle of the floor and leave him spread out upon the rug before the dressing table. "Hopefully, he'll regain consciousness before Farris arrives." His brows lowered and specks of silvery-blue light darted across his eyes. "I shall have a few choice words for our host, too."

If she thought it'd do any good, Clara would've considered a further tongue-lashing from herself. But the idea of speaking more than a few words felt nigh impossible at the moment. At least the world had stopped spinning some time during her dressing.

Her head was feeling a fair bit better and her would-be assassin had indeed woken enough to understand the gravity of his circumstance by the time Farris and Thad arrived at what remained of her door. The pair faltered at the entrance, shooting each other worried looks, before venturing inside with their hands on their sword hilts.

"What happened?" Thad enquired, his gaze taking in the room.

Farris' barely took in the area, glancing only at the man in passing before turning to Clara. "My lady, are you unharmed?"

"No," Lucias replied to save her from doing so. "Fortunately, she will recover. I thought you said this castle would be safe for the duration of our stay?" The specks of silvery-blue light in his eyes had faded during their wait. They now flared with full force.

Farris blinked. "It is. I've doubled patrols and tripled the guards on all the entrances."

"Then explain how *this*—" He dealt a swift kick to her would-be assassin, sending the man rolling across the rug. "—festering pustule of a creature managed to get close enough to risk her life."

Farris scratched his cheek. He stared at the man, at the room, the windows, the doorways. His grey brows knitted together, further wrinkling his face. "I can't rightly say how, but you can be assured that I'll find out before the day's end."

"No need." The light all but filled Lucias' eyes now. Only the whites were left, and they were fast ceding to the unearthly glow. "I will have the answer from him now."

"Please, no." The man scrambled to his knees. "I'll tell you whatever you need to know."

"Yes," the word left Lucias' lips in a low hiss. "You will." His voice took on that all too familiar tone. No matter how many times she heard it, that guttural sound never failed to lift the hair on her body.

But he had always been in the Citadel dungeon when taking souls. She had no idea that he could do so whilst outside the old fortress' grounds.

Clara slid off the bed and took a few wobbling steps off to the side. On the edge of her vision, she spied Farris and Thad hurriedly looking away. Had neither seen Lucias do what all Great Lords had done?

Lucias laid his hand upon the gibbering man's head. Words poured from his lips. Words she didn't understand. Words she didn't *want* to understand. And yet, she knew they were different to the ones he usually spoke.

The air grew hot. Charged. A ring of glowing, seething glyphs surrounded the pair. The symbols circled slowly before embedding themselves into the stone floor where they flared in silvery-blue bursts.

Clara backed further away, taking pains to keep her slippered feet from touching the lines. He'd always been very explicit about that whenever she was there to witness punishments. She shielded her face with a hand. The light blazed around them in a ghostly flame arcing between the pair.

And still, Lucias continued on in that strange tongue.

At last, the light died and he stood over the man, a ball of light resting in his hand. Lucias stared at it. He seemed to be, for a moment, considering what he had just done. Then he flicked his hand and the ball vanished to wherever the stolen souls went.

"Stand," he commanded of her would-be assassin.

The man scrambled to his feet, his back straight and his eyes carrying the same dullness that every other one of the Great Lord's men bore. This was his life now. Unless Lucias died without an heir to take on the Great Lord's curse, this man's soul was lost to him forever.

Had he not attempted to strangle her only moments ago, she would've felt a smidgen of pity for such a fate.

"Who sent you?" Lucias demanded.

"The Lady Raven."

Clara didn't need to hear any more information than that; she only knew of one Lady Raven and that was Lucias' mother. *Lenora.* She'd expected the scheming witch to return in some manner, to finish the job her pet barbarian had started back in the Citadel several months prior.

Targeting Clara made sense, especially after all this time. *Kill the heir before it's born.* Well, Lenora was fresh out of luck there. For the moment.

"Were you behind the attempted poisoning of my mistress?" Lucias asked. The question got mirrored frowns from Farris and Thad. Clearly, the two lords had no idea what had transpired beneath their own roof.

"Yes," the man replied.

Lucias nodded, seemingly pleased with himself. "You will go with them." He indicated the two lords with a twitch of his head. "You will show them how you got past the defences and into this room."

The man bowed. "At once, master." He vacated the room, followed rather swiftly by Farris and Thad.

Clara hugged herself as she eyed where the glyphs had branded their design into the stone. "I didn't think you could do that outside of the Citadel." Although her voice sounded dreadfully raspy, there was no pain.

"It's a little harder. A little more draining, but it's what Kerwin would've done to his enemies when forging our kingdom."

Our *kingdom.* There it was again. Never just his, but *theirs.* He wanted an equal. She wasn't certain if she'd ever truly attain that status, but she was willing to try. "I need to dress."

"I thought you were."

"Not in this." Her dress had been suitable to maintain modesty in the presence of others not of her family, but she couldn't very well walk around the castle in it without drawing attention. And there was the matter of her neck. She'd several gowns that wouldn't touch the bruising, but also bore lace that would obscure it. "This won't do."

Lucias shrugged. "I will defer to you on that. Following the court's mercurial fashion trends has never been an interest of mine." He turned his back to her, but made no effort to remove himself from her room.

"Shouldn't you be leaving?"

"When you have no door?" he shot back whilst still looking straight ahead. "I hardly think that would be a good idea. Although, it does remind me..." He waggled a finger in the air. "I must send for another. You may have to make do without the symbol, though." He glanced over his shoulder. "I thought you were changing?"

She nodded. "But you're here and—"

"My dear, you were just attacked. No one will consider it as the atmosphere for intimate ideas." He waved his hand at the dressing screen. "By all means, clothe yourself as you deem appropriate. I am merely here to guard your person. I swear, peeking like a pubescent boy is the last thing on my mind."

Gathering the required garments from her travelling chest, Clara slipped behind the dressing screen. She set about exchanging the loose-fitting tunic dress for a slightly snug one in the familiar style of her village. It wasn't exactly a new style, relying more on the bodice to hold everything in place rather than a corset, but it enabled her to get away with looser lacing.

Throughout the change, she could hear Lucias moving around the room. The tromp of his lazy footsteps wandered from one end to the other.

Clara peeked around the edge of the screen to find him idly examining various objects. Did he search for traps? The man had already admitted to poisoning her food, what other innocent items could he have tainted?

Fully garbed once more, she stepped out from behind the dressing screen to find Lucias examining her dagger with much suspicion.

"Where'd this come from? Did he use it on you?"

"No." Clara took the weapon from him. "It's mine." It

took but a moment to wipe the short blade on her skirts and secure it back into the sheath already nestled within her bodice, watching Lucias' brows lift to their highest as she did so. Whilst the bodice didn't hold the dagger quite as comfortably as her corset, it remained in place nevertheless.

"Well, now," he murmured. "That's quite the concealment. Gettie's idea, by chance?"

She inclined her head. Whilst she'd been hesitant at having the weapon at hand, she'd come to appreciate the old woman's insistence.

Lucias mimicked her bobbing head. "I wonder if you would meet me in the training grounds come the afternoon? Tommy knows the way."

Curiosity tweaked her nose. "Of course."

With a grimace trying to warp his features, Lucias brushed a finger just below where her neck still ached. "In the meantime, I would recommend having a doctor look over you. There should be one employed in the castle, Thalia's midwife might also be a possibility. You should see about that at once." He fixed her with a stern look. "No excuses."

Clara nodded. Although the stubborn, rebellious piece of her wanted to wriggle out of agreeing, a doctor would be a wise choice. "I'll have Tommy take me there." Her page had already visited the man not long upon their arrival to Endlight, seeing to a cut he'd garnered in the stables. The boy was likely in the room with the rest of the children given his marked absence in the doorway.

That served her well. She could check on them in passing and perhaps usher them towards the doctor for him to check over.

CHAPTER THIRTEEN

The clang of steel greeted Clara's ears as she neared the training grounds. She hesitated in following Tommy down the corridor before continuing on, ensuring to keep close to her page without giving off the appearance of a mouse flushed from its hole.

The corridor was deserted. Not the emptiness of all-but-servants that they'd come across on their way down here, but fully uninhabited save for Tommy and herself. Visibly, at least. That meant no one to see if anything untoward happened to their soon-to-be Great Lady and her page, but also no one to watch her scurrying steps.

They exited the castle and made their way down a covered path winding around the building. In this late afternoon, much of the guard was on duty. Most marched along the outer wall, little more than helmeted heads bobbing along. Occasionally, one would step a little closer to the inner edge of the wall. Peering her way, she was sure of it.

She halted and glanced over her shoulder, hugging herself to mask the subtle check of her dagger's clearance.

Even with Thad's insistence that not all of his father's men were as savage as the one who had dared the attempt of forcing himself on her some months back, she still wasn't willing to find herself alone with one of Endlight's numerous, and free-willed, guards.

A part of her craved the normality of the Citadel, however oddly perverse it was for her mind to easily slip into thinking of the soulless army as ordinary. Like most of her hometown, she hadn't known the truth behind the army before they'd snatched her off the streets. Even with living on the Citadel's doorstep.

Despite the lack of a soul driving their desires—some of them quite disgusting, based on the reasons for their punishment—there wasn't the hollowness she'd once attributed to them. She'd grown fond of a few, like Gutting Gettie who'd earned her nomenclature via way of retribution for the things her lecherous victims had done to young girls.

But, even with the men and women in the Citadel being punished criminals, Clara could count on them to have her health and safety in mind. Even if it was only because that was what the man who possessed their souls demanded.

Here was different.

Those who weren't guarding the castle would prefer relaxation or some other form of entertainment to sparring, unlike the soulless people of the Great Lord's army. Their routine was one she'd become accustomed to during her time in the Citadel. No matter the day, it was always the same people in the same places.

"Killed you!" Lucias' voice rang out from somewhere ahead of them, breaking Clara's attention on the guards above.

More clanging and general scuffling followed the declaration. She jerked her head around, searching for the source. The curved wall of a building stood not far from them. An archway led inside where two figures danced around each other, sunlight glinting off their weapons.

"And again," Lucias announced to whomever he fought. "Honestly, this is the worst technique you've shown in years."

"Do excuse me, my lord," Thad snapped back in answer, his words a touch slurred. "I'd a few drinks this morning and wasn't exactly expecting a sparring session."

Lucias' gleeful answering laughter tweaked Clara's lips.

It always sounded so young and just that little bit wistful.

Now she was certain he waited just ahead, Clara hitched up her skirts and hurried to the archway. She stepped beneath it to find the two men shirtless and standing in the middle of what had to be the training grounds. The circular space wasn't all that bigger than the one in the Citadel. The addition of an interior ring of pillars did much to lessen the clear space to practice.

In the centre of the grounds, Thad staggered back from his old friend—he seemed ready to fall at any moment—whilst Lucias effortlessly twirled his sword about in one hand. Neither one seemed to have spotted her in the entrance.

Clara took the opportunity to scurry behind the closest pillar before they did, waving Tommy to join her as he entered the archway shadows. She hadn't seen Lucias spar with anyone beyond the soulless men in the Citadel training grounds, which had also become a place of magical healing thanks to being ringed by glyphs some centuries back. Seeing him spar against not only a friend, but in a place where he'd need to be mindful of not actually harming his opponent would be interesting.

" 'Twas more than a few." Lucias pointed his sword at the sorry mess who was his opponent. "I'd wager you downed a whole barrel on your own."

Thad gave a lopsided grin and paced in front of Lucias, cutting the air with his sword at each wobbly step. "I'd be passed out on the table if that'd been the case." Without warning, he dove for Lucias.

It was a move that Lucias easily dodged, leaving Thad skidding right on by to barely stop himself from falling on his rear. Turning on his heel with a burst of drunken grace, Thad lunged once again for his opponent, his sword raised.

Lucias easily blocked the attack with a backhanded swing. His eyes narrowed and Clara watched, wide-eyed, as the air shimmered behind Thad.

The man gave a yelp. He rubbed furiously at his backside, muttering a few curses which would've sent her mother in search of a strap. "You swore you'd never use magic in our sparring."

"I thought I'd see if it would sober you up."

"Ha!" Thad spat. The glob hit the dirt, hardened by countless years of practising soldiers, and remained unwholesomely intact. The man turned his head further, finally spotting Tommy and herself. "We've an audience, it would seem."

"Well, if it isn't my preferred sparring partner and her page." Beaming and with his arms spread wide, Lucias strode to her side. "How are you feeling, my dear? Better?"

Clara nodded, casting a sideways glance at Thad. The lord leant on his sword, blinking owlishly at them. He swayed on the spot, but managed to remain upright all the same. The last time she'd seen a man drunk, it'd been the man who'd assaulted her. Even though Thad was far more likely to give her a stern telling off than attempt to rape her, the thought hovered over her head like a wasp.

"You look a little pale," Lucias said, his brow furrowing as he gently lifted the hair from her forehead. "Tell me you've seen the doctor?" Relief visibly relaxed his features as she nodded again, leaving only a sliver of concern tightening his eyes. "What did he say?"

She shrugged. The man had been dismissive of her injuries, examining her under great duress and going so far as to question her recollection of the events. "As far as he's concerned, I can walk, talk and comprehend matters, so therefore I must be fine."

Lucias' frown returned, the wrinkles between his brows creasing to their fullest. "I should've sent you to the midwife for her opinion," he muttered, sheathing his sword.

"I can have her drop by Clara's room tonight?" Tommy offered.

"Good man." Lucias gave the boy a hearty pat on the shoulder that brought a flush of colour to Tommy's olive cheeks. "See if you can't track her down for me. You might want to suggest your father gets a new doctor," he added over his shoulder to Thad as Tommy eagerly scampered off to obey Lucias' gentle request.

"The man's here to set bones and mend flesh amongst the guards, not tend to every minor injury in the castle."

"What about your servants?" Clara pressed. The kitchen alone would have quite a number of injuries that would heal better with proper treatment. In the Citadel, that used to mean briefly slipping into the training grounds, but she'd since stopped all but the most serious cases from taking advantage of Lucias' power. "Who do they see when they've been injured whilst under your service?"

Giving an indifferent shrug, Thad scratched at one side of his jaw. "They probably have their own means of dealing with whatever ails them."

"Then perhaps I should've had Tommy seek out those people," she retorted. "Because I certainly don't want him near my children." She'd gone as far as the doctor's door with them, leaving without giving the man a chance to do more than glance at their departing forms. The gleam in his eyes as he'd spied Sweetie had been all the warning she'd needed.

"And how are our children?" Lucias asked, his voice overtly light and clearly meant as a distraction.

"Not yet conceived," Thad muttered.

"Shut up," Lucias flung over his shoulder at the lord.

Thad's smirk fast became a scowl. "You should have chosen a mistress long before now. Had a dozen children, just to be safe." The way he spoke, the frustration behind his voice…

They'd definitely had this conversation before.

Lucias' nose wrinkled at the mention of children as if the entire contents of a midden had been dumped before him. "I'd forgotten how much of a mongrel you become when you're drunk. You'd be wise to watch your tongue before I cut it out." He shook his head. "Forgive him, my dear," he said, directing his full attention to Clara. "He gets like this with every approaching birth and his wife is somewhat overdue."

She recalled how large the lady who'd greeted her arrival was. *Ready to burst.* Clara shook the image free from her thoughts. "Our children are well. A little shaken." Especially poor Poppy, who'd wailed as if Clara had actually died. "But Derek managed to calm them down." The boy had to be wondering just what sort of nightmare he'd led his charges into. Only Tommy's assurance that the Citadel was safer by far had kept Derek from bundling everyone out of the castle.

"Where are they now?"

"In the solarium. Thalia offered to watch over them."

Thad's face darkened at the mention of the children's location. "Spreading more disease," he muttered.

"They don't look ill, never mind diseased." Beyond their obviously malnourished frames, she'd spied nothing in the way of lesions or unexplained scabs that couldn't be put down to sunburn. Frequent bathing and grooming would see to any fleas or lice.

"What of the pasty girl and the piebald boy?" Thad sneered. "They'll bring nothing but death."

Rage blinded Clara for a moment, all thought thrown back to when she was just five years old. *He dares?* The baker in Everdark had been accused of similar by a travelling merchant. She'd been so scared and confused as to why the quiet, gentle mountain of a man had grown so angry.

She opened her mouth, but little more than unintelligible noises escaped her throat. Clara hugged herself to keep the anger from quaking through to her bones. How could Thad not know the lack of colour in someone's skin, or the white patches Derek bore, were circumstances of birth rather than disease? She tried again.

This time, her voice was stalled by the pressure of Lucias' hand on her shoulder.

"*Thad.*" There was a winter's worth of ice gusting out with the man's name. Even though it wasn't directed at her, a shiver still skittered its way along her skin. Silvery-blue specks of light danced in Lucias' eyes. "I think you should go back to bed and sober up."

Reason seemed to flicker to life in the lord's eyes, it moulded his face, slackening his jaw and raising his brows. There was a spark of hesitancy in that green gaze as it darted between Lucias and herself.

She glowered back, giving no quarter, and continued to do so even as Thad seemed to decide that taking Lucias' advice was a logical course of action.

Only when the training grounds held just the two of them did she turn her attention to Lucias, surprised to find him over by the weapons rack. "Did you at least manage to get anything further from my would-be assassin?"

"We did. After the doctor stitched up his wound, of course. You've excellent aim, by the way." He grinned, the tone of his voice swelling with absolute delight and—

Pride. That was what her ears caught. It had been so long since she'd heard anyone be prideful of her actions.

"But your assassin was most helpful in laying out all his plans, including how he got into the castle in the first place. Farris has him combing through the newly-recruited servants as we speak." Lucias stooped over to fish a long, slender bundle from beneath the foot of the weapons rack. "He was working alone and indeed in service to my mother, but it pays to be thorough with this sort of thing."

Clara nodded. Once, not that long ago, she would've dismissed it all as paranoia.

"What did you hit him with? Your dagger was clean and I saw nothing in your room capable of creating such a neat slice."

"A candlestick."

Unadulterated glee crinkled the corners of his eyes. "Wonderful," he breathed. "You are simply amazing. I worry so much about you and your safety and here you are fending off assassins with candlesticks." He cleared his throat, a flush of red creeping across his suntanned face. "But that isn't why I asked you here." He offered up the bundle. "I have something for you."

Another gift? "Lucias," she moaned. He'd started with the dresses, which had seemed quite practical at first. She couldn't, after all, wear the same outfit day after day. But *twenty-four* of them? She'd never owned more than three at any one time in her life. "You know how I feel about the gifts."

Then there were the jewels. He hardly had a single item of jewellery on himself, yet she had ended up with enough necklaces to adorn the necks of an entire village, more rings and bracelets than she could ever want to wear and, even after several months, her ears still tingled when she thought of all the earrings he'd bought her. "You really must stop. You know it's not necessary."

"Is it not?" He chuckled. "Clara, you are—" His gaze slid from her face as she pinned him with a stern glare. "You are to be my wife, I have—"

Clara crossed her arms.

Like a fool, he grinned and continued. "Even without any marriage vows, you are my mistress, which means I still have every right to bury you under a mountain of gifts if I so choose." He placed the long, wrapped item into her hands. "*This*, however, was to be my wedding gift to you, but in light of the current circumstances, I'd feel better knowing you have it at hand now." His grin widened. "Should you find yourself bereft of a candlestick."

She stared at the bundle. The thing beneath the cloth was unforgiving and not at all as light as she'd expected from something so lean. *What* had he given her this time? What would he consider as a wedding gift? *He hasn't...*

Peeling back the layers revealed the decorative hilt of a weapon she'd grown all too familiar with. "It's a sword."

He inclined his head. "I thought it prudent for my wife to have one of her own for when I couldn't lend her mine."

Clara examined the hilt. The steel had been bound with leather. The top was gilded and engraved with a delicate braid. In the middle sat a gem that she wouldn't be surprised to find was the same shade of red as her hair. "Even though you know I'm no good with swords?" Despite all her training after his departure, she still couldn't wield the weapons quite like his men. She was getting better, granted, but the blades were just that smidge too unwieldy.

"My wife will need to be. And you might find this more to your liking." He urged her to take up the weapon with the tilt of his head. "I had it made for you, after all."

Free of the cumbersome cloth, the sword did seem a little shorter than the ones she'd trained with back at the Citadel. She hauled the blade from its scabbard, which she gently laid down on the cloth whilst her gaze never left the weapon. Her name had been engraved in the fuller.

The blade wasn't as long as Lucias' hand and a half, and bore an edge sharper than anything she'd wielded before. Clara gave it an experimental swing, listening to it slice through the air at the twitch of her wrist. *Perfect balance.* She shouldn't have been surprised—she'd seen Lucias swing his own monster of a weapon with scalpel-like precision— but she hadn't expected the blade to react so swiftly to her command. "I love it."

The faint, steely hiss of drawn metal pulled her gaze up. Lucias stood before her, his sword at the ready. "Are you feeling well enough to try it against an opponent?"

Nodding, she walked out into the centre of the training grounds. Her heart pounded, powered by exhilaration and a faint tinge of fear. She'd never sparred with Lucias more than a couple of times, and never outside the Citadel training grounds.

Clara raised the sword, instantly grateful for the extra fabric the seamstress who'd made this dress had added to the sleeves. She kept herself just loose enough to react to whatever attack her opponent made. It didn't help that Lucias silently circled her like a hound measuring its prey before it struck.

She rotated on the spot along with him, always keeping one eye on his left side. He might fight right-handed—doing everything else with the left to always keep his sword hand free—but the left side was where his tells lay, in the twist of his hip and the weight of a single leg.

Sure enough, his stance shifted. The left leg took on more weight than in the other steps. He rushed forward, the slight drooping of his right shoulder indicative of a low attack.

Clara angled her own sword down and stepped to one side, sweeping his blade out of harm's way. The sibilant whisper of silk rubbing against itself slithered along with each movement. Not exactly stealthy, but she never trained for silence.

The twist of Lucias' foot warned of a sudden shift in direction. She scuttled backwards a few steps, giving herself room to counterattack. The heft of her skirt and petticoat hems thumped her calves, no more hindering than a solid cloak. Thankfully, there was a distinct lack of train on this particular dress. The hem all around was likewise lifted to the ankle rather than the floor-sweeping designs she'd witnessed on several ladies during her stay here.

As she expected, he followed her tactical retreat.

She feinted and lunged. The sides of their blades clashed before she could pull her sword back.

Lucias beamed at her over the crossed blades, an odd gleam in his eyes. "You've been training."

"Did you expect me to sit around all day and sew?" Granted, she did quite a bit of that along with other activities, but mostly because it gave her hands something to do whilst reading up on the kingdom's history or listening to the Citadel steward's daily report on everyday life in her home village, both of which often consumed much of her time.

His gaze silently traversed her form and the mild heat of exertion turned into a furnace-like assault on her cheeks. Was he measuring her stance? It'd be hard to see precisely where her feet lay with the bulk of her skirts in the way. Or did his thoughts slink to something a little more primal?

When he spoke again, his voice had become hoarse and choked with emotion. "You are going to make a spectacular Great Lady fighting like this. And in such cumbersome attire, too."

"It's nothing," she babbled. "The skirts aren't hampering me in any fashion. See?" She tapped the front, sending the layers swinging. "Hardly any weight to them."

Lucias scoffed. "You're being coy. I wouldn't be able to *walk*, much less fight, in them." Nevertheless, he gave the edge of her skirts a nudge with his boot, his head cocked to one side as they shifted with ease. "Do you think you could teach the children? Especially the girls."

She twisted from side to side, basking in the admiration. "I'd have to improve a great deal for that."

"Nothing perseverance won't plough through, I'm sure. You wear determination like a shawl."

"I'm still nowhere near as good as you," she professed.

He dismissed her self-deprecation with a snort. "I've been training for as long as I could lift a sword, you started a few months ago. If you improve at your current rate, you will surpass me sooner than you think." He untangled their swords and stepped back. "Care to go again? I wouldn't want to over-exert you after your run-in with our newest recruit to the army."

"Again." She resumed her ready stance.

Lucias inched closer, watching her moves, a little more cautious now. Those little tells of his still worked in her favour, allowing her to close and react with greater speed.

She pressed him whenever he showed an ounce of hesitancy, forcing him back past the pillars and along the outer ring. He grinned with every back step, praising each well-placed swing, offering suggestions to improve when an attack didn't quite go as she'd planned.

Finally, his sword dropped to react to a weapon that was no longer there. The lower length of the blade slid along her skirts, the edge pushed away from her legs by the fabric.

Barely pausing to think, she swept her free hand before

her, bringing it low. The cool weave of silk brushed her fingertips. She grabbed a fistful of fabric and twisted, leaving Lucias' sword trapped in her gown.

With a jerk of her hips, she sent his sword clattering onto the compacted earth. Clara watched the dust settle around it and gave a satisfied huff. "I've always wanted to try that." She examined her skirts for any sign of damage. A few slashes on the outer fabric, nothing that some needlework couldn't fix. She might even be able to hide the cuts in some embroidery.

The absence of any sort of reply from Lucias had her lifting her head.

He stared at her, his dark eyes at their widest. Then he straightened, his arms spread. "I love you," he murmured. Before she could think of the ramifications of letting her opponent embrace her, he'd wrapped his arms around her waist, bodily lifting her and tipping her onto the ground.

Her back hit hard, a grunt tightening her throat. Her sword jolted from her fingers and skittered out of reach.

"S-sorry," he stammered like a clumsy child. He stumbled in an effort to pull her back to her feet, succeeding only in tumbling atop her. "I didn't mean for you to land so roughly. Are you all right?"

Nodding, Clara attempted a half-hearted bid for freedom. "I'd be better if you got off me."

Rather than shift his weight, he pinned her shoulders to the ground. "So, you concede? I win this round?"

"After I disarmed you? You've got some cheek." She struggled a little harder. Alas, with the bulk of her skirts tucked beneath her, there was no chance she could throw him off. Admitting defeat seemed to be the only option. "You win," Clara announced with a sigh. She peered through the tangled strands of her hair when his weight didn't move. "Did you not hear me? I *concede*."

Lucias brushed the hair from her face. She had expected to find his mouth warped into that insufferable smirk he always got whenever he won. Its absence only added to the guilt bubbling in her stomach.

He leant close. "Clara." His breath danced along her throat, its warmth aiding in the pounding of her heart. "Tell me you're fine." Each hushed word slunk across her skin, more intimate than any touch. "Look me in the eye and say it. Make me believe you're no longer thinking of the attack."

Clara parted her lips, drinking in his breath. It was always hard to think straight with him so close. Her body strained against him, no longer seeking a way to be free of his weight. *This is wrong*. She willed herself to lie still. It left her bitterly hollow, but to do otherwise would only give rise to rumours and wouldn't be doing the Great Lord's reputation any favours if he was seen in such a compromising position in public.

Her thoughts sluggishly turned to his question.

Did she still dwell on the attack? In a way, her mind tumbled over various scenarios. Was she scared? She had been at the time. But once her would-be assassin had been taken care of, what was there to fear? He'd been working alone and was in no position to poison her or... or...

"I—" She couldn't bring herself to speak whilst looking at his face. Her gaze dropped, fastening on his bare chest. The way it rose and fell in rapid bursts only served to warm her cheeks. "I'm fine," she finally mumbled.

"Liar."

The stark certainty behind the word drew her gaze back up. He dared to call her that? She glared at him. *There* was the hint of smugness she'd expected earlier, tempered by the ghosts of fury and heartache. "I am *not*," she insisted vehemently.

His laughter shook both of them. "Lying about lying, now?"

She pushed herself off the ground until their foreheads touched. Their noses also pressed uncomfortably against each other, but she wasn't about the pull away right now. "Let more come, if they dare," she muttered, each word clipped. "They will see I am *not* afraid."

Something dark shimmered in the back of his eyes as she spoke, flickering at her single falsely-uttered word. His lips twisted wryly. They were so close to touching hers that her skin tingled. "I don't believe you."

Of course you don't. If she couldn't believe her words, then what hope did she have of deceiving him with something as plain as an outright lie? The magic he'd inherited from his mother's family practically guaranteed she couldn't. "I can't be the Great Lady our kingdom needs, the one you want, if I'm scared of a little assassination attempt, can I?"

Heartache darkened his eyes and deepened the lines on his face. "Clara..." The back of his fingers caressed her cheek; soft and slow as if she were some half-tame alley cat. "Did you not hear me when I told you that you will always be everything I want?"

She bit her lip and searched for a fresh escape route. There wasn't one. "Get off me."

His weight finally shifted, but he didn't heed her. Instead, he straddled her waist. "Not until you admit you are lying. No one's asking you to never be afraid. Fear is an understandable response. But the last thing I'd ever want is for it to rule you. All I ask is for you to tell me what haunts you and I will do my best to put those ghosts to rest."

"I know you will." Her gaze drifted to her sword. She couldn't rely on his help forever. Was that not the purpose of her wedding gift? "I am afraid," she whispered. "But not for me." His death would have a far greater impact on the kingdom than hers, for now at least. That the assassin chose to come after her could only mean they thought she was with child. "I don't want you to die."

"You're asking for me to be immortal?" He shook his head, the wisp of a mirthless chuckle escaping his lips. "I can't offer you that. Our lives are finite, for all that my ancestors have tried to prove the world otherwise. Being strong is something I can do, for the both of us if need be."

"I can be strong, too."

"Then we'll do so together." He stood, offering his hand and hoisting Clara to her feet. Lifting her chin, he met her gaze. "Think on what ifs only when you must, but never seek to bandage your head before it's broken."

Chapter Fourteen

She met Thalia's midwife that night, the woman having been escorted to her door by Tommy. Abby, as she'd insisted on being called, had checked her neck and determined she was well.

Clara had her check over the children, too. They'd a relatively good outcome on that, bar the sunburns and malnutrition. Abby had left them with strict instructions to eat only until full and not to gorge themselves just because the food was there. Clara hadn't considered that as a hazard beyond making an overeater ill, but the woman had spoken quite seriously of witnessed instances where people had died from simply eating too much.

The children had certainly believed her, all listening with the widest eyes Clara had ever witnessed on a group. In all, it made for an interesting night of sleep, with several of the children piling into her room after nightmares of their bellies exploding like trodden fruit.

The morning bells had seen her groggy and not at all willing to clamber out of the middle of a pile of equally sleepy, little bodies. Only the hesitant rapping of knuckles upon her new door—made of sturdy, brown oak—had kept her from sinking back into a dreamless sleep.

She'd been greeted outside her door by one of the castle's many servants only a few hours ago, the woman bore a message from Thalia. An invitation for Clara to join the lady of the castle and the other noblewomen in the solarium. Unrolling the note had revealed an addition scribbled hastily in the corner, insisting that the children also come along.

Ushering the children into their rooms to change had been quite the task. Fortunately, they'd rather enjoyed themselves with mingling yesterday and chasing them up had consisted of reminding the younger ones that they couldn't wander through the halls in their chemise or wearing no trousers whatsoever. At least she'd Derek and Tommy to help with the latter fussing, convincing Poppet that her dress didn't need to match Clara's had taken several trips between the girl's room and her own.

But they'd finally made their way to the solarium door, where Thalia waited in the doorway with her hands firmly planted on her broad hips. "You finally made it, I see. For a while there, I thought you'd opted to stay all shut up. I simply couldn't allow that."

"My apologies for our late arrival," Clara gabbled, impulsively adjusting the large dark-red ribbon Poppet had insisted on wearing in her hair. "We'd a few issues with getting dressed."

Thalia flapped her hands, brushing off the apology as if Clara needn't had said a word. "Servants, my dear. We've plenty who'd be all too happy to help. Do make use of them. In fact, I'll send Tammi your way; she's excellent with settling our young ones." Clasping Clara's hand, she whisked Clara in through the solarium doorway. "But you're here now and you simply must join the rest of us noblewoman. You'll feel much better around people."

Clara nodded. With her would-be assassin's failure still fresh in everyone's minds, having other people nearby seemed like a good plan. After all, what were the odds that everyone in the room was out to kill her?

The solarium was filled with what had to be close to every noblewoman in the castle, if not all of them. They crowded around the lit fireplace and had been chatting amongst themselves quite exuberantly until she'd been spotted. Now they talked in almost hushed tones, occasionally glancing her way. They either drank from little porcelain cups or waited on those who did the former.

"I must admit—" She trotted after Thalia, trying to keep up with the woman. For someone so heavily pregnant, she moved deceptively fast. Clara leant close to the woman's ear. "—I'm uncertain what a lady of the court does with her time." Whilst alone in the Citadel, bar the Great Lord's men, she typically engaged each new day with whatever took her fancy the most.

Thalia halted, her lashes fluttering as she stared incredulously at Clara. "Why, we do the same thing every other woman does when there's a group of us. Sit around the fire, drink tea and talk."

She recalled a few hazy memories of her own mother engaging in such talks, back when her father had been alive. Generally, it was nearer festivals. "I've never done that," she confessed. "Mother always said it was for women."

The older woman's fine brows twitched together, confusion clouding her eyes. "I see. Is that an Everdark custom?"

Clara shrugged. She'd never thought to ask, merely taking her mother's words at face value. But tea was expensive and having an extra mouth consuming even a small amount would've used it that much faster.

Thalia laid a comforting hand on Clara's arm. "Well, it's no matter either way. You're not far off from getting married." She tipped her head and smiled over Clara's shoulder, no doubt at the children who warily tailed them. "And you've several simply adorable little ones under your care. I'd say those two points alone class you as being a woman." Her gaze drifted further over Clara's shoulder.

Turning to discover what had caught the woman's eye almost had Clara colliding with her page. The boy practically hovered at her elbow.

"Is there anything you need?" Tommy asked, his gaze flicking to the young women milling around the steaming kettles. His eyes suddenly widened, realisation flashing in their depths that he'd an audience. He bowed to Clara, his hands clasped before him, and stammered, "I-I mean, m-my lady?"

"Not at this moment." Clara laid a hand on his wrist, stilling the tapping his fingers had started up. Whilst he didn't mind crowds when they were outside, he'd gotten progressively less happy being around even small groups of strangers. "Go relax with the others." She gestured to the children with a sweep of her free hand. Already, they'd all scuttled over to a table laden with an assortment of delicacies designed to tempt children's bellies.

Nodding, Tommy joined the others in taking a sample from each plate before settling on a bench near the solarium entrance to eat in peace.

"Your page," Thalia said. "Is quite the peculiar young man."

Clara bristled at the remark. Her lips parted, ready to defend Tommy the very instant the wrong words came out of the woman's mouth.

"Why, just the other day," Thalia continued, seemingly heedless to the change in Clara's expression. "One of the stable hands caught him in a stall talking to the moodiest of our warhorses. Well, I thought we'd have to send him to the doctor or, Goddess forbid, a priest. But he had the beast nuzzling him and eating apples like the most docile of ponies."

"Tommy prefers the company of animals to strangers," she replied, fighting to maintain a civil tone. There was certainly nothing peculiar about an animal liking someone who showed it proper respect. She'd seen guard dogs when they weren't on duty gambling down the streets like puppies alongside their owners; it wasn't a stretch to imagine a warhorse had that same playful nature. "And they always prefer him."

"Oh?" The remark tore the woman's gaze from Tommy to focus back on Clara. "My father employed a woman like that. Best milkmaid I'd ever seen. Practically had the goats lining up to be done."

Clara frowned, trying to picture Tommy milking goats. "He's at his best with horses."

"Our Great Lord has designs on making your page his stable master, correct?" Thalia smiled when Clara inclined her head. "Then I am certain he'll do a marvellous job." She swung to the women, all of whom had gone deathly quiet in the close presence of the lady of the castle. "I fear most of these faces will be quite unknown to you. You already know my dear daughter-in-law, I trust? I hear you're from the same village and you two were in the Citadel at the same time."

"Yes," Clara murmured. She wasn't sure just what the woman knew about Brenna, but she also wasn't looking to form any rifts in anyone's life. Thalia could even be aware of everything, right up to Brenna having had the possibility of being the Great Lord's mistress in lieu of Clara. None of that was any of Clara's business and she intended to keep her nose out of it.

"Well, I—" Frowning, Thalia rubbed her belly.

Her thoughts immediately turned to Lucias' remark yesterday of how the woman was past the usual nine-month mark on her pregnancy. The women she'd witnessed go into labour generally felt no pain at the beginning, though. "Are you well?"

She smiled and patted Clara's shoulder. "Extremely so. The little one's just being a touch more energetic than usual. If you will excuse me, I must sit down."

"Of course." Clara moved to escort Thalia to her chair by the fireplace.

"Please, my dear lady," one of the servants said, scuttling to Clara's side. "Allow me." She deftly clasped Thalia's elbow and laid a hand on the pregnant woman's back.

The noblewomen seemed to realise just who she was, for they jolted to their feet and gave her a deep curtsey, waiting until she replied with the small bob of her head before any of them dared to return to their seats.

Was this what Lucias had to deal with on a daily basis from the court? Small wonder he preferred taking patrols.

Clara settled on the bench seat next to Brenna. Not because they shared a commonality in their birthplace, but she figured the woman was the least likely person to treat her as some unearthly being.

"My lady," Brenna murmured, demurely lowering her head. "I would offer another curtsey, but…" She rubbed her belly. This close, the bump was almost as huge as Thalia's. "My back sadly cannot hold up as well as it did a few months ago."

"I quite understand." Her mother had loaned her services to several expectant mothers who either had young ones that were too young to help or were otherwise alone and not in the position to clean or cook. For some, birthing seemed to be the easiest part.

They sat there for a while, their silence broken only by a servant offering tea. Mercifully, they left them the option to sweeten it on their own rather than subject them to a sickly brew.

Clara sipped at her cup, savouring her tea. A pea-sized glob of honey had been just the right amount to cut back the sharp bitterness of the leaves. Her gaze slid to Brenna. "So," she drawled, her mind racing to think of anything beyond the obvious topic swimming at the fore of her thoughts. "I hear you chose to swap your husband for a younger version?"

Brenna snorted and lowered her cup, resting it on the saucer delicately clasped in her other hand. "You mean Lord Farris? He wasn't my husband. He *was* going to be," she admitted with a shrug. "But… Well, I'm sure you've heard all the sordid stories. They do like to gossip here."

She nodded. Although much of what she'd heard had come from Lucias, there'd been snippets here and there amongst the court chatter of border squabbles and what she'd deemed as the usual complaints of taxes and trade.

"Leonard has as many excellent qualities as his grandfather," Brenna insisted before Clara could utter a single word. She rubbed her belly. "And, this way, I'll be giving him his heir instead of another half-uncle." Her dark eyes narrowed. "What of you? Everyone's been wondering how you convinced our Great Lord to marry you."

"I didn't convince him of anything, he proposed." She hadn't even realised marriage was an option before then. Everyone knew the Great Lords only ever had mistresses.

One of Brenna's perfectly arched brows lifted higher. Her painted lips twisted in disbelief.

Clara didn't care. Some people were content to believe in lies even when faced with the starkness of truth. She had long since given up expending her time where any impact would fail to matter. Instead, she turned her attention to her children.

They currently played at the other end of the room with the Endlight lords' younger children, having been introduced to the majority of them yesterday. Except for Derek, who was considered too old at thirteen by local standards to mingle with unrelated children below his age. Instead, he sat near the door, speaking with Tommy and casting the odd protective glance at his siblings.

None of the children seemed at all concerned as to the origin of Clara's little group. But she'd seen that sort of mingling on the streets of Everdark, where the boys and girls from wealthier families would happily include others without a care they were from less well-off homes. The desire for separation often came at the parents' behest.

A few in the group seemed enamoured with Sweetie's hair. Others would shuffle up to Derek and speak with him, darting back, their eyes wide, to divulge what he'd said to those who'd remained behind. They seemed focused on his skin. Curious about the difference—and her heart had pounded out an entire symphony before she had come to that realisation. If only she could find a way to get closer and be entirely certain. All she could really console herself was with the fact Derek seemed content.

Brenna leant on her, peering around Clara's shoulder. Her soft rumble of humour shook the both of them. "They're such nosy things at that age, aren't they?"

"Forgive the gossip, but Thad seems to have..." Clara hesitated, trying to think of a polite way to mention the prejudice she'd witnessed in the training grounds yesterday. Something that couldn't get easily spread. "...particular views."

The gleam in Brenna's eyes spoke of knowing precisely what Clara meant. "You mean about the older boy?" She nodded before Clara could respond. "I think he might've gotten that from his mother, Lord Farris certainly doesn't give a whit what people look like so long as they can do the job they were hired for. Thank the Goddess' good graces that she sent Lady Thalia this way."

Clara caught herself frowning before she could smooth the expression. From the way Lucias spoke about the woman, Lady Jennah certainly hadn't sounded like the type. She'd been generous, kind and like a mother to him. That in no way exempted her, but he'd never mentioned anything in the way of flaws.

Perhaps time had eroded those memories.

"You might find a few things are different here," Brenna continued. "That's the influence of the moor nomads."

Clara grunted noncommittally. Despite being part of the kingdom, for over a century at the very least, there was little literature to be had in the Citadel on the people or their customs. Much of what she'd learnt about them had come from Lucias and what he'd experienced during his time amongst them. Blatant prejudice had either been swept from his mind or never reared its unsavoury head in the presence of what would've been the Great Lord's heir at that time.

The solarium entrance opened, granting passage to a pale-faced woman with dark-brown hair and full rosy lips— and a curvy figure Clara would give anything to flaunt. She looked suspiciously like the woman she'd spied draped all over Lucias a couple of nights back.

Brenna nodded towards the woman. "I see you've spotted Farris' current piece of skirt." She leant close enough for Clara to feel her breath. "I hear she came straight out of a local brothel."

"That's not a crime." Her mother might've considered it as such, but Clara had always tried to keep an open mind about people's choices. At least, when those choices didn't wind up with them stealing from those who couldn't afford the loss or harming others in whatever manner.

The woman wasted no time in sashaying over to their little bench seat, pointedly paying Clara no mind. "Brenna, darling. It does me great pleasure to see you mingling on this fine morning. Has the wee one finally chosen to settle down?"

Brenna's hands crept across her belly as if protecting it from the woman's words. Her gaze flicked to Clara and relief washed over her face. "Allow me to introduce you to Clara Weaver, the Great Lord's Mistress." She twisted in her seat, opting to face Clara more than the woman. "Clara? This is Marie."

Marie? Why did that name sound familiar? Had she heard it somewhere before?

Marie's bright red lips curved. From afar, it could be mistaken as a smile. Up close, there was nothing pleasant about the expression. "Of course." Those brown eyes, rimmed with smoky powder, traversed Clara. "We met briefly upon your arrival, but it is a pleasure to see you again. How is Lucias? I've missed our little talks."

I know that voice. She'd heard it just the other day in the corridor after growing weary with dancing. This *was* the woman who'd been propositioning her future husband. "My betrothed is well. Although, I doubt he'd appreciate you being so familiar with his name."

The woman shrugged. "I must say, you would have to be very good at what you do for him to gift you so many liberties."

Clara gawped at the woman, taken aback by the personal way she uttered the words. "Excuse me?" she growled, her teeth clenched. A sideways glance revealed Brenna to be in a similar state of shock.

Marie waved her fine-boned hand in the air, flipping it back and forth. "All this trouble he's going through to wed you, the current whispering rumour going around that you're a virgin—of all the things to lie about, that has to be the most preposterous—and now you bring in these orphans off the streets. You must be very good in bed."

Rage stole her voice for a few heartbeats. Bristling, Clara straightened in her seat. "How dare you," she rasped. "What gives you the right to make such a statement?"

The woman's smile grew twisted. Those smoke-rimmed eyes practically glittered with malevolent glee. "Why, by being someone who knows the Great Lord far better than his mistress, it would seem. In ways your sweet little mind wouldn't dare to think of."

Clara bit her inner cheek in an attempt to remain composed. She folded her arms in some vain hope it would help stave off the wedge of dread trying to bury itself into her chest. "Lies," she curtly replied.

Still, her mind was abuzz. She couldn't help notice the confident way Marie planted herself before them. *She comes from a brothel.* Lucias admitted to spending much of his past in such houses. Was she one of the women he'd given money to lie with? It would certainly explain why he'd preferred not to speak of the woman when Clara asked.

"Oh?" Marie laughed, showing an obscene amount of teeth. "I do believe I have the truth of it. Tell me, is he still a taker? You don't have to lie to me, I know precisely how lacking in tenderness our Great Lord can be." Marie bent over, her red lips pulled into a horrid smirk as she whispered, "Or are you *really* still the innocent little petal?"

Tears pricked the corners of her eyes. It was one thing to know her husband had lain with such women, quite another to find herself face-to-face with one of them. And such a wretched creature as this, to boot.

Steeling herself, she opened her mouth to object.

Brenna got there first. The woman rocked to her feet, the pregnant bulge of her belly lurching forward like an avalanche. The crack of Brenna's hand across Marie's face echoed through the room.

Marie scuttled back, clutching at her cheek. The paleness was gone, wiped clear of powder by Brenna's hand. She stared at the pregnant woman, shock having her mouth gaping like a dead fish. "You *hit* me?" she whispered. She rubbed at her cheek. More white powder transferred onto her fingers. "You little..." Her other hand rose, the back of it ready to retaliate.

Clara was on her feet and grasping the woman's wrist before she could think of her actions. "You would sink to striking a pregnant woman?" she asked, incredulous at Marie's audacity and surprised at how even her own voice was.

Anger blazed across the woman's face. She snarled like a caged street mutt. "Let go of me, little girl."

"You spiteful harpy," Brenna hissed over Clara's shoulder, all but spitting in the woman's face. "You dare to speak that way to the future Great Lady? After you also have the hide to insinuate she is *lying*? You would be wise to take your leave and do so swiftly if you wish to remain within these walls."

"I only—"

Clara held up a silencing finger, its mere presence making Marie flinch. "Do as she says," she whispered. "Leave now whilst you've still a shred of dignity, or I will have the guards throw you out." She cocked her head as a new thought came to mind. "Or perhaps you'd like to explain your actions to my dear Lucias?"

Marie stared at her. Whilst her powdered face couldn't get any paler, her painted lips opened and shut wordlessly. Then her whole body sagged as she opted to silently back up to the exit.

Settling onto the bench seat, Clara continued to watch the woman's departure. Was it possible Marie knew the extent of the Great Lord's power? Who had warned her? Lucias? One of the servants? Just how much did the Endlight people know about their ruler that Everdark was ignorant of?

Brenna collapsed next to Clara onto the bench with a rumbling sigh. "Everything she said was true, wasn't it?" she murmured, her voice barely audible. "You've not lain with him." The words were more statement than question.

Nevertheless, Clara felt they deserved an answer. "I haven't. Yet." She glowered at Marie's departing form. "Not that it's anyone's business." Everyone seemed a little too interested in that topic.

"Of course it isn't," Brenna replied. "It must seem strange having such gossip about you. No one back home would talk about sex, you know?" She scrunched up her nose. "Or perhaps they did with you, coming from a common background. I guess we moved in very different circles, didn't we? Funny how things work out, both of us winding up here."

Clara stiffened in her seat. "I didn't *wind up* anywhere. I chose this." Lucias had already arranged a carriage with enough money to see her settled beyond their kingdom's border. Then his mother and her pet barbarian had attacked and...

Only when Clara had been faced with him dying, had she realised she didn't really want to leave him.

Brenna's gaze dropped. Beneath the dusting of pink powder that tinted her pale skin, her cheeks steadily turned redder. "I'm sorry. I just assumed that, being the Great Lord's mistress, you—"

"I had no say in any matter?" Clara finished for the woman. Quite a few people seemed equally as puzzled as to Lucias' actions. None seemed to consider the obvious answer. "Don't assume next time, it'll make you seem less the fool."

Surprisingly, Brenna merely nodded in reply. A far cry from the rather physical response she'd displayed to Penny Tanner, the cobbler's daughter. That'd been some months back, when five young women, including herself, had been whisked off by the Great Lord's men as a potential mistress. Was it being out from under the stern control of her father that'd changed the woman, or the pregnancy?

A shriek from the far end of the room turned all heads and banished all questions from her mind bar one. *Who—?*

Thalia lay on the floor, clutching her stomach. Women gabbled and fluttered around her like startled pigeons, terror shaking the wits from them.

Clara leapt to her feet and was at Thalia's side before she realised she'd taken a step. Speculations of poison raced to the forefront of her mind. Had her would-be assassin lied about being the only one? Could he speak anything but the truth whilst under Lucias' control? It didn't seem possible.

Her knee rested in something wet. Clara dropped her attention from the woman's pained face to the floor. A puddle of red seeped across the rug, emanating from Thalia. The woman's skirts were already dark with blood.

Clara had been present at a few births, mostly fetching this item or that thing for those more knowledgeable, but she knew the early stages of labour weren't like this. *The midwife.* If anyone knew how to proceed, it was Abby. "Fetch the midwife," she said, the words surprisingly steady despite worry shaking her to the core.

The command, or perhaps the tone, seemed to snap a few of the women out of their frightened state. "What are you just standing there for?" one of them demanded of the servant who'd frozen near the door. "You heard my lady. Now!"

"Quickly!" Clara shouted after the man. Giving Thalia's hand a comforting squeeze, Clara stood. With her arms akimbo, she took only one look at the noblewomen running about. "You two," she snapped at a pair who seemed hearty enough to carry a bucket between them. "Fetch some water. You!" She singled out a middle-aged woman who wore the brown and yellow garb of a personal servant. "Gather some cloths, the softer the better. You three, help me get Lady Thalia off this cold floor. We could be in for a long wait."

CHAPTER FIFTEEN

So much blood. Clara sat in a corner of the study, looking out onto the castle gardens, her thoughts awash with the vision of the past few hours.

The whole court was alive with the chatter of Thalia's newborn. Celebrations of the birth had begun almost immediately. Some prattled on about how lucky Thad was to have another son, whilst others voiced their many concerns about Thalia's current state—which was the reason why Thad was at his wife's side rather than basking in the traditional adulations.

Even without the presence of either parent or child, the small bundle dominated most talks. That was to be expected. Whilst the baby had a relatively low chance of ever inheriting his grandfather's title of Lord of Endlight, the newborn's life was another strand for the Endlight line to continue down, to forge new alliances and strengthen the old ones. For now, those talks also brushed aside mention of the Great Lord's impending wedding.

Clara had swiftly excused herself from such revelry to pursue what little peace of mind this alcove overlooking the gardens afforded her. Laughter and music invaded her sanctuary from time to time, shattering the illusion of solitude.

Her chambers would've given her the complete quiet that she sought, except she wasn't entirely certain she could make it to the door unnoticed never mind through the corridors. Leaving now would bring questions she would prefer to leave unasked. The last thing she wanted was to taint anyone's evening or draw attention away from the extremely fortunate family. That left her the option of waiting for the crowd to thin.

She wouldn't have minded joining in on the revelry had her mind not been flooded with the vision of the birth.

Clara squeezed her eyes tightly shut, trying to block the memory. The midwife had opted not to move Thalia. Those who could help had. *So few*. The flurry of panicked women had only added to the chaos. And the rest...

The solarium had been transformed into a world dominated by Thalia's screams. *And blood*. There'd been so much of it. *Too much*. Clara knew giving birth wasn't always an easy process, but none of the births she'd assisted in had ever involved the Goddess attempting to take the mother's life whilst bringing another into the world.

The air before her was disturbed. The subtle aroma of warm leather and wine wafted into her nose.

"Clara?"

She opened her eyes at the sound of Lucias' voice, an act that did nothing to banish the memory of a woman soaked in her own blood and sweat.

Lucias had laid claim to the seating on the opposite side of the alcove. His arm draped down one side of the chair, a goblet dangling between his fingertips. "I thought you'd be with the other noblewomen."

She shook her head. It didn't feel right. One of their own had almost died right before them and they all still chattered so frivolously. "I'm not in the mood to mingle tonight." If she'd been forced to, she would've given them a piece of her mind.

He sipped from his goblet, staring at her over the rim. The gentle concern on his face fast melted into barely contained distress.

Clara sucked on her bottom lip, refraining from speaking. Her face burned so intensely that she was certain her cheeks must be glowing like a beacon. *Goddess, is it too much to ask you to make the ground swallow me where I stand?*

As always, such a plea went unanswered.

Just when her face could grow no hotter under the fire of his scrutiny, he took another sip from his goblet. His actions a little too calm and precise. "You're troubled." The verdict slipping quietly through his lips came soft and sure. "What is it?"

Fiddling with the loose curls of her hair, Clara shifted her gaze to the wide archway where the crowd still seemed oblivious to her presence. How she wished Lucias couldn't hit the truth so easily. Her parents were never this hard to convince.

A glance back at him revealed he still patiently waited for an answer.

Might as well tell him the truth. Whatever she said, if it was anything but the truth, he'd catch—or perhaps feel or however the magic let him know—the little lie in her response. She exhaled long and noisily. "I've never seen a birthing like that before."

Gentle understanding moulded his face. "And it bothered you."

That was putting it mildly. "Have *you* ever seen a woman give birth?"

His brows merged. He shifted in his seat. "I... have not. As I'm sure you well know." Lucias spoke slowly, seemingly more concerned with setting his goblet to one side than conversing. "But, from what I've heard tonight, it was dreadful."

"I don't—" She ducked her head, plucking at the embroidery on her skirt. "Do you think that's what's in store for me?"

Her gaze lifted in time to see the colour draining from his face. He stared at her for what certainly seemed like forever, his mouth silently opening and closing. "*What?*" That single, strangled word seemed to be the only thing capable of passing his lips. "I would never let—"

"I'm sorry," she murmured. "I didn't mean to imply you would..."

Her words fell away as Lucias scrambled across the space to kneel at her feet. She cast a surreptitious glance towards those beyond the alcove archway. No one seemed to have noticed their Great Lord's sudden, ungainly burst of speed.

He grasped her hands, squeezing her fingers tight as if anchoring her. "You're always apologising for things you've no control over. Stop. Nothing that has happened is your fault." He drew himself to his feet, leaning over her. Warm air bathed her hairline before his lips brushed her forehead.

Clara breathed deeply of his scent. She tipped her head forward and burrowed her face into his jacket, trying to banish the tears that threatened to soak the dark cloth. She couldn't cry now. Not when everything had turned out all right.

Untangling himself from her grasp, Lucias sank onto the other half of the seat. He wrapped his arms about her shoulders, drawing her close. "I've never considered the thought that you might have the same complications as Thalia during the birth of our child. That I might lose you in such a way..." He shook his head, his face strained as he combed back his hair. "None of that has ever occurred to me until now."

She pressed her lips together, still fighting to keep them from trembling.

"Come." He stood, offering her his hand. "Let us converse further in private."

Their passage through the study was one heavy with the gazes of others. Leaving the room wasn't exactly a frowned upon action, and it was quite late into the night. For the Great Lord to leave with his mistress would be a perfectly normal thing.

Still, Clara's stomach twisted. She clung to Lucias and did her level best to match the relaxed attitude in his pace as they sauntered through the corridors. She'd attempted such a feat many times before and had never quite managed that balance of nonchalance and danger.

The sun had dipped behind the castle walls, throwing the gardens into shadow. A chill breeze nipped at her skin, caressing her face with its icy fingers. She briskly rubbed at her arms in the hopes of staving off the cold before it could burrow into her skin.

They strolled through the gardens under the cover of smoky lantern light. They wandered by a trio of large windows. Through the dusky panes, she could make out the curious stares of people. Men and women twirled about, clearly enjoying themselves. To think she should've been one of them.

"Where are our children?" Lucias asked, his voice light

Clara smiled at his attempt at small talk. Never mind she had wondered the same thing once other thoughts were able to return from the calamity of the solarium. Every single child had been bundled out of the room once the midwife arrived. To where, she'd not known until she'd stumbled upon them in the gardens, practising swordplay with sticks alongside the noble children. "I sent them off to bed."

"Prudent."

She slipped free of his touch to lower herself onto a bench surrounded by the sleeping buds of roses. Not looking up at him, she fussed with arranging her skirts to fall just so. This would not affect her. She couldn't let it. "I suppose this is where you're going to tell me that there are a million differences between Thalia and myself. That I shouldn't worry." It'd been easy to tell herself those very words that morning, but now he stood before her, she couldn't bring herself to lift her head, to look into his eyes without wondering.

"There are and you shouldn't worry. You've no reason to. But I am picking that reason and logic fled some time back." He plucked the handkerchief from his jacket pocket and offered it up.

Clara accepted the handkerchief, dabbing at her eyes

with a corner. "What if I decide I don't want children? Ones I've carried and given birth to, I mean."

In the soft lantern light, she barely made out the flattening of his lips. "You know I need an heir." He sank to one knee before her. His head tilted to one side in an obvious attempt to see her expression. Concern creased his brow. "You know *why*."

"But the child doesn't *have* to be mine." Lucias might seem confident that she would be the one to give him his first child, but who was to say he hadn't already unwittingly impregnated someone like Marie? "There's nothing special about me."

"That is..." Lucias frowned, his gaze sliding to one side. "...technically true, I suppose. Although it's a point that could lend itself to some heavy debates."

Clara sat in silence, picking at the handkerchief's deep red embroidery—rows of stylised fires she'd stitched into the dark silk three months ago. None of what he'd said came close to an answer.

"I..." Sighing, Lucias clambered onto the bench and buried his face into his hands. He remained silent for some time before wiping his face and staring vacantly out at a vine-covered trellis shielding them from the wind. "I don't know what you expect me to do. Obviously, no one is asking you to carry a child before you're ready."

Clara peered at him through her lashes, trying to decipher whether he spoke the truth. "I'm quite certain there are a fair number who expect news of a child right away."

Lucias wrinkled his nose, amplifying the hook-like angle. "They can sod off with their expectations. Forcing someone to carry my heir was never an option I felt at all comfortable with taking. I am certainly *not* about to change my mind on that. I can wait."

"But can the people? Is it not selfish of me to demand you risk every life in the entire kingdom just because I have reservations?" She tugged at her sleeves, vainly trying to cover more skin than they'd been cut to manage. No matter how hard she tugged, the great swathes of red and black fabric just didn't seem decent enough. "You can't hold off producing an heir forever."

"If the assassination attempt rattled you, I am more than capable of ensuring you come to no harm." He fingered a lock of her hair, tucking it behind her ear. "My love, I will do everything that's in my power to ensure your wellbeing. If that means waiting until such a time that you've allayed your fears, then so be it."

"But that's just it, isn't it?" she blurted. "You could protect me from any number of attempts on my life. What if something goes wrong that you *can't* fix?" she pressed, falling back to picking at the handkerchief. "Yes, your magic was powerful enough to bring you back from the brink of death, but it's not endless."

She'd learnt of the limitations behind the healing glyphs ringing the Citadel's training grounds, of why such magic was kept to one tiny section of the kingdom. If a person was to place enough mortally injured people within the glyphs boundaries, the magic would tear the life from him whilst trying to mend them.

Lucias grew very still and silently stared at her for some time, his eyes black in the shadows. "It'll be enough. I'll make sure that it is."

She didn't waste her breath on asking how. He'd never tell her. She took a deep breath and spoke in a rush. "What if the bleeding won't stop? What if the baby gets stuck? Or it takes too long and suffocates? Or the cord strangles him?" She could almost feel something wrapping around her own neck at the thought. There were so many ways a birth could go wrong. She'd never seen any complications before Thalia but she'd heard of plenty. "Or... or—"

He clasped her hands, drawing them to his lips. Concern creased his face and lit the dark depths of his eyes. "Or maybe nothing bad will happen at all." He ran his thumb over her cheek, wiping the dampness from her skin, before drawing her close. "You're letting fear run away with you, my dear. Don't allow it an inch."

Clara glared at the ground, unable to bring herself to pull away and face him. Her eyes burned with the desire to resume spilling a thousand angry tears. How easy it was for him to say when he wasn't the one expected to carry and bear the next Great Lord. "It's not that simple," she mumbled.

"Then let me attempt to allay your fears." His breath warmed her ear. "We'll be back at the Citadel when the time comes, I'll make sure of that. Gettie has ample experience with midwifery; she helped deliver both my father and myself, amongst others, and my mother certainly didn't make things easy for her."

"I bet." After trying to kill herself, Lenora likely found the idea of dying in childbirth and taking the heir of her kingdom's enemy with her an acceptable option. "You won't push me, then? I'll be given time to come to terms with what I saw?"

"We've all the time you could possibly desire, far more than I did when we first met. You gave me that, how could I not reply in kind? We'll have a baby when you're ready to and no sooner."

She blinked furiously for a second, just to convince herself that her eyes hadn't bulged out of their sockets. "What if I'm never ready?" she whispered. "You can't wait forever."

His brows lowered in thought, his lips thinning as he pressed them together. "We don't have to come up with that answer now. And whether there's a child in the near future or not, I still want you as my wife."

"And that…" She sniffed back a few tears. "That means I'll need you to stay healthy for me. You can't needlessly endanger yourself." She poked his vest. "No running off to join the guards or patrol the borders. The Great Lord can't afford to be so irresponsible with his life. I know you like to taunt the assassins, but it'll only take one stroke of luck on their part to throw the land into chaos."

His mouth twisted, failing to contain his mirth. "I think I

can restrain myself there."

"You had better. I don't want to become a widow anytime soon."

Lucias bowed his head, effortlessly mimicking the stance of a scolded boy. "I swear, I shall endeavour not to die." He caressed her cheek, his calloused thumb cool against her flushed skin. "You're right, though, it *is* selfish to wait."

Her heart skipped a beat. Irrational fear welled in her chest for a breath before deflating under the pressure of logic.

"But I've waited so long already. You were also right in that I cannot hold off forever, but a month? A year? *Two?* Why would I chafe at that passing of time when I have you to share it?" There was a twinkle in his eye as he glanced up. "I can also put up the same glyphs as those in the training grounds in whatever room in the Citadel you desire, for when you are ready."

"*If*," Clara stressed. "As far as either of us knows right now, it may be never."

"I am aware. Forgive me for misspeaking. *If*," Lucias echoed. "But the hour is getting late and we both have a busy day ahead of us." He bounced to his feet before she could begin to formulate a response and offered her his hand. "May I escort you to your chambers?"

She took hold of Lucias' hand and let him hoist her to her feet. She may very well change her mind after a few months of marriage or a year. *Or more.* There were so many years ahead of them, likely more than any other Great Lady. How many had ascended to their titles at seventeen years of age? *None.*

And as long as she was given the time to consider the idea, she could face the world at Lucias' side.

Chapter Sixteen

*T*he imperious banging on her door jolted Clara from her sleep. She had dozed fitfully throughout the night, her dreams a mess of memories and nightmares all stitched together at the wrong angles. She recalled staying with the children until their eyes just couldn't remain open, which had her retiring to her own bed quite late.

How long had she slept?

A quick roll of her head to one side gave her enough of a view of the windows to know the inky darkness of a late morning still lurked beyond the curtains. *Only a short time, then.* Her head pounded along with the thumping on the door. Had she not known otherwise, she would've claimed it to be too much wine. But her tongue hadn't tasted a single drop during the scant meal she'd woodenly eaten last night.

"My lady?" a man called from the other side of the door, the voice unfamiliar and desperate.

As much as she wished it was, ignoring the stealer of her sleep clearly wasn't going to be an option. *This had better be important.* If she was to avoid tripping over her tongue when it came to her marriage vows tomorrow, then she needed her sleep now.

Clara stretched, her hands slipping beneath the pillow to grasp the dagger lying there. A part of her chided how such a weapon was unnecessary, but after the attempt on her life, little seemed ridiculous. "Coming," she called out.

Clutching the crosspiece so that the naked blade laid flat against her forearm, she padded across the room to open the door a crack.

A man stood in the hallway. He straightened, snapping her a salute. The rattle beneath the thump of his fist suggested chain mail hidden under the green and golds of his livery. A guard in service to the castle rather than a servant. "The Great Lord wishes to see you, my lady. In the gardens. Said it was a matter of some importance."

Clara frowned. He seemed familiar, but she couldn't recall where from. Her gaze flicked down. Only now did she register the man's sword. There was something in the way he gripped the hilt, his fingers flexing as if restraining an urge to use the weapon.

It roused a nagging suspicion in the back of her mind. She inched the door closed a little more. If there was danger to be had, Lucias wouldn't call her towards it. "One moment, if you please?" She eyed the doors opposite hers. Neither one was open. "I am in a frightful state of undress. If you will allow me a moment to make myself presentable?" She swung the door, jumping as the oak panel connected with his booted foot and went no further.

That nagging thought rushed to the fore, screaming at her. She wet her lips, resisting the urge to scream for her page. There was nothing Tommy could do against an armed man except get himself killed. Or the children, should they seek to exit their rooms.

The guard's thin lips curved upwards. She'd always been of the opinion that nothing could be creepier than the glassy smiles of the soulless army under Lucias' command. Being proven wrong wasn't any better. "Excuse me, my lady, but he was most insistent that you come now."

"Come where?" Tommy's voice echoed down the otherwise silent corridor.

Grimacing at the sound, Clara opened the door far enough to confirm Tommy was indeed in the hallway. She should've known someone banging on her door would wake her page as the boy had always been a light sleeper.

And it appeared to have woken not only Tommy, for Derek stood behind the older boy, crowding the open doorway to their room. Both seemed to be in varying states of dress, with Tommy clearly missing a jacket and Derek still half in his nightwear. Whether the rest of the boys were awake, she couldn't tell.

The guard turned towards the two boys, one side of his face twitching.

"Lucias has asked for my presence, that's all," Clara replied before the guard could react. "Pop back to bed." Smiling sweetly, she turned her attention to the guard. A brush of her fingers on his forearm him focusing on her. "I shall just be a moment. My future husband wouldn't want me wandering the halls in just my nightgown." She barely waited for the twitch of the man's head in acceptance before scuttling back through the doorway.

The door still refused to shut fully. A glance at the floor confirmed that the toe of the guard's boot remained in the gap.

Clara backed away, aiming for the sword propped against the bedside table. Her dressing gown hung not far from it, giving her an excuse should the man choose to burst into the room. She swiftly donned her dressing gown, eyeing the door and keeping one ear out for the smallest creak of dried door hinges.

Tucking her now-sheathed dagger beneath the additional layer of clothing was a simple matter, but she would need to close with the guard to use it. And if he managed to draw his weapon first...?

She needed a longer blade.

Her gaze settled on her sword. The garnet set into the top shone balefully back at her. Should she dare attempt its concealment? *No.* The very folds of fabric that would shield the sword's shape would also hinder its drawing.

She could grab it now and face him here, but she'd be isolated with only Tommy for backup and a gaggle of innocent children that the guard could use to his advantage. Playing the man's game seemed the best way to put him in a place where armed assistance could arrive in a short enough time.

Tightening the sash of her dressing gown, she grabbed her cloak and threw it across her shoulders before opening the door wider. "Where did you say he was?"

"The gardens, my lady." He waved for her to take the lead, frowning when she didn't move.

"Oh!" she exclaimed loudly. She pressed a hand to her lips, trying her best to look unthreatening and entirely clueless. "Could you perhaps lead the way? I get so lost walking around here." Clara fluttered her lashes at him.

Smiling in that same skin-crawling manner, the guard bowed and took up the lead. She padded wordlessly behind him, her bare feet making little sound over the clink and tramp of his boots.

Whilst they travelled at a brisk pace, they wound through corridors and side passages she hadn't been escorted down before. Each place was lit with dim lanterns and Clara expected to find someone waiting behind each corner. But everywhere they went, it was just them. No guards patrolling the inner halls, no servants tending to the running of the castle that few higher up gave a thought to.

She stared at the back of the man's head. He continued to look straight ahead, confident of his path. How many times had he walked these passages at this time to be certain of their emptiness? The green and gold livery he wore looked worn—mended tears that spoke of being used in a fair bit of fighting rather than age—but the garb fit him as if tailored.

A blast of cool air greeted them as they strode down the open corridor that led to the gardens. Unlike inside the castle, only watery moonlight lit their path. The breeze continued to ruffle her dressing gown and shook her thoughts free.

There would be time later for introspection of how the man was able to integrate himself into the castle guard, but only if she survived the now.

Slipping her hand into her dressing gown under the guise of seeking warmth, she wrapped her fingers around the dagger's crosspiece and drew the blade to the beat of his footsteps. Dare she make the first blow? The guard wasn't the tallest man. A few inches higher than herself, perhaps. Whilst her dagger wouldn't penetrate the chain mail, the man's neck lay dreadfully exposed. A stab to the spine would see him fail whatever task drove him. Likewise would a slash across the throat.

Both options were rather final, though. What if there was truth behind the man's words? He'd made no gesture to her that could be determined as an absolute threat. And whilst she could be certain of a distinct lack of punishment should she react on her feelings and be proven wrong, the idea of killing because of a perceived threat didn't sit well with her.

Her gaze slid to the mostly-naked bushes and sleeping trees that lined one side of the corridor. If Lucias was really here, then surely there'd be illumination of some sort. Nothing moved out there. No hints of men skulking through the shadows, no guards beyond those atop the wall.

The softest of changes in her escort's gait had her returning her attention to him. The guard's casual interest in keeping a hold on his sword hilt had shifted into an outright grasp. Her ears picked up little beyond their footsteps and the occasional muffled clink from the guards on the ramparts.

With her heart hammering—surely, loud enough for him to hear—she skittered closer to the guard. The path grew rougher as they marched, with gravel and specks of dirt littering the stone slabs. Clara bit her lip, desperate to maintain his pace without giving away her closeness. There was a risk in remaining within arm's reach, but closing would hopefully limit his ability to use the sword's full length.

The faint crunch of a boot grinding into gravel narrowed

her focus.

The guard's torso twisted, his elbow lifting in the act of unsheathing his sword. The blade gleamed dully in the moonlight.

Clara rushed him, shoving her shoulder into the middle of his back to throw him off balance.

Sure enough, the guard pitched forward, clearly not expecting her to be directly behind him. *First mistake.* With one hand, she jabbed her dagger into the pit of his sword arm. The blade met resistance in the chain mail, but it was enough of a distraction for her to purloin the man's own dagger. Sadly, the attempt didn't have him dropping his weapon.

Armed with a longer blade, Clara swung the man's curved dagger up to his neck as he turned. The act had him freezing instantly. She wrapped her free arm around his to keep his sword in check. Hopefully, she was strong enough to maintain the grip should he struggle. "Don't move," she snarled. "Or I'll slit your throat."

She dared to glance at the wall looming before her. Guards marched across the ramparts and carried crossbows, but the dark of the garden shielded Clara and her attacker from their sights. "Help!" she screamed. The men on the wall could do nothing in the moment, but there would be messengers waiting to send news to relevant folk.

"You down there!" a voice ordered in the dark, coming from somewhere above. "What is going on?"

"Betrayal!" she replied. "Send guards at—"

Her previously subdued attacker suddenly arched back, tipping his head away from the dagger at his throat, and threw her to one side with a push of his elbow in the same smooth motion.

Clara stumbled, the soles of her feet barking on the path's rough surface. Only the presence of a wall at her shoulder kept her from pitching right onto the ground.

He regained his balance far faster than she. Grasping the hilt of his sword in both hands, he swung.

She slammed the daggers together, locking their cross-pieces, and jabbed towards the oncoming blade. The sword struck. Her arms shuddered under the strength of the blow, but she pushed further until the unsharpened length below the cross guard slid into the V-formation of her dagger blades.

She glared at the man over their locked weapons. If she'd worn any sort of footwear, she would've attempted a kick to his groin—although the skirt of her nightgown did much to limit outward movement there. *Chain mail above.* And solid leather boots protecting his feet. What of between? Did the thick linen of his trousers contain more armour?

Clara aimed a swift kick to his leg, her heel slamming into the inside of the man's knee.

The guard pulled back, hobbling and swearing.

She followed, swiping in the direction of his throat, his arms, anything that dared to put itself within reach. Lucias' training rang in her ears. *Keep them on the defensive.* This wasn't like her duels with the Great Lord or his men, both of whom would fail to use their full strength even within the confines of the Citadel training grounds.

Her pilfered dagger struck the man's forearm, eliciting a hiss from him.

Instantly, the man's demeanour changed. He dropped his sword and kicked it into the bushes before throwing up his hands in surrender.

Before Clara could fully ponder the sudden transformation—she didn't believe him wounded enough to warrant a sudden shift into defeat—the pounding of booted feet down the corridor at her back reached her ears. *Reinforcements.* She peered at the guard before her. For who?

The thunder of feet stopped. Light danced at her back, throwing shadows over the man.

Clara swung, keeping the wall behind her and a dagger still trained on her attacker. Several men filled the corridor's width, one at the fore bearing a lantern and the rest with their swords drawn. Each one wore similar attire to the other guard, although it was harder to determine the livery colours in such a light, she assumed them to also be the same.

"What in the world?" one man blurted.

"Grab them!" another demanded.

The men surged forward, closing around her. Rough hands latched onto Clara's arms, tearing her away from the guard and disarming her. Despite the order, none made a move to restrain her attacker who suddenly seemed a lot surer of himself.

"What in the Goddess' dear name is going on here?" the second guard said. He turned to her attacker. "Lieutenant Dean?"

"She's as mad as the Great Lord," the man muttered, straightening his attire. "A harlot, too. Just look at how she's dressed. Lured me down here garbed like that, then tried to have her way with me."

"I did no such thing," Clara snarled. She strained against the men holding her. Where had she heard that name? It was elusive to her, just as trying to grasp where she'd seen the lieutenant's face before.

"I told her I wasn't about to disrespect the Great Lord like that, then she attacked me with my own dagger. Look!" He displayed the cut on his sword arm as if it were a mighty gash. The wound still bled, although not as profusely as she would've liked. A few stitches and a bit of bandaging would see him back to swinging his sword freely in a week.

"Lucias!" she growled. "Get him. He'll be able to determine the truth." She wasn't certain how many outside a close few knew of the ability he'd inherited from his mother's family, but it was about to be a lot more.

The other guards glanced from Lieutenant Dean to her and back.

"Don't just stand there, fetch him!" Clara snapped at the men, all of whom continued to disregard her orders. She squirmed on the spot, seeking a way to free her arms. In that respect, the guards holding her remained firm. "Do you want it to be your heads he seeks when word of this gets out?"

"I don't think it's my head you should be worried about," the leader replied, leaning close enough for her to smell his heavily-meaty breath. "Considering the situation you've been discovered in and all."

Barely-contained rage seethed in her veins. Somehow, Clara managed to hold her tongue. Lucias would believe her, even without his magic telling him she spoke the truth. He would believe her word over theirs in a heartbeat.

The steady tramp of people on the move caught her ear as she considered her next move. Judging by how a few of the guards shuffled their feet and glanced about uncertainly, she wasn't imagining the sound and nor were they expecting it.

Lieutenant Dean swung to address the leader of the Endlight guards. "Did you send for reinforcements?"

The other man shook his head. "The other two ground units are on the far side of the castle as per orders." A slight frown tweaked his brow as he spoke. "There's no chance they could've gotten here that fast even if I had."

A group of unidentifiable men rounded the corner. They marched in formation and there was little doubt of them being armed. Even with them still in the shadows, the dark livery of the Great Lord was evident.

Relief weakened Clara's legs. It was a whole unit of soulless guards.

"What are you lot doing here?" the leader of the Endlight unit demanded.

The other group entered the range of the lantern's light. Her gaze alighted on the man leading the rest of the soulless unit. *Henry.* He'd travelled with her from the Citadel and, although he'd had his soul taken by Lucias only a few months ago, was quite reasonable in dealing with most situations bloodlessly. If anyone could see that bringing Lucias here was the best course of action, it'd be him.

"All of the Great Lord's men have been ordered to respond to any announced threat within the castle grounds," Henry replied. "We were merely the closest unit." He bowed his head at Clara. "What's all this, my lady?"

"They—"

"That's what we're attempting to determine," the Endlight guard said right over the top of her.

Clara glared at the man. How was she going to set this straight if he didn't let her talk?

Henry frowned. No doubt if any emotion had been able to shift the dead flatness from his eyes, it would've been annoyance. "That question was directed her ladyship," he murmured. "It would be wise of you to hold your tongue unless directly addressed." Like a bird, his head twitched in her direction. "Has the Great Lord been informed, *my lady?*" A sliver of ice slipped free on his tongue at the address. By the way his gaze remained trained on the other man, the caustic tone hadn't been for her.

"No," she replied. Unable to move her hands, thanks to the vice-like grip the Endlight guards maintained on her arms, Clara jerked her head towards the man who'd interrupted her. "He—"

The Endlight guard shuffled from one foot to the other, doing his best not to meet the soulless man's gaze. "We don't need to wake him for what seems to be a simple case of a liaison gone awry."

"You dare accuse me of such without a chance to prove my innocence?" Clara snarled at the man before directing her attention to Henry. "Send for him. One of their own attacked me."

Henry nodded to one of the guards in his soulless unit. "You know where the Great Lord currently sleeps, fetch him." Before the ordered guard could vanish from sight in his quest to rouse Lucias from his slumber, Henry's flat-eyed gaze swept to another pair in his command. "Hold him."

"Is this really necessary?" the Endlight guard persisted

even as his unit reformed to stand between the Great Lord's men and Clara's attacker. "Look at him." He waved his hand at Lieutenant Dean in emphasis. "He was unarmed when we found him, whereas she'd a pair of daggers trained on him. Clearly, he's not the one at fault here."

"He doesn't have a weapon because he tossed it into the bushes. That way." Glaring at the guard accusing her of infidelity, she twitched her head again to single out the most likely place for them to search. "Surely you heard it hit the path."

The Endlight guard frowned, uncertainty tightening the lines around his eyes.

Henry barely hesitated in having his unit search the surrounding garden and his men swiftly unearthed the sword in the direction she'd indicated. "Seize him," he snapped.

The Endlight guards tightened their formation before Lieutenant Dean, stalwartly denying any access to the man. The two holding Clara dragged her behind them.

Surprise stole her voice. Were these men truly so far under the thrall of their lieutenant's lies that they'd defy the word of a Great Lord's man? *They can't be serious.* No one back in Everdark would've dared to stand in the way of a single man wearing the black and red of the Great Lord, never mind challenge a direct order.

Henry frowned. "I would suggest stepping aside." His fingers twitched. Not towards his sword, but in a little curling movement.

Most people forgot—or didn't even know to begin with—that the Great Lord's men had been criminals before meeting this end. Whilst the men could no longer act on their own desires, heeding only the Great Lord's wishes and orders, they still remembered their lives before having their souls stripped from their bodies.

In the case of this unit, most had been part of Henry's little gang of highway robbers. Lucias preferred keeping the men together, for their leader had specialised gestures that, on the surface, seemed innocuous. But Henry had taught her a few during their travels. He had sent a few men to circle the group and come up from behind.

"An innocent man has nothing to fear from the Great Lord," Henry continued. Those who'd brought the man and his troop to Lucias for their final punishment had claimed Henry to be a smooth talker, often stealing valuables from travellers without a drop of bloodshed. He'd lost the nuances along with his soul, but a ghost of that man remained. "If your lieutenant is indeed guilty of the accused crime, then the Great Lord may consider your acts as treasonous. I need not remind you gentlemen the punishment for that."

The men standing before her shuffled on the spot. A couple of them gripped their swords.

One by one, the guards parted like sheep before a herder, exposing Lieutenant Dean. The man was swiftly snaffled by the two guards that had been sneaking up on the Endlight troop's back.

"You chose wisely," Henry said, clasping his hands before him as if the spectre of a brawl hadn't been in the air only moments ago. "Now we all wait for the Great Lord."

Chapter Seventeen

By the time Lucias arrived, the sky had gone from the dark shade of eternity to a velveteen indigo colour. The sickly light creeping over the castle walls gave the world an unflattering grey tone. Through it all, Lucias shone like a beacon as he marched down the path. His dark gaze ran over her, his lips twisting as the concern dulling his eyes flared into smouldering anger.

Farris and Thad walked at their lord's back. The pair shot each other worried glances, but seemed content to silently tail Lucias. Had they also been roused from their respective slumbers or had they been awake and merely caught up?

The guards standing on either side of Clara stiffened and saluted as Lucias halted before her. All the while, the men maintained their gentle but firm hold on her personage. It did little to soothe the ire burning in Lucias' eyes.

"My lord," one of them said before Lucias could open his mouth. "Your mistress says that—" The man's words dropped into silence as Lucias lifted his hand, donning the aloof manner of his title.

For one brief moment, pity for her restrainers rose within her. The men were only doing as ordered. *No weaknesses.* They'd be punished, not perhaps as severely as their commander, but the Great Lord couldn't afford to appear inept.

"My mistress can speak for herself." Lucias settled a pointed glare at the guards' hands. Specks of light fluttered across his eyes like deadly butterflies. "I don't recall asking you to restrain her, nor do I deem it necessary for you to have your hands on my betrothed."

The guards released her as though they'd been holding a red-hot branding iron.

Clara put further distance between herself and the guards, tugging her dressing gown back into a respectable position. They'd not even afforded her that dignity during their time waiting for Lucias' presence.

"Now, what happened, my dear?"

She swung her attention to Lucias, who waited with his head tilted to one side and that dark gaze questing across her for any hint of needed violence. It didn't show on his face, but the quiet fury seethed in his gaze. Whatever the man had said to bring Lucias here, it was plain that he knew she'd been insulted, manhandled and had suspicion thrown upon her.

I could have this entire troop executed. The thought floated queasily alongside her indignation. He wouldn't question her ruling. "That man," she pointed at the guard in question, still being held by a pair of soulless men. "He—"

"Dean?" The name flew sharply from Lucias' lips. His brows rose, familiarity gleamed in his eyes as his gaze swung towards the man. Just how many of the castle guards could he know? Dozens, surely. "What error in judgement did he make?" He frowned at the garden that still mostly stood in darkness. "Why were you even down here?"

"Because of him." She jabbed a finger at Dean, snarling as the man merely smirked and shook his head. "He lured me down here with some story about you asking for me and *then* he attempted to kill me."

Shock parted Lucias' lips. He tipped forward, cocking one ear to her. "I beg your pardon? He did *what*?"

Dean laughed, the sound little more than a nervous burble. Did he only now realise his predicament? "It's such a ludicrous accusation, I know. The truth of it is far more embarrassing, my lord, I assure you. You see, she attempted to seduce me. I dare say, she must've been in the wine this morning. I assure you, I made no such attempt on her life."

The dark shimmer in the back of Lucias' eyes darted across them like an enraged wasp as the man continued to dig his grave with each word. Inhumane rage warped Lucias' features, stealing any semblance of the man she'd fallen for. Specks of silvery-blue light swelled as they came to life in his eyes. He turned to face the guard. "Say that again," he growled.

All around them, men reared back as if faced with a viper. Only the Great Lord's men remained unfazed. They closed around Dean as if heeding an unspoken order. For all Clara knew, that was true. Lucias spoke very little about his control over the soulless people his heritage let him command.

Dean sank to his knees, slipping free of the men holding him. He made no attempt to escape. In the lantern light, his olive-toned face had grown ashen and drawn. "I-I—"

"The truth, you said?" Lucias whispered, the words little more than a hiss. "How about a few more? Who is your master? Which land do you hold allegiance to?"

"M-my lord," Dean stammered. "I am forever your humble servant."

Poor choice of words. Clara didn't need to see Lucias' eyes to know he'd sensed the lie.

"Yes," Lucias hissed. "You will be."

Something dark shifted across the guard's face. His brows lowered. "You'll not take me." In one smooth movement, he pulled a dagger from his boot.

The Great Lord's men surged forward to protect their master. Shocked cries and orders to restrain the man muddied the air.

The men who'd been holding him lunged for the dagger.

Dean's blade slid effortlessly into his own neck. Blood oozed from the wound, soaking his clothes and the ground as he collapsed onto the path. He convulsed, throwing up more blood as he fought to breathe.

The sight had Clara rooted to the spot. Her stomach bubbled and her throat constricted. Swallowing fast became difficult. Nevertheless, she held her head high and waited for the moment in which her attacker would grow still.

She hadn't ever witnessed a man die before. Aftermaths of death, yes. There'd been the mutilated remains the barbarian had left of the guards when Lady Lenora stormed the Citadel with her one-man siege machine. Lucias had been close to death by the time she'd dragged him into the training grounds to heal, but that had been nothing like this. Before now, she'd thought any major injury to the neck—that wasn't an outright beheadal—meant instant death.

Finally, all hint of life left the man.

A hand clasped her shoulder. It took a moment for her to realise Lucias stood at her side. The silvery-blue light had vanished from his eyes. "Have him put in the cellar," he ordered Henry. "And fetch our newest recruit, I want him to have a good look, see if he recognises him. Be sure to go through his belongings whilst you're at it."

The man saluted and snapped a hearty, "Yes, master." A few swift gestures had the dead lieutenant hoisted by his arms and legs to be carted off into the shadows whilst one of the men ran off to, presumably, find Clara's previous would-be assassin.

"I also want all the gates, every single entrance, closed and your men posted before them. No one goes in or out until I say so."

"Is that measure necessary?" Farris enquired, his head turning back from watching the soulless guard rush off into the castle. "My men—"

"—were compromised. *Twice* my betrothed has been targeted. She's only been here five days and the fifth has barely begun. We are to be married tomorrow and I'd prefer not spending the ceremony looking over my shoulder for an attack." He swung on his heel to face the old man. "Line up your men, every single one who is stationed at the castle. It's past time I tested their loyalty."

"All of them? But there are hundreds."

Lucias' eyes narrowed. "One of our own almost managed to slaughter your future Great Lady."

Farris opened his mouth, shutting it again as his son clasped his shoulders.

"I'll give the order," Thad said. "But Dad's right, it could take hours and you've a rehearsal to attend."

Grunting, Lucias flapped his hand between them. "Forget the rehearsal. Ensuring my future wife shall be safe for the duration of her stay here is paramount."

"Of course," Farris babbled. "It was not my intention to—" He fell quiet as Lucias raised a silencing hand. Instead, he nodded to his son.

Giving the much older man a pat on the shoulder, Thad directed his father over to the group of Endlight guards still milling near where Dean had fallen. Thad spoke at great lengths to the men, his voice too quiet for Clara to make out.

"One through the servants, one through the guard..." Lucias muttered, catching her attention. He eyed where Dean's body had lain, gnawing on his bottom lip. "How many more could she have sent?"

"You seem particularly troubled by this one." The whole reason the castle guards travelled in groups was to deter the threat of an assassin being disguised as one of their own, but what better way to blend in?

"The servant, your would-be assassin, he was here for only a few days. His execution was sloppy and the castle guards had latched onto his trail the morning of his attack. But Dean..." Lucias shook his head. "I thought I knew that man. He lived alongside us, fought at our side, drank with us and the other guards. I shared sleeping quarters with him and several others in the barracks. We went on regular patrols. There was never any hint of a lie when he spoke and it was always with respect."

She frowned in thought. The man *had* seemed agitated.

She'd dismissed it as being solely anxious about being caught before fulfilling his task, but maybe there'd been another reason. "Did he have any family? Children? A spouse?" She didn't doubt Lady Lenora would stoop to kidnapping and threats in her pursuit of killing her own son.

"Just an older sister, as far as I know. She used to visit him every seventh day. Although..." He fell silent as he tapped his lips with a forefinger. "Now I think about it, her visits stopped a few weeks back. I'll be sure to have a few of the men check on her. She at least deserves to be told her brother's dead."

Clara nodded in silent agreement, her gaze idly traversing the wall top where guards continued their duties. What would they do if the woman was found to be missing? *A path to choose when we reach that fork*. Knowing Lucias, he would insist on tracking her down. Even if only to ensure her safety.

"What I don't understand is, if he was working for the Raven Household, why would he attack you?"

"The baby," she blurted. "He..." Clara cast a glance at the surrounding guards. There were less now, with most sent away at Thad's command. But who amongst them could they trust? *Probably for the best to assume no one*. "He must've thought it would be easier to kill me first." The logic seemed sound to her. Why persist with killing the current Great Lord when his power would only be transferred to his unborn child? Far better to ensure any chance of the magic skipping to that child was dead before striking at their sire.

The lines between Lucias' eyebrows deepened. His lips pursed as if he'd eaten nothing but limes. Had the thought of her becoming a target never crossed his mind? Not even after her status as his mistress was made public?

Bending to scoop her dagger from the ground, Lucias handed over the short blade. "Allow me to escort you back to your chambers to dress."

Clara nodded as she sheathed her dagger and wrapped her dressing gown tighter around her. It took little to remind her she stood in the middle of the gardens garbed in very little. Even a pair of slippers would've been welcomed to her poor freezing toes.

They strode through the corridors in relative peace, taking what had to be the same path Lieutenant Dean had led her down. A few servants scuttled on by every now and then, barely pausing to bow or curtsy. She eyed each one. Could they be the next threat to her life and the kingdom?

No. Lucias had already led her first would-be assassin through the servants. He hadn't identified any as dangerous. But did that truly rule them out? If the man didn't know another had been sent... *He didn't know about Lieutenant Dean.* Alone, the first man had said. That clearly hadn't made him the only.

But what solution could possibly be viable there? Lucias planned to speak with every guard in the castle as it was. That would take up a good chunk of the day, if not all of it. To add servants on top of them... *We'd have to push back the wedding.* Which ran the risk of giving whoever meant ill more time to act.

"Are you well?"

She jerked her head to stare at Lucias. He'd said little for much of their journey, but even in the sooty lantern light, the concern lining his face was palpable. "I'm fine."

"He didn't harm you?"

Clara shook her head. Had the man truly been trying, though? She'd never know the answer there.

"I can't believe you held him at bay with a pair of daggers." The pride in his voice was palpable and swelled her chest.

"I *did*."

Wrapping his arm around her shoulders, Lucias pulled her close enough to plant a kiss on her cheek. They remained no further apart as they strode down more familiar corridors. Her chambers weren't far. "I was going to suggest we stay for a while after the wedding, but I think we should instead return to the Citadel."

She nodded. "Probably for the best." And if they journeyed elsewhere afterwards, she would've had time to settle the children into their new home.

They halted before the closed door to the bedchamber. She didn't recall shutting it. Did it mean a well-intentioned servant had passed this way, or something far more sinister?

The handle gave a squeak as she opened the door. *Unlocked?* A peek inside revealed nothing out of place or missing. Nevertheless, she offered no objections as Lucias checked over this room whilst she waited in the doorway.

It was only once he had casually emerged from the bathing chamber that Clara dared to enter. She padded to her bedside table, setting the dagger down.

Yawning, she sat on the bed. How long had it been since the lieutenant woke her? Hours? Dawn was certainly happening on the horizon. "I guess sleeping a little longer is out of the question." She wasn't sure just how well sleep would come, but resting would likely see her far more alert for anything tomorrow.

"You are welcome to try. Although, I doubt your ability to do so." He bowed, stepping out of the doorway and into the hall. "Be well, my dear. I shall see you in the evening."

Her stomach fluttered at the reminder that he would indeed be sharing this room, if not her bed, tonight. *Is that wise?* So far, the assassins had concentrated on her. At least, Lucias had made no mention of an attempt on his life beyond the ambush outside the city walls. But to have what Lady Lenora would've certainly described as both targets in the same room...

Before she could voice such concerns, Lucias had closed the door.

"Wait. I—" Clara leapt off the bed as the latch finished clicking shut. Tugging her dressing gown tightly around her, she rushed out into the corridor. The cold air slapped her skin. Shivering, she searched up and down.

No sign of her betrothed.

She cocked her head, listening for the telltale hint of someone on the move. Noises reached her over the hushed rasp of her own breathing. Snoring mostly, interspersed with the muffled bumps and murmurs of others in the rooms above and below stirring at this early hour. No footsteps.

How did he manage to disappear so quickly? Was that yet another facet of his magic?

Clara glared at the empty corridor, fervently wishing Lucias would suddenly appear. They were going to have a serious talk about his magical abilities after the wedding. He may not wish to brag about what he could do, but it just wasn't right for a wife not to know the full extent of her husband's power.

For now, there was little she could do except return to her chambers and dress.

She set to work with cannibalising her attire to form one wholly unrestricting outfit. Fortunately, the overall black and red motifs matched with little effort on her part, leaving her with a loose-fitting shirt and overcoat sitting primly over a much wider skirt than they were designed for.

A timid knock on her door reached her ears.

Clara finished tying the last of the laces securing her boots and scuttled across the floor for her sword. Quietly drawing the blade, she softly trotted to the door. If whoever wanted her presence also sought to do harm, they weren't about to find her an easy target.

She flung open the door, her sword levelled.

The children milled around the doorway, wide-eyed and confused.

Clara hastened to lower the weapon. She fell to her knees and embraced the smaller ones. A few quick questions, and further hugging, confirmed that everyone was unharmed. The guard had come only for Clara. *Just like the first one.* Had Dean also worked without the knowledge of others making the same attempt? How many assassins would Lucias' mother send before she gave up?

"Can we stay with you today?" Poppet asked.

"Well..." Like Lucias, her only expectation had been to attend the rehearsal at midday, to ensure they both remembered their vows and whatnot. She hadn't given much thought to the rest of her day. "I don't see why not. But not here." She waved her hand to indicate the room with its black and red decor. "How about we all trot downstairs for some breakfast, then retire to the library and see if there's any suitable reading material for you to study?" She laid a hand on Ruby's shoulder. "Except for you. We might start you off on a little writing. Have you attempted it before?"

Ruby nodded, her eyes uncertainly rolling from one side to the other. But there was a sudden determined edge to her walk.

Beyond the girl's eagerness, the latter half of her suggestion was met with a few groans, but Clara merely hitched up her skirts and strode into the corridor. Studying would be an excellent distraction from the morning's upheaval, not only for the children. She could do with forgetting about the lieutenant's corpse, the thought of possible attacks on her person, and the very real prospect of spending tonight with her betrothed.

Chapter Eighteen

*T*he new lock resisted her efforts to turn the key. As stiff as the mechanism was, the faint clunk it gave still seemed too loud.

Clara laid her forehead on the door and sighed. *One more day.* The better part of five days had passed since her arrival and she'd only begun to appreciate sealing herself away from others just to sleep.

The day was done. The morning had been bliss, filled with children listening as she read aloud the various stories in the castle library, then listening to them in turn whilst they showed her what they understood.

Now here she stood, locked within the supposed safety of her bedchamber for another night. A part of her longed to return to those carefree months of being sheltered behind the Citadel's thick walls. Would she ever feel so secure again?

Odd, too, for Lucias to expressly demand she made it difficult for anyone to enter. Surely he would prefer to be unhindered. He may not be adhering to the local custom and taking his bride on the night before the wedding, but he had firmly stated they were to share the room.

Together. Why did her stomach flutter at that thought?

He'd been strange for most of the afternoon, overly formal and polite as he guided her through the hours before the evening meal. Much of the time was a blur, stuffed with the mindless chatter of people she knew little about but was forced into small talk with.

They'd gone on to feast in a similar manner to the previous nights, although thankfully without a reoccurrence of Farris' embarrassing drunken declaration. Then, with a large portion of the hall cheering them on—and a few bouts of lewd advice for Lucias which set her face aflame—they exited the great hall together only to have him leave her here.

Clara pressed her ear against the door. The only sounds to reach her were the steady trump of her heart and the rasp of her breath. Had he changed his mind about tonight?

She pushed away from the door, her stomach churning with equal relief and disappointment. Obviously, he would much prefer their wedding night to this, but was he really going to just leave her here because tonight wouldn't be in his favour?

"Fine," she mumbled as she marched across the room, stripping off the outer layers of her gown. "If he thinks I'm spending the night waiting for him to show up, then he is sadly mistaken." She discarded the last of her petticoats, viciously kicking it aside, and attacked the laces of her corset.

A strangled grunt came from outside.

Clara hastily donned her dressing gown. Was someone at her window? *Impossible.* She was several floors up. A person would have to be mad or extremely desperate to attempt climbing so high. *Another assassin?* She scrambled for her sword and slunk across the room towards the window. They would not find her unprepared this time.

Throwing the curtain to one side offered no more than the view of the moors. She fancied seeing dark shapes moving on the distant grassland. *Cattle.* Perhaps the wind had carried their cry, warping it along the way.

The windowpane rattled. A hand flattened itself against the glass.

Clara jerked back, a scream lodged in her throat. She

clutched the sides of her dressing gown to her chest and, with the sword levelled at the panes, inched backwards in search of the door. What sort of madman would dare to enter her chambers via the window?

Her gaze fastened onto the small metal latch which was all that kept her intruder at bay. The latch turned. No one touched it, yet its ponderous movement was unmistakable. The two sections of the window swung into the night. A forearm thumped onto the sill. The other arm joined the first, followed fast by a head topped with dark hair and a familiar face.

"Lucias?" Clara couldn't help the relieved laughter escaping her lips as she scurried to his side. Of course, only *her* madman would dare to attempt something so foolish. So much for his vow to not risk his life. "What are you doing out there?"

He grinned up at her. Sweat flattened his hair, yet the wind still managed to move a few strands. "Trying to get in?"

"Through the window?" She glanced back at the door. It was held shut with a simple lock. Such a mechanism hadn't stopped him in the Citadel and the effort he could've put into magically manipulating the latch had to be far less than scaling the castle. "I thought you were another assassin."

Lucias paused in hauling himself onto the ledge, his face scrunched in more than mere effort. "I… didn't think of that," he confessed with a sheepish grin. "But the custom demands me to enter my bride's chamber through an alternative entrance." He swung his legs over the sill and jumped into the room. The windowpanes creaked shut behind him. "Which, admittedly, would be easier had this been a tent. Fortunately, this room's within easy climbing reach."

She thought back to the words someone had uttered upon her arrival at Endlight. Of the view and how she wouldn't be doing much in the way of admiring such a sight. The person who had arranged this room to be hers must've known what was planned and had been deliberate in their choice. "So what happens now?"

His smile grew crooked. Those dark eyes dropped to run over her clothes, or rather the lack of anything decent, before returning to her face. A spark of silvery-blue light flickered to life in his pupils and then vanished. "We spend the night together."

She drew her dressing gown tighter. Her face felt aflame. "Yes, but how?" He once swore to teach her ways where they could be intimate without actual sex being involved. She had agreed back then, but now he was standing here, expecting more from her than kisses and...

Clara wasn't quite so sure she was ready to go any further.

He frowned and leant back against the window ledge. "Would you prefer I left?" Gone was the cocky teasing he had clung to over the days. A quiet, almost understanding, affection took its place. "It won't be any fun if you're uncomfortable in my presence."

"Yes... no!" She clutched at his arm, although he hadn't attempted to move. "I don't know!" she wailed. Clara plucked at the linen of his shirtsleeve. She'd no clue what she was meant to do. The women she'd asked had tried to be helpful, but it was such a conflicting jumble she wasn't certain of the truth anymore. "I can't... I... I mean, I don't think I could..."

Lucias smiled. "A brave woman like you? Sure you can." He brushed the back of his fingers over her cheek. "We'll take it slow and, I swear, go no further than I promised. But first..." His hand dropped to his sword belt. "I won't be requiring this." He tossed the sheathed weapon aside. The scabbard and sword slid across the ground to hit the dressing screen with a clatter.

"Are you certain? We might be attacked by brigands in the middle of the night."

Laughter creased his eyes. "I assure you, they'd be greeted with a rather chilly reception before they made it this far." Leaving her side, he sat on the edge of the bed. "Come." He patted the bedding. "Sit with me."

She hugged herself, torn between staying put and doing as he asked. This was going a little faster than she'd hoped. What if she did something wrong? What if she didn't like what he did?

She bit her lip. *Then he'd stop.* He'd promised her that he would. "Lucias..."

"Back at the Citadel, you entered my chambers wearing less than you do now, intending on more than I do at this point in time." Again, he patted the bed. "Sit."

Her limbs woodenly obeyed, positioning her on the bedding. The mattress shifted under Lucias' weight. She stiffened before realising his attention had turned to a crystal wine decanter and matching goblets sitting on the bedside table. Gifts from Farris, no doubt.

"My dear, you simply must relax." He twisted back around, a goblet in each hand. Candlelight glittered off the rims. "I don't know what you've been told, but I'm not about to turn into some senseless beast. I won't break my word."

She knew that. But knowing didn't help unravel the massive knot nerves had made of her stomach. "This is new to me," she murmured, graciously accepting the wine.

"I know." The top button of his shirt popped with the slightest touch of his fingers. "And if there was a way I could ease your concerns, I would. It pains me to think you are uncomfortable in my presence."

But there *was* a way, was there not? She ran a finger around the goblet's rim. "Would compelling not work, then?" He had stopped her from being captivated by her fear when the barbarian invaded the Citadel, surely it worked on other emotions.

His nose wrinkled in disgust. "It would all too well. Is that what you believe I would do?" Loathing warped his features for a moment before shifting back into concern. "I've no desire to trap your true feelings behind such a mask. If I could come to you without a drop of magic in my veins, I would, and gladly so if it quelled your unease."

"So… under my own power or not at all?"

He inclined his head. "Precisely." He unbuttoned more of his shirt and flapped the fabric. Dark hair peeked through the gap forming in the linen.

Clara swiftly turned her head. Seeing him throw off his shirt to spar with his men and watching this gradual removal were two completely different things. Her hands itched to run across his bare chest, to dig her fingers into his hair, to feel the heat rolling off his skin.

She didn't think her face could get any hotter, but her cheeks made a valiant effort. She stared into her goblet, hoping her thoughts would grow neutral. "That outfit…" It was not his usual attire. There was too much soft cloth and not nearly enough leather.

"This?" He plucked at the shirt, loosening another button. "I did not wish to try scaling the castle walls in armour."

"You—" It was quite the drop from her window sill. *If he had made one wrong move on the way up…* Her mouth was suddenly too dry. She took a sip of wine. It didn't help. Nor did the several gulps that followed.

"Clara? Are you—" He took the empty goblet from her unresisting hands and set it back on the bedside table. "You're trembling." His thumb ran along her bottom lip. "Like a cornered little rabbit. I didn't mean to frighten you."

Clara shook her head. Whilst his appearance at the window had shocked her, she'd already recovered from the scare. "We're meant to be intimate tonight," she whispered.

"Are you afraid of that? Of *me?*"

Her gaze lifted to stare right into his rich, dark eyes. Genuine concern creased his face. "I'm not scared of you." A touch nervous, perhaps. She was allowed that, given the circumstances. Wasn't she?

His concern melted into quiet amusement. "You should be. I'm a dangerous man."

"But you're not a bad one." She eyed the sleeve of her

dressing gown. His fingers had worked the fabric down her arm until her entire shoulder was bare. "Just a little naughty," she muttered, deftly hoisting the sleeve back where it belonged.

He chuckled. "And you are far too lenient with me, Miss Weaver."

"You won't be able to call me that come tomorrow."

One corner of his mouth lifted. "No, I guess not. Such a pity when it rolls off the tongue so deliciously well. It'll be a shame to have you saddled with my name, but I guess that can't be helped." A single brow arched high. "I should endeavour to call you Miss Weaver as many times as I can tonight." His gaze slid down to her mouth. He wet his lips, drew closer and tentatively kissed her.

Clara flung her arms around his neck, surrendering herself. This she was used to, although her actions were met with an intensity that she hadn't anticipated.

He pulled her against him, gently slipping the dressing gown from her shoulders to pool around her wrists. She let the fabric continue its tumble onto the bed before gliding her fingers up his chest. How was it that he could have her heart pounding and craving his touch with a simple kiss?

Her fingers continued the task he'd started on his shirt, undoing the rest of the buttons and sliding the dark linen off his shoulders. His chest heaved beneath her fingertips. The hot breath of his whimpering moan heated her skin.

He clasped her hands and withdrew the fabric from her grasp. "As much as I would like to go further... Truthfully, I'm not sure how well I could contain myself in that circumstance and I'd rather you didn't find out the hard way." He took up his goblet, taking a sip. "Let us just spend tonight enjoying the wine, the food and..." Smiling, he indicated her with a tilt of his goblet. "...the exquisite company." Even so, he shrugged out of his sleeves and tossed the shirt aside.

Try as she might, Clara couldn't keep herself from staring at the vertical scar running along his abdomen. His torso had always been covered in faint scars from his days scrapping in the training grounds. *Likely even before then.* This particular mark was about a handspan in length, just right for a broad sword blade. She already knew it had a matching one on his back.

"What are you—?" His gaze dropped. One hand wandered across his belly, disturbing the dark hair. He ran a finger down the scar. "I don't think it'll heal further." Like a tear in fabric sewn back together, the healing magic within the Citadel's training grounds might do a decent job in fixing whatever ailed those within the circumference of the glyphs, but it couldn't undo what had been done. "I thought I was going to die that day."

She recalled the amount of blood he'd lost on the way to the training grounds. *So much.* Any more and that would've been the end of the Great Lord. And of the kingdom.

"You gave me a second chance at life. I don't think I could ever thank you enough." His breath escaped in a husky sigh. "My dear Clarabelle," he purred, her name rolling across his tongue and sending a hot jolt down her spine.

She opened her mouth to object to him using her full name. He was aware of her dislike for it.

"You know, your very presence has consumed my thoughts since the day we met. I've never wanted to be with anyone as badly as I crave you at my side. *You* and no one else."

"You mean the naive young woman with hair as red as freshly-spilt blood?" she teased, recalling precisely how he'd described it the day he picked her as his mistress. She was used to standing out from the crowd, but it was her hair that drew people's attention, not herself.

"Your hair may have caught my eye to begin with, but such superficial attributes would mean little to me if you were anything less than your charming, tempestuous self. And you aren't as naive as you believe. If anything, I underestimated how much you knew of the world."

She snorted, disbelieving both points. "I'm certain you've met women you have misjudged before."

His attempt at stifling a laugh trumpeted through his nose. "Only on how far I could trust them. They're all paint and perfume and will belong to any man who can pay." He slumped forward, resting his arms on his knees. "Believe me, I know exactly how petty some people can be."

She laid a hand on his shoulder. How many times had he been lied to, been used, just because of who he was? Of who he would become? A mantle he'd no choice in taking up.

"But you." Lucias sat back, his head almost colliding with hers. "When I'm with you, nothing else in the world feels as real." His lips brushed the corner of her mouth. "And come tomorrow," he murmured in her ear, his breath hot on her skin. His arms slid around her shoulders, the gentle embrace of his magic keeping her from slipping off the bed and onto the floor. "I place the future of the kingdom in your hands."

She shivered and pressed against him, seeking the warmth emanating from his bare skin. "I love you," she whispered.

He jerked back, his mouth dropping open before his lips became broadly skewed.

"Why are you grinning like a halfwit?"

Still beaming, he tucked a wayward lock of her hair behind an ear. "That's the first time you said it."

She closed her eyes, nuzzling his palm. "Said what?"

"That you love me. You've never told me that before."

It was her turn to stare incredulously at him. He was mistaken. Had to be. This couldn't be the first time she'd admitted it. "I must have."

He shook his head. "Not once. I've told you countless times, but you've never replied in kind."

"So you doubted my feelings when I chose to stay?" She leant closer, laying a hand on his chest. "We are to be married tomorrow, do you doubt it still?"

Lucias shrugged. "People all over the world marry each other without being in love. Some even go on to have children. I'm a prime example of a couple not requiring even fondness for them to create life."

Yes, she'd heard in great detail—from both him and the Great Lord's men—what had transpired before Lucias' conception. If the former Great Lord had ever held any capacity for love, it'd burnt out long before he'd kidnapped the young Lady Lenora and forced her to bear his heir.

"I'm not one of those people." She clasped his head. Nose to nose, she glared at him. "I would not have stayed if I didn't love you."

His eyes closed at the declaration. The years, the strain of his position, seemed to drop from his features.

Their lips met and Clara sank into his arms, surfacing only when she felt his fingers entwining with the laces of her corset. "If you will permit me," he breathed, the heat of his words slinking along her neck. "I would like to remove this."

Clara nodded. She could hardly sleep in the thing and, even without the corset, she still wore a chemise. Like the rest of her clothes, they were in black and dark red. Far more clothing than he wore and yet... she felt as if she were naked.

He worked diligently at the laces, threading through enough for her to wriggle out without unthreading the entire thing.

"Now," he said as she resettled on the edge of the bed. "If I can remember rightly enough, this should help you relax." His hands fell upon her shoulders, his fingers moving in soft, slow circles.

Her skin tingled. She leant against him, her bare arms tickled by the hair on his chest. His lips fell upon her neck and worked their way up, brushing her earlobe.

Giggling, Clara shied from the touch. His breathy laughter puffed into her ear.

The loose short sleeve of her chemise slid off her shoulder. She hauled it back where it belonged only for him to work the sleeve back down. "Stop that."

"But I just want to do this." He kissed her bare shoulder.

"And this." His lips once again brushed her neck. "A thought comes to mind." The heat of his breath shivered its way along her skin to settle in her cleavage. He slithered off the edge of the bed. "Come with me."

Clara trailed after him as he vanished into the bathing chamber. "Just what are you planning?" She huffed and rubbed her hands together. Strange how she could forget just how cold it was when in his arms.

"I'm going to run a bath for you."

She eyed him, then the empty tub. Whilst she wasn't aware of the full extent of his magical talents—a conversation she would definitely need to have with him once they were married—she did know that conjuring water out of the air wasn't in his power. "Won't calling for someone to fill it create more talk?"

Lucias indicated one of the clunky taps at the base of the bath. "Did no one tell you these are functional?"

She shook her head, curiosity shuffling her closer.

"That would explain why you had them do it manually last time." Lucias grinned at her. "Observe!" He turned a tap with the deft twist of a hand. The pipes rattled and clear water poured from the spouts. In a very short time, steam also rose from the taps.

Clara crept closer. "I've heard of this." She lightly traced the pipes with a forefinger. The pipe beneath her finger was cold and steam did not rise from the water it supplied. She didn't dare touch the other. "Plumbing, right?" There'd been snippets of gossip about ways to bring hot water inside without having to heat it, but as far as she knew, it hadn't yet caught on anywhere within Everdark, not even the more expensive houses.

Lucias nodded. "Farris likes to latch onto everything new. He's had the kitchens, laundry and his family suites all piped for a good year now. *This*—" He patted the bath as if it were a favoured pet. "This is the newest installation. Just a few months old." With a few firm twists of the taps, the water flow was shut off. "Now, then. If you'd be so good as to hop in before the water cools."

She clutched at her chemise. "I'm not taking this off."

He bowed low and offered her his hand. "If my lady wishes." He glanced up. "Be quick, my dear, before I toss you in."

Clara dipped one foot into the bath, then the other. Warm water lapped at her legs. She sank to her knees, then with a sigh, swivelled around to stretch out along the length of the tub. She slipped further beneath the surface, almost floating. Even then, her feet failed to reach the far end.

Movement from where Lucias stood caught her attention. Just what was he planning and just why was he bent over so ridiculously? She lifted her head out of the water enough to peek over the bath's rim.

Lucias popped back up, one of his boots in his hand. Already, the belt helping secure his trousers was undone.

Heat flooded her face. Clara turned away and closed her eyes as he further undid his trousers. She listened to the soft grunt of him pulling off his other boot, the rustle of fabric and the clank of metal as the clothing hit the floor.

Then there was silence, broken by her harsh breathing.

Lucias' fingers curled around her hair, drawing it back from her ear. "Still so shy, Miss Weaver?" His lips fell upon her shoulder, his breath further heating her already warm skin through the fine linen. "You've seen me less dressed than this."

He was right there. The first time they'd met, he wore naught but a towel. "That was different." She'd been trying to escape and he…

Well, he had levelled a sword at what he had seen as an intruder skulking about his fortress. At least if he remained in his undergarments, he wouldn't run the risk of them slipping off.

The splash and rock of the bathwater had her opening her eyes. *He hasn't…* Clara peeked through her fingers to the image of Lucias standing in the tub. At the opposite end, granted, but still *in* the tub with her. Even a few hard blinks didn't change what she saw. "What are you doing?"

"Getting in. I'm cold, so scrunch up." He settled into the tub, stretching his legs out until his rather chilly feet lay on either side of her buttocks. Groaning, he leant back with his eyes closed. "I've missed this."

"Bathing?" She was pretty certain he'd scrubbed himself down at least twice since her arrival.

His shoulders shook with silent mirth, disturbing the water's surface. "Relaxing. There aren't many baths this big outside of the family suites, so I've not been able to indulge since your arrival."

"This was where you slept, then? Before I got here?" Had she inadvertently kicked him out?

One corner of his mouth tweaked upwards. "Did the symbol on the old door not give it away?"

Not really. The castle was huge, definitely far wider than the Citadel, if not as tall, and more like a rabbit warren than the backstreets of Everdark. For all she knew, there could've been dozens of rooms bearing the Great Lord's emblem. "If this is where the Great Lord is supposed to be, then where have you been sleeping?"

"Never in the same bed, that's for sure. Yesterday was in the barracks. Tonight? Well, I'm looking forward to bunking somewhere soft and warm. The beds in the western wing are not the best the castle has to offer."

"You don't deem it safe for you to spend more than a night in the same bed, yet you have me sleep in one place for almost a week?"

"I spent every night here before you arrived. It's supposed to be the safest part of the castle. I guess that's no longer true."

She laid a hand on his forearm, sliding down the underside to companionably link fingers. "Maybe it's only safe when you're here."

Lucias hummed noncommittally, his free hand idly rubbing the top of her foot. "This room is warded against those who seek to do you harm. At least, it's meant to be. Clearly,

I need to tighten the parameters on just what that means." His fingers slowly circled her ankle as he talked, gently lifting her leg onto his lap.

Before she could ask just what he had in mind, he slowly began massaging her calf. Never had she thought a touch so simple could be so soothing. It had to be some work of his magic.

She closed her eyes, trusting he would go no further up her leg. In any case, there were her rather sodden breeches to contend with should he dare sneak past the knee.

They remained in silence for quite some time. Just when Clara was convinced her muscles had been massaged into jelly, he swapped to her other leg. His hand slipped further up as he did so, tickling the back of her knee. Her leg jerked, splashing water.

After a muffled curse and a swift apology, Lucias went back to his previous actions. He hummed a soft tune every so often as his fingers kneaded their way along her skin.

Clara tipped her head back, sliding down until her shoulders were just below the water's surface and her head rested on the bath rim. Her mind wandered as she lay half suspended in the water. They were to be married in the morning. He would speak his vows and she would say hers, everyone would rejoice.

And then?

"Lucias?"

His fingers paused briefly. Silence reigned in the room once again.

Once they were married, she became his wife. That was the only outcome, but he was the Great Lord. So she would be... "What will I be called?" She couldn't wait until they were standing before the altar to find out what new title she would wind up with. *Not mistress, that's for sure.* When Brenna had faced down that nasty woman, she had declared Clara would become the next Great Lady, but that title had been forsaken for several successions.

"You already know my family's name. You'll be Clarabelle Dark."

"I meant my title." She cracked open an eye and peered at him from beneath her lashes. Surely, he couldn't be that dense. "I'll no longer be your mistress so—what?—my title changes to the Great Lord's wife?"

He shook his head, repressed laughter shivering across his shoulders. "You'll be known as the Great Lady, of course. Although, since the kingdom has been so long without one, I could, if you like, change your title. How would you feel about the people calling you their queen?"

Queen? There were times, especially when they were alone in the Citadel, when she forgot the title of Great Lord meant Lucias ruled this land. But being here, spending time with the court, had pushed that to the forefront of her mind. "You won't change your family's name but you'd have me referred to as a queen?"

Shrugging, he resumed massaging more vigorously. "There's hardly any difference in calling you Great Lady or Queen. After all, I'd merely be gifting you with the title you would have had this been any other kingdom."

Not all. The Ebony Court that ruled the neighbouring kingdom certainly didn't have a queen. If her studies were correct, then the Raven Household was the closest anyone there got to being royalty and they were only in power because of the same lie-detecting abilities Lady Lenora had inadvertently bestowed upon her son. "If I am to become queen, does that mean you'd be willing to name yourself king?"

He chuckled. "No thank you. If you've read any tale involving kings, you'd know they're far too stuffy for my tastes."

Grinning, she withdrew her leg from his grasp and sat up to rest her elbows on her knees. "I think it would suit you, your *majesty*."

Lucias gave a disgusted snort. "No, no." He waved a hand in the air, clearly batting away the horrid little thought. The act sloshed water violently up and down the bath and flung droplets from his fingertips. "None of that. There is nothing majestic about me."

Clara laughed. "I couldn't have said it better."

He wrinkled his nose. "That's not what I meant."

"So," she murmured. "I become the Great Lady, Clarabelle Dark. Correct? No queen without her king." Even so... *What a mouthful that's going to be.*

He reached across the gap between them to brush her cheek. A trickle of water wove a path down her skin. "As you wish, Miss Weaver. By tomorrow evening, you will be my Great Lady Dark." Somehow, the address seemed even more intimate coming from his lips than when he addressed her by her old family name. The way he purred the words, drawing each one out as if his lips were hesitant to let them go, prickled her skin.

She slipped deeper into the water, letting the wavelets lap at her chin. It was the cold air that was affecting her, not his voice.

"It's late." Lucias stood and clambered out of the bath. He grabbed a towel from the pile folded neatly on the nearby stool and wrapped it around his waist. "We should go to bed. Tomorrow will be exhausting enough without adding a lack of sleep to it."

Chapter Nineteen

The muffled clang of temple bells intruded upon Clara's dreams. She stirred, reluctant to heed the call of morning. It was warm in her bed, snuggled securely beneath her sheets and with the flickering light of fire dancing across her closed lids.

Clara rolled over to find herself staring into Lucias' dark eyes.

He lay atop the blankets, smiling at her. Stubble adorned his face. Mercifully, the silvery-blue light that had become a common occurrence these last few days did not flicker to life in his eyes. "Good morning, beautiful."

She answered with a grin. A spark of memory fluttered awake in the depths of her thoughts. They'd snuggled into bed whilst he told her tales of the kingdom's history—quite often, that meant tales of his ancestors' misdeeds, but he'd refrained from such talk for neutral ground. Wrapped in his embrace, she had dozed off listening to his voice.

"Did you sleep well?"

Clara nodded. Last night had indeed been the first she'd slept soundly. "And you?" Judging from the ruffled state of his hair and the distinct lack of clothing beyond his drawers, she gathered he'd been nowhere else.

The suggestive twist of his lips warmed her cheeks. "Can I tell you a secret?" His gaze roamed over the walls, his expression one of mild distaste. "I've never liked sleeping here.

It's always felt so isolated." The sudden grin adorning his face seemed directed entirely at the window. "But last night certainly changed that."

She sat up, taking in the room. Everything was just where she remembered it. The fireplace blazed merrily away, its warm light peeking through the elaborate iron screen.

Clara dared to peek at what she wore, surprised to find herself not only firmly ensconced beneath the comfortable layers of winter bedding but also covered by her voluminous nightgown. Half of her had expected to still be clothed in the same sodden chemise and bloomers she'd been wearing yesterday.

"What happened last night?" She could recall everything clearly enough, right up until she'd begun to drift off. *And Lucias...*

He'd wrapped his arms around her, pulling her close to him.

Gasping, she buried her face into the pillow and mumbled, "Please, tell me we didn't—"

Her plea was cut off as Lucias rolled back onto the bed and laughed. When she lifted her head to glare at him, he only laughed harder. Her chest tightened. He thought this was a joke?

"Nothing happened," he managed to wheeze. "I swear, you'd remember if it had." His easy smile took on a smug, predatory edge before it vanished. "Do you not recall changing before we sought the bed?" He pointed towards the far corner of the room. "You hid yourself behind the screen, remember?"

Now he had said it, she'd a vague recollection of darting around the screen of blackened wood and red silk. *Then what?* Obviously, she'd changed, but... she recalled his closeness, the warmth of him against her body and the tingling caress of his hands gliding across her bare arm as she drifted off to sleep.

"We spent the night together," she murmured. Perhaps

not quite like what the people beyond this room would believe, but very close to it.

He inclined his head, his smile faltering. "As I promised you." His gaze traversed her and the dull glow of light took his pupils for but a moment. He cleared his throat, launching himself off the bed. "Since you're awake," he said amidst the flap and rustle of linen. "I should ready myself and leave you in the capable hands of Thalia's ladies until the afternoon."

Afternoon. That was when they were to marry. When she would be required to recite her oath before a hall full of people. *And if I mess it up...* Her stomach twisted. She couldn't think about it or she would make a mistake purely because she believed it would happen.

Lucias strode towards the open entrance to the bathing chamber, halting only once he reached the doorway. "Feel free to get dressed without fear of interruption, my dear. I shall be a while."

Clara slithered out of the bed and, over the carefully muffled sigh of pulling on her dressing gown, listened to the peculiar sounds emanating from the open door. *Water?* There was a definite liquid quality to the noise. Did he bathe? Again?

She slunk up to her clothes chest and hauled out a fresh pair of knee-length bloomers. Her chemise sat with the rest of her wedding attire, a piece that was cut wide at the neck and decked in lace even though few were likely to see it. The women in the Citadel who'd made her gown had offered to stitch together a pair of bloomers to match, but plain linen had always served her fine.

The sound from the other room changed as she hastily donned the garment, turning into something that reminded her of patting wet cloth. She picked up her chemise to the accompaniment of furious, and soggy, scrubbing.

Then there was a disturbing silence.

Pausing with the chemise to her breast, she cocked her head. Nothing indicated anything serious or wrong going on in the room. So what *was* he doing in there? Did she dare have the courage to creep up to the half-open door and peer inside? She took a hesitant step towards the bathing room.

A knock came from the other door.

Clara jumped, a scream barely contained in her throat. She hastened to the exit, her fingers halting upon the key. "Who is it and what do you want?" The words came out a little harsher than she intended, but she wasn't about to repeat yesterday's attempt on her life.

"Ewan, your ladyship," a wobbly voice answered. "I-I was told to bring the Great Lord's clothes here?"

Clara turned the key halfway around before another thought came to mind. "Put the clothes on the floor and turn around." Already, she could make out the hurried movements of the man's obedience. "Knock on the door to your right and ask for Tommy, he'll take it from there."

There was the hollow knock on another door, then silence reigned from the other side.

Clara turned from the door. It would take a moment for Tommy to wake, if he wasn't already up, and a little while longer for her page to see to it that the corridor was absent of servants. She could at least get her chemise on. *Dressing in instalments.* If people kept interrupting her, she'd be fastening her last button at the altar.

Three knocks, all brisk and no-nonsense, rattled the door.

Slipping her dressing gown over the clean lines of her chemise, she strode back to the door. The silken fabric whispered against her skin with every movement. "Tommy?"

"A boy left clothes here," her page replied. "Said they were for Lucias? I waited until he'd left like you asked."

Excellent. There were times when she wasn't sure if he'd heard her specific requests and she was certain he'd blatantly refused a few from others. She unlocked the door and opened it to find Tommy already clutching the bundle of clothes. "I hope he didn't wake you."

Tommy shook his head. He certainly seemed a little too

well-dressed for a sudden rousing from slumber. "You look less tired."

"Thank you." She glanced over her shoulder to the other door, still sitting slightly ajar. "I'd a good night's sleep for once." She'd lost count of the night's Tommy had woken her from a nightmare during her journey here. Knowing people hunted her specifically certainly hadn't helped matters.

She never recalled what had disturbed her, but he always spoke of her yelling and crying in her sleep. Had she always slept so fitfully? She'd never know, no one at the Citadel lingered close enough to her chambers to hear and if her mother had ever noticed, then she had clearly preferred to let Clara wade through her dreams.

Clara held out her hands for the clothes her page still carried. "May I?"

With a heavy blush further darkening the olive tone of his skin, he shoved the bundles toward her. "S-sure. Sorry."

Waving away the apology, she tucked the clothes under an arm. "Why don't you get a little more rest? The wedding won't start until late afternoon and I shan't have need of your time until then." Even then, that would consist mostly of him aiding Derek in rounding up the children for the ceremony.

Nodding, Tommy turned and crossed the hall to his assigned quarters as Clara shut and relocked the door.

She examined the bundle of clothes. It seemed to hold nothing more.

As quietly as she could manage, she peeked around the door. Hopefully, Lucias wasn't naked.

He sat on a stool set before a small table, hunched over a mirror. A tray sat before him. What drew her eye the most was the foam covering his face and the wicked-looking blade he had pressed to his cheek.

She held her breath as the blade's edge glided across his skin, taking the foam with it. He wiped the blade clean on the towel draped across his shoulder and went to scrape more off.

He paused in lifting the sharp edge back to his face, the blade not quite touching his skin. Slowly placing the shaving instrument onto the tray, he swivelled on the stool. "Was there something you required in here? Forgive me, but I thought everything you needed would be in the other room."

Clara shook her head, her gaze drifting to the tray. She couldn't make sense of the assortment of pots and brushes. One held what seemed to be a bar of soap, whilst another was clearly the same foam on his face. "When did they bring that in?"

"It was here last night. Didn't you notice?"

No. He had rather ensnared her full attention then, doubly so once he turned on the taps. She held out the bundle of clothes. "A servant turned up with these."

"May the Goddess bless you, Farris. I thought I'd have to hunt them down." He waved his hand towards the bench. "Leaving them there will do, if you don't mind."

She did as asked and stood back to examine what he did with the blade. Shaving wasn't something she'd ever witnessed. The blade looked very sharp. How could he run it across his face, removing the foam a bit at a time, without cutting himself?

"Was there something else?"

Clara ducked her head, her cheeks heating. Composing herself, she faced him once again. "I've never seen a man shave before."

The blade slid across from his ear to his jaw, scraping away more foam to reveal smooth skin. "Not even your father?"

"He had a beard." And he must have occasionally trimmed it, for it couldn't have been more than two inches long, but she never caught him doing that either.

Lucias grunted and ran his hand across the shaved side of his jaw. "I'd a moustache in my late teens." One brow arched in her direction. "I could grow it again if you like."

"That won't be necessary." His face was intense enough now without adding the imposing touch brought on by an excess of facial hair.

He chuckled. "Thank the Goddess. Thalia said it made me look far too sinister."

"I could well imagine." Clara sidled over to stand at his back. "I thought you'd have someone else shaving you." Surely the average nobleman did not tend to these matters himself.

"Oh yes." He tipped backwards, until his head nestled upon her breasts, and screwed up his nose. "Because I'd delight in the thought of having a stranger's hand wielding a blade near my throat."

"Point." She supposed for someone who customarily slept with a dagger close at hand, letting another shave him would be a problem. "But what of your men?" The soulless guards under his command couldn't lift a hand towards harming him no matter how much they might've otherwise desired it.

He shrugged. "I've been shaving myself for years." His attention returned to the mirror before him. "It wouldn't seem right having someone else do it for me."

Clara watched his hands, failing to find the slightest tremble as the blade's sharp edge slid along his jaw. Was he not as nervous as she was about later? *Of course not.* Why would he be? He'd probably spent years learning his vows, even if there was little chance of saying them.

Finally, he slid the blade over his face one last time before patting off the scant remains of foam with a clean towel. In the mirror, Lucias' eyes flicked up. He frowned, then carefully finished running a hand across his cheek before wiping the blade clean. "You look troubled, my dear. What's bothering you?"

"Nothing new." She tried to smile, but her lips quivered something dreadful. "Just nerves, I guess."

He reached back, his fingers spread and seeking.

She stepped closer and his hand clasped hers, giving them a reassuring squeeze.

"You'll do fine. Just don't believe Thalia's women-in-waiting. I'm sure they'll be here once it's confirmed I've left." Releasing her hand, he returned to the mirror to twist his head this way and that. Likely checking for any lingering remains of stubble.

"Why would they come here?" Thalia wasn't even going to be able to attend. Not that Clara had expected the woman to be there given Thalia was still recovering and the midwife insisted on bed rest.

"To help you get ready? To chat about whatever women talk about amongst themselves on the morning before the ceremony." There was a certain twinkle in his eye that suggested he knew precisely the topic they generally spoke on.

Heat bloomed in her cheeks, steadily marching across her face like an invading army. Gettie had prepared her as best as she could, but the old woman possessed only so much personal knowledge. And, to add to everything, she'd spent a somewhat unconventional night with her betrothed that no one would truly believe had transpired.

"Now, if you could leave me to dress." Swivelling on the stool, Lucias stood and examined the bundle of clothes. He separated them with meticulous care, pausing only to lift something slim from the beneath one article. "There appears to be a letter here." He held up a folded piece of parchment, held closed by a green wax seal. "For you."

Taking up the letter, she broke the seal and scanned the words within. The words were brief, not entirely rude or commanding, but bereft of the flowery wording she'd come to expect from the nobility. "It seems Thalia requests my presence in her chambers once I'm adequately dressed."

Grunting, Lucias unfurled his undershirt from the pile with the flap of his hands. "I guess she wants to express her condolences for not being fit to attend the wedding in person."

Clara's thoughts darted back to the image of the woman giving birth. She shook her head, squeezing her eyes shut in hopes of banishing the memory back into the darkness. "There truly is no need. It's quite understandable that she wouldn't be capable."

"Knowing Thalia, she will be upset nevertheless. But if you could please?" He gently wiggled his hands at her in a half-hearted shooing motion. "Standing here in just my undergarments loses its appeal after a while." He glanced at her over his shoulder, the gleam of his gaze barely visible through the loose strands of his hair. "Unless you plan on watching me get dressed."

Clara retreated back into the other room and set about garbing herself. She snatched up her knee-length bloomers, hauling them on before fishing out a pair of dark stockings from her clothes chest—along with a set of red, heeled shoes—and plonked herself on the end of the bed.

She paused in tugging the stockings on, stretching a leg to admire the curiously diaphanous weave. Done, Clara hopped back onto her feet and slipped into the shoes. With the aid of a little hook she was most grateful for Gettie gifting her, she made short work of the tiny buttons running up the sides.

With her lower half appropriately clothed, she strode behind the screen where the rest of her garments awaited. The heels forced her to set each foot down with purpose or risk toppling. However was she going to make it up to the altar in these, let alone dance afterwards?

Breathe. All she could do was hope her balance would adjust or pray Lucias caught her if she stumbled.

Her fingers fumbled with the laces as she set about donning her corset, a knot she'd tied a dozen times just within the last few days eluding her like a fickle alley cat.

The creak of a door alerted her to Lucias' nearing presence. The gentle tap of his boot heels on the bare floor, then muffled as they trod the rug, spoke of him walking across the room.

Clara held her breath, waiting for him to pop around the edge of the screen.

"You've been quite a while behind there."

Grumbling, Clara continued her battle with the accursed

corset laces. What was wrong with the blighted thing? She'd been doing this on her own during her time here and even through the journey beforehand.

"Do you need my help?"

"Not at all," she muttered, finally able to tug the errant lace back into position and secure them into a bow. Getting into the rest of her clothes was a far simpler matter, requiring the tying of a few light, soot-coloured petticoats around her waist. They swished about as she turned to collect the next layer, tickling her legs through the fine stockings.

The blood-red skirt, whilst heavy and long enough to sweep the floor behind her, was modestly decorated with black lace. She bounced on the spot, shaking all the layers into place before turning to garb her torso a little more thoroughly.

With the chemise and bodice cut wide enough to expose the beginning curve of her shoulders, she opted to forsake her corset cover. It'd been made in a rush by the woman back at the Citadel and she rather feared the sleeves would slide further down her arms than designed. Having one less layer would be better for dancing in anyway.

The bodice easily slipped on and she made swift work of tightening the laces at her back. There was a small splash of embroidery down the front. She'd spent a fair few nights stitching the design; the flame of the Great Lord picked out in black and gold thread with wisps of smoke creeping up to the neckline.

A massive sash was the last thing to add. Clara eyed it distastefully as she secured the bodice lace. It was a heavy thing of velvet, designed to be supported by a cage. By rights, her skirts should also be draped over a crinoline. However, after so many horror stories of women being burnt alive because of them, she refused to wear one.

Finally garbed as was considered appropriate by the current fashion, she stepped out from behind the dressing screen. "No comments," she warned. "I'm not yet done."

Lucias froze, his foot still half off the floor. "Not done?

You look as heavenly as always."

Clara stroked her hair, trying to ignore her steadily warming face. "This still needs brushing and styling."

"Perhaps Thalia's ladies can help you there."

They likely could, and probably better than she was capable of. "There's also this." She held out the sash. "I can't tie it myself."

"Allow me." He swiftly wrapped the length of velvet around her middle. It took more time than she'd figured, much of it taken by Lucias fussing with how the massive bow he'd made from the fabric draped across the rear of her skirts. "I hope I've done it justice. Dressing people isn't exactly a skill I've—"

"The children!" Clara gasped, his words jolting the task from the forgotten depths of her mind. "I must get them ready." Hitching up her skirts, she strode towards the door. Did they even have anything to wear beyond the few hastily thrown together garments they'd worn yesterday and their tatty street clothes?

Her feet left the floor. Not by much, but enough to halt her forward progress.

"I'll see to them," Lucias said as he set her back onto the rug. "But first..." He held up a necklace that was a chain of silver ovals and squares with garnets set into their centres. One of the first pieces of jewellery he'd gifted her. "I do hope you weren't thinking of leaving without putting this on."

She wordlessly held up her hair, idly rocking back on her heels as he fastened the clasp. Icy metal stole her breath for the moment it took for her skin to adjust.

"Now go." Lucias opened the door, indicating she exit first with a bow and the sweep of his hand. "See what Thalia wants."

Clara entered the hall, turning only at the sound of a door shutting to find Lucias at her back. He waved her on, but not before blowing a kiss in her direction. She touched her cheek, swearing she had felt the fleeting pressure and warmth of his lips against her skin.

CHAPTER TWENTY

*C*lara ducked her head as she walked through the doorway into Thalia's bedchamber, not quite sure what she'd be confronted with. It had taken a little wandering, some asking and, finally, an escort to find her way here. The servant who'd arrived earlier with Lucias' clothes had probably been sent for that very reason.

A gasp from the opposite side of the room had Clara lifting her gaze from the green and gold rugs dotting the floor.

"Why, aren't you just stunning?" Thalia gushed. The woman sat primly at the head of the bed, propped up by a small mountain of frilled pillows. "Isn't she?"

As they had in the solarium, much of the younger nobility drifted around the room. Like a flock of disturbed chickens, they babbled and clucked out their agreements.

"I didn't expect you to come so soon," Thalia continued amongst the noise.

Clara halted halfway across the room. Even seeing how at ease Thalia seemed, the recent events that'd occurred to the woman did not easily slip from Clara's mind. "I can come back later."

"No, no." Thalia all but threw her cup and saucer at a nearby lady whilst simultaneously attempting to sit straighter. "I called you here because I wished to speak with you and speak, we shall." She patted the mattress. "Sit."

Clara obeyed. Her stomach churned a little as she

walked to the bedside. *So much blood.* Such marks would be gone from the solarium now, scrubbed clean by the castle servants until the only remnant was in her head.

She wished she could wash the sight from her thoughts as easily.

"Forgive me if I falter, my lady," Clara said, choosing her words carefully. "I am uncertain if you mean to follow a particular tradition." They'd a few customs back home revolving around weddings, but the preparation of the bride was reserved for relatives. She wasn't certain if this was yet another diversion of the tradition she knew or if Thalia actually considered her as family despite the lack of ties.

Thalia clicked her tongue. "I am no priest judging how you adhere to convention, girl. Although, I do hope you'll forgive me for not getting up. Abby gets quite cross with me when I try." She shot a smile in the direction of the far left corner and Clara belatedly realised the midwife stood there, carefully lowering a small bundle into a cot.

"Of course, you need time to recover." Clara settled on the edge of the bed. "How have you been?"

"I've *been* better, that much is certain," Thalia quipped, looking mighty pleased with herself. "Never fear, Abby says I'm improving. But how are *you*?" Those brown eyes seemed to grow twice their size as Thalia peered at her. "I heard there was another attempt on your life."

Nodding, she swiftly filled the woman in on Lieutenant Dean's treachery to the accompaniment of horrified gasps and murmurs from various women around them.

"How ghastly," Thalia said once Clara had finished speaking. She patted Clara's hand. "But we mustn't let that mar the day. Their failure will only make us stronger. Have you eaten yet?"

Clara shook her head. Food had been a distant thought.

"Goodness. Brenna?"

There was a grunt from behind the gaggle of ladies and Brenna trotted into view. She curtsied before the much older woman, as much as her gravid state would allow, at least. "How may I be of assistance, my lady?"

"There should still be some food in the solarium," Thalia continued with little indication that she'd seen or heard her daughter-by-marriage. "Do see that our future Great Lady has at least something in her belly."

Thoughts of venturing into the solarium after witnessing the woman giving birth there had Clara's stomach roiling. "I'm really not hungry." Eating was one thing. Keeping it down might be a far bigger issue.

"Now, my lady." Thalia shook her finger as if admonishing a child. "It simply won't do to have the bride faint before the altar. Nerves are a poor excuse to starve oneself." Her gaze swung to Brenna. "See to it."

Inclining her head, Brenna wordlessly indicated for Clara to follow her with a twitch of her hand. Other women trailed them in their departure of the bedchamber.

Rather than lead the way to the castle's solarium as Clara had expected, Brenna headed for a nearby entrance. Soft morning light crept through the open doorway, illuminating the room in the pale glow.

The room itself wasn't anywhere near the size of the other solarium, maybe a quarter. A fireplace, its flames licking forlornly at a charred log, sat opposite of the doorway. Two chairs sat either side of the mantle. One long table, still laden with a healthy selection of food, took up the length of the right wall whilst floor-to-ceiling windows broke up the monotony of the grey brickwork on the left.

Brenna guided her to the head of the table whilst one of the ladies, who seemed to be the leader of the gaggle, loaded two plates up with a little piece of everything. One was placed before Clara, the other set at a nearby seat that Brenna swiftly claimed.

The fare placed before her seemed more in line with what her mother would offer than anything the kitchens had cooked for her over the past week. Beans and what she hoped was scrambled eggs, alongside a few thick slices of bread and a small chunk of cheese. All good foods for someone still recovering.

"Sorry about the leftovers," Brenna said, dipping a piece of bread crust into some sort of brown sauce. "There was chicken, but Thalia's cooks nicked off with that over an hour ago. I can send for something else, if you'd prefer."

"This is fine." If she could manage to keep down this simple food, then she might consider taking Brenna up on her offer.

The rest of the women slowly settled along the table as Clara ate. Some picked at the remaining food whilst others chattered and giggled about what was to come. They nattered on about past weddings, either theirs or someone close to them. A daring few delicately asked her how last night had been.

Clara tried to answer as well as she could. Outright lying no longer came naturally to her and these people likely saw nothing wrong with their enquiries. She stuck with simple answers between bites: "Yes, he spent the whole night" and "No, he was gentle". Her face still heated with each word.

They stopped trying to pry answers from her only once Brenna had cleared her throat one time too many.

Once Clara was finished with her meal, Brenna tucked her arm beneath Clara's and guided her upright. "It's all right," she murmured. "They'll calm down soon enough." She flicked a curl of Clara's hair out of the way. "We really should do something about this." She clapped her hands twice.

The group surrounding them seemed to close in on Clara like a pack of wolves around a humble little fawn. She was towed towards a stool standing before a mirrored dresser.

The world became a flurry of hands. Her hair was combed, styled, pinned and perfumed.

She dared attempt a peek over one woman's shoulder. Alas, the mirror's angle was tilted too far back. Straightening her back allowed her a view of the very top of her head and nothing more. If she was just able to stand and see what they'd done.

The balls of her feet had barely taken her weight before someone at her back laid their hands on her shoulders. "Close your eyes," Brenna said, the tone more in line with a suggestion than a command. "You wouldn't want powder in them or to be reciting your vows with them all red."

Clara followed the simple request and swiftly found her face bombarded by something impossibly light and fluffy. *Two somethings.* Whatever they were, they bounced across the face like little wisps of unspun wool. She held her breath, fighting the urge to wrinkle her nose.

Then the sensation vanished, leaving her face feeling dry and dusty.

Around her, the women chatted amongst themselves, discussing this colour and that. Clara hadn't much experience with makeup and certainly hadn't worn it before. Her mother had deemed it as the mark of a harlot and refused to let Clara try even a few of the cheaper products the travelling merchants would bring to the store. She'd always wondered why the nobility would also paint their faces if that was true. *Another lie.*

She cracked an eye open, peeking warily from beneath her lashes. All discussion had stopped, yet her limited view revealed she was still surrounded by people. Only one stood before her.

A brush, similar to one a painter used, descended upon her cheek. Whilst it didn't rid the dry feeling of the powder, the sweeping did have an oddly soothing quality. She closed her eye again. Another brush—smaller she was sure—ran across her eyelids and brows.

Something wet, and slightly tacky, brushed along her lips. Clara flinched from the sensation, peering down at the woman's hands to what looked like a pot of reddish paint. The woman continued on as if Clara wasn't currently staring at her, her focus clearly narrowed only to the lips she painted.

Finally, the woman straightened. "All done!" She

stepped back, granting Clara full view of herself in the mirror.

Clara stared at the reflection whilst a few women at her back continued to fuss about with the mass of her hair. To her dismay, the blood-red curls seemed all the more vibrant now they'd painted her face. But that wasn't what drew her gaze.

She could barely believe the woman in the reflection was herself. Whilst she wouldn't call the light olive brown of her skin the darkest of shades, the white dust they'd applied to her whole face gave her a ghostly appearance. A few pats of rouge had returned a soft, if not entirely healthy, glow to her cheeks whilst dark powder rimmed her eyes, giving them a smoky facade. And her lips... they might not have been the same luscious red as a few of the women at her back, but they were still extremely bright.

Was she getting married or going to war?

With her deemed ready, the group escorted her down to the entrance to the lesser hall, where they left her alone and entered through the massive doors.

Clara paced the width of the corridor, her heeled feet giving a muffled clack on the rug with each step as she quietly ran through her vows. Her face itched beneath the powder. She fisted her hands into her skirt, trying to ignore the sensation. Even with the distraction, the words she was to speak before the altar came freely.

A low whistle caught her attention and she spun about to see Lucias marching up, still adjusting his jacket. She'd been too consumed with her own attire to previously notice just what he wore.

Beneath the jacket was a dark red shirt and black waistcoat, the latter of which was so heavily embroidered with the stylised fire emblem of the Great Lord, it might as well have started off as red. His hair was tied back, although a few unruly strands were fighting their way free. A simple silver coronet bearing a single garnet adorned his brow.

Belatedly realising her mouth had dropped open, Clara

closed it with a click. Instantly biting the tip of her tongue. "S-shouldn't you be inside?" she mumbled.

Lucias chuckled as he stopped beside to her, fussing with the jacket collar. "Did no one tell you? Here, custom dictates that we walk to the altar together." His dark gaze raked over her, seeming to drink in every inch. How she wished to know what thoughts sparked through his mind to have him look at her so hotly without a flicker of silvery-blue light. "As equals."

"Equals?" He held the power to destroy an entire kingdom, how could she possibly be considered his equal? *Us?*

One brow arched in her direction. "Do you doubt it?" His gaze had settled on her face now, unwavering in its non-committal appraising of her painted visage. Did he not like it? This was the first time she'd ever been this dressed up and he didn't seem as impressed as he had a moment ago.

Her bottom lip trembled. She wanted to bite it, but daren't. "I'm not your equal."

"My dear, if you aren't, then I don't know who could be." He lightly ran a finger over her jawline and frowned, concern creasing his eyes. "You're shaking."

"I'm nervous," she said, fastening onto the most familiar of fears. He'd think it foolish for her to be upset over something as small as him not liking the makeup. "I'm going to get the vows wrong."

"Still? Come here." He drew her into his arms, holding her tight against him even as she valiantly strained to keep from marking his clothes with the makeup. "My love, you won't get them wrong. Even if you do, it won't matter."

Clara pulled back to stare incredulously at him. "They're the most important words I'll ever speak." Did they not carry the same significance to him? And what of the people she must recite the oaths before? Lucias may not care if she fumbled, but they would.

"I can think of a few other words which would rank higher. If it bothers you to say them out there..." He entwined their fingers, holding her hands to his chest. "I,

Lucias Dark, swear in the name of the Goddess that I have the right to take the maiden Clarabelle Weaver as my wife." He leant forward until their foreheads all but touched. "This is where you say your bit."

Laughing, she spoke the last piece of her oath, "And I, Clarabelle Weaver, accept this man's claim of being my husband." The words came so easily, but it was never the final portion she was worried about.

Lucias step back and, with a mighty flourish, bowed. "And now we are wed."

She bent her head. Her eyes burnt from the strain of holding back even these tears born of joy. "In the eyes of the Goddess, maybe, but not before the altar."

"In my heart, we already are." He cupped her chin, tilting her head up. "To me, the priest's talk is mere words and the altar naught but a marble slab. A ceremony, no matter how grand, won't change how I feel for you. If I thought I could get away with it, I'd rather have a quiet little wedding in some temple, especially if it would ease your distress."

"You mean the kind where you gift the priest a few coins for his time and he blesses our marriage?"

He grinned. "Precisely."

If only it were so simple. If only he wasn't the Great Lord so it could be *that* simple. "But we can't." Such a wedding would not do for the ruler of a kingdom.

"No." Lucias tugged at the lace encircling his wrists. "Clara?" He peered at her face, seemingly attempting to pluck free the true source of her worry. "You *are* aware of how to make children, aren't you? Gettie spoke with you on that?"

Smiling, she clasped his shoulders. "I know." There weren't many people her age back home who weren't vaguely aware of the mechanics. Gettie's talk had merely given her a more in-depth awareness.

Relief smoothed his forehead. "Good," he mumbled.

"Did you think you were going to have to explain the act to your newlywed wife?"

"Briefly, yes." A smile curved one side of his mouth, although his gaze suddenly refused to meet hers. "By the way, don't drink too deeply of the Cup."

The Cup? Did he mean the Goddess' Cup? The one richer people drank from after they exchanged vows? Many couples in Everdark wed without such ceremony, but she'd heard of its use. For a bride and groom to drink from the Cup at their wedding was meant to gift them with the Goddess' blessing. "Why not?"

"It'll be spiked with *tiāpe*. I've warned them not to put it in, but I can't be certain if they listened."

She nodded distractedly. "Sure." Of course the people of Endlight would twist the ceremony by spiking the Goddess' Cup. *Tiāpe.* Had she heard the word before? "What is it?" She swore it was the same word Gettie had uttered some time back, although she couldn't recall the reference.

Lucias ducked his head and peered up at her, his grin cocked to one side. "An aphrodisiac."

"They wouldn't dare," she breathed.

"They would."

Her lips parted in horror. "To a *virgin?*"

The snort of unrestrained humour gusted out his nose. "Clearly you haven't heard the rumours spreading about last night."

She felt her face warm until she had no other choice but to look away or die of embarrassment right then and there.

"Let's just say no one believes you're untouched." He sidled closer and squeezed her hand. "Just take a sip from the Cup. You've my word that I shall do the same."

"You will?"

He bobbed his head. "I desire to keep my wits about me tonight. It's probably better if we wait until we're back in the confines of home to consummate our marriage. However..." He leant closer. His breath fell hotly on her ear, sending a cool jolt down her back. "This day is something we'll only experience the once, Goddess willing. It should be remembered without some herb clouding either of our minds."

The doors to the lesser hall swung open, stilling any thought of a reply.

Sunlight streamed through a multitude of windows, flooding the room beyond in its soft, yellow-amber glow. Clara squinted, trying to make out more, giving up as her eyes watered. She blinked furiously, trying to keep herself from tearing up and smearing the makeup.

"Well then, Miss Weaver," Lucias said as he offered her his right arm. "Shall we?"

Shocked, she lightly placed her hand in the crook of his elbow. She wasn't used to being on his right side. Ever since they'd first encountered each other, he stayed left-handed in everything except sparring. "Would you not prefer to keep your sword arm free?"

He smiled and the world seemed to melt into a soft, warm realm lit by the same rich light emanating from the lesser hall. "In this, my dear Clara, you *are* my sword."

Chapter Twenty-One

*S*he wasn't sure why they referred to this hall as the 'lesser' of the castle's two mighty rooms. The title certainly did not allude to its opulence. Immense marble columns held up a ceiling of gilt and glass, allowing great shafts of golden light to illuminate the room and make the walls glitter.

Dozens of people lined the space between the thick pillars and the aisle. The crowd turned in unison as Lucias escorted her into the room. The jingle of bells greeted their entrance, accompanied by the delicate notes of a harp. Clara caught the faint tap of a drum, wavering on the edge of hearing and pounding in tune to her panicking heart.

All at once, they became the centre of the world. Her legs faltered for one brief moment. Everything whirled on without her. Only Lucias' firm grip on her arm kept her from collapsing. He gave her hand a reassuring squeeze, the faint narrowing of his lips at odds with the calm facade that had taken the rest of his face.

Clara hoped her smile appeared more confident than she felt. With luck, her face was plastered with enough makeup that her steadily heating cheeks were adequately masked. *Some sword I am.* A fresh loaf of bread would offer more resistance.

"Relax," Lucias whispered out the corner of his mouth, the words barely audible over the singing which had started up. Count Farris had apparently decided to head in the direction of extravagant when it came to preparing for the Great Lord's wedding. "You're halfway there."

She hugged his arm, her chest tightening. How she wished she could draw on his strength and have as much faith in her not messing up as he did. But whilst they were halfway to the altar, they hadn't come close to being in the middle of the ceremony.

At the far end of the aisle, a massive stained-glass window took up much of the wall. In the middle sat the symbol of the Great Lord, rimmed by the light pouring through the panels of green and gold. Like the flame the symbol represented, the dark red glass glowed and seemed to flicker in the afternoon sunlight.

The rays illuminated the priest waiting upon the dais. Being in Endlight, the man's official robes were the green and gold of the city's ruling house. After a lifetime of seeing the men and women of Everdark's clergy garbed in grey and pale red, it looked a little comical.

She turned her gaze to the front row of seats where her children were, decked out in their red and black attires. They sat all prim and proper alongside some of the highest nobility in the court.

Poppet waved as Clara glided by, the girl's eager movements stilled by Ruby's gently restraining touch.

They reached the short flight of stairs leading to the dais without any further stumbling, a miracle in itself considering she'd envisioned herself breaking an ankle in the heeled footwear. The singing stopped and the music faded away until there was only the faint drumming to fill her ears.

Or perhaps the beat truly was her heart pounding away. Was it this hot a second ago? She was going to pass out, she was certain of it.

Fanning herself with her hand was not an option, so Clara settled on discreetly puffing. *Breathe, breathe.* Absorbed in her personal struggle, she barely felt the increasing pressure of Lucias' grip on her fingers.

The droning voice of the priest as he spoke the words which would, by the ceremony's end, unite her and Lucias in marriage seeped into her consciousness. She caught a few words of a prayer, the familiarity soothing her. *I can do this.*

At last, the priest fell silent and bowed to them in turn. "Do you both agree you are of sound mind and of an age to enter into this union?" His grey gaze settled on her as they both nodded. "And you, dear woman, do you also declare you come before the altar of your own free will?"

Clara straightened. The fluttering in her stomach that had been with her for what seemed like forever had suddenly stopped. She knew this part. Could it be that Lucias was right and she'd no reason to worry? "This is true."

The priest inclined his head, the dark red light filtering through the window turning his cap an unflattering brassy shade. "Then kneel and centre your minds."

They followed his orders, sinking to the floor with their knees brushing the dais. Out of the corner of her eye, she spied Lucias remaining quite still and seemingly calm, his gaze steadfastly locked on the carpeted step before them.

She closed her eyes, seeking the same peaceful state. No matter how she tried, there was no possible way her mind would centre itself, not with her heart thudding so desperately. Why did the sound not echo throughout the hall? It seemed loud enough.

The priest cleared his throat and addressed the crowd at their backs, "My good people, my lords and ladies, we are gathered here, under the blessing of the Goddess, to join this man and this woman in a binding of lifelong commitment." He laid a gentle hand on her head. "On this most merry of days, if any man or woman does seek to declare any impediment on why these two may not be coupled, whether it be by the Goddess' Law or those of the realm, now is the time to speak."

Clara held her breath, the pounding of her heart drowning out all sound. Already, sweat ran down her back. Her lips moved in silent prayer that no one would seek to stop this.

The priest lifted his hand from her head. "Arise as one, my children, and step before the altar with the assurance that none here seek to disrupt your union."

She rose to her feet, aided by the subtle touch of Lucias' magic. Was her unease so obvious? Did he think she would faint? *Was* she going to faint? Her head felt light enough. *Goddess, please give me the strength to hold out until we've kissed.*

Together, they stepped onto the dais. Her gaze fell to the altar, a huge block of marble carved with intricate knot-work. Atop it, glittering in the afternoon light, sat an ornate golden chalice.

The Goddess' Cup.

The priest walked to the altar, turning his back to them. "There is much which could be said about marriage," he said, picking up the Goddess' Cup. "Yet it is not a path which can be determined by others. As in all ways of life, it does not come without its challenges, but in facing these trials together, you can step forward knowing you are united with someone to share your burden as willingly as they partake in your triumphs."

Clara's fingers twitched as the Goddess' Cup was lifted above their heads. She heard the liquid within—the traditional dark red wine—slosh about. *Not yet.* Soon, she would be required to take hold of the chalice's wide bowl. She could not be too eager to grasp the chalice or risk dropping it.

"Above us lies the sky just as the earth lies below," the priest rattled on. "Take heed in these constants and remember your hearts may be likened to the earth and are in need of nurturing, just as the soil must be tilled for each harvest. Yet, you should not let it rule you entirely, for like the sky, the mind presides over all and thoughts are ever-changing. The Goddess gifted us with this understanding so we may guide ourselves throughout all stages of life. So may the combined strength of your wills make you not as one, but as two of a whole. Possess the other as you are possessed in turn and be free in giving your affection and warmth. But above all, have patience with one another, for though the sky is ever above, it not always clear. Storms are as constant as fair weather, as is their passing."

She caught Lucias' lips twitch into a gentle smile at the last sentence. His dark eyes were locked on her face. Tiny beads of sweat adorned his upper lip. The bobbing of the slight lump in his throat was more pronounced than usual. Not as calm as she first believed. And seeing his discomfort relieved some of her own nervousness.

The priest lowered the Goddess' Cup between them and Clara placed her hands on one side, supporting half of the chalice as Lucias did on the opposite side.

Their fingertips touched. Within the deep bowl, the dark red wine rocked and stilled. *Perfectly balanced.* That was meant to be a sign of the Goddess' approval towards their union. She hoped it was true.

"As the wise Goddess decreed in times past, only those seeking to unite in marriage have the right to bind themselves to the other." He nodded to Lucias. "If your wish to seek this woman as your wife is in earnest, then say so at this time and declare before all your pledge to her and may the Goddess find favour in your words."

Lucias licked his lips, his face reddening. "I do ask before the Goddess and the court for she who already claims my heart to become my wife. I stand here in full acceptance that none shall be above her, for her heart, her love in exchange for mine, shall be all I desire, be it in this life and beyond. I promise to love her completely, never seeking to change her in any way, for she is already perfect and none could convince me otherwise." He took a deep breath and when he spoke again, there was a definite catch in his voice. "Instead, I vow to be her shield against those who would do her harm and her sword when she cannot stand on her own. These things I swear as true."

As he fell silent, the lesser hall overflowed with the susurration of many hands hastily dealing with their tears.

The priest kept his head down and waited until silence once again fell over the room before leaning her way. "Do you, dear maiden, judge this as fair?"

With her eyes misting and her throat barely letting her breathe, Clara sniffed back her tears and nodded. "I do." As if she would rebuff him now.

Over her shoulder, she heard approving whispers.

"Then speak as to what you have to offer your intended husband," the priest said.

"I—" Her tongue froze. She searched for the words, for the oath Gettie helped her to recite for weeks, the very one she'd recalled perfectly just outside this room, but could not find them. "I..." Her fingers slid down the goblet's bowl and the surface of the wine rippled. Fresh tears, each one a bitter drop of frustration, filled her vision and trickled down her cheeks.

She couldn't remember a single word!

"Clara?" Lucias drew his head closer. "Don't start crying," he whispered over the Goddess' Cup. "Please? You're doing fine. Just calm down and repeat after me."

She blinked, clearing her vision as best she could without relinquishing the chalice. He knew both vows? *Bless the man who can recite a bride's oath.* Clara parroted him as he whispered the vow to her. So engrossed in quoting them precisely, she barely heard the words spilling from her mouth, until her ears caught, "...vow to be his shield..."

A wave of surprised murmurs rippled through the crowd as she continued. Those weren't the words she was meant to say. Only the man was to promise safety. She was meant to promise...

She still couldn't remember.

"...and his sword when he cannot stand on his own." A warm hearth. *That* was what she was meant to offer. *And children.*

Grinning, Lucias continued on as if she hadn't made the biggest muddle of her vows in the history of weddings. "I, Lucias Dark, swear in the name of the Goddess that I have the right to take the maiden Clarabelle Weaver as my wife."

No way to fix what she'd done now. Forward was the only option left to her. "And I, Clarabelle Weaver, accept this man's claim of being my husband."

With his lips pressed into a thin line, the priest placed his hands upon their shoulders. "You are now joined in the Goddess' eyes and, upon anointing your blood into her vessel, you may at last drink your fill from her cup."

Blood? Clara gawped at the priest. No one mentioned blood being involved in this ceremony. Was this another Endlight addition to the usual ritual? Did they expect her to spill it, or perhaps be smeared with it?

A horrid thought swam through the chaos of her mind. Did she have to *drink* blood?

Lucias' muffled hiss drew her attention. With his jaw clenched, he hooked his thumb over the rim of the cup, allowing a single drop of blood to slide down the curve of the bowl and into the wine.

Staring at the cup, she suddenly became aware of the spikes adorning either side of the bowl, just above where her fingers sat.

She pricked the side of her thumb on the sharp point, biting the inside of her lip to limit the volume of her whimper. Mimicking him in hooking the digit over the rim, she pressed her thumb against the cool metal until a drop marred the inside of the chalice bowl. The chalice shook, the motion aiding the blood drop's descent.

Clara steadied the Goddess' Cup, helping Lucias guide it to his mouth. The wine touched his lips. Whilst he tentatively licked the droplets from his skin, he helped her keep the liquid from tipping too far her way as she went to drink.

Tepid wetness graced her lips. Bitter wine washed over her tongue. She tried not to gag at the thought of what she could be drinking. Sucking on her finger after pricking it was one thing, she'd done it enough whilst learning how to sew. But willingly imbibing another person's blood? Her stomach churned at the very idea.

It's just a sip. If she was quick, then perhaps there would be naught but wine in the mouthful.

Having swallowed all she was prepared to drink, they lowered the chalice.

The priest took it from them and handed Lucias a delicately wrought, silver tiara. Her heart jumped at the sight. She silently cursed herself for not expecting this. Marrying him meant more than going from mistress to wife. She'd become the first Great Lady in the last three centuries, if not longer.

The tiara settled on her head, its weight barely discernible as the ends slid into her hair. She watched Lucias' features soften as he fussed with the tresses. Whether through outward pressure or conscious command, his eyes remained free of any silvery-blue light.

Clara laid a hand upon his chest, feeling the tightness vibrating through his body as she glided her fingers up his waistcoat to rest at the base of his neck.

His lips curving at her touch, Lucias' dark gaze dropped from the tiara to her mouth. The sunlight caught his coronet, glittering off the deep red garnet. His fingertips delicately snaked along the curves of her ears, trailing down her jaw where the powder wasn't so thickly applied to cup her face. He wet his lips, pulled her closer and bent his head as if he meant to kiss her. Then he seemed to think better of it.

Instead, he wrapped an arm about her waist, gently turning her towards the already chattering crowd. "My lords and ladies," he said, the words booming over their talk. "I present to you Great Lady Clarabelle, the Great Lord's Shield."

There was a pause, then, starting from the front, a cheer burst forth from man and woman alike, stoking the growing fire in her cheeks.

Feeling emboldened and a little bit cheated, she leant closer to her husband and whispered against his shoulder, "Is this not the part where you're meant to be kissing me?" He'd been so eager beforehand. Why the sudden distance?

His gaze flicked to her face before returning to eye the crowd. Lucias watched them with barely veiled disinterest as the music started up again and the people began to form little groups amongst the whole. The longer he stared wordlessly ahead, the more knotted her stomach became.

At last, he spoke. "And here I thought you weren't keen on participating in public displays of affection." His gentle smile widened. "If I start kissing you now, I fear I wouldn't be able to stop and, although Endlight's people are tolerant of much, I think even *they* would baulk at seeing their Great Lord eternally fused at the lips to his wife."

She'd been thinking of something quite a bit more restrained than that. "You would be comfortable being so forward with all of these people watching us?"

"I'd prefer to think most of them would seek out an alternative place to engage in revelry. As for comfort, I'm pretty sure my mind would be on other things." He lowered his head until his breath tickled her ear and ignited an irrationally hot thumping throughout her whole body. "Of course, we could leave now if you don't fancy lingering."

Unbidden, her grip tightened on his belt, the sturdy leather biting into her palm. She clung to his waist. To do otherwise was to risk collapse. Her thoughts quickly settled on the room she'd left only hours ago and the bed awaiting them.

Sudden uncertainty stabbed into her ribs. Naturally, his mind had raced ahead to then, and she didn't think any less of him for harbouring the thought of coupling with his wife.

She mutely shook her head. She couldn't face the prospect of *that* yet.

Lucias pulled back, his lips pressed flat and his brows bunched together in worry. He cupped her cheek. "You're trembling." His thumb brushed across her chin. "I misspoke again, didn't I?" He squeezed his eyes shut and clutched at his forehead with his free hand. "I didn't mean to suggest you must choose between remaining here and being ravished. If leaving straight away bothers you, we can socialise as long as you want. Or, if you prefer, dance for a while." His head snapped up, the silvery-blue light in his eyes flashing for one brief moment. "You *do* still enjoy dancing, don't you?"

Clara inclined her head. Perhaps, if they danced long enough, he would be too tired come nightfall. "As long as we stay vertical."

One side of his mouth lifted. "You have my word. But, if it's merely a case of nerves, might I suggest you drink a little more from the Goddess' Cup? In small doses, *tiãpe* has been known to have a relaxing effect."

I bet it does. She crossed her arms. "Is that your way of tricking me into drinking your blood?" She was pretty certain no married couple in Everdark had ever been required to do such a thing. And who knew what the magic infused in his body would do to her.

His shoulders shook with deep, sad laughter. "Believe me, it would be worse the other way around." He took hold of her hand, gently resting it in the crook of his elbow. "Come, we've tarried long enough. If you wish to stay, then there are formalities we must attend to before the people grow impatient."

Chapter Twenty-Two

*C*lara walked beside her husband in a daze as he escorted her to various factions around the room. She smiled and nodded at all the right social cues, leaving Lucias to do all the talking.

Her mind simply refused to stop focusing on what he'd said back on the dais. How would it have been worse for him to drink her blood instead of the other way around? She desperately wanted to ask him, but in private.

Yet if she sought that privacy, she wouldn't be able to return to the revelry without sparking more rumours. It wasn't as if she'd heard even a whisper about the Great Lords of the past using blood to augment their power or anything of the like.

"*There's* the happy couple!" Farris boomed, pulling her full attention back to the room. The old count strode through the parting crowd to embrace his lord, giving Lucias' back a hearty pat. "Come now, lad, don't be shy. No point in hiding her amongst the low nobility, trot her out."

"Trot?" Lucias bit the corner of his mouth, the other side already on its way into a grin. "She's my wife, not a prized filly."

The count clapped his hands onto her shoulders. "No, she's a fine woman. One, I might add, I haven't seen you kiss." He bent close to Lucias as if to whisper, but the words came louder than ever. "If you won't, someone will have to."

With that declaration, he kissed her cheeks multiple times before relinquishing her. "Couldn't help but notice a little flaw in your vows there, my lady." Farris elbowed his lord in the ribs. "You'll regret not having her promise you a warm hearth when you get older."

The soft smile Lucias gave was one she knew came from thinking on his own mortality. "I think her sword and shield will serve me just as well in the future as it has done in the past."

Farris scrubbed at his chin. "You've men aplenty for protection and retaliation."

"I'd rather have her."

The count shook his head and laughed. "It gladdens my heart to hear you say that, lad. Reminds me of myself with my dear Jen." He clapped an arm around Lucias' shoulders, hugging him tightly. "But you must come mingle with the other lads. Let your woman have a moment with the highborn ladies."

Lucias untangled himself from the count's grasp. "I'll be along shortly." Sending Farris off with a gentle shove, he waited until they were alone once again before turning his full attention to her. "It seems they seek to part us for a while."

"Not too long, I hope." The music grew louder, not quite masking the bustle coming from the nearby room. There would be feasting soon, and dancing. She snuggled into his embrace, letting him rock her from side to side. "You promised me a dance."

"Did I?" Smiling, he brushed his lips across the tip of her nose. "Then I'll make sure to return as soon as I am able."

"Lucias darling," a woman called as he went to follow Farris.

He froze, his brows merging in horrified bewilderment. His gaze darted over Clara's shoulder and his whole face paled. "Marie?"

Curious, Clara swung about to find the dark-haired woman with the full rosy lips standing there. Her gaze swept over the woman's low-cut neckline and split skirt. *She dares?* Even without flaunting a style that would've looked more appropriate in a private setting, the gown was in shades very close to the Great Lord's colours of black and dark red.

Marie sashayed over to Lucias' side, trying in vain to drape herself on his arm. "It's a *pleasure* to see you again."

Clara bit her tongue, diverting her focus to keeping her expression neutral and discreetly balling her hands lest they flew to the woman's throat of their own volition. *How dare she!* Clara stood right there and the woman practically purred! *I am not going to do a thing.* She refused to start the first few hours of their marriage by getting jealous over some tart's flirting. *With* my *husband.* He belonged to *her,* not *Marie.*

Mine. All mine.

"A pleasure?" Lucias mumbled, jerking back from the woman and drawing Clara closer in the same move. "Is it?" His gaze shot to Thad and his face doubled its effort in regaining its colour. His grip on Clara's waist tightened, the press of his fingers verging on painful. "I suggest you cease with this display of familiarity and remove yourself from this court immediately before I have you dragged out."

Marie stepped back, the smoky-grey dust on her lids serving to make her wide-eyed stare seem bigger. "My lord? I—" She laid a hand atop the bare upper half of her bosom. "I do not understand. Have I done something to displease you? You've always been so happy to see me in the past."

Lucias' face darkened. Silvery-blue light blossomed in the centre of his eyes. "No," he whispered, the word akin to the distant rumble of an approaching storm. He pulled Marie to him, close enough to whisper in her ear. Like the time an Endlight guard had assaulted Clara back in the Citadel, the words weren't loud enough for her to make out. All the same, they pulled at something within her.

When Lucias finally stepped back, the woman's dark eyes had taken on the unearthly glow.

In the same low tone, Lucias continued to order the woman, "You have no business being here, certainly not at my wedding. You will depart immediately and not return to this place until we have left. Understood?"

Marie nodded, unable to resist the compulsion spell Lucias laid upon her. She bowed to them and slowly made her way out of the room.

"I thought compulsion only lasted a few hours," Clara said, unable to take her eyes off Marie until the crowd blocked all hint of her. Lucias had never given her a precise timeframe—too many variables, he had claimed—but she knew it was long enough for a man to march up the steps of the tallest tower in the Citadel and defenestrate himself.

"She'll have shaken the spell by the time she returns home. I'm just hoping she'll also have the sense to heed my words." He slowly relinquished his hold on her. "If you'll excuse me, I must speak with Thad. I'd rather not have any more unwanted surprises." With that, he slipped into the crowd.

Clara followed his path to where the Endlight lord now stood with a cluster of men around the same age near the lesser hall's north-facing wall. The group chatted and laughed amongst themselves, stilling only as Lucias stalked up to drag his friend from their midst before redoubling all talk.

Try as she might, Clara lost sight of the pair after that little display. She wove through the crowd, bowing her head to those who acknowledged her presence and accepting their good wishes with what little grace she could muster as her cheeks burned brilliantly beneath the makeup.

"Mummy!" a small, and somewhat distinctive, voice rang out across the hall.

She turned, certain she knew the voice's owner. *Poppet?*

Sure enough, the small child Clara had taken off the street raced towards her as if they'd known each other all their lives. The girl flitted through the gaps between skirts and trousers, dodging startled people with all the expertise of a gambling puppy through the market square.

Clara knelt, scooping the bony child into her arms.

"You look like a princess from one of Derek's stories," Poppet gushed.

With Poppet settled snugly on Clara's hip, she wove through the crowd in the direction the girl had come from, searching for any sign of the other children. None seemed to appear in the immediate vicinity. "Where are your brothers and sisters?" Surely if the smallest of their group was wandering amongst the court, then the rest had to be nearby.

"They've all gone to eat. I'm not hungry." She puffed out her chest. "I *was*, and I tried eating some of this bird. It tasted weird, though. Trubs said it was because the bird had eaten nothing except oranges, but I don't think that was true."

"That does sound a little implausible." Although, having seen some of the meals the castle kitchen wheeled out, she wouldn't be entirely shocked.

"Then I heard there was dancing and Derek said I couldn't dance on a full belly, which I thought sounded a little silly. You dance on the floor, not a belly."

Repressing the urge to laugh, she gave Poppet the most serious face she could manage. "I suppose if you'd really tiny feet, you could." Clara hopped briefly onto her tiptoes and scanned the room, but true to the girl's word, none of the other children were nearby.

Poppet bounced in her arms. "Like that time the baker's dog jumped all over the fat man in the street. Although, Derek said I shouldn't call him fat, but Woden started it so it's not my fault. I thought he was pregnant at first, but Sweetie told me men can't get pregnant, but I think she might be wrong, because he was really big. Like this." She extended her hands as if clutching an apple basket and puffed out her cheeks.

Clara swung her gaze from side to side as Poppet continued her chatter, hoping to spot Lucias amongst the crowd. If she could get a moment alone with him, then he might be able to help locate the other children with little fuss.

Sadly, it seemed he was just as absent from sight.

She widened her hunt for Farris and the group of old men wishing to speak with their Great Lord, but the count was nowhere to be seen. She'd even settle for Brenna's presence, for pregnancy seemed to have mellowed the once haughty woman.

Snippets of other people's conversations reached her ears as she squeezed by small, gossiping groups. People speculated on the small child in her arms. Not really *hers*, surely. *All* of them? Maybe the younger ones. Couldn't be the Great Lord's, though. What an utter disgrace she was to flaunt the children of past lovers. And at her wedding, of all things.

Clara shook her head. Had their brains fallen out their backsides? How could anyone even entertain the suggestion?

Still, each new group she passed whispered their version of the tale.

She felt thoroughly hounded by the time she finally found Lucias. He stood amongst a group of older noblemen, quietly sipping from his goblet and nodding to the men, who chatted away with all the eagerness of washerwomen.

Clara wove past servants bearing trays of food and pitchers of wine to dive into her husband's surprised, but no less accepting, grasp.

"Hello love." He grinned at Poppet. "And a good evening to you, little lady. You haven't been running your dear mother ragged, have you?"

Poppet shook her head, her curly hair bouncing and swinging in all directions. She seemed as oblivious as Lucias to the sideways glances and whispered words spoken behind fans and palms.

"Come here." Lucias held out his arms. "Give your poor mother's arms a rest."

Like a fearless kitten, Poppet wriggled out of Clara's grasp and vaulted into Lucias' embrace.

Around them, the hushed chatter increased. She couldn't be the only one to notice. What did they gossip about now? Did none of them have the brains to realise that she, a woman of seventeen years, could not have given birth to these children? Was the kingdom really run by such vapid minds?

"Clara?" Lucias whispered, tipping their heads together. "Is something wrong?"

She focused on smoothing her features into a neutral expression, not entirely certain she had succeeded. "Not at all."

"Are you sure?" He cupped her chin. "Forgive me if I choose to not believe you, but you're crying."

She sniffed and fluttered her lashes. The moisture brushing her cheeks was merely sweat. "I'm not," she insisted, noting the shimmer in his eyes at the outright lie. Now wasn't the time to be concerned of such things. She refused to show any weakness whilst others hovered within earshot.

She was the Great Lady, sworn as Lucias' shield before the altar and the Goddess. Nothing could be seen to upset her.

His thumb ran across her cheek, disturbing the warm wetness lingering there. "Well then, my dear, your tears are lying to me."

"Stop it." She stumbled back a step, wrenching her head from his hands. "You'll smear the rouge."

The ghost of a laugh escaped through his lips. "I don't care about that." He took her by the elbow, leading her away from the group and towards the nearest marble pillar. "Won't you tell me what's wrong? Please? Let me fix it." He pulled her into his embrace, squeezing her tight.

Poppet's little hands joined in the hug, patting Clara's shoulder.

"It breaks my heart to see tears when you're supposed to be happy," Lucias whispered against her hair.

"I'll be fine," she mumbled into his shoulder. Already,

the mortifyingly strong urge to crumple into a weeping ball of silk and flesh ebbed with being in his arms. "Just a few silly rumours getting to me."

He leant back enough to shoot her a quizzical look.

Clara explained the past half hour of her search for him, briefly relaying the chatter about her and the children. Hearing the words from her own mouth served only to make them sound even more absurd.

He laid a silencing finger on her lips. "I... I get the idea." His gaze slid across the court. "Utter foolishness. None of them look a thing like you and..." Lucias combed his fingers through his hair, disturbing the coronet. "I could almost believe this little one was yours." He bounced Poppet in his arms. "Although you would've been very young and the thought of anyone being with a girl of such an age makes me a little sick, to be honest."

Clara pressed her lips together. Keeping her mouth shut on that topic was likely the best course of action. Was Lucias aware there were a few mothers in Everdark as young as thirteen? Most had been kicked from their homes, left to struggle on the streets or do the jobs no one else wanted for a pittance, but they existed.

"The rest is just—" He shook his head. "I don't think there's a word for how inane a thought that is. Has anyone said anything to you directly?"

"Not yet." She had already steeled herself for when someone did find themselves bold enough to ask.

"All this talk will die down as soon as the court has something of greater import to speak of, don't worry about it. I—"

"There you are!" a voice pierced through the indistinct chatter of the hall. Woden came barrelling through the crowd. He skittered to a halt at the sight of them, relief sagging his shoulders. "Poppet," he puffed. "Derek told you to stay close."

She clung tighter to Lucias. "I am."

"I'm pretty sure he meant sticking with the rest of your

brothers and sisters," Clara said, garnering a sheepish smile from the girl.

"And he's right that you should," Lucias said, setting the girl onto her feet. "Even if you did stick with us. This is a big place and I don't want a single one of you getting lost in it."

"But the city's heaps bigger," Poppet countered. "I never got lost there."

"That's because we were all there with you," Woden said.

"But I wanted to—"

The first screech of a bow against strings reverberated through the room.

"—dance!" Poppet shrieked over the sound. "Derek said there'd be dancing soon and you were all stuffing your faces. And he said no one could dance after they'd eaten, but I didn't eat anything. So I can dance." She jabbed a finger at her own face before turning the digit on Woden. "And *you* can't."

"It's a dance you want?" Lucias interjected as the jangled chords settled into a harmony that was easier on the ears. "I'm sure I can accommodate you there." He lifted her off the ground, the faintest cinch of her dress at the waist the only hint that his magic cradled her.

Whilst a few nearby people gasped, Poppet merely squealed in delight. They twirled across the dance floor with Lucias taking the proper steps whilst Poppet floated along like an angel.

"That—" Woden mumbled, his pale face drained completely of colour. "That'll take some getting used to."

"Would *you* like to dance?" Clara asked.

"*D-dance?*" Immediately, the boy's pallid cheeks flushed a spotty red. "I don't know how."

"That's all right." She took up his hands, holding him at arm's length. "I didn't know the steps to begin with either, but my dad used to say that we all have to start learning something new at some time or another. Just watch my feet and follow. Can you see them from there?" With the bulk of her skirt in the way, she certainly couldn't.

He nodded.

She took the first step to the side. "The important thing is to not stand on your dance partner's feet." Thankfully, the tune lent itself to a simple four-step, something that they could shuffle to without any trouble.

Woden smiled shyly up at her before dropping his full attention to the floor between them. "I think I can manage that."

They circled their little corner of the room in carefully-measured steps. Woden slowly grew a touch more confident with each rotation. He stopped staring at his feet and his back straightened, allowing his movement to grow more fluid. *If I could get a sword in his hand.* Clara shook the thought free. There'd be time enough for sword training. For all of her children.

The song eventually petered out and Clara led him into the final steps before curtsying. "See? You got the hang of it."

The boy puffed out his chest, his cheeks glowing with a mixture of pride and embarrassment. "I did!"

The soft notes of another song began. The tune was a little slower than the last and just bordering on audible.

Clearing his throat, Lucias returned to their side. "Why don't you and your siblings see if we can't get some livelier music for proper dancing?" he asked of Woden, setting Poppet down.

The pair dutifully trotted off. Poppet scampered at the fore with Woden struggling to remain at her side. With the musicians playing in earnest, Clara saw no chance of the children convincing anyone to play something different.

Still watching the children, Lucias held out his hand to her. "Care for another dance in the meantime, my lady? Although, I'm afraid I shan't be as spry as your last partner."

She sagged gladly into Lucias arms, following the same slow steps she'd walked with Woden. It seemed Lucias also preferred the seclusion of their little section of the lesser hall rather than swinging them into the midst of the crowd.

Thankfully, her husband also favoured not striking out for any intricate steps as the train of her dress had yet to be tied up and would've made moving quickly a bit of a challenge.

A thought came to her as the last notes drifted across the room. Something he'd said that had fled her mind until now. "What does having you drink my blood do, precisely? Why would it be worse than me drinking yours?"

"It—" Lucias frowned. "It's been a long time since I was told about it, but I believe it would've formed an unbreakable bond between us. I'm not entirely certain how much is required, but one drop could've been all it took for me to have known where you were at all times." He shook his head, disgust twisting his lips. "My ancestors used to do it with their wives." He muttered, his eyes unfocused and staring at whatever dark thought his mind had taken him into. "My father probably did it with my mother."

Clara numbly followed his steps. What better way to ensure they knew where their heir was at all times than to bind themselves to the walking vessel carrying the child? "You could've done that to me back in the citadel whenever you wanted," she whispered. She never would've known.

"But I *don't* want—" Sighing, he wrapped his arms around her shoulders. "To bind you to me in such a fashion. You—" He tightened his embrace. "You are your own person and to place such a beacon above your head for the rest of your life... that wouldn't be an equal marriage."

She clung to his jacket. *One drop.* He might've claimed it as pure speculation, but there'd been a note of chilling certainty in his voice. "When we return to the Citadel, you're telling me everything your magic is capable of. No more surprises."

Lucias chuckled. "Whatever my lady asks."

Chapter Twenty-Three

The sun set and the music played on into the night, stuffing her head with enchanting trills and thumps. Clara twirled her way around the grand floor of the lesser hall, letting herself become lost in the heavy rhythms and the various, intricate steps.

She'd changed dancing partners a number of times over the course of the evening, mostly older men of the upper nobility. Their idle chatter was welcome and mercifully distracting. No one brought up the incident with Marie except for Farris and she could've done without him peppering apologies and explanations throughout their dancing.

A few people in the crowd had dispersed, either to bed or other places around the castle, whilst the larger portion preferred to prance their way across the room in time to the music. The temple bells had struck the midnight hour some time back, she was certain of it. Who could possibly mistake their muted clanging?

For now, Clara was content being in her husband's arms with his cheek pressed to her temple as they gently swayed on the spot to the lulling notes of various string and woodwind instruments.

"Are you hungry yet?" Lucias asked, his breath tingling across her ear.

She shook her head. After the first few dances, most of the crowd had excused themselves to the adjoining room where they partook of the lavish feast the cooks spent hours preparing for this occasion, then returning here to chat or dance further. Clara had sat at her husband's side as was proper, but done little beyond nibbling on some fruit before abandoning the idea of eating altogether. Her appetite just wouldn't come and, the later it got, the more her stomach knotted.

He kissed her forehead and led her through a few slow, twirling steps. "As you wish." There was a definite tinge of concern in his voice. Although she'd stopped all attempts to starve herself within the first few days of being confined to the Great Lord's Citadel, Lucias still seemed intent on ensuring she ate what he considered a decent meal.

If only he believed her about the little she survived on whilst living in the village with her mother, then he'd realise she already consumed far more than she was used to.

The room continued to spin long after her body had stopped moving. A sudden flush of heat engulfed her face, sliding across her skin to pool in her gut. For a moment, she thought her stomach sought to reject the meagre amount she'd eaten.

Then, with less warning than its arrival, the queasiness dissipated. Was this some side effect of the *tiāpe*? But she'd barely taken a sip of the wine. "I feel strange," she mumbled. "Hot."

Lucias pressed the back of his hand to her cheek and then, as his brows lowered in a heavy frown, her neck. "It *is* quite warm in here. We can leave, if you want?"

Clara nodded. Going somewhere less conspicuous would be nice. She certainly couldn't dance any longer and the nearby balconies were already far too crowded with other couples seeking relief from the heat.

With his hand settling in the small of her back, he gently guided her towards the exit. The cooler air beyond the lesser hall caressed her skin. "Would you prefer a stroll through the gardens or going to bed?"

She snuggled against him, pillowing her head on his

shoulder. "Bed sounds good."

He was silent whilst they crossed the anteroom and began winding through the hallways. Just as she was beginning to wonder if she'd said the wrong thing, Lucias' caressing touch on her jaw coaxed her head up. The smile he gave was soft, but a hint of mischief tweaked the corners and sparkled in his eyes. "You mean *sleep*, don't you?"

Clara blinked and frowned up at him. What else could she have possibly meant?

Lucias shook his head, chuckling. "Of course you do. Let us go to bed, then."

The chill air did little to banish the fresh inferno dancing upon her cheeks. "Us?"

"Well, yes. Where else am I to sleep if not at my wife's side?"

Wife. So easily he spoke the word, seeming to relish in the way it rolled off his tongue, as if he'd waited his whole life to declare he'd found his equal. She rocked onto her toes and planted a kiss upon his cheek, her lips brushing the corner of his mouth.

Silvery-blue light flashed across his eyes. The delicate grip his arm maintained about her waist tightened, pulling her hard against him, whilst his lips greedily consumed hers. They staggered across the hallway until their path was blocked by the cool, smooth curve of an alcove cradling her back.

Only then did he relinquish his hold.

"Forgive me," he huffed. His face was as flushed as hers felt and lacking in anything resembling remorse. "I've wanted to do that all day." The words escaped his lips in a voice rough and low, heavy with the passion he clearly struggled to keep in check.

"Me too." Clara closed her eyes, revelling in this awareness as it soaked through to her core. She didn't need anyone to tell her how great his desire for her was. It blazed across his face like a second sun.

Lucias gave a gloriously booming laugh, which only

served to heat her further. "Have I been remiss in my husbandly duties so soon?" His hands slapped the smooth brickwork either side of her. He leant on the wall, pinning her up against the stone with the full length of his body.

It was just as well that he had, for when their lips met again, she was certain her knees would've preferred to dump her at his feet.

His kisses came harshly at first, a feverish crush of lips that screamed of a desperate need to consume all. Her fingers slid into his hair, curling at the nape of his neck, where she was then able to coax him into gentler, but no less fervent, kisses. He moaned into her mouth, the sound guttural and dark, and pulled her tighter against him.

Her restraint slowly melted away as she found herself held fast to her husband's firm body. She clung to his shoulders, his flesh trembling beneath her fingers as she sought a way to relieve the pressure of the brickwork at her back.

Lucias' trembling hand snaked down her side to grasp at her skirts. The fabric lifted.

Although she knew, in some far-off manner, she was still covered with copious amounts of silk, the sensation of his knee slipping between her thighs overpowered all thought. Her mind spun, barely able to comprehend what was happening, and for one irrational moment, her leg lifted, seemingly of its own accord, yet with her full consent.

A tendril of cooler air wound its way about her legs, chilling the small gap between bloomers and stockings, and sharply reminding her they were still in the public hallways. Clara slammed her foot down, the jolt bringing her fully back into herself. And still, he had not let her mouth go.

Just when she thought she'd have to push him away or allow things to slip into the realm of indecent, he released her lips and pressed their foreheads together.

Clara gasped. How brightly his eyes blazed. The silvery-blue light so intense, they verged on white. The very air around him shimmered. Shivering, she ran a hand up his arm. Tiny sparks of light danced between them. Was he aware of the change? "Lucias?"

Drawing her back into his arms, his lips brushed over her cheek, slowly trailing down her neck and back up to her ear. His hands slid over her back, the gentle pressure through her corset having her straining her chest against his. Such a simple pleasure, just being in his embrace. Comforting.

But this glowing-eyed beast wasn't her Lucias.

"Stop."

He obeyed the command, relinquishing his hold on her. The glow in his eyes was fast fading to its customary silvery-blue colour. She would've preferred if it vanished altogether. "I..." The passage of his fingers trailed across her bare collarbone, heating her skin.

Then, without warning, he turned and slammed his fist against the wall at her side.

Clara winced. Had she imagined that crack? Had he just broken his hand? He showed no sign of pain.

One blink and the light vanished, returning his eyes to their usual dark shade. "It appears I'm having more trouble restraining my own want for you than I had factored. It would also seem that someone was not at all honest with how much *tiãpe* was in my drink." He peered at her, his brows scrunching together. "Did you say you weren't well?"

"I wasn't." Clara hugged herself, silently trying to figure out just how she felt. Hot, cold, slightly giddy and more than a touch wicked. Each sensation demanded a different course of action. She wasn't entirely sure which one to strike out for. "I feel a little better out here. Maybe I just needed some air?"

He ran an appraising eye over her before bringing the back of his finger to her cheek. "You still seem flushed. How much wine have you drunk since the ceremony? Did you take the full vial of antidotes this morning?"

"I've only had a sip of wine all night," she replied. It was certainly less than he could say after having witnessed him down two full goblets with his meal. In truth, after hearing the Goddess' Cup had been spiked, she'd declined everything beyond water. Could they also have put *tiãpe* in that? How much of this aphrodisiac could she have consumed without her knowledge? "And yes, I downed the whole vial, just as you told me." It'd fast become an early part of her morning routine since the first suspicious instance of poisoning.

One of his dark brows arched high, along with a corner of his mouth. He nodded, relief sagging his shoulders.

Clara shook her head. *Insane. All of them.* The sooner she was out of this crazy city with their bizarre customs, the better. "I want to go to bed," she mumbled. Whether tonight would lead them towards sex or sleep, she would decide once within the privacy of their chambers. "Take me there."

"As you desire." He linked an arm with hers and resumed escorting her down the hall. "I shall take my leave and gather what little of my things are scattered about the castle once you're within." Lucias raked back the loose hair from his face and turned from her. "That should give me time to cool down. This way." He guided her into the corridor leading to the grand entrance.

"Thank you."

Lucias froze in the middle of the hallway.

"What—?" Clara fell silent as he held up his hand.

The unmistakable clash of steel upon steel reached her ears. Was the castle under attack? *The bells.* Perhaps the clanging hadn't come from the temple. But no one had seemed bothered by the noise.

She clutched at Lucias' sleeve. *He's unarmed.* Likely for the first time in years.

Lucias scrabbled at his jacket, swearing as he, too, came to the realisation he bore no weapon. "Go!" he ordered, shoving her back the way they'd come. "Return to the lesser hall. I'll come for you once I've dealt with this."

"Don't be a fool." Clara tightened her hold, refusing to be shaken off. Just like when the barbarian had stormed the

Citadel, Lucias was heading straight into danger. She was even less willing to risk losing him now, certainly not with the healing properties of the Citadel's training grounds sitting days away. "You can't go in there without any way to defend yourself." *And I promised to protect you.* She would kill to keep him safe.

"I always have a means of defence at hand." Lucias disentangled himself from her grip. Caressing her cheek, he stepped out of reach. "But I can't focus if I'm consumed with whether or not you're safe." He turned from her. "Do as I ask and leave this area. I've no desire to compel you into obedience." Without waiting for an answer, he marched around the corner.

You'll not sway me so easily. She refused to stand idly by whilst her husband threw himself into danger. His magic wasn't limitless. All it would take to end his life was a single misstep coupled with a lucky strike from some man's blade or arrow.

Behind her came the hurried tramp of boots.

Clara paused only to determine that the pounding footsteps were headed in her direction before fleeing via the only route she was familiar with: the one leading towards her husband and the fighting.

How many hallways intersected this one? How many men were behind this attack? Enough to surround the castle? To block every exit and close in like a snare around a bird's leg?

She wished she knew.

The clash of weapons and the hair-lifting screams of the wounded grew louder. Rounding the corner, she spied the sight of armoured men fighting other armoured men at the far end of the corridor.

Clara raced onwards, slowing only once she'd exploded into the grand entrance. Keeping close to the walls, she relied on her dark attire to blend with the shadows whilst searching for Lucias in the chaos. However did they tell enemy from ally?

Her fool of a husband had managed to procure a sword and now darted through the fighting, intent on the entrance where, filling much of the doorway, stood—

It can't be. Clara rubbed her eyes, pleading to the Goddess that someone was playing tricks with her vision. But no, the hulk of a man casually lopping off men's heads with his great battleaxe was the same barbarian who'd all but killed Lucias three months ago.

No. This was her worst fear come to life.

"Dark One," the barbarian bellowed. "I see you still live." He swatted aside an impending attack with all the effort of batting away a fly. "You will not be so fortunate this time."

Snatching a sword from a fallen soldier, Clara raced towards them. Terror had the weapon dragging at her arms, but somehow, she lifted it. To do otherwise was to let her husband die.

A shadow fell over her, she spun in time to witness the horrified contortion of a man stabbed through the chest.

Other men, garbed in the green and gold of Endlight, surrounded her, their blades trained on keeping everyone from her. Beyond their ring of swords, the fighting continued. Lucias had reached the barbarian and, for now, appeared to be holding his own.

"My lady." Thad stood over her would-be attacker, his fine clothes torn and blood-splattered. With the man dispatched, the lord wrenched his sword from the crumpled armour and faced her. "This is not your fight." His strong arms wrapped about her waist, hoisting her onto his shoulders before she could object. The sword slipped from her grasp and clanged to the floor.

Clara bounced up and down as they left the battle behind, the motion threatening to empty her stomach. "Put me down!" she shrieked, pounding her fists upon his broad back. "That's an order!"

Thad did as commanded, lowering her to the ground. "You must be protected."

She planted her feet and glared up at him. She'd had

enough of everyone seeking to maintain *her* safety. She could look after herself. *"That's* who you must protect," she snarled, jabbing a finger in Lucias' direction. By the noise reaching down the corridor, the barbarian was in the room now. The brute would be hounding her husband whilst she was stuck here arguing. "Go help your lord."

"But he—"

Unthinkingly, Clara backhanded him. This was not the time for a lengthy discussion. "Did I mishear the priest?" she screamed into his face. "Is he not my husband? Am I not your Great Lady? Go, Lord of Endlight, do your duty and help the man you claim to serve!"

Thad paled. He drew his sword. "Men!" he roared at the guards flanking him. "To your lord!" He rushed back up the corridor, aiming for the hulk of muscles and steel battering at Lucias' defences.

She withdrew into the shadows even as she followed the guards, wary of being taken by surprise again.

Now she knew what to look for in the fighting, she could make out various clusters of heraldic colours. What she couldn't place was the dark garb that appeared to belong to the enemy.

So many men. How was it they'd gotten into the castle? Endlight was the most fortified place she'd seen. But how many nobles attended this wedding? Dozens? Hundreds? Each one would've entered these walls with their own guard. How hard would it be to slip in one more group of armed men?

A hand clapped over her mouth. She lurched forward, sudden terror blanking her mind, only to be dragged back by an arm about the waist. The unseen man tossed her over his shoulder as effortlessly as Thad had done.

Clara struggled. She kicked out, trying to connect with more than air. When that failed, she clawed at her kidnapper's jerkin, making her way down to his belt. Her hand fell on the hilt of a dagger. Tearing the weapon from its sheath, she slammed it into the man's back.

The man collapsed with a piercing scream, sending her tumbling across the floor.

Aching, she crawled over to where her would-be kidnapper lay writhing. There appeared to be no identifying marks on his clothes, but she didn't need them to suspect this man worked alongside the barbarian. And that meant Ne'ermore and Lucias' mother were involved.

She hauled the dagger from the man's back and, as he howled, scrambled to her feet. The man could've killed her. Instead, he sought to carry her off. *Why?* What did they have to gain by taking her now?

A hushed gasp broke through her panting and the man's groans.

She whirled, her pilfered weapon held at the ready.

Sweetie stood in the hallway, her brown eyes at their widest and trained only on the blade sitting inches from her nose.

Clara hastily lowered the dagger. "What are you doing here?" The girl should've been abed hours ago, along with— "Where are the others?" she demanded, frantically taking in their surroundings. No other little faces popped out from behind the decor. They were alone, except for her deathly quiet would-be kidnapper.

"I don't know," Sweetie mumbled. Her gaze refused to lift from the weapon in Clara's hand. "Maybe their bedrooms? We were all heading there when we heard—"

A roar of anger and pain boomed from the man. "I'm going to kill you!" His hand wrapped around Clara's leg, attempting to tug her off balance. His efforts got him little but the heel of her shoe on his hand. "And you, monster," he snarled at Sweetie, using the train of Clara's skirt to claw his way along the floor. "Skin you both alive like the demons you are."

Screaming, Sweetie raced off down the hallway.

"Wait!" she called after the girl, the word out before she could stop to think if she would be heard by others. The direction Sweetie had fled was the same one the man had been attempting to cart Clara down.

"You're not going anywhere," he growled.

Unable to turn with his weight pinning her to the spot, Clara slashed behind her with the dagger. A hissing cry, followed by the absence of his weight, told her she'd struck.

Not waiting to see if the man was dead, she raced after the girl. Wherever her would-be abductor had planned on taking her, Clara was certain he wouldn't be attempting the feat alone.

Sweetie's path took them down a dark hallway. It curved ahead. A pale glow, such as the beacon that marked the grand entrance, emanated from the corridor. A way out? Would the man really have taken her back into the thick of the fighting?

Clara rounded the bend and slid into a small, round intersection. Moonlight illuminated the area through a pair of tall windows, throwing long shadows across the space. The room didn't seem at all familiar. Had she taken a wrong turn? She could've sworn her would-be kidnapper had kept a straight path. Perhaps the man had aimed to carry her to a less guarded part of the castle and some obscure exit.

She peered about, wary. Wherever this place stood in the castle, it was devoid of men. Not even a sign of any fighting.

The faint snuffle of hastily-stifled tears drew her gaze to a statue set into one of the four alcoves. Sweetie huddled at its base.

Clara skirted the edge of the intersection, checking each hallway entrance before proceeding. The clack of her heeled shoes boomed through the silence. She rocked onto the balls of her feet and continued on to kneel next to the girl. "It's all right," she whispered, wrapping an arm around the too-slim shoulders. "I'm here."

"S-sorry," Sweetie whimpered.

"For being afraid?" She wiped the girl's cheek dry with a sleeve. "That's nothing to be sorry for. But we can't stay here." Clara stood, gently lifting Sweetie to her feet. They couldn't risk going back. There could be other men waiting and, whilst she would've considered it a calculated risk were she alone, she had no inkling of what they might do to the girl.

That left going forward. Several corridors branched off the room, all as equally dark as the passageway at her back.

Keeping her dagger high, she led them down the nearest hallway.

The hushed pad of another's feet upon the stone was all the warning she had before a sack dropped over her head, throwing the gloomy world into complete darkness.

Then the only sound was Sweetie's screams piercing the air.

Chapter Twenty-Four

*S*everal men carted her through the castle with all the ease and care she would've afforded a bolt of cloth. Her unseen captors had worked fast to bind her hands at her back and haul her away. She wasn't even sure how many men there were, a definite two if she was to judge by the arms hefting her about. But the footsteps suggested more people trotted alongside them.

Clara struggled against the bonds, thrashing about like a cornered rat. The coarse rope bit into her wrists. Sweat fast soaked her back, adhering her clothes to her body just as the sack clung to her face. She tossed her head, finding it increasingly difficult to breathe in the humid air. The cord securing the sack about her neck dragged at her throat and set off a bout of coughing.

She'd tried screaming, giving up when a particularly shrill attempt gained her only a mouthful of dusty hessian. Clearly, help wasn't going to come at her call. If she could get just *one* arm loose, then perhaps she stood a chance of freeing the rest of her.

So far, her numerous tries were proving themselves no more helpful than her shrieks.

Would a leg be easier to free? Her foot twitched at the thought. They hadn't bothered with tying her ankles together, but between the way one man had his arms wrapped about her knees and how her skirts tangled about her legs, they might as well have.

The peep of a whimper reached her ears. Not hers. That could only mean…

Sweetie.

Fresh rage flooded her senses. They had taken the girl. Likely trussed the same and terrified out of her mind.

Clara fought the bonds. The rope dug deeper into her skin as she strained. Still, they held fast.

The back of her ankle smacked against what she guessed was a hip. If only she could get enough purchase to distract at least one of them. A swift kick in the side with her heels would be enough to win her freedom.

"Wriggles something fierce, doesn't she?" one of the men quipped to his companions. "Ye would think she'd be grateful to be free of the man."

Clara stilled, straining to hear over her own panting. It was the first time any of them had said a word since her capture. She had assumed these invaders came from neighbouring lands but, if she wasn't mistaken, wherever the man called home now, his accent had originated from within this very kingdom.

Did that mean the enemy had a foothold within their realm?

Another man sniggered. "I hear they teach their women that it's an honour to be his mistress or some rot like that."

"An honour?" the first man scoffed. "To bring another soul-sucking demon into the world? Aye, if ye came from the abyssal swamps yerself."

"Will you two shut it?" a third man said, this one closer to her head and, if he truly was the bulk pressing against her back, with a far higher voice than she expected from someone so large. "We're not in the clear until the lady's got the girl."

Lady? Did he mean Lucias' mother? *That can't be right.* The last Clara had seen of the woman, Lenora seemed more intent on killing her son and ensuring there was no heir. Had the failed attempt on his life changed the lady's plans?

Silence fell over the group, punctuated by the odd grunt as they shuffled her through what she assumed must be several doorways. Even with the sack muffling all but the closest voices, she heard the harsh clash of steel alongside the cries of injured and dying men. The sounds came faintly at first, growing louder before fading again.

Was Lucias amongst them? Did he even still live? Would anyone hear if she screamed now? *Probably not.* Her voice was likely to be lost altogether if not mistaken for another poor victim amongst the fighting.

They lowered her to the ground, seemingly content to leave her to sit quietly. She wriggled, searching for Sweetie. Had they discarded her? Or worse?

"This *is* the right one, is it not?" one of her captors asked. "I don't want to be risking my neck only to find we've snagged some prettied up servant like that woman earlier on."

"It has to be her," the high-voiced man replied. "She's wearing the Dark One's colours and this one's hair is the right shade. Red as blood. Is that not what the big guy said?"

Murmurs of agreement followed his question.

So the barbarian led these men. How deep did their loyalties to the behemoth run? Were they less servants of Ne'ermore and more mercenaries?

There was the hushed, carefully placed, pad of a boot, then the squeak of a hinge in dire need of oiling. Some sort of rarely-used entrance? "Wait here," the high-voiced man said. "And be quiet whilst I see if the path is clear. If they catch us, we'll end up just like those poor blighters who took on the Dark Lord."

Did he mean recently? If that were true, it meant Lucias was still alive. Enraged and possibly unaware of her full predicament, but alive.

"He should've let me put a bolt through their heads when I had the chance," the second man grumbled. "It would've been the merciful thing to do."

"And have ye give us away? Ye can't say they weren't warned. Did ye see how fast he got out those glowing symbols? And that voice..." There was a faint vibration to Clara's left—a leg, perhaps—as the man seemed to shudder. "If that didn't come straight from the deepest parts of Hell, then I'm a Punegeain veil dancer."

Clara leant back. She wriggled her hands, trying to curl her fingers around far enough to work at the knot.

"What do we do with the other one?"

"Leave her," the first man suggested. "Can't do nothing all tied up. Can you, lass?"

A muffled scream was Sweetie's only reply. Gagged.

"And if she escapes?" the second man demanded. "Be better to slit her throat now and be done with it."

Another scream, higher and definitely pleading.

Clara thrashed, she bumped into someone's legs. The man staggered, but seemed to regain his feet. "Don't you dare touch her!" she shouted around the mouthful of sacking.

Whether or not they understood her, Sweetie's screams fell to whimpers.

"We'll bring her with us," a fourth man said, the tone brokering no room for quibbling. "They'll want a way to control the Dark Lord's whore and she seems eager enough to see that the girl lives."

Her knuckles brushed against the smooth, chill stone at her back. She felt along it, seeking a rough edge to help cut the rope. Mortar turned to dust under her fingers, revealing a corner. The rope ran along the edge, sliding without a sign of growing weaker.

Abandoning the effort, she turned to slowly squirming her way along the wall, aiming for the sounds of fighting. If she could draw the right kind of attention her way...

"I thought I said to shut your traps?" a high voice suddenly hissed. A hand fell on her shoulder, the thick fingers digging into her flesh. "And where did you think you were going, my lady?"

More hands grasped her. There was the softest of grunts as they lifted her back into the air, then the door squeaked once again. A cold breeze hit her damp skin. She was out of the castle and, from the feel of it, fast ascending a flight of stairs. With her heart attempting to pound its own way free, Clara redoubled her efforts to escape.

Somewhere above them, bells clanged. Had their presence been noted?

"Quick," the high-voiced man snapped. "We haven't much time before the big guy leaves."

Her ears, already straining for any sound of pursuit, caught the click of a carriage door. Her side thumped against a floor that gave with a rocking, creaking motion. The weight of a small, screaming and thrashing body landed on her. *Sweetie.*

The door slammed shut. Something banged on the side and their surroundings lurched to the clatter of shod hooves upon cobblestone.

Wriggling her way between the seats, Clara found enough purchase to haul herself into an upright position. One wrist—slick with sweat or blood, she didn't know—slid within the bindings. She tugged some more, using the edge of the seats as leverage.

One hand slipped free, then the other. Tearing the sack off her head, she took in her surroundings. A carriage, not too dissimilar to the one Lucias' men once shoved her into.

Sweet Goddess, please, not this. She couldn't be confined like this again. *Anything but this.* Screaming and with the walls seeming to shrink with each breath, Clara clawed at the door handle.

Locked.

Undeterred, she pounded on the door, first with her fists, then lashing out with her feet until her heels were sore. The wood protested eagerly enough at each thump, but refused to yield. She slammed a shoulder against the window. It might as well have been made of stone.

Dashing the tears blocking her vision, she rested her

forehead on the smoky glass to stare at the world beyond. In the late night, her only witnesses were dying torches and a few alley cats. How long would it take the castle inhabitants to realise she was gone?

Sweetie cringed on the opposite seat. In the gloom, her eyes were dark holes in a ghostly face, but they were at their widest. "What'll happen to us?"

"To you? Nothing bad, I'll make sure of that." Clearly, they didn't want her dead or she'd already be so. That gave her leverage.

But first, she would need to meet her kidnapper.

A mighty boom shook the carriage. She scrabbled across the seat and peered through the back window just in time to see a great cloud of dust and fragments of stone burst from the side of the castle.

Up and down the street, dogs barked into the night whilst people shouted for an explanation from their windows and doorways. She watched them with the bitter knowledge that, should she choose to scream for help now, no one would hear her.

The sharp crack of a whip pierced the noise. Clara tumbled about the carriage, clinging to the seat, as they lurched forward. Again, the driver wielded his whip, pushing the horses faster still. She braced herself, every bump they hit jarring through her spine.

Eventually, the way became so bouncy that even the driver must have considered it rough, for the carriage slowed.

She risked a peek out the window. They'd left the city boundaries. She caught sight of the castle again as they climbed a hill. The dust had settled and a portion of the building was missing.

Lucias. What had happened to him? Had the barbarian finally completed his task of slaying the dreadful Dark Lord?

"What are we going to do?" Sweetie asked, still huddled on the opposite seat.

If Lucias was dead, then why would they take her? The answer there was simple. They wouldn't. *So I am to be used as bait.* Clara punched the carriage roof, biting off a few choice swears that would've had her mother reaching for the switch. She felt so helpless like this.

Think, girl. If she was bait, then clearly someone thought he would come for her or they wouldn't have gone to the trouble of kidnapping her. So logically, if the enemy wanted him to leave the kingdom, he should take the opposite course of action.

That would mean forsaking her.

Clara sat back in the seat, the thought chilling her. Was she not expendable?

Although she would never admit it to a single soul, the answer could only be a rather stinging 'yes'. Even as his wife. It wasn't as if there was the slightest chance of her being with child. Lucias might consider her as his only option there, but realistically, any woman of childbearing age could give birth to the next Great Lord. He didn't have to love them, or even like them, to get the deed done.

Thinking of what should be an intimate act between lovers in such a clinical fashion twisted her insides into a thousand knots, but that seemed to be how everyone else viewed it. *Not him.* Lucias would not have waited if he felt the same way. *And he swore he'd tear apart the world for me.* Whether he did so because she wished it or to rescue her, wouldn't matter to him.

"Lucias will come," she murmured, partially to reassure herself as well as Sweetie.

"So, we wait for him to rescue us?"

Did he know Sweetie was missing along with Clara? Did it matter when they were together? He'd come for Clara.

And when he did pursue her, he would no doubt do so without thinking of the consequences.

Nothing she could do about that except pray there was someone in the castle he would listen to who had enough sense to come up with a plan before acting. But who would even know where to begin his search? Or what to look for? She could've sworn no one saw the carriage leave, for surely they would've stopped these men from completing their kidnapping if they had any idea.

Just like their tales. Wasn't that the basis of some Endlight folktale Thalia told her about, where the bride was abducted before her husband got to consummate their marriage?

Clara shook her head. The one thing she *wasn't* doing was waiting around for five years in the hope that someone would aid in her escape. *Or marry my kidnapper.* Once a lifetime was enough.

She would need to win their freedom and return to Endlight well before her husband had a chance to mount a rescue party. She just needed a chance.

"No," she said, her thoughts still ticking over the consequences of any action. "We're not going to wait."

"Then what?"

Where were they headed? *Ne'ermore.* There was a good possibility that was their destination. She may not be able to elude her kidnappers out in the wilderness, but if Ne'ermore was anything like the rabbit warren of streets back home, then she'd be in her element.

The walls may keep her husband from getting in, but they wouldn't stop her from getting out.

Unfortunately, such a plan involved entering the city in the first place and that gave Lucias far too much time to do something stupid, like believing he could enter enemy lands without an army at his back. *You better have more sense than that.* She refused to think she might have just married an idiot.

Her gaze flicked to Sweetie. Away from the shadows of the city buildings, the weak moonlight filtered through and illuminated the girl's pale skin. Just as Clara's hair singled her out, the girl would have a lesser chance of casually blending in.

So what could they do?

Clara straightened in her seat. "We are going to rescue ourselves."

THE END

ABOUT THE AUTHOR

Born and raised in New Zealand, Aldrea Alien lives on a small farm with her family, including a menagerie of animals, most of which are convinced they're just as human as the next person. Especially the cats.

She discovered a love of crafting other worlds at the age of twelve when she first conceived the idea of *The Rogue King*. Since that that fateful day, she hasn't found an ounce of peace from the characters plaguing her mind, all of them clamouring for her to tell their story first.

It's a lot of people for one head.

www.ingramcontent.com/pod-product-compliance
Lightning Source LLC
Chambersburg PA
CBHW021643110726
47902CB00007B/1805